W9-CPD-722

THE
BROTHER-IN-LAW

THE
BROTHER-IN-LAW

Dave

Enjoy my
autobiographical fiction
F.X. Biasi Jr.

F. X. BIASI JR.

Copyright © 2012 by Francis X. Biasi Jr. All rights reserved.

No part of this book may be duplicated, reproduced, or transmitted in any form or by any means, electronic or mechanical, including photocopying, recording, storing in any information storage and retrieval system, or sharing by e-mail or website — except in the form of brief excerpts or quotations in critical articles and reviews — without written permission from the author.

Contact F. X. Biasi Jr. at fxbiasijr@gmail.com

This is a work of fiction. Names, characters, places, and incidents either are the product of the author's imagination or are used fictitiously, and any resemblance to actual persons, living or dead, business establishments, events, or locales, is entirely coincidental.

Cover and interior design by Williams Writing, Editing & Design

ISBN 978-0-9848781-2-3

This novel is dedicated to the memory of
Al Bonavita. I wish he were still here to read it.

PROLOGUE

Tuesday, September 4, 2001
Queens, NY

Bart LaRocca felt a bead of sweat begin running from his hair down the back of his neck. His forearms and the backs of his hands were slick with perspiration. Although the evening sun was only a pinkish glow on the horizon, the hazy late summer day was still stifling. After weeks of living on the street, he no longer noticed the ever-present sour aroma of rotting food blended with a myriad of animal excrements. A well-nourished rat cautiously scurried along the base of the brick wall, stopping periodically to examine his surroundings. In the distance the city's never-ending cacophony resonated. Bart glanced at his watch. *Seven forty-five. It feels like rain.* Just then, out of the corner of his eye, he saw the Lincoln Town Car turn onto the block. *Right on time . . . OK, pre-game warm-up starts now . . . stay calm . . . control your breathing . . . it will be dark in another couple of minutes . . .*

Bart had been crouched for half an hour in the shadows, alongside a green dumpster, in the alley directly across the street from the Elmhurst Italian-American Social Club. It wasn't really a social club; it was actually the headquarters of the Leucchi crime family. The 1930s two-story brick building stood a half block off Queens Boulevard on Sixty-Ninth Street, which actually put it in Woodside, not Elmhurst. For nearly two years he had planned for this day. This was the day Bart would take down

1

Al "Little Nicky" Nicosia, one of the most powerful bosses in the New York Mafia.

Bart watched as Little Nicky's driver, Tony the Animal, extricated himself from behind the steering wheel of the Lincoln and scanned the area. The 6-foot, 260-pound gorilla then walked around to the passenger side, opened the back door, and scanned up and down the street one more time before his boss made a rapid beeline for the protection of the social club's alcove. Little Nicky waited as his bodyguard cautiously opened the door leading to the staircase and the two upstairs apartments. Just as they had the other three times Bart had scoped out them out, Little Nicky waited at the foot of the stairs while Tony checked upstairs. Bart silently instructed Tony, *OK, turn on the lights.* He had hardly finished his thought when a glimmer of light burst through the shades. Moments later, getting an all-clear sign from his driver, Little Nicky climbed the stairs to the apartment on the left.

Good. Now, Tony, come back out and get in the car. Fifteen seconds later Tony's massive frame reappeared in the alcove. Almost as if it were an involuntary muscle reaction, he checked up and down the street again as he made his way to the car. "Have a nice dinner at Pepe's," Bart muttered under his breath. The first Tuesday he had staked out the club, figuring that Tony would not stray too far from his boss, Bart hurried down the block after the Town Car trying to get a glimpse of where the driver was headed. He just made it to Queens Boulevard in time to see Tony make an illegal turn from one service road, across four lanes of traffic, and onto the service road headed in the opposite direction. He squeezed the big Lincoln into a parking spot in front of Pepe's Trattoria. During his last dry run, Bart had checked the boulevard a few minutes after Tony left and verified the Lincoln was parked a couple of doors down from Pepe's.

So far right on script; plenty of time, after the girls get here, to make sure Tony is having his pasta. If everything continued on schedule, he knew he had another fifteen minutes before the two prostitutes arrived. Once they were upstairs, he could take a quick walk up to the corner and make sure Tony was a man of habit. Smiling to himself, Bart wondered what the gossip columnists would dare write if they knew their "Mafia Casanova" had to get his rocks off with two S&M professionals every Tuesday night.

Except for the streetlight fifty yards up the block and the faint illumination from the neon lights on Queens Boulevard, it was dark when the pros arrived. When he was sure they were in the apartment, Bart went out the back of the alley and headed to check on Tony. The Lincoln was right where it was supposed to be. Checking his watch again, he verified it was 8:15. One more hour and it's game time . . . *There's still time to call this off. No way! I've waited too long to get even with this bastard.* Feeling reassured, he turned around and headed back to the alley to go through his inventory of weapons one last time. Satisfying himself that he had everything he would need, he took his disguise out of the daypack and began to get ready. He was wearing a pair of well-worn black Levi's over running shorts and a T-shirt with a NYU logo. He first strapped on a flak jacket, like the ones NFL quarterbacks wear. Over the flak jacket he slipped into the Vietnam-era army fatigue shirt he had been wearing for his reconnaissance over the last few months. The name tag over the right breast pocket had been removed, leaving its dark outline. The sleeves also revealed the outline of discarded master sergeant chevrons. He began the rest of his physical transformation back into the homeless derelict he had portrayed for the last two months, hoping the absence of his beard would not be noticeable in the darkness. He removed the two-tooth temporary bridge from his lower jaw, leaving a conspicuous gap. He affixed to his head a shoulder-length, salt-and-pepper-wig that was identical to his own hair before his haircut the previous week. He traded the white Titleist cap for the same faded Mets cap he had been wearing as part of his covert identity. Inspecting himself in a small round mirror, he couldn't hold back a sneaky grin. *All right, you look like a destitute Vietnam vet again . . . Oops, almost forgot the glasses.* Out of the breast pocket of the fatigue shirt he retrieved a pair of black-rimmed prescription eye glasses that were held together with a piece of white adhesive tape on the bridge. Besides a visual diversion from his real features, the glasses would be left behind as "evidence" confirming the perpetrator was near-sighted, which was exactly opposite of Bart. *Perfect! Nothing left to do but wait for the girls to leave; then I can get revenge on my bastard brother-in-law.*

A quick peek at the $10 Seiko knockoff watch verified he only had another forty-five minutes before Bart LaRocca, one way or another, would no longer exist.

CHAPTER 1

The last of our children's families had just left following Marie's sixty-fifth birthday party when I received the mystifying phone call. I knew it was an international call by all the numbers showing up on caller ID. I didn't know it originated in Monaco until I hung up and checked the front of the telephone book for the 377 country code. Since Marie and I had retired and moved out here to Westhampton, I was under the assumption that only family, my literary agent, and a few close friends and former business associates had our telephone number. So I answered apprehensively, "Hello."

Speaking in what sounded like a Spanish accent, the caller asked, "Is this Charles Stanfield, the attorney and author?"

Damn, I thought, *who's giving out my number to strangers?* I considered hanging up, but Marie always told me that rudeness was unbecoming to my personality. "Yes, and to whom am I speaking?"

"My name is not important; I am calling as a deathbed favor to Bart LaRocca. Are you familiar with the events surrounding his disappearance?"

Having been a pretty sly attorney for over thirty years, I contained my surprise at the mention of Bart's name and played dumb. "No, did something happen to Bart besides the fact you just told me he was dead?"

Sounding surprised and disappointed that I didn't know the

history of my former classmate, the caller replied, "During the first week of September in 2001, there was an incident in Queens, about which Bart had some relevant information involving a Mafia bigwig. Before he died last year, he told me the whole story; he thought it might be an interesting theme for a novel. He beseeched me to try to find a writer to whom it might have some appeal."

I interrupted him. "Wait a minute, you did say he died last year?"

"Yes, and on his deathbed he gave me a list of writers to contact. You were the first name on the list. He also provided some money to finance the writing of his story."

"Well, you flatter me, but I'm no novelist. Since I retired from the law, I've only had a few articles published in the *New Yorker* magazine; certainly nothing that would qualify me to write a novel."

Undaunted by my humility, the caller countered, "Bart believed that your credentials along with the fact the two of you played football together made you uniquely qualified to tell his story."

Unimpressed and still highly skeptical, I responded, "I'm flattered my ex-classmate thought of me first, but this whole telephone conversation sounds a little fishy to me. I mean . . . out of the blue, a stranger calls me about some kind of a Mafia incident, claiming he has information from a deceased acquaintance whom I haven't seen or heard from in decades. You wouldn't be the same guy who emailed me you'll have $60,000,000 wired to my bank account if I'd just provide you with all the right codes, would you?" Not expecting a reply, I added, "If this is for real, why didn't he just have you call the *New York Post* or the *Daily News*?"

"Because, Mr. Stanfield, it is not just the one incident, it's a forty-year chronicle of two innocent lovers whose lives were destroyed by their family association with the mob. Besides, they would probably assign it to some twenty-three-year-old apprentice who has no appreciation for the era."

"OK, if I told you I wasn't intrigued, I'd be lying . . . especially about how he managed to disappear for over eight years. By the way, you still haven't given me your name."

"You're right, but at this point, my name isn't really important. You're either interested in Bart's story or not. Who I am shouldn't make a difference. If you are interested, we can get more familiar; if you're not, we'll both move on."

"Fair enough. I'll tell you what, let me have a week or so to think about it, and then I'll give you an answer as to whether I am interested in the story. Can I reach you at the number you're calling from now?"

"No, this is a pay phone. I'll call you back in two weeks."

It did seem a little melodramatic, but it also revived some vivid memories of Bart. He was one of the stars of our championship football teams in '60 and '61, and an outstanding sprinter for the track team.

The first thing I did after hanging up was consult my Bishop Ott High School yearbooks. Bart first appeared in our junior year. The classic headshot in the front of our senior yearbook identified him as F. Bart LaRocca. I also found pictures of him putting a move on an opposing player and taking a stick handoff in a relay race. Other than sports, his activities were minimal, no National Honor Society, no academic clubs. He didn't even list any of the bullshit clubs like judo and senior server. He signed my book, "To Chuck, A great teammate and a class act. Best of luck at Fairfield." *Chuck.* I had almost forgot I went by that name back then. I haven't used that moniker since college, preferring the more attorney-like Charles.

A few days later, out of curiosity, I stopped in at the Westhampton library. All periodicals before 2003 were still on microfiche. Fortunately, being an old guy, it was probably just as easy pulling up the microfiche of the *New York Post* from 2001 as finding it on the library's computer. The *Post* loved to sensationalize anything to do with the Mafia, so it was more likely I would find an article in there rather than in the *Times*. I had a vague recollection of Al Nicosia, the darling of the New York media at the time, being involved in some kind of an incident. The tabloids, especially the *Post*, had given the tall, dark, handsome ladies' man a rock star image rather than the criminal status he deserved. Anything the mobster did was big news. Bingo! Front page on September 5, 2001, I read "Mafia Don Attacked." The article went on to explain the reputed head of the Nicosia crime family and his driver were brutally attacked outside the Elmhurst Italian-American Social Club in Queens. Alfonse (aka Al, aka Little Nicky) Nicosia was listed in serious but stable condition, but the article did not elaborate on the nature or extent of his injuries. His driver, Anthony (aka Tony "the Animal") DeMateo was expected to be released from the hospital that morning. Nowhere in the article did it mention Bart LaRocca or whether police had any leads on the attacker.

Follow-up stories shed little light on the attack or Little Nicky's injuries; they just reaffirmed his injuries were extensive but non-life-threatening. It quoted an unnamed source as stating the Mafia boss would have to undergo a long series of surgeries and rehabilitation and that he might never fully recover. The articles also chronicled Little Nicky's colorful past, including his ability to escape prosecution and a long list of the celebrities he had reportedly dated and bedded. Anonymous NYPD sources expressed doubt the attack was mob-related. The paper speculated the assailant might be a jealous husband of one of his many lovers. After September 11, 2001, the story disappeared from the papers as the World Trade Center attacks totally consumed the news. OK, I thought, *this might be an interesting story, especially if Bart was somehow involved. Let's ride it for a while and see how it plays out.*

A few days later, I was talking on the phone with another classmate, retired NYPD captain Dave McCarthy. Dave knew Bart even better than I did. They both attended Blessed Sacrament K through 8. For the last several years, Dave had been Bishop Ott's go-to guy for updating contact information on alumni. We were working on updating our class list to get ready for our fiftieth reunion. I asked Mac, "Do you have anything on the whereabouts of Bart LaRocca?"

Snickering, he answered, "I'm sure you heard Bart disappeared back in '01. I wasn't involved in the investigation; but as an old friend, I kind of followed it pretty closely for a few days. When the World Trade Center thing happened, we all became preoccupied for quite a while. Bart was a person of interest in the attack on his brother-in-law, the head of the Leucchi crime family, Al Nicosia. NYPD and the FBI suspected Bart was somehow involved in the attack. Bottom line was, following the attack, they believed Al either had his brother-in-law whacked or Bart successfully disappeared. Since Little Nicky and his bodyguard claimed they did not recognize their assailant, there really wasn't any evidence LaRocca was involved except it was widely known by law enforcement there was bad blood between them. Dave was pretty sure no charges were ever filed. He doubted there was an ongoing investigation, but if Bart was still alive, he assumed there was still a contract out on Bart, saying, 'Those wise guys have a long memory.'"

"So what do you think, was he the one that attacked Little Nicky?"

"Hell, I don't know. Early on, all of NYPD's attention was focused on finding some homeless derelict. The FBI, on the other hand, liked Bart for this but came up with nothing except he disappeared along with a couple of million bucks he had stashed away. For me, it's hard to believe he had the cojones to pull this off. I mean, he was a damn accountant who never even got a speeding ticket. He didn't even see combat in Vietnam."

We sat in silence for a few minutes while he let me digest what he had just told me. Finally he said, "Bart has a sister, Fran; I'll try to locate her. Maybe she can give us an update."

The next day he called and said he located Fran in Huntington; but as far as she was concerned, Little Nicky had him whacked. I got her phone number from Dave and called her. I persuaded her to meet me for coffee. Fran explained Bart had been reported missing from his Charlotte, North Carolina, apartment by his golf buddies, who became concerned when he did not return from a fishing trip. A few weeks later, Bart's car was found in a shopping mall parking lot somewhere in Virginia. There were a few minute traces of his blood in the trunk and front seat, but the inside of the car had been wiped clean of prints. That was the last piece of information Fran had on Bart. Visibly upset, Fran blurted out, "I know that bastard Little Nicky had him killed."

I played dumb. "What did Bart have to do with the Nicosias?"

"You don't know?" Fran asked. "He married Little Nicky's sister, Gina. Bart was convinced his son-of-a-bitch brother-in-law, Al, was behind their divorce and somehow responsible for Gina's and their son Peter's deaths. A few days before Gina died, Bart told me he and Gina were going to get back together. Following her funeral, I overheard Bart and Al arguing over some bogus story Al had relayed to Gina. After a heated argument, Little Nicky and two of his goons jumped Bart in the men's room, beating him up and putting him in the hospital. Bart swore he'd get even with Little Nicky — and maybe he did." After a momentary reflection Fran continued, "The guy you need to talk to is Gina's other brother, John; he is a doctor and moved away from the family years ago."

"Do you know where I can find him?"

"Phoenix, I think," replied Fran.

I checked the AMA directory for Arizona and found a Dr. John Nicosia, cardiologist, listed in Phoenix. I called the listed number and the receptionist said Dr. Nicosia was retired; she would not give me a home phone number. Doubtful of having any success, I called directory assistance anyway. To my surprise, they gave me a number for John and Patty Jo Nicosia. I dialed the number and got Patty Jo. When I asked for John, she hesitantly replied, "Uh, John is not up to talking right now. May I ask who is calling?" I gave her my name and told her I was a friend of Bart LaRocca. Her reply was swift and caustic, "Bart's dead and John won't talk about him." Then she hung up abruptly. I thought about the call for a few moments and decided to wait a day and call back to lay all my cards on the table.

About an hour later my phone rang. The area code indicated Phoenix, but the number was not the one I had just dialed. When I answered, I heard Patty Jo's unmistakable New York accent. "Tell me again how you know Bart and got our name and location." I told her we had been high school classmates at Bishop Ott. I told her about the call from Monaco, and that Fran had suggested I talk to John.

When I finished she sighed and offered, "Sorry I was so abrupt with you when you first called. John and I have to be very careful what we talk about concerning his brother Al and Bart. Over the years, we've come to believe that our phones have been bugged. I am calling you now from a safe phone."

She continued, "I've known Bart for sixty years; he introduced me to John. In spite of Bart's issues with the rest of the family, the three of us remained good friends. We moved to Arizona thirty-five years ago to get away from John's family. Periodically, while Bart and Gina were together, they came out here to visit. John and Bart would spend all week playing golf and hiking in the desert. Gina and I shopped until we dropped, and the four of us had many wonderful times in and around Phoenix.

"Unfortunately, even John couldn't convince Gina to break away from New York and the rest of their family. Ever since we were teenagers, Bart and John's older brother Al despised each other. Al constantly filled Gina's head with exaggerations and lies about Bart. Bart was always crazy about Gina, and in her own strange way, she loved him. Even after their divorce and despite all the bullshit he took from her and Alfonse, Bart always dreamed that, one day, they would live happily ever after, and before her death, they almost did. If he could, John probably would have talked to you about some of the stuff that went on with his family, but unfortunately he developed early-onset Alzheimer's about five years ago. He is no longer capable of distinguishing reality from delusion."

At that point I sensed Patty Jo was all talked out on the subject; I told her I would like to have met John before his disease set in. I then thanked her for talking to me. Before she hung up, she said something strange: "It might be worth your while to listen to your caller from Monaco." Although the call did not shed much light on the attack, at least I was able to get some sense of the family dynamics that probably put this whole thing in motion and perhaps some kind of limited endorsement for my mysterious caller.

CHAPTER 2

As promised, exactly fourteen days later I received another call. This time the country code was Spain. The caller asked if I had done my research and made a decision. I told him about my newspaper findings and what I discreetly obtained from my NYPD classmate. Hearing this, the caller sounded upset and expressed concern about repercussions from the inquiry with the retired police captain. When I assured him it was an innocent discussion revolving around contacting missing classmates for our fiftieth high school reunion in 2012, he seemed relieved. I also assured him there had not been any visits or inquiries from law enforcement since that conversation. I never told him about my telephone conversation with Patty Jo. In retrospect, I should have realized there had to be a reason why the caller became nervous when I mentioned the retired policeman.

The caller then identified himself as Carlos Diaz and asked again if I wanted to hear the whole story and take on the book project. I told him it sounded like a fascinating story but I had some reservations. I then asked, "When are you going to be in New York, so we can meet in person to discuss this further?"

He laughed. "What's the weather like in New York?"

"Mid-20s and snow flurries."

"I don't think New York is someplace I'd like to visit just now. It was in the low 60s here today. Ever been to Spain?"

"No, my wife and I have been meaning to take a trip to Madrid, but haven't gotten around to it."

"Suppose I send first-class plane tickets to Spain for you and your wife? I could rent you a villa in Malaga. The weather is really balmy there this time of year. The tickets for your return flight would be open-ended. If you don't like what you hear, you can return to New York whenever you want." After a brief hesitation he added, "Check with your wife. I'll call you back in two days. If you're up to a winter vacation in Spain, I can have those airline tickets in your hands the following day."

Marie was apprehensive, but I reminded her that when we retired we promised ourselves we would travel. What better way to start than with an all-expenses-paid winter vacation in Spain? She did make me promise if things didn't feel right, we would come home immediately.

■ ■ ■

Marie and I boarded Iberia Airlines' New Year's Day nonstop red-eye at New York's JFK airport for our flight to Madrid. As soon as we settled into seats 2A and 2B in first class, the flight attendant was on us like she was expecting a big tip or something. Handing us the first class menu, she asked, "Can I get you something to drink, Mr. and Mrs. Stanfield?"

Disregarding all the sound advice for avoiding jet lag, I ordered a Beefeater martini; Marie asked for a bottle of water.

I have never been a fan of gourmet food; just give me a rare-barbecued beef or tuna steak, a potato, and salad, and I'm in heaven. If I have to go to an ethnic restaurant and it's my choice, I always pick Italian. When I looked at the menu, I was a little apprehensive. Fortunately, since English is the universal language of the airlines, the menu was in both Spanish and English.

I was able to determine *solomillo de vaca con salsa de trufa y gratten de patata con queso manchego* is actually steak and potatoes. Marie has a slightly more sophisticated palate and went for the *guiso de pollo de corral con vino y vanilla*, which is chicken in wine and vanilla sauce.

Marie fell asleep about ten minutes after dessert. Oh, how I envy an uncluttered mind. I, on the other hand, spent the rest of the flight reexamining the peculiar events that led up to our imminent "winter vacation" in Spain.

I think I actually did fall asleep as we passed over the Azores, but before I did, there were four burning questions left on my mind. First, how did a kid from Hicksville ever get involved with a New York City Mafia don's sister? Second, what did the F stand for in F. Bart LaRocca? Third, did Bart really have the balls to attack his brother-in-law? Lastly, if he did, how did he avoid detection for so long?

CHAPTER 3

I hate red-eyes. Even in first class you get off the plane feeling dirty and stiff as a board; except for Marie. Do you think it was not having the booze that allowed her to bounce off the jetway like a thirty-year-old? It was ten o'clock when we finally cleared customs at Madrid's Barajas International Airport. Marie immediately spotted a uniformed driver holding a MR. & MRS. STANFIELD sign. Marie caught the driver's attention and we negotiated through the maze of people to reach each other. He greeted us with only a smile and a nod. Our driver took Marie's suitcases and handed me an envelope while beckoning us to follow him. It was already a sunny 51 degrees when I dragged my tired aching body, along with two overstuffed suitcases, out of the terminal. I waited to open the envelope until we were safely in the backseat of a black Mercedes sedan. The typed note inside read:

Mr. & Mrs. Stanfield,
  Relax and enjoy Madrid for a few days. All
your expenses will be covered. You will be
contacted about the rest of your itinerary.
  Carlos

The thirty-minute drive from the airport was a harrowing experience. Horns blared as we drove through the central city and past the Prado Museum, stopping less than one hundred yards away and right in front of the palatial Ritz Hotel. Marie, a retired art teacher, was still gawking over her shoulder at the Prado when we entered the large marble-floored lobby with ornate pillars, high ceilings, and handmade carpets. "Oh well," she exclaimed, "I guess this is acceptable for a few nights."

The gorgeous young desk clerk with classic Mediterranean features checked us in and confirmed, in perfect English, "You have an open-ended booking and all charges, including meals and all other hotel amenities, will be covered." *First-class airline tickets, limo, five-star hotel, all expenses paid, not bad,* I thought.

The desk clerk signaled the same young valet who had picked up our luggage from the Mercedes. After he had scurried over with the luggage cart, the desk clerk instructed us, "Please follow Damien to the elevator. He will take you to your suite and make sure you have everything you need. Please enjoy your stay with us and do not hesitate to contact the front desk with any questions."

Before we left the desk, Marie asked the clerk, "Do you know how late the Prado is open?"

"Until 8:00 p.m.," the desk clerk responded.

When we were finally in the room alone, Marie asked, "Don't they eat dinner real late in Spain?"

"Yeah, I think they start dinner after 8:00 p.m."

"Great," she said. "Let's take a quick nap, grab some brunch, and then hit the Prado."

Happy to hear the word *nap,* I yawned and replied, "Sounds good to me."

Marie was excited when she woke me at 1:30, a mere two hours after I'd conked out. "Hurry," she ordered. "If we don't waste too much time eating, we can have five hours at the museum." She was already showered and dressed; I quickly followed suit. At the tapas bar in the lobby, we grabbed an antipasto, which consisted of wonderful pancetta, olives, cheeses, and bread. Fifteen minutes later she had us dashing across the street to the Prado.

For the next five hours Marie was in heaven. I couldn't remember seeing her so excited since our honeymoon in Bermuda forty-two years earlier. She practically drooled at El Greco's *Nobleman with his hand on his chest*. I thought I saw a tear in her eyes as we viewed Goya's *The Third of May 1808 in Madrid: the executions on Principe Pio hill*. It went on and on, Rembrandt, Titian, Raphael, Fra Angelico, and Rubens.

Marie was still giddy over dinner at the hotel's Goya Restaurant as she revisited the many masterpieces we had just observed; excitedly she prompted me, "Which one was your favorite?"

When I nonchalantly replied, "Ruben's *The Three Graces*," she kicked me under the table and whispered, "I should have known you'd like the nude women." I signed the check, and hand in hand we beat a hasty retreat to our room.

On Sunday morning we attended High Mass at San Francisco El Grande, the finest church in Madrid, modeled after the Pantheon in Rome. By Sunday night, I was getting antsy. Over dinner I commented to Marie, "I don't understand why this Carlos character is making us cool our heels here in Madrid. He said he was going to get us a place in Malaga."

"What's your problem, Charles? You don't like spending a few days alone with me in this romantic city?"

"Of course, that's not the reason. This is great! I'm loving every minute, but his not showing himself makes me wonder if this whole thing was bogus from the start."

"Look babe, we've got return tickets and the receptionist told us everything in the hotel was paid for. What's the worst case? We get tired of waiting and use the tickets to go home."

"I guess you're right," I agreed. For the next three days we enjoyed both the classic luxury of the five-star hotel and never-ending wonders of the old-world city. Finally, on the afternoon of the third day when we returned to the suite, I found an envelope that had been slipped under our door. The note read:

> Mr. & Mrs. Stanfield,
> A driver will pick you up in the lobby
> at 7:00 a.m. tomorrow morning.
> Carlos

CHAPTER 4

January 5, 2010
Madrid, Spain

Promptly at 6:45 a.m. I called for a valet to pick up our luggage. Ten minutes later we arrived at the main entrance and were greeted by the same driver who had collected us from the airport.

Assuming we were to be driven a few hours south to Malaga, we were surprised when the driver headed in the opposite direction. Twenty-five minutes later we arrived at a small private airport, Madrid-Torrejón. A small two-engine Beechcraft Baron 58P was waiting for us. Again we had to wait on the tarmac for about fifteen minutes. Finally, a man wearing tight jeans, cowboy boots, a black safari hat, and sunglasses hurried out of the terminal and walked briskly across the tarmac. He bounded up the steps. Stopping at the top of the steps, he turned to take one last look around the airport. Apparently satisfied by what he saw, he pulled the cabin door shut. The new passenger greeted the pilot in Spanish, then turned and headed directly back to the passenger seat facing us in club-style seating. There were two open single seats at the front of the plane, so we were somewhat surprised by the stranger's seating choice.

While the pilot was revving up the engines and taxiing to the runway, I couldn't help staring at our fellow passenger. He seemed familiar, but I couldn't place him. Besides his clothes, his physical appearance was definitely Mediterranean with brown eyes, wavy black hair, a mustache, and a week-old scraggy salt-and-pepper beard. His age was elusive; the sparkle in his eyes, his physique, his mannerisms, and his choice of clothes said fifties; yet, up close, the wrinkles of his skin and graying of his beard and mustache suggested ten years older. He must have noticed me staring at him because he acknowledged me with a brief nod, which quickly transitioned into a broad smile. I returned the smile but with what must have been a quizzical expression.

Astutely, the stranger said, in what I assumed was a put-on New York accent, "How you doin'?"

"Fine," I replied. Then, not to be outdone by a foreigner, I countered with, "How you doin'?"

Smiling, the stranger replied, "You don't recognize me, do you?"

"There is something familiar about you, but I don't know from where. Enlighten me."

"It was a long time ago, Chuck; or do you now prefer to be called Charles?"

"Charles," I automatically responded, continuing to study the other man's features for several more seconds, silently admonishing myself for not being able to place the face. Finally, I saw the resemblance. "Damn! Is that you, Bart?"

"I was wondering how long it would take you to recognize me. I've had a few facial adjustments since we last met twenty years ago. I'm also twenty-five pounds lighter and significantly more buffed, don't you think?"

"So, this whole Carlos thing was a ruse?"

"Obviously, the being-dead part wasn't true but everything else is; along with probably most of the stuff you've dug up. I am in hiding from my brother-in-law and I want to tell my story to somebody who will use it as the foundation for a novel. I didn't put up a couple of grand to get you over here just to yank your chain or catch up on old times."

"OK," I smirked. "So anything new in your life, Bart?"

He must have liked that, because he let out a hearty laugh.

After an exchange of brief pleasantries, Bart offered us coffee and pastries from a cabinet neatly hidden under the table between us. While we ate, Bart explained the reason for the ruse, including the stopover in Madrid, was for security reasons. "I assume there is still an open contract on my life, and law enforcement may still have an interest in finding me. I had you waiting for the last four days in Madrid to make sure you were not being followed."

He then coyly asked, "So now you know that I am alive and under a Mafia death sentence, how are you feeling about this trip?"

I was about to respond when Marie injected, "I am more concerned about potentially aiding a criminal than about being caught in the crossfire of a Mafia hit."

I added my concurrence and asked the $64,000 question: "Did you do it? Did you really attack your brother-in-law?"

Bart's response was so immediate it was obvious he had anticipated the question. "If I told you definitely one way or the other, would it make a difference?"

Marie and I both expressed the opinion that, if we knew for sure he had been involved in a felony, we would feel a moral and civil obligation to inform the authorities.

"Fair enough," said Bart, "so I guess I won't give you my answer too soon. In the meantime, can we agree that neither of you will reveal anything about what I tell you until after you have heard the whole story? Then if you want to go to the authorities, do it."

Warily we both agreed to his conditions.

Seeing my chance to have some of my burning questions answered, I asked, "So, how did you ever get involved with Gina? Weren't the Nicosias from Brooklyn or someplace in the City while you grew up out on the Island?"

A mischievous grin crossed Bart's mouth. "I slapped her on the butt with a ping-pong paddle."

Marie chuckled, and I responded, "Yeah right, hotshot! You're telling me you just walked up to the daughter of a Mafia don and slapped her on the ass. Give me a break!"

"Really, it was at a party during our senior year in high school; when I did it, I didn't realize she was a Nicosia."

"Oh, I gotta hear this story. Go on, lay it on us."

Bart began, "Remember how easy it was for us football players to crash parties all over the Island? Well, one Saturday night after a Bishop Ott basketball game at Holy Cross High School, a few of us crashed a party in Jamaica Estates. It was at the house of a Mary Louis Academy girl whose parents were away for the weekend. As usual, our notoriety and a case of beer was enough to get us in. We weren't there very long, and I was playing ping-pong with one of the Holy Cross guys when the ball got loose on the floor and one of the girls bent over to pick it up. What could I do? She's bending over, three feet from me with her ass virtually staring me in the face. I couldn't help myself. I slapped her on the butt with the paddle. The girl, surprised and outraged, turned, saw the paddle in my hand and punched me square in the gut. Fortunately, she missed my solar plexus. Somehow I managed to appear undaunted and not double over. We stared at each other for a few seconds and then she exclaimed, 'I know you. You're Bart LaRocca. I'm Gina Nicosia, Al and John's sister. No wonder Al hates you. You're a jerk.'

"While this feisty Mary Louis girl was berating me, I had a chance to check her out from head to toe. She was a classic Italian beauty with an olive complexion framed by gleaming jet-black hair that draped halfway down her back. She had the same dark brown eyes as her brother Al, but on her they somehow looked soft and inviting while Al's made you nervous and wanting to look away. She was nearly as tall as I was, and wow, what a body. This wasn't the same flat-chested eighth grader I met a few times when I used to hang out with her brother John.

"When she finished shouting at me, I matter-of-factly said, 'Sorry, I thought that spider might crawl up your skirt.' She gave me a funny look; then she just laughed out loud. A slow song was playing so I asked her to dance. She hesitated, then said, 'Sure, as long as you promise not to let anything crawl up my skirt.'

"As soon as I put my arm around her, she seemed to ease into my caress, letting her head rest on my shoulder. My senses went into overdrive. I had never experienced anything like it before. The silky feel of her hair on the side of my face, her tantalizing smell, and the electricity pulsing through my body as we gently brushed together transported me to a new emotional dimension. We never stopped dancing that night until the guys dragged me out to go home."

Marie and I were mesmerized by Bart's story. We just sat there absorbing it for a minute. Eventually I said, "So you knew Al and John before you started dating Gina?"

Before Bart could answer, the pilot announced we would be landing in ten minutes. Peering out the window, Bart suggested, "We should continue this later. By the way, you'll probably think I'm really paranoid, but we are not landing in Malaga; I thought it would be safer here in the Algarve region of Portugal."

▪ ▪ ▪

As we disembarked the plane into the balmy 65-degree sunshine, Bart turned and said, "Here I am known as Carlos Diaz, but if it's easier for you, you can still call me Bart and I would really like to call you Chuck."

"What the hell, all of a sudden Charles sounds so stuffy. It's Chuck from here on out."

We quickly passed through the small terminal and straight to a Range Rover parked in the nearby palm tree–lined lot.

Bart headed south on N125, which the Portuguese would call a secondary highway; I'd call it a narrow country road. For the next fifteen minutes we wound south through open fields until we finally entered the small city of Portimão on Portugal's southern coast. Crossing over the Rio de Alvor, he continued for another forty kilometers. My first impression of southwestern Portugal was exactly as the travel brochures advertise: picturesque towns, flower-covered hillsides, broad sandy beaches, and breathtaking cliffs overlooking a vibrant blue ocean.

Approaching the oceanfront city of Albufeira, there was a noticeable increase in traffic and pedestrians. Bart explained the Albufeira area is a popular tourist region in Portugal frequented by both retirees and vacationers from all over Europe. Bart gave us a quick tour of the town; first driving through the Old Town with its charming labyrinth of narrow streets lined with shops, then through New Albufeira, the touristy part of town populated with scores of cafes, restaurants, and bars. We finally wound up at a luxurious beachfront resort consisting of single family homes, four-unit villas, and a magnificent oceanfront hotel. His first stop was at the rental office. After verifying our villa was paid for the rest of the month, I signed the lease. Bart then led us to a ground-floor, one-bedroom villa with an outstanding palm tree–framed view of the ocean. He assisted us with our luggage and gave us a quick walk-through of the apartment including the fully stocked pantry, refrigerator, and liquor cabinet. He had done a fine job planning our stay. He supplied us with maps of the resort and local area along with a number of the standard tourist brochures.

While we unpacked and changed into our resort clothes, Bart made a pot of coffee. He was quite the tour guide. Over coffee he went over the maps and brochures, filling us in on places of interest. Lastly, he took us on a walking tour of the resort.

Around 1:30 he asked, "Do you like seafood?"

Marie enthusiastically responded in the affirmative, I just nodded unenthusiastically. He drove a short ten minutes to Ze do Peixe Assado Restaurant on Estrada de Santa Eulalia. On the way he explained this restaurant was the best place in the area for local seafood prepared in the classic Algarve style. It was a simple place. The motif was white stucco walls, red tablecloths and a few framed lithographs of boats and the sea. There was little to draw your attention, except for the wonderful aroma of fish and garlic and the fact virtually every table was still full at nearly 2:00 p.m.

Bart spotted a booth at the far window. Walking past the tables, it was obvious to me this was a favorite place for both locals and tourists. I picked up on a smattering of Portuguese, Spanish, German, French, and Cockney English. Our waitress soon arrived and greeted Bart in Portuguese as if they knew each other. Then, turning to us, she asked in English, "Americans, right? Have you dined here before?"

This wasn't the first time during our trip that a waitress automatically knew we were American. It's funny how Europeans can spot Americans right off. Somebody once told me it's the shoes, but this time our feet were hidden under the table.

Marie replied yes, we were Americans, and no, we hadn't been there before.

"I believe you'd describe us as home-style. There is no menu; courses of fish will be periodically delivered to your table and you take what you want. In addition, I will bring a jug of wine, a bowl of potatoes, and a bowl of fresh salad."

When she departed, Bart got down to business. "Look, we need to decide how we are going to work. I don't know how long this is going to take, but you can't spend a month in Portugal without taking some time soaking up the culture and experiencing as much as you can of the Iberian Peninsula. Do you have a preferred schedule you would like to follow?"

"No, I don't, but Marie and I have discussed it; and she definitely prefers not to be involved in any of our business discussions."

Shrugging, Bart offered, "If you want, Marie, I can suggest some interesting places to go and things to do in the area." Turning to me he announced, "Tomorrow morning a friend of mine will deliver a rental car. All charges will be prepaid through the end of the month. You will probably just have to sign for it."

After a brief hesitation he asked, "Do either of you play golf?"

"We both took it up since we retired. We're not very good but we do enjoy being outdoors and the challenge of the game."

Obviously pleased, Bart replied, "You'll find golf here in the Algarve rivals anything in the States. I can rent you clubs and get you passes for golf at some of the nicer courses within thirty kilometers of Albufeira. If Marie is interested, I will hook her up with a group of gals that play on Tuesday and Thursday mornings at a nine-hole course on the ridge overlooking the ocean. It is a well-maintained course with a Pebble Beach–type finishing hole.

"If it's OK with you, Chuck," continued Bart, "we can start weekday mornings at 8:00 a.m. and go until either of us decides he wants to do something else. We can break it up with golf and fishing occasionally. How's that sound?"

"It sounds good; I look forward to starting in the morning."

By then, the waitress had delivered the wine, potatoes, and salad and was making the rounds to each table with a platter of fish. Her first offering was whole trout. She followed that with deliveries of tuna steaks, whole sardines, salmon, prawns and some kind of white fish. Everything was cooked in a simple olive oil and garlic seasoning. The wine, a local red table wine, seemed to get much better as we drained the second jug. Two hours later, having exhausted both our appetites and our memories, Bart paid the bill in cash and to my surprise soberly drove us back to the villa.

CHAPTER 5

January 6, 2010
The Algarve, Portugal

The next morning, bubbling over with enthusiasm, Bart arrived at our condo shortly after 8:00 a.m. "Ready to go, Chuck?"

"Absolutely, I can't wait to get started!"

"So, where's Marie?"

"She left for the resort's health club about fifteen minutes ago," I responded.

"Well good, glad to see she is already making use of the resort's amenities. How would you like to take a walk down to the beach?

It's really nice this morning and I could use the exercise and feel the fresh sea breeze on my face."

With the seashell path crunching under our sandals and the palm branches gently flapping in the light morning breeze, Bart said to me, "The reason I chose you is not only because you're a former classmate and writer, but you are also an attorney licensed in the state of New York. Even though I am not currently accused of any crimes, some of what I am going to relay to you is terribly incriminating. At some point, I may need a pretty broad spectrum of legal representation. Chances are New York state, the federal authorities, and perhaps even some foreign governments will consider charges. Under those circumstances, I would require one key person orchestrating the whole defense. I was hoping you might be willing to fill that role."

While I was considering his proposition we arrived at the beach. As we were removing our sandals, I hesitatingly pointed out, "First of all, I have not practiced criminal law since I left the Boston DA's office thirty-five years ago to work in my grand-father's firm. Second, I don't see how I could maintain client confidentiality and still write an accurate story."

Dodging the last gasps of a surprisingly long-running wave, Bart matter-of-factly responded, "Who says you have to publish anything before the legal issues are resolved and why does it have to be accurate? I always figured this would be a work of fiction based in part on historical events, sort of like one of those James Michener epics. Hell, at our age, we have a hard time remembering what happened yesterday, much less decades ago. I am going to tell you a story based on my faded memories. You, on your part, can take literary license to make it even more compelling and marketable. You can use fictional names and places. You can even put in a qualification that it is a work of fiction loosely based on some historic events."

After a momentary pause he added, "If you agree to represent me, I will pay you a $10,000 retainer and you can keep half of any proceeds from the book. The other half can be used to cover any legal expenses. Whatever you don't need can be split with my sister Fran and Bishop Ott High School. Oh, yeah, if there are no book proceeds, I still have enough money to cover quite a bit of legal expenses.

"But," added Bart, "as far as you no longer being a criminal lawyer, I don't believe that will be a problem. I think the kind of attorney I need is more of a negotiator than a trial lawyer."

"Why's that?" I asked. "Are you planning on pleading out?"

A sneaky smirk crossed over Bart's mouth as he put his arm around my shoulder. "Buddy, I believe I have a get-out-of-jail-free card."

We continued along the shoreline in silence.

Curious, I said, "So what makes you think you can get a legal pass on all this?"

"I have irrefutable evidence that links Al Nicosia to the killing of a New York state trooper. Don't you think the authorities would be willing to overlook my transgressions for the opportunity to put Al in the electric chair?"

"When can I see this evidence?"

"I don't have it in my possession; it has been carefully guarded for over three decades, waiting for the right moment to turn it over to authorities. Now is not the right time to reveal its location; I think we are close but if even a hint of this gets out before certain events take place, the lives of several really good people would be at risk."

I pondered this a few minutes as we turned around and headed back in the direction we had just come. I never liked my clients keeping stuff from me and this was no exception. But if the evidence was real and I walked away now, I'd probably kick myself. "I'd like to be part of this," then with a well-timed pause I added, "but I can't provide the appropriate counsel if I can't judge for myself how good our case is."

A rogue wave crashed a short distance from us, and the wash caught us off guard. We both scurried back up the beach before our Bermuda shorts were soaked. When we were clear, Bart offered, "Look, you've already agreed to hear me out before you decide whether to contact the authorities; let's leave it at that, but my offer still stands. I believe, before we are done, you will be convinced I have iron-clad evidence and my not revealing it to you now is the right thing to do."

Trusting he was right, I cautiously replied, "I can live with that for now."

"Good" was his cheery reply as he turned to shake my hand.

While we wandered along the beach and the sun began to warm the chilly morning air, I asked Bart, "So what does the F stand for in F. Bart LaRocca?"

"Congratulations, most people never notice my first name isn't Bart, and I don't advertise it. In fact, Bart is nowhere on my birth certificate. My real name is Fagan Bardon LaRocca. Yeah, I see that look in your eyes saying, *What kind of a name is Fagan Bardon for a guinea?* That's exactly what my father thought over in France when he received the letter from my mother announcing my birth. His name was Francis and he always hated it. Before he was shipped out to Europe for the Normandy invasion, he and my mother could not agree on a boy's name. So the last thing he said before he left was, 'If it is a boy, I don't care what you name him, as long as it is not Francis.' My mother, Margaret, took that to mean naming him after her father, Fagan Bardon O'Boyle, would be a perfect solution.

"My father finally got the letter during the celebration for the liberation of Paris. Needless to say, he was beside himself. He always said the names fit together like corn beef and spaghetti. He had another year in the maelstrom of WWII to contemplate what he was going to call his male heir. Several of his smart-ass buddies suggested 'Fag.' By the time he boarded his liberty ship heading back to the States in August of '45, he had settled on calling me Bart after his CO whom he respected, plus it wasn't too far off from Bardon. The nuns in grammar school were determined to call me by my given name and wouldn't even grade my papers when I signed them Bart. Finally, when I was in the fourth grade, Sister Claire complained to my father at a parent-teacher conference that I was giving her a hard time about using my baptismal name. He told her he also despised the name Fagan and she should loosen up. They worked out a compromise: she would call me Bart if I signed my name F. Bart LaRocca."

After a few minutes of quiet strolling I suggested, "Let's get back to your involvement with the Nicosias. You knew Gina's brothers before you two met at the party? Tell me how that came about."

"I met them when I was going to Christian Brothers in Brooklyn. John and I were in the same class, and we played football together; Al was a year ahead of us."

"Now that you mention it, I have vague recollections of you playing against us and scoring a few touchdowns. In fact, I remember how psyched we were when you showed up at Bishop Ott's preseason football practice at the beginning of our junior year. But why did you ever go there in the first place? That's was one hell of a commute from Hicksville."

"I always wanted to go to Bishop Ott but my father lost his job the year before and we couldn't afford the tuition. In spite of that, my parents along with the priest who ran the CYO sports programs in Hicksville were adamant that I not attend public school. Father Bolling arranged for me to have a tryout with the track coach at Christian Brothers. Apparently, they liked what they saw and offered me a track scholarship. My father, like you, thought it was a too long a commute. When my grandmother heard what the options were, she insisted I stay at her house during the school year. I gotta tell you, the track coach wasn't too happy when I tried out and made the freshman football team, but after he saw me play the first game, he was cool with it as long as I ran indoor and spring track."

"You know what, now I even remember the Nicosia brothers; I hadn't made the connection before. I recall Al was a mean son-of-a-bitch and John was a tough running back. So you knew those guys pretty well, from the football team at Christian Brothers?"

"Oh yeah! Unfortunately, that's when the whole thing started between me and Al.

"John and I were among the eighty-four candidates trying out for the freshman team during our first week at Christian Brothers. The coaches' very difficult task was to pare the group down as quickly as possible. The school only had enough uniforms, pads, and helmets for thirty-eight freshmen; more than half the candidates had to be cut before they had a chance to prove themselves with contact.

"It was easy to pick out the guys who had played on an organized team. They already understood the concept of numbers for positions, had a sense for formations, and generally excelled at the drills. There are usually a few boys who never played organized football but showed real promise. John Nicosia was one of them. He was bigger than most of the other candidates but he was always right near the front during wind sprints. John and I made the cut and picked up our pads and uniforms on Friday after the first week of tryouts. First contact was on Saturday, when the coaches scheduled a double session, which meant workouts in the morning and the afternoon.

"It was in the morning session we first hit it off. We were both trying out for the backfield. All through the morning drills, in oppressive heat, the coaches paired us together. We went one-on-one in blocking and tackling, pushed around the two-man sled, and ran all the same drills alongside each other. By the end of the morning, with every inch of exposed skin caked in a thin layer of dusty sweat, we had developed a strong appreciation of each other's athletic skills and toughness.

"You must remember what a reprieve lunch break was. Two and a half hours to shower, change into street clothes, have lunch and muster up the energy for the afternoon session. At Cathedral, the players usually went to the German deli a couple of blocks away for a sub sandwich and drinks. Most of the guys would then head over to W. E. Sheridan Playground to eat in the shade and recharge for the afternoon session. John, aware of the tradition from his brother Al, who was a sophomore on the varsity team, led a contingent of us freshmen to Sellerberg's Deli then over to the park. It was at the playground that I first met Al Nicosia. Al, as a sophomore on the varsity, was hot shit, and he knew it. Like his brother John, he was big, almost six feet tall and one hundred eighty pounds, but it was his eyes and physique that really caught your attention. Since starting high school, his body had burst out of adolescence; so now, as a sophomore, he had the chest and arms of a full-grown man. He featured dark Italian bedroom eyes with long eyelashes, but they weren't inviting. There was something foreboding about them; maybe it was just the way he seemed to stare right through you. Then there was his walk; well, it wasn't really just a walk; it was somewhere between a swagger and the prowl of a big cat.

"John eagerly introduced me to his brother Al, who inspected me from head to toe. Al then let out a phony laugh and said, loud enough for everyone to hear, 'You're kidding, is this the punk you've been talking about all week? He looks like he should be trying out for the bowling team.' That brought a boisterous howl from the rest of the nearby varsity players. I was seething, but momentarily bit my tongue. It was right then and there that the seeds of our hostility were planted.

Not content with his initial put-down, Al followed up with 'Hey runt, didn't I see you on the bus a couple of times?'

"Still smarting from Al's first shot, I couldn't let this second barb slide. I made sure the seeds of our loathing would germinate by mockingly replying, 'You mean to tell me a big varsity man like you still takes the bus?' Now that pissed Al off, he didn't take too well to returned wisecracks, especially from a lowly freshman."

CHAPTER 6

We were silently sitting on the treacherous cliffs of Cabo de São Vicente, watching two old fishermen standing on what looked like a precarious sliver of granite and casting the lines on their fifteen-foot poles out over the edge to the boiling maelstrom seventy-five meters below. I broke the silence by announcing, "By the way, I didn't get a chance to tell you. I spoke to Patty Jo, and she told me how close the four of you were over the years. It also sounded as if the Nicosia family was associated with the mob long before Al became involved."

"You talked to Patty Jo? How is John doing?" Bart queried excitedly.

"Not good," I sighed. "He apparently can't distinguish reality anymore."

"Damn!" Bart spat out as he unconsciously picked up a nearby stone and tossed it over the cliff. With a far-off look in his eyes he added, "Well, I guess it was inevitable, given the diagnosis."

Um, that's interesting, I thought. *They must have had some contact in the last five years.*

Bart seemed to be in deep thought for a few moments. Then out of nowhere he said, "Let's get back to my introduction to the Nicosias. You know, at the time, their father, Pietro, was an underboss in the Leucchi family."

"Didn't you know that when you met John and Al?"

"Shit no, I had heard of the Mafia but unlike most of the guys from the City, it had no significance in my world. During my two years at Cathedral, I heard guys whispering about their family connection but I didn't pay any attention to them. For the longest time, all I knew was I really liked John and wanted to avoid his brother." Almost without hesitating, he changed thoughts again and his mood brightened. "You know, I've known Patty Jo longer than I've known John. In fact, I introduced them. She lived next door to my grandmother, and from the time I was five years old, I looked forward to seeing Patty Jo whenever I visited Grandma. Until high school, she was a better ballplayer than most of my male friends. Hell, when she was twelve, she could throw the ball better than Jason Giambi could when he played for the Yankees. She was cute, too; not the kind of cute I was attracted to. I always liked the Mediterranean type, but John sure had the hots for her as soon as they met. With her ponytail, she looked like a teenage Debbie Reynolds."

He continued with his now upbeat demeanor, "They are almost the only family or friends I've had contact with over the last nine years. I knew John was a big deal in the International Association of Cardiologists. In '03 I read the association was having their annual convention at the Atlantis Resort, in the Bahamas. At the time, I was still in hiding in the Caribbean. I surprised the two of them in one of the bars while they were waiting for a table for dinner. You should have seen the look on their faces. Anyway, John said he understood why I did what I did to his brother, and he was OK with it. But then I always knew he would be. Before we parted we worked out a way for him to contact me in case of an emergency. He would run an ad on Craigslist in Phoenix under the sporting category. The ad would read '1972 New York Yankee team picture $25.' He would list a random phone number. We figured there wouldn't be too much interest in a picture of a team that finished six and a half games behind the Detroit Tigers. I committed to check Craigslist once a week. Since I always knew how to find him, we agreed I would call. I was to make the call from a pay phone at an international airport and say, 'Honey, I'll be home on such and such date.' Whoever answered would reply, 'Sorry, you've got the wrong number.' The day I mentioned would be the day we'd meet in Nogales, Mexico, at the famous La Roca restaurant at 8:30 p.m. How appropriate is that, La Roca's?

"John first ran the ad in early November of '06; I established December 12 as the day we would meet. When we met at LaRoca's, Patty Jo was with him; they told me of his recently diagnosed condition. He tried to make me think Patty Jo knew nothing about this by asking her to go powder her nose, but I'm pretty sure she knew what he was going to tell me. That's when he told me, for the first time, about the get-out-of-jail-free card. He handed me an envelope with a copy of an affidavit in it. The handwritten document testified to an incident that occurred during John's residency at Yale New Haven Hospital. His father, Pietro, called and told him to be at a marina in Bridgeport at 4:00 a.m. It was June 15, 1971, about 2:00 a.m.; John was scheduled to be at the hospital in four hours, so he had to get someone to cover for him. His father's yacht, with its running lights off, arrived at approximately 4:15. John was ushered on board, where he found his brother Al in serious condition with a bullet in his left leg.

"His father explained that a private ambulance was going to pick them up and take them to a nearby clinic where John could discreetly fix his brother up. Knowing that, as a doctor, he was required by law to report all bullet wounds to the authorities, John reluctantly followed his father's plans. It turned out the ambulance took them to a veterinarian clinic owned by, as his father put it, 'a friend of ours.' John removed the bullet before the clinic opened for business and spent the next two days at a motel watching over his brother. From that day forward, John was always afraid if anyone ever found out what he had done he would lose his license to practice medicine and perhaps do time in prison.

"Neither his father nor his brother ever told John how Al got shot. John never dared ask. However, curious to know what kind of mess his family had gotten him into, John did some checking in the New York papers. It didn't take much for him to discover the front page story about a New York state trooper who stumbled upon an attempted hijacking of a tractor trailer. When the trooper endeavored to thwart the hijacking, a gun battle ensued and he was killed. Based upon blood evidence at the scene, it was believed that, before he died, the trooper was able to wound one of the hijackers. When John returned to work at the hospital, he discovered a bulletin had been issued to all emergency rooms and doctors in a thirteen-state area looking for a cop killer with an unreported bullet wound.

"There wasn't much John could do about the incident, but he made up his mind he would never let his family suck him into something like that again. He documented the incident in the written affidavit and saved the X-rays along with a small, sealed test tube containing the extracted bullet. He then gave the evidence, in a sealed envelope, to a young attorney friend for safekeeping. He never revealed to the attorney what was in the envelope. His instructions to the attorney were that, unless he heard otherwise from John, in the event of John's death he was to turn it over to the FBI. At that time, he wasn't sure if he would ever need the evidence as leverage against his brother, but he figured it wouldn't hurt to have a trump card. John also decided that as soon as he finished his residency, he and Patty Jo would get as far away from New York as they could.

"So, I now have a copy of the affidavit, and John has told the attorney friend he should follow my instructions. If John was right about how his brother was shot, the bullet containing Al's DNA should be a match to the dead trooper's gun and the X-ray should correspond with a healed wound on Al's leg."

"Wow," I exclaimed. "That's dynamite. I would think you do have enough for a free pass . . . and Little Nicky's balls in a vise. But why didn't John ever use it?"

"Well, as I said before, he was concerned that, even if he wasn't prosecuted as an accomplice, he probably would lose his medical license; but I really think it had just as much to do with the 'code.' Even though John is a good person, he just couldn't bring himself to rat on his brother. When we met in Nogales, he figured someday I might be able to use it to come home."

"Yeah," I responded, "this might clear up your legal problems, but that wouldn't stop Little Nicky from sending people after you even if he is on death row."

Nodding, Bart said, "I don't know about you, but I've had enough for today. How about we go have a beer?

"By the way," he added, "when I die, I would like my ashes tossed into the ocean right here."

On the drive back, we stopped at a small bar and restaurant overlooking the ocean. While we were sipping on bottles of

Sagres Preta, Bart suggested, "You ought to bring Marie up this way over the weekend."

CHAPTER 7

The next morning Bart showed up bubbling with enthusiasm and announced a round of golf was on our agenda. When we arrived at the Millennium in Vilamoura, about twenty kilometers from Albufeira, the pro shop paired us with two Spaniards who did not speak a word of English.

In between shots Bart continued to relay experiences from his two years at Christian Brothers High School. The Nicosias also lived in Middle Village, so the teammates rode the bus together. Al, being a hot shot, would often get a ride to and from school with one of the upper classmen. Fortunately, this meant Bart was able to avoid his antagonist. Bart and John Nicosia were stars of the freshman team and soon became close friends. On one of their evening bus rides Bart referred to Al by the nickname he had heard whispered around school, Little Nicky. John's horrified response was, "Don't ever call him that to his face." Surprised by John's emotional reaction, Bart pressed his friend for an explanation. Even though his brother was not on the bus, John whispered the story as if somehow Al would hear him reveal the legend of the nickname Little Nicky.

During Al's first few weeks on the freshman football team, he was caught dogging it during wind sprints. As was the custom, the coaches made him run laps after practice. Because 120 football players can't shower at the same time, the freshman, JV, and varsity teams ended practice about a half hour apart. The freshman team always finished up first, but on that day Al's extra laps put him in the shower with the JV team. One of the JV players, a big tackle, started making fun of the freshman, who was a few months short of his manhood blossoming. Pointing to Al's private parts, he pronounced to the other JV players in the shower, "Get a look at Little Nicky over there!"

The younger, smaller boy was furious but held his temper. That evening, Al clandestinely followed the big tackle home. It turned out the young man, who lived in Bayridge, had to walk through a park after he got off the bus. The next evening, after practice Al quickly took an earlier bus to Bayridge and waited for his tormentor. It was just getting dark when Al saw his victim. Concealing himself behind a tree, he stealthily waited until the other youth approached the tree. Al suddenly sprang out from behind the tree and surprised the bigger boy with a hard kick to the groin. The kid went down, and Al was all over him, punching his face and kicking his ribs. It didn't take long for the bloody and beaten teenager to beg for mercy, but Al was having too much fun to stop. Finally, after what must have seemed like an eternity, the out-of-breath Al Nicosia scornfully told the beaten and bloody youth that if anyone ever called him Little Nicky again he could expect another ass-kicking. He also warned him that if he wanted to live, he better not tell his parents or the cops who beat him up. The terrified teenager apparently decided he didn't want to chance another beating, so he never returned to Cathedral.

■ ■ ■

Bart had covered a lot of ground the last few days and I needed some time to sort out my notes and spend time with Marie. When he ended our round of golf with the disturbing Little Nicky story, I told him I wanted to spend the weekend alone with Marie. He was fine with that but suggested we get an early start on Monday. He said he would pick me up at 5:00 a.m. He suggested we could continue just as well fishing in a boat as sitting on my balcony. Reluctantly I agreed, telling him, "That's fine with me just as long as we continue to move this along." Before he dropped me off, he promised to reveal some interesting stuff on Monday.

■ ■ ■

36

On Saturday Marie and I hung out at one of the five pools at the resort. She did some really interesting still-life sketches and I consolidated my notes. When I got to my notes on the Little Nicky story I told it to her. Her response was "I can't believe he got away with that. It would not turn out like that these days."

I thought about that for a moment and replied, "You're right, today the kid would probably show up in the cafeteria with a gun and blow Al away."

"That's not funny," she said.

Sunday I took Bart's advice and drove Marie up to Cabo de São Vicente. She brought along her sketch pad and pencils. We wandered around the many rocky outcroppings that make up the cape. She popped out a dozen or so sketches of soaring eagles, nesting storks, and waves pounding the cliffs, but her best was of one of those local fishermen casting his line over the precarious edge. It now sits above the mantel on our fireplace.

We capped off a wonderful relaxing day with dinner at a small restaurant in the village of Sagres.

CHAPTER 8

Right on schedule, Bart picked me up at 5:00 a.m. Monday morning. We drove to the marina in Vilamoura where he purchased a fishing permit for me along with containers of frozen bait fish and squid strips. He then rented a small, brightly painted wooden skiff with a 35-horsepower outboard motor. We loaded up his fishing box, two rods and reels, and a cooler loaded with water, sandwiches, and a six-pack of local beer.

Just before we cast off I quipped, "Thank God you're not taking me to fish off the cliffs at Cabo de São Vicente."

His chuckling response was "That kind of scares me, too."

We headed south at full throttle, hugging the coastline for about a half hour. When we stopped and threw out the anchor, we were over a reef and barely in sight of land. Bart explained that this far south on the Atlantic we were starting to get the effects of the warmer Mediterranean waters and its wide array of fish.

He showed me how to bait the hook with the squid strips. Then we each let out a line in about thirty feet of water. After fishing for about an hour, we had each caught and released a few small mackerel and sea bream. As the sun began to warm the cool morning air and the temperature reached a comfortable point, I decided to ask the question that had been bothering me since he told me about his first meeting with Gina. "The other day you said Gina's first words to you were that her brother Al hated you. That couldn't just be from the one incident at the park between double sessions, could it?"

He snickered. "No, there was one other incident at a different park that occurred while I was still attending Christian Brothers. On its own, it was probably enough to solidify his animosity toward me, but the third incident definitely iced it.

"On our rare free days, John and I would meet at Juniper Valley Park in Middle Village. We loved to just mess around playing handball, knocking around in pickup games of basketball, or just hanging out. Periodically, we'd run into Gina and her friends, or Patty Jo and her friends. John was smitten with Patty Jo and pleaded with me to introduce them. It didn't take long for the two of them to become a hot item. I on the other hand had no such feelings for Gina. To me, Gina was a flat-chested eighth grader beneath my social standing.

"By the middle of our sophomore year Patty Jo usually hung out with us at the park. In spite of the fact she could generally beat both of us, John loved to play handball against her. One day during Easter break, Al and his wiseass friends showed up while Patty Jo and John were having a match. Al, being the big shot he was, said he wanted to play the winner. When Patty Jo wins, Al turned into the gaping screaming asshole that he was. He started ragging on his little brother for losing to a girl and predicted how he would beat the pants off her. Well, Patty Jo beat him in the first game. Now Al's buddies are ragging on him. He's pissed and insists on a rematch. Patty Jo beats him again.

Humiliated, he made a half-assed attempt to be gracious, but it was obvious that he was furious. As he and his guys left, we heard them all tossing barb after barb at Al."

"Wow! That's a great story, but how does that get Al on your case?"

"Well," replied Bart, "by then, John and Patty Jo were more than friends. They were dating and I think they were making out. The following Saturday afternoon I came home from a track meet to find Patty Jo sitting on her front stoop. I could tell she was upset; in fact I was pretty sure she had been crying. I sat down next to her. 'What's the matter?' She didn't want to tell me, but I persisted. Finally, she told me she was at the park with her girlfriends, and Al and his boys showed up. Al, needing to get even for the humiliation earlier in the week, couldn't help himself and started mouthing off. He quipped, 'So, how's Patty Jo the dyke? Oh, wait a minute; is Patty Jo really short for Patrick Joseph? I bet one of these days my little brother is going to reach down into those panties and grab a handful of cock.'

"I was livid; I wanted to beat the crap out of him. But first I put my arm around her shoulder and told her what a jerk Al Nicosia was and everybody knew it. Besides, it didn't make any difference what Al said or did, John was the one that really mattered; and he loved her. This seemed to make her feel better, so I told her I had something to do and headed straight over to the Nicosias' house. On the way over, I pondered what I was going to do. Tell John? No, I would handle this myself; John didn't need to be put between his brother and his girlfriend.

"So how was I going to confront Al? No way did I want to get in a straight-up brawl with him. I had heard the stories about the fights he had been in. He was supposedly unrelenting. You could hit him with a brick, and he would just get up and come at you again and again. He had never lost a street fight; and when the fight was over, the other guy's face always looked like a pepperoni pizza. As a result of this reputation, he had not actually been in a fight in quite some time. I'd seen him in a few confrontations and it always went the same way. He would get straight up in other guy's face and tell him that he was going to crack his head open. Each time the other guy backed down and begged Al's forgiveness. So I figured if I got him alone, that's what he would try with me. But I couldn't let him get away with this without at least a verbal rebuke. Perhaps if I could catch him at his house, he'd use his standard intimidation; but when I didn't back down he might not want to get into a bloody confrontation within earshot of his family.

"As luck would have it, Al was alone in the driveway washing his recently acquired 1956 Chevy convertible. I walked up and said, 'Hi asshole, rumor has it you were your normal jerk-off self and tried to humiliate Patty Jo in front of a bunch of other kids. Let me tell you, she is more of a woman than you are a man, *Little Nicky*.'

"Well, I was wrong on both counts. He instantly went ballistic. Perhaps it was my emphasizing the Little Nicky thing. He didn't try to intimidate me, and he would start a fight in his own yard. Dropping the hose and sponge he charged. I was about ten yards away. As he charged, he yelled something that was unintelligible and then, lowering his shoulder, he tried to put one of his infamous crushing tackles on me. Being the nimble back that I was, I sidestepped and put my best straight arm to the side of his forehead. He went down, half on the driveway and half on the grass. Just as he was about to get up and come at me again, John burst out of the house.

"Flabbergasted, he shouted, 'What the hell is all the commotion about?'

"Containing my adrenalin surge I managed an unruffled, 'Oh, Al was just showing me how to fall without getting hurt.'

"The look Al gave me could have melted glass, but he said nothing. I looked at John and said, 'Hey, I just came by to see if you wanted to go down to the avenue and get a pizza.'

"'Yeah,' said John. 'Want to go, Al?'

"Swallowing his rage, Al snarled, 'Nah, I have to wax my car.' We left Al simmering in the driveway."

Awed with Bart's brashness, I couldn't contain my reaction, "Wow, that was ballsy! Did Al ever come after you again for that?"

"Nope, it turned out I was half right. Given time to consider the consequences, I guess he decided kicking my ass wasn't worth his brother finding out what an asshole he was with Patty Jo."

"Now you really have me curious. What was the other incident?"

Before Bart could answer, my pole was nearly ripped from my hands. The seven-foot graphite composite rod immediately bent into a crescent shape and the line started screaming off the reel. Bart carefully made his way across the boat, urging me to keep the tip up. I helplessly watched the line race out into the ocean, and Bart began tightening the drag. When he had adjusted it to where he wanted it, he began advising me to keep just enough pressure on the fish to prevent him from diving into the sharp rocks and coral where the forty-pound line could be severed, then to work the fish until it tired out. He told me to work the fish by slowly pulling up on the rod then letting it relax while frantically reeling up the slack.

I worked the fish for ten minutes before we even got a glimpse of it. When it did flash near the surface, it seemed smaller than its fight. Then as quickly as it surfaced, it dove and made a frantic run away from the boat. Another ten minutes of working the rod and winding the reel, and I had him at the side of the boat where Bart could scoop him into the net. As my hands and forearms went into spasms, Bart unhooked a forty-pound corvina.

"Well, looks like we have tonight's dinner and plenty left over to freeze," Bart announced. He dropped my catch in the empty cooler and transferred some ice from our food cooler. He turned to me and said, "There goes the ice. I guess we'll have to eat our lunch and drink our beer now."

So that's what we did, ate sandwiches and drank beer. We never put another line in the water. After we replayed my epic battle with the "sea monster" several times, Bart recounted his next confrontation with Al Nicosia.

■ ■ ■

In early spring of Bart's sophomore year, two events again changed his life. First, his father finally got a good-paying job that afforded the LaRoccas the luxury of paying for Bart's Catholic school tuition. The second event was when his grandmother suffered a stroke. Although it was minor and she quickly recovered, as a precaution, the brothers decided she should move in with her eldest son in Westbury. For the last month of the school year, Bart had to take the train from Hicksville to Jamaica and then catch the bus to Williamsburg. Although Bart was now relatively happy at CBHS, he did not relish the commute all the way from Hicksville. Fortunately, his father also felt the commute was too long. Over the summer, father and son convinced Christian Brothers High not to contest Bart's eligibility if he was to compete for another Catholic high school in their league. With this release in hand, Bart was accepted at Bishop Ott High School in Mineola. Of course, it helped that Bart, as a freshman and sophomore, had been a thorn in the school's side in both football and track.

"Al was pissed when he found out I had transferred and was going to be playing for Christian Brothers' archrival Bishop Ott. But there was one incident that sealed the deal. Do you remember the Christian Brothers game our junior year?"

"I'll never forget it; that had to be the maddest I ever saw Coach Thomas. I think we were down 21 to zip at the half."

Bart grinned in acknowledgment. "He sure gave us hell at halftime. Remember, he benched most of the seniors to start the second half."

"Boy, did we come out of that locker room fired up."

"We sure did. Remember Toche took that second half kickoff and ran it back eighty yards for a TD. Then on the next series Tiny was so pumped, he took out their tackle, linebacker, and safety all on the same play; and Toche followed him up the middle for fifty-five more yards to get us to 21–14. That's when it got interesting because the linebacker Tiny leveled was Al Nicosia. I could tell by Al's eyes and the spittle coming out of his mouth as he cussed his teammates and us, he was now out for blood. I remember that we stopped them again and started marching down the field. We were on about their forty-yard line and Ed

Doerr called a quarterback rollout pass with an option to run. I no longer remember the name and number of the play but it called for me to set up out on the flank and do a flare-out about fifteen yards downfield. So I did my thing, and Ed decides he has an open field and starts around the corner. Well, Al, who was playing middle linebacker on the play, first backpedals to cover a short pass over the middle, then when he sees Ed head for the corner, he starts sprinting diagonally to cut him off. I realize Ed is going to run so I start back in to make a block. I picked up Al charging toward Ed; I could tell through his face mask that Al couldn't wait to put a hit on our quarterback. He was so intent on delivering a lethal blow to Ed he never saw me coming off to his side. When he was about two yards from pounding Ed, I ran my shoulder straight into his thigh, just above the knee. He went ass over teakettle and landed in a lump on the turf. Ed got all the way down to the fifteen-yard line. After the play was over, I tried to help Al up, but he just yelled, 'I'll get you, LaRocca.' Al was down on the ground for a full minute and had to leave the game for a couple of plays. While he was out we moved to the one-yard line and scored again on Ed's quarterback sneak. I then caught a little flare-out pass for the two-point conversion and we were ahead 22–21 with less than three minutes to go."

Bart's description of the game brought back vivid memories for me. "God, the way you've described it makes it seems like it all happened yesterday! I can still recall their next offensive series when Tiny almost took the quarterback's arm off. They were moving the ball pretty good down the field when their QB went back to pass. Tiny came in from his blind side and went for the ball just as the QB cocked his arm. I could hear the quarterback scream when Tiny swatted his arm like a big grizzly bear and the ball came out. Do you remember that I recovered it?"

"Of course I do, that was like the cherry on top of the whipped cream." Bart paused to regain his train of thought then continued, "So, after the game, we were walking to the center of the field for the traditional handshake and Al made a beeline for me. Fortunately I was sandwiched between Tiny and Billy Sellers who were probably the only two guys on the field Al figured were as tough as him. Al comes toward me and starts yelling, 'LaRocca, you little prick, I ought to kick your ass right here.'

"Tiny and Bill pick up on this. Billy steps between Al and me while Tiny moves his 6-foot-4, 275 pounds menacingly closer to Al. Not being completely stupid, Al stared at Tiny for a second then quietly turned to walk away. Feeling pretty safe, I yelled back at Al, 'I'd rather be a little prick than have a little prick.' He didn't even turn around, but I thought I saw smoke coming off his head."

Chuck and I laughed until we almost pissed in our pants, then we had another beer before pulling up anchor to head back to the marina. Bart shouted over the engine noise, "I bet you can't wait to show your woman what her brave and cunning mate has provided for supper."

CHAPTER 9

January 12, 2010

Bart arrived at our villa promptly at 8:00 a.m. Just before he left the night before, he promised to get back into his courtship with Gina. After hearing his story the previous day, I was also curious to learn how their dating ever got past Al.

■ ■ ■

The Saturday after Gina and Bart met at the party in Jamaica Heights, Bishop Ott had a home basketball game against Christian Brothers. John showed up with Patty Jo and Gina. Seeing them walk into the gym, Bart bounded down the stands enthusiastically greeting John and Patty Jo, but he was "too cool" to reveal the excitement he felt at seeing Gina again. Even though it was Gina that talked her brother into attending the game, she too played it cool. They all watched the game together. Bart was sitting between John and Patty Jo, but he couldn't stop sneaking peeks over at Gina.

Bart had little trouble talking the three of them into staying for the sock hop after the game. It was Patty Jo who finally broke the ice between Gina and Bart. After watching them pretend to be uninterested in each other for most of the afternoon, she chided them, "Enough, you two, it's obvious you're hot for each other, get out there and dance." Anxiously gazing into Gina's eyes, Bart gave her an inquiring expression; in response Gina took his hand and led him out on the dance floor.

In spite of their feelings, halfway through their first slow dance, an awkward vibe still hung in the air. Their bodies hardly touched and each seemed to have retreated into their own universe. Neither of them said anything for a long while; finally, Bart ratcheted up the courage to unmask his true emotions by announcing, "I couldn't stop thinking about you all week. Maybe I didn't show it but I was so excited to see you walk in the gym."

Looking up into his eyes, Gina instantly burst into a broad smile. "I got goose bumps when I saw you headed toward us."

Gina's acknowledgment of her emotions unleashed a tsunami of exhilaration through Bart. With a great effort to contain his eagerness, he gently drew her up against his body. "In that case, we should probably dance a little closer." She did not resist.

They danced every dance together, with Gina declining every offer from other guys to cut in while Bart glared at each interloper. By the end of the hop Bart confidently asked, "So you want to go out on a date, just you and me?"

"What did you have in mind, a movie?"

"I don't know yet, there's usually a party somewhere Friday or Saturday nights. I haven't heard about any yet, but it's still early. If there is going to be something, I'll know by Wednesday."

"When you decide something, call me. I'll have to get my parent's permission to go out alone on a date, but John will put in a good word for you."

On Tuesday Bart heard about a Friday night party in Roslyn at

Skip Tyler's. Skip's parents had both been killed in a car crash a few years earlier. Skip and his twenty-five-year-old single brother inherited the house and a small fortune.

Bart called Gina and told her about the party in Roslyn. He didn't say anything about the wild unchaperoned parties that made Skip a legend. She got her unsuspecting parents' permission to go to the party with Bart, on the condition he would first come over for dinner. Having dinner with a date's family was always a scary proposition; in this case, with Al being away at college and having been good friends with John, Bart was actually looking forward to Friday evening. Following track practice he drove the 1954 Ford he inherited from his father into Queens.

In spite of his relationship with John, Bart hadn't spent much time at the Nicosias' home. He had met Mrs. Nicosia a few times and he had gotten good vibes from her. She always seemed pleased to see him with John. He had met Mr. Nicosia after some of the freshmen and JV football games. John's father always made a point of coming over to congratulate the boys after a good game. Bart had heard the rumors John's father was connected to the Mafia, but Bart was totally naïve as to what that really meant.

He showed up at Gina's around five. The old three-story house was large and built on a long, narrow lot. It had a two-ribbon concrete driveway that made its way to the backyard and a detached garage. Gina answered the door dressed in jeans and a tight white sweater underneath a red apron. The loose apron hardly detracted from her exceptional figure. Again, his senses went into overdrive, but this time, besides the electricity he felt being in Gina's presence he was acutely aware of the tantalizing aromas emanating from the depths of the house. Enthusiastically she greeted Bart and apologetically explained she was helping her mother make dinner and had to get back in the kitchen. Bart followed her through the living room and dining room into the kitchen.

Mrs. Nicosia was busy over the stove when Gina and Bart walked in. Eleonora Nicosia was the epitome of a middle-aged Italian mother. She was a little plump but still attractive. Her short dark hair was peppered with gray. She had on a baggy flow-ered housedress and, of course, the ever-present apron. Appre-hensive of how she might feel about him dating her daughter, Bart had elected to start with a formal greeting. "Good evening Mrs. Nicosia; thank you for inviting me over for dinner."

With a glowing smile Eleonora surprised him by saying, "Oh, Bart, how you have grown up to become such a handsome young man." Embarrassed, Bart became flushed, but Eleonora imme-diately put him at ease by asking him how he liked Bishop Ott.

A few moments later John bounded into the room, inquir-ing, "Are you really interested in my sister or just my mother's cooking?"

Bart's retort was "I'll let you know about my intentions for your sister after I taste the food." They all laughed and Gina told them to get out of the kitchen.

The boys retreated to the enclosed front porch, waiting for Mr. Nicosia to get home. Soon Gina brought them fried dough and a small dipping bowl of marinara sauce.

John and Bart talked about school, their college intentions, and how they thought Al was going to react when he found out Gina had gone out on a date with Bart. John was of the opinion that as long as their mom and dad approved, Bart had nothing to worry about from Al.

Mr. Pietro Nicosia pulled into the driveway at 6:00. He entered the house through the front door dressed in a dark suit, white shirt, and striped tie, sporting a black fedora. Bart's first thought was *He sure doesn't look like a gangster*. He sort of looked Italian, but he was fair-skinned with refined features. John stood to greet his father. "Hi Pops, how was your day?"

In a soft, pleasant, New York accent Pietro replied, "Nothing special, just the normal dog-eat-dog business stuff." Turning to Bart, he said, "I am so glad you could join us for dinner. I've been looking forward to seeing you again. Good thing Al's not around, he's probably still seething from that great football game the season before last. It cost Christian Brothers the CHSAA championship. I admired the way you guys came back and won it. You beat us again this past year in Brooklyn; what was it that time, 12 to nothing?"

"Yeah," replied Bart. "John played a good game this year, but they just couldn't put the ball over the goal line."

"That's the way it goes. Now let me go in and say hello to Eleonora and Gina before I get cleaned up for dinner."

As was the traditional Catholic requirement on Fridays, Mrs. Nicosia had prepared a meatless meal. The rest of the fried dough was out on the table along with a wonderful salad of sliced beef-steak tomatoes, red onion, and bufala mozzarella cheese drizzled with balsamic vinegar. Gina and Bart both picked off the onions. The main course was a delicious fish stew Mrs. Nicosia called "cioppino in red gravy." There was a jug of red wine on the table, but they all mixed it with club soda. Apparently, from a young age, drinking wine at dinner was normal for the Nicosia children.

Following dinner, Gina and her mother cleared the table while John mysteriously vanished. Mr. Nicosia quietly motioned for Bart to follow him out back. Bart apprehensively trailed Pietro through a small pantry then out into the backyard. He turned to Bart and said, "After dinner I like a few puffs of a cigar but Eleonora won't let me smoke in the house. She says it stinks the place up. Normally I just go out the back door; but when it's cold, like tonight, I go into the garage."

Neither of them had on a coat but their bodies slowly began to adjust to the sudden change in temperature. Pietro bit off the tip of his cigar and methodically lit the other end with a cigar lighter. After a few healthy puffs, he was satisfied his stogie had an even burn. He turned to Bart. "LaRocca . . . that means *the fortress* in Italian; that's a good trait for a family man."

"I never thought of it translated into English. To me it's just a name. What does Nicosia mean?"

"It's a little mountain village in central Sicily where my family was from." Quickly changing the subject, Gina's father said, "You know, you are the first boy I've let take my daughter out alone at night in a car." Not waiting for a response he continued, "From what I have seen and what John has told me, you are a respectful young man. My daughter is at an age when it would be easy for a deceitful person to take advantage of her. I expect you will treat her the way you would want your sister to be treated. Please do not let me down . . . and have her home by midnight. Now go inside and make my daughter happy."

When Bart walked back into the kitchen alone, Gina had just finished drying the dishes. She gave him a sheepish smile and told him she was going upstairs to change into her party clothes. Shortly after she left, John reappeared and led Bart back to the front porch. John inquired, "Did Pop give you The Talk?"

Bart replied, "I don't know if it was The Talk but I did gain a clear understanding of his expectations."

"That's good," John emphasized. "If you meet his expectations you won't ever have to worry about Al."

Dinner had taken over an hour and Gina spent another half hour getting changed and finalizing her makeup. When she walked out on the porch, Bart almost bit off his tongue. Gina looked gorgeous. She had on just enough lipstick, makeup, and eyeliner to make her look several years older, and the tight white sweater had been replaced by a red one. *Wow*, thought Bart, *whoever lands this beauty is going to have to fight off half the guys in New York!*

CHAPTER 10

It was after nine by the time the couple arrived at Skip's party in the exclusive North Shore Village of Roslyn Estates. Apparently the party had been going on for some time because there were at least twenty cars filling the driveway and parked all around the cul-de-sac. Empty beer cans and plastic cups were strewn all over the driveway and front lawn. Music could be heard blaring long before you walked in the front door. Skip's brother was nowhere to be found and couples were making out on every available sofa and chair. Many of the underage teenagers appeared drunk, and one girl could be heard puking her guts out in one of the downstairs bathrooms.

Gina seemed to be taken aback by the scene. "Is this typical?" she asked.

"No, Skip's parties are a little wilder than most." Sensing a critical moment, Bart injected, "We can have a good time without getting drunk, and I won't do anything you don't approve of."

Seeming appeased, she allowed Bart to lead her to the basement where there were several seemingly sober couples dancing. They did have a good time for about an hour. Bart had one beer and Gina took a swig. They danced and talked, and she met both his sober and drunk friends.

They were slow dancing to Elvis Presley's "Are You Lonesome Tonight?" when it happened; Gina loosely put her left hand on the back of Bart's neck and began lightly stroking it. Then she took his left hand in hers and brought it to rest on her right breast. Their movement slowed down, and when the record finished, it was replaced with Ray Charles' "I Can't Stop Loving You." Then the third slow song in a row, the Marcels' "Blue Moon," came on. By now, their feet were hardly moving, but their pulses were pounding.

Bart couldn't stand it anymore; he kissed her on the lips for the first time. She responded by tightening her hold on his neck and pulling him closer. Before either of them realized what was happening, their tongues were feverishly exploring each other's mouths and both of Bart's hands had moved to Gina's firm butt. Disregarding Pietro's warnings, Bart began slowly grinding his now rigid manhood. If Gina was shocked or surprised, she didn't pull away. When "Blue Moon" ended and Roy Orbison's "Running Scared" began blaring they were both breathing hard and Bart was left with a protruding lump in the front of his pants. Gina, realizing she had just reached a new level of physical and emotional excitement, abruptly bolted for a bathroom.

Instead of a bathroom, she accidently walked into a bedroom with a naked couple engaged in "the act." This graphic scene both shocked and scared Gina; she did an about-face and made a beeline back to Bart. Grimacing, with ice dripping from her tones she declared, "Take me home, I'm not ready for this stuff." Much of the ride back to Queens was completed in silence. It wasn't until Bart asked, "So what's the problem? I thought you were enjoying it as much as me. I'm sorry if I got carried away."

"It wasn't just you, I was enjoying it, too; I wanted you to keep going." Then she told him about the couple in the bedroom. When she was finished, she concluded by saying, "It just got me wondering if either of us could control how far we go. Hell, we weren't even alone in that room."

They finished the ride home in silence. When he walked her to the front porch, she kissed him and said, "Bart, I really like you and enjoy being with you, but I am only sixteen and not ready for the emotions I felt tonight. Don't call me for a while." Then she said good-bye and went into the house. It was only 11:30.

CHAPTER 11

Gina's abrupt ending to their short romance threw Bart into the doldrums. He was so disappointed he skipped track practice twice the next week. Friday night he returned to party crashing with his buddies, but this time he had a new purpose. Instead of just having a good time, he was obsessed with finding the girls that were easy makes. He discovered he had a knack for zeroing in on a vulnerable mark, and over the next several months his conquests mounted. In spite of his successes, he always felt unsatisfied.

In mid-April John called and invited him to a Sunday game at Yankee Stadium. Pietro had given him four tickets to the game. John explained that Patty Jo and Gina would join them.

Bart was ecstatic; he couldn't wait for Sunday to come, when he would get to see Gina again.

Unable to contain his excitement at seeing Gina again, Bart arrived at the Nicosias' early. Gina was still getting ready but John and Patty Jo were in the kitchen with Mr. and Mrs. Nicosia. It was obvious by their reaction to Bart's arrival they were unaware of what had transpired between Gina and him. Mr. Nicosia told the boys that Whitey Ford was scheduled to pitch and the line was 8 to 5 on the Yankees. Bart had no idea what 8 to 5 meant, but he feigned interest. Gina did not join them for another half hour, but when she did her mood appeared buoyant and playful. She greeted Bart as if nothing had changed since the family dinner the previous week. It seemed to Bart nobody in the room knew about Gina's feelings. Of course, that wasn't true. Gina had confided in Patty Jo and she in turn had played matchmaker again by convincing John to invite Gina and Bart.

They took the subway up to the Bronx. It was a good game. Whitey pitched an eight-inning six-hitter and Johnny Blanchard hit a two-run homer for a 3–1 win for the Bronx Bombers. Bart sat next to Gina the whole game and was in heaven. They talked and joked as if nothing had happened between them. On the subway ride back to Queens, buoyed by her demeanor, Bart invited Gina to his senior prom.

Looking away, Gina sighed, "I can't. I'm still afraid of what was happening with us. I'm just not ready to get that serious with anyone yet." Devastated, Bart avoided speaking to her the rest of the trip.

After picking up his car at the Nicosias', Bart drove Patty Jo home. On the way, Patty Jo revealed her thoughts on Gina. She believed Gina was sincere about being afraid of the possible consequences of their relationship. She suggested he give Gina time. Patty Jo was convinced that Gina would realize she missed him more then she feared the consequences of their emotions. Little did either of them realize this wouldn't be the last time Bart would have to wait for Gina to sort out her feelings.

Bart attended his prom with a Hicksville High School girl

whom he had known since grammar school. After the prom, they bounced around between several of the after-parties then went out for breakfast with a small group. Bart dropped her off at her front door at almost 6:00 a.m. and received just a peck on the cheek. It had not been a particularly memorable night for either of them.

CHAPTER 12

Bart showed up at our villa on Thursday morning about 9:00 a.m. He appeared melancholy. When I asked him if something was wrong, he shrugged and said, "I received a message from Patty Jo. John's not in good shape. He might not make it much longer." He then plunged back into the chronicle of events from the '60s.

In those days, colleges required commitments by May for the fall semester. However, most graduating high school seniors planning on attending college made their commitments during the winter. John was recruited to play football by Lehigh and Boston College, but had enough of the sport in high school. He applied to Yale, Johns Hopkins, and Columbia. With his 1350 SAT scores and extracurricular activities, he was accepted to all three. He chose Johns Hopkins in late March.

Patty Jo applied, and was accepted, to Beth Israel School of Nursing in Manhattan. Bart was recruited by Bowling Green and Hofstra, and to everyone's surprise, he received an invitation to visit the University of South Carolina during their spring practice in March. When Coach Thomas received the telephone call from USC requesting game tapes, he initially assumed that they were interested in one of his two high school All-Americans, tackle Tiny Reiser or fullback Duke Kiley. When the recruiter said that they were interested in Bart LaRocca, he was overjoyed and spliced together an impressive collage of Bart's performances.

■ ■ ■

Before the completion of Interstates 95 and 20, it was a long two-day drive from New York to Columbia, South Carolina; but the transition from winter to spring made the drive exhilarating. While signing in at the athletic complex, the answer to the mystery of USC's interest in Bart was solved. The student assistant registering Bart told him his player-escort for the weekend would be Joe Zielinski, or "Joe Z," as he was called. Bart had played Connie Mack baseball two summers earlier with Joe. Joe Z was huge at 6 foot 3 inches and over 300 pounds, but he was extremely agile for his size. As a catcher, he could get out from behind the plate and field a bunt as well as others half his size. South Carolina had recruited Joe to help them compete with the giant linemen the University of Maryland had lured out of the coal-mining towns of Pennsylvania and West Virginia. Besides his size, the coaches were impressed with the energy he brought to the field. The coaching staff asked Joe if he knew any other Yankees who might like to come on down to the Carolinas. He gave the coaches a short list that included Bart.

Trading New York's windy 40-degree temperatures for South Carolina's 70s was an unfair recruiting advantage. Bart fell in love with the weather and the palmetto palms. The girls weren't too bad either. In May, when he got the letter officially inviting him to come down in the fall and try out for the freshman team, he was ecstatic. Although the school did not offer a scholarship, the letter indicated that, if he was able to secure substantial playing time on the freshman team, a scholarship would be offered. It was all the encouragement Bart needed. He accepted the offer.

■ ■ ■

Al Nicosia completed his freshman year at the University of Rhode Island; he was a star linebacker on the freshman team. He and the coaching staff fully expected him to start on the varsity in the fall. The University of Rhode Island provided Al with familiar surroundings and a local family connection. Mrs. Nicosia's sister, Agnese, had married Rafaele Patrone. It was common knowledge in the Providence and Boston area that Raf, as he liked to be called, ran the New England Mafia from his adopted home state of Rhode Island. Ever since the children were very young, the Nicosias vacationed for several weeks each summer with their cousins at the Patrones' beach house in Narragansett.

. . .

In spite of the emptiness he felt from Gina's rejection, Bart plunged into the summer with the euphoria of a typical new high school graduate who knew he was about to embark on the most exciting adventure of his young life. As soon as track season was over in mid-May, Bart was able to pick up additional spending money caddying. A new private country club opened in early May in the elite North Shore incorporated village of Muttontown. The caddy master, Gene Miles, had come from Bethpage State Park, where Bart had taken caddy lessons four years earlier. Gene remembered Bart and was also a huge Bishop Ott football fan, so when Bart showed up one Saturday shortly after the course opened, Gene gave Bart favored treatment.

Bart was generally able to pick up a couple of bags on both Saturdays and Sundays, and on really busy weekends he might get in two rounds a day. Each bag paid $5, but most of the members were pleased to give healthy tips to an energetic, college-bound young man with a great personality. Once school ended in late June, Bart was able to also pick up rounds almost every weekday. Through the summer of 1962, Bart averaged $100 in cash per week, no taxes and no deductions. With gas at less than 20 cents per gallon and a six-pack of Pabst's Blue Ribbon at $1.05, Bart had plenty of money for his meager social life during the summer and enough spending money to get him through most of the school year.

It was on the golf course, one Saturday morning in July, when he first heard about it. Bart and another college-bound caddy had picked up a regular foursome of lawyers every Saturday morning at 8:30. All four were in their midforties with single-digit handicaps, plus they were generous tippers.

Bart rarely read anything in the newspapers except the sports section, so it was news to him when he overheard their discussions about the big scandal involving the construction of the Long Island Expressway in Suffolk County. According to an article in Friday's *Newsday*, police arrested an expressway subcontractor for cheating the state and federal government out of tens of thousands of dollars. The contractor, Bruno Cefelo, through his company, Cefelo Excavation & Trucking, had a multimillion-dollar contract for grading and landscaping on the still-incomplete Long Island Expressway. Cefelo's company was responsible for excavating the topsoil of the future roadbed and replacing it with stone and gravel. The topsoil was supposed to be stockpiled until it was needed for landscaping the roadside after the concrete was laid. His scheme was to pilfer one out of every five truckloads of topsoil. He would either sell it to landscapers or stockpile it for a later sale back to the state for the expressway landscaping. He was also overstating the weight of the gravel he was delivering. It was a brilliant scheme. He probably would have gotten away with it if this forty-five-year-old father of three teenage daughters hadn't been caught by his wife out on a late lunch with his good-looking thirty-year-old office manager, who was hanging all over him. His jealous, infuriated wife insisted Bruno "fire the bitch" because it was obvious she had designs on her husband. In reality, he had been screwing her for years. Bruno unwisely complied with his wife's demand and consequently the pissed-off office manager went to the cops, exposing the scheme.

The story also went on to speculate that Cefelo had ties to the Leucchi crime family from Queens. Specifically mentioned was the fact that Pietro (aka Pete) Nicosia, a reputed Leucchi associate, was on Cefelo's board of directors. This last tidbit got Bart's attention, causing him to anxiously scan *Newsday* for follow-up stories.

Two weeks later Bart ran across the story on page two: Bruno Cefelo was found floating in Long Island Sound off Port Jefferson. He had been shot in the back of his head, in what the paper called "gangland fashion." He apparently had been chained to a boat

anchor but had somehow come loose. The coroner estimated he
had been dead for a week to ten days. At the end of the article
the newspaper promised to publish a weekly exposé on mob
influence in the New York area.

Bart eagerly awaited the first installment in the series. It came
out the following Saturday and recounted a brief history of organized gangs in New York, all the way back to the Irish gangs of
the nineteenth century through the emergence of the Italian
and Jewish gangs of Prohibition. Many of the names seemed
familiar; he remembered hearing his father and uncles talking
about the mobs over drinks at family gatherings. He never paid
much attention, but many of the names they mentioned stuck in
his memory and were now printed in the articles he was reading. He saw it as a fascinating history of brutal men preying on
their fellow immigrants, then rising out of the ghettos during
Prohibition to amass fortunes out of the nation's puritanical
prohibition of the "demon rum." Of course, none of this had
anything to do with him.

Episode two the following week recounted the transformation
of the exclusively Sicilian gangs into multicultural organized
crime syndicates led by Meyer Lansky and Lucky Luciano during
the 1930s. It detailed the Five Families, where they operated, and
their violent and parasitic nature. It took the reader through the
'50s, starting with the Kefauver hearings in 1950, and chronicling
several of the more sensational assassinations of the era. There
were photographs of Frank Scalise's bloodied body on the floor
of a Bronx produce market, and the famous photo of Albert
Anastasia after he was gunned down in the Park Sheraton Hotel's
barbershop. It concluded with an almost comical tale of sixty
mafiosi in Apalachin, New York, scurrying through the woods
in their $500 suits and $100 Italian-made shoes when a rural
state cop accidentally discovered their ill-fated national meeting.

The third installment detailed both successful and failed pros-
ecutions by authorities. It enumerated illegal activities in which
the Mafia was believed to have been engaged. It postulated from
"informed sources" the current leadership and territories of each

of the five families. There was a brief mention of John and Gina's father as a key figure in the Leucchi family. It alleged he ran the rackets for the family in Queens and Nassau.

The fourth article in the series painted a gruesome picture of mob influence on Long Island. It cited numerous convictions of mob associates for violent crimes and illegal activities in garbage, trucking, gambling, prostitution, and drugs. The paper went on to quote anonymous law enforcement officials claiming the La Cosa Nostra (as the FBI now called it) controlled these activities on Long Island along with wielding influence over the teamsters, dockworkers, and construction trade unions. The final installment attempted to leave the general public with the belief these hoodlums were involved in their everyday lives.

When Bart finished reading the exposé, he was less than impressed. Though he tended not to doubt that some of this was true, he had never witnessed any crimes. He was left with the feeling the existence of a massive organized crime conspiracy was sensationalism. The fact that he knew one of the alleged kingpins, Pietro Nicosia, and observed him to be a loving family man, tended to reinforce his belief.

Two days later, on the front page of all the New York papers, was the news of a brutal attack on Philip Reinhart, the author of the exposé. A lone assailant accosted the newspaperman as he was returning home from work by throwing acid in his face. The crusading journalist was severely disfigured and blinded by the attack. This was too coincidental even for Bart; he began to question his judgment about Pietro Nicosia and the Italian Mafia.

■ ■ ■

"Are you kidding me, Bart? You're telling me that up to this point you had no inkling the Italian Mafia was an entrenched criminal organization routinely involved in violent activities?"

"Yeah, I really didn't have a clue. I thought being called a wiseguy was the same as being a smart aleck. I mean, I knew there were bad guys, but the notion there was this whole Italian underworld controlling the rackets using violent tactics just never made it onto my radar."

"Incredible! You didn't have a clue even after you spent two years at CBHS in Brooklyn and staying with your grandmother in Middle Village where half the goombahs lived? That's not naïve; that's having your head up your ass!"

"Yeah, I guess it was," sighed Bart. "But you know, until the late 1950s even the FBI ignored the existence of a Mafia conspiracy. It wasn't until the Apalachin thing that J. Edgar Hoover was forced to recognize the national scope of organized crime. Even after that, it was another five or six years until Joe Valachi testified before the senate investigations subcommittee and the proceedings were broadcast on radio and television. It wasn't until these hearings the term Cosa Nostra was first introduced to the public. It is so easy today to look back and say, 'Of course there is a Mafia that violently runs all kinds of rackets,' but remember in 1962 there were no *Valachi Papers* to read or a *Godfather* trilogy to watch."

"So, after the Philip Reinhart thing, were your antennae up?"

"Sort of, but it wasn't until John invited me to another baseball game that I really began to take notice. The tickets and trip were arranged by Mr. Nicosia's brother Paul. John, his dad, and I met about thirty 'relatives' at Paul's bar off Queens Boulevard in Woodside. By the time we got there about 11:30 a.m., most of John's uncles and cousins were already half drunk. I'm not sure that some of them weren't left over from the night before. We all piled on this bus, about thirty of us with ten cases of beer, two cases of hero sandwiches, and about six boxes of Cuban cigars. We had a police escort all the way across the Triborough Bridge. About halfway up to the Polo Grounds, I finally figured out the terms 'uncle' and 'cousin' did not necessarily denote a blood relative. I kept asking John how he was related to different guys, and he explained he really wasn't a blood relative but he was part of the 'family.' It was also obvious John's father was the de facto head of this group. He was treated with incredible reverence. He never had to light his own cigar or open a beer can. All of that was done by one of the nearby 'uncles.' But it was apparent there was a pecking order below Mr. Nicosia. Only certain 'uncles' got to sit next to or near him. They were all about his age or older and they rarely initiated a conversation outside their little group. Even when we got into the stadium, the seating was arranged to maintain the hierarchy. On the bus ride half of the conversations of this small group of elite were carried out in Italian and in muffled whispers.

"It's a funny thing about stereotypes; they are generally based upon fairly accurate observations. Take the then generally accepted stereotype of a young Italian from the city, a greasy-haired loudmouth wearing a T-shirt with a pack of Camels rolled up in the sleeve, using terms like 'youse guys' and 'wazup,' and greeting each other with a hug or some kind of secret handshake. Well, I can tell you, they all might not be like that — God knows, John wasn't like that — but at least ten of his cousins fit the bill almost to a tee."

Smiling, I asked, "What about Al, didn't he go to the game with you?"

"Thank god, no. He spent most of the summer up in Rhode Island with the Patrones. I often wondered what the dynamics would have been if he had been there. However, I doubt John would have invited me if Al was on the trip.

"While most of the young guys were loud and verbally ragging on one another, John and I sat off to the side quietly observing the ritual. It was obvious he was not into all this goombah stuff. During the trip, the only other guy besides me John spent any time with was his real cousin Paulie. Paulie was the only child of his father's brother. He was a couple of years older than John but had some kind of a mental handicap that caused him to act about twelve years old. He was a nice kid and he adored John. For his part, John treated him like an equal. I later found out Al treated Paulie the same way. In fact, after both Pietro and Paul died and John moved to Phoenix, Al became Paulie's protector and his sole financial support.

60

"Anyway, this trip was a peek into a completely different world for me.

"The game was something else again. The 1962 Mets only won forty games and were really as horrible as their record. The fans were unrelenting on the hapless Mets players, but our group was even worse than the rest. Every time there was a pop-up or fly ball they would all shout, 'I got it, I got it,' mocking the numerous collisions Richie Ashburn and shortstop Elio Chacon had that season. And that was the tame part; you wouldn't believe the expletives they were yelling. John and I were so embarrassed we left to get a hot dog and didn't return to our assigned seats until the ninth inning.

"On the ride from Paul's bar to the Nicosia house, Pietro asked me what I thought of his family. When I hesitated, Pietro picked up on my caution and replied, 'I know sometimes they can be quite unruly and crude. I am sure your family has its own characters that make you cringe. Unfortunately, when you hang with my family and friends, this is pretty typical of what you get.' Message received loud and clear!"

CHAPTER 13

Driving to South Carolina in a non-air conditioned car is a lot different in the late summer than it is in the spring. Double sessions in Columbia's heat and humidity turned out to be a real struggle for Bart. He lost fifteen pounds the first two weeks of practice and wound up with frequent bouts of leg cramps. By the third week his body had adjusted to the heat and humidity and he finally started to show promise in the flanker position. He was fast and had good hands. In early October, when the temperatures finally cooled down to the 80s, Bart really began to shine, especially in game situations. He became a favorite target for the team's starting quarterback. By midseason he had received the scholarship they had promised.

First semester classes were not difficult. Without much effort, he was able to maintain a B average. The social life was good, especially for a football player. Many of the freshman football players pledged a fraternity, but that never appealed to Bart. The humiliation of pledging went against his basic nature plus he thought living in the sports dorm would give him more control over his free time and choice of friends.

He discovered the social life of a college athlete was similar to high school; jocks found out about the parties and could generally crash them if they brought beer. Many southern girls seemed to find Bart's New York accent and mannerisms intriguing. There was only one exception in Bart's four years at USC. Once he mentioned the Civil War in a small group and one coed corrected him with, "You carpetbaggers insist on referring to the war of Northern aggression as the Civil War, when there was nothing civil about Sherman's march to the sea." Though he doubted it was original, Bart actually thought it was a clever retort. In later years, whenever he retold the incident, the timbre of the sweet southern inflection oozing out of her mouth, like melted brie, still made him smile.

Bart figured it wasn't a random selection by the student housing department that the Italian from New York was matched with the only Jew on the team. Bart's roommate, David Tanner, was an anomaly for a South Carolinian. His family could trace their roots in Charleston back to the 1750s, but it was not one of those blueblood English families that were deeded vast amounts of land by the Crown. Charleston was one of the first colonial cities to allow Jews to practice their faith without restrictions, and David's ancestors were among the first German Jews to immigrate to the city. While worshipping in the Kahal Kadosh Beth Elohim congregation was made easy by the city's religious freedoms, doing business was not as easy. As suggested by their name, the Tanners were leather workers. In precolonial times Charleston was the hub of the colonies' deerskin trade. Europeans clamored for more and more of the skins that were so plentiful in the New World. David's family was at the forefront of that industry for over 200 years. In spite of the initial recalcitrance of the southern Christians to do business with German Jews, the Tanners' honesty, persistence, and outstanding craftsmanship eventually won over the local merchant community. It didn't take too many generations before the Tanners prospered both economically and socially. After the Second World War, David's grandfather financed his returning veteran son in the low country's commercial real estate business. By the 1960s the only remnant remaining of the original leather goods business was a very high-end retail leather goods store on King Street. However, the family also owned and rented out numerous other buildings in Charleston's bustling retail district. Because of his Jewish heritage, David never gave pledging a fraternity a second thought. Columbia was not Charleston.

In late October, over parent's weekend, which Bart's parents didn't attend, David's mother suggested that he invite Bart home with him for Thanksgiving. While it sounded like a better idea to Bart than the long drive back to New York in what was now becoming a very temperamental 1954 Ford, he was apprehensive about staying in a Jewish household over the Sabbath. Growing up he never had any Jewish acquaintances so the traditional rituals that were practiced from sundown Friday to sundown Saturday were a mystery to him. As the weeks leading up to Thanksgiving flew by, Bart and David's friendship strengthened. In spite of their growing camaraderie, Bart was still reluctant to stay with David's family over the Sabbath. A solution presented itself when Joe Z told him he and a couple of the other football players were going to spend Thanksgiving break in Myrtle Beach, playing golf and partying. This development gave Bart the opportunity to spend Wednesday and Thursday with the Tanners but leave on Friday to meet Joe Z and the other guys 100 miles up the coast for the rest of the weekend.

Bart found his stay at the Tanners' antebellum mansion on The Battery to be another unique cultural experience. These two days solidified Bart and David's friendship. The rest of the weekend with the guys at Myrtle Beach also solidified a decades-long relationship for Bart. Although it was still early in Myrtle Beaches' development as a golf mecca, Bart fell in love with the courses and the beaches. He went back to the region for vacations many times during the succeeding decades.

■ ■ ■

Bart tried not to think about Gina even while he was home for the three-week Christmas break. John and he exchanged one letter during the semester, but the content revolved around how they were adjusting to college life; he made no mention of his sister.

Bart loved the winter weather in Columbia. There were generally three or four days of "cold" 40-degree weather followed by three or four days in the 60s. He played a lot of golf that winter. His course schedule remained relatively easy and interesting. Spring football in March was OK. He wrote John that he might get some limited playing time as a wide receiver in the fall. John wrote back he had taken up lacrosse and had made the freshman team as a walk-on. Johns Hopkins always had the premier college lacrosse team in the country, having won twenty-four national championships between 1898 and 1961. For John to make the team without having played the sport in high school was a major accomplishment, and Bart was proud of his friend.

Out of the blue, Bart received a letter from Gina inviting him to her senior prom. The prom was scheduled for the week after Bart expected to return home for the summer. This invitation proved to be a dilemma; part of him was excited with the thought of being with her again, yet part of him was leery. He could still feel the pain from her rejection. Did he want to risk getting all worked up over her again only to be rebuffed a second time? Fighting off his urge to accept, he decided not to answer her immediately. He would catch a ride home with Joe Z for Easter break and try to talk to her face-to-face.

He arrived home on Good Friday and called John on Saturday.

When Bart mentioned the letter and invitation to John, he didn't sound surprised. Following a frank discussion, John agreed it would be best for Bart to have a frank face-to-face discussion with Gina. John also suggested Bart meet him Monday afternoon at Patty Jo's house; he promised to try to get Gina to be there too.

Bart drove his father to the train station on Monday so he could use the family car to get into Queens. He met John, Patty Jo, and Gina at Patty Jo's house. John had chosen Patty Jo's because Al was also home for Easter and he didn't want to complicate the day.

As soon as he saw her, Bart was smitten again with all the intense emotions he had been trying to suppress for all these months. The best part was Gina seemed genuinely happy to see him. It was a beautiful spring day and the four of them sat among the blossoming trees and fresh flowers in Patty Jo's backyard chatting about school, gossiping about friends and all the little stuff young people talk about. Bart learned that Gina had applied for and was accepted at Manhattanville College and St. John's in New York plus Trinity College in Washington, DC, but she had not made up her mind where she wanted to go. They talked for an hour before Gina asked Bart to take her for a ride. Patty Jo, always the matchmaker, interjected, "That's a good idea, Bart. John and I have something to do anyway." Of course, Bart didn't really need any encouragement to be alone with Gina.

Once they were settled into his car Bart asked, "So, do you have someplace special in mind?"

"Not really." After a thoughtful hesitation she added, "Someplace where we can talk. How about Flushing Meadows Park?"

Nodding his agreement, Bart responded, "We can do that."

On the drive to the site of the 1939 and the coming year's World's Fair, Gina began relating events from her senior year. At first, it was the classic teenage girl stuff about teachers, friends, classes, parties and home life, but then all of a sudden she threw out, "I assume you've guessed I've been dating other guys and I'd be surprised if you hadn't been going out with lots of those southern belles."

Confused as to where this was headed, Bart downplayed

his response. "Yeah, I've had a few dates, but nothing serious," when in fact he had been with someone almost every weekend. Granted he wasn't serious with any of the many coeds he had gone out with, but he wasn't celibate either.

Glancing at him, she tried to maintain a matter-of-fact tone. "I've gone out with a half-dozen or so other boys. We've gone to parties that were almost as wild as the one you took me too." She waited for a reaction from Bart.

Now he was really perplexed; he pulled over to the curb, turned off the engine, and turned to face her. "OK, now you have my attention. Where is this going? Are you expecting me to get pissed or something, or is this your way of reneging on the invitation to your prom?"

She could see by the flush on his face he was on the verge of losing it. Regretting her initial approach to this very touchy subject, her voice took on an apologetic tenor. "Absolutely not! What I am trying to tell you is that I'm not scared of us anymore."

Bart's eyes narrowed as he scoffed, "Huh, so let me see if I've got this, you're saying, now that you screwed around with other guys, you're finally ready to screw around with me?"

Exasperated, Gina screeched, "No! How could you think I would screw other guys? Yeah, I necked with one or two but that did nothing for me." Surprised by her own emotions she stopped, forced herself to regain her composure and said calmly, "Look, my whole point is, none of them made we feel the way you did. Making out with them was . . . well almost clinical or mechanical or something, not emotional. Am I making any sense?"

Bart shrugged. "I guess."

Undaunted by Bart's noncommittal reply, she continued, with tears slowly trickling out of the corner of her eyes, "It made me realize, if I am going to make out, I want it to be with someone who will make me feel the way you did. Please forgive me for how I handled this; I know how hurt and confused you were, but I needed to discover this on my own." Sighing, she stared at him expectantly.

Paralyzed by Gina's revelation, Bart couldn't do anything but return Gina's gaze. What could he do to tell her she had just made him the happiest man in the world? He didn't even realize he had choked out the words until he had his arms around her and there were tears welled up in his eyes. "Gina Nicosia, I fell hopelessly in love with you the first time we danced, and nothing over the last year has changed that."

Gina stopped sniffling, rubbed the tears from her eyes, smudging her eyeliner, and after a thoughtful pause, pulled back, looking him in the eyes as she playfully prodded him. "So, does that me you'll take me to my prom?"

Now fully recovered, Bart returned her taunt. "Only if you promise to let me kiss you."

"Just one thing, lover boy, I don't want to get knocked up; *capisci?*"

With a wicked chuckle and a renewed sparkle in his eyes, Bart shot back, "Is that the only limitation?"

"I'm not sure, but no matter what, we can't let me get pregnant."

"You don't have to convince me; I'm not sure who I'm more afraid of, you or your father."

Instead of stopping at Flushing Meadows Park, Bart continued driving over to Alley Pond Park, exiting off the Cross Island Parkway onto the service road that runs between the parkway and Little Neck Bay. He parked the car behind a stand of trees, and before they knew it they were all over each other. It was still the middle of the afternoon, but they were oblivious to the traffic whizzing by on the parkway. Before they could get into too much of a compromising situation, a cop car pulled in behind them and let out a short bleep on his siren. Message received, they both laughed, and Bart started up the car and pulled back onto the parkway.

On the drive back to Gina's they were both giddy, knowing it was just a matter of time before they would be alone in the right place to finish what they started that afternoon. They made a date for the next night, assuming Bart would be able to borrow his father's car again.

As it turned out, Bart was not able to use the family car for his date the following night. He did, however, get it during the daytime on Wednesday. By the time Bart arrived at Gina's, Al had already gone out with his friends. Sitting in her backyard, the lovers talked about their future together, which they agreed included lots of children and a little house out on the North Shore of Long Island.

When Al found out Gina and Bart were now dating and going to the prom together, he went ballistic. He ranted and raved about "that no-good traitor who would betray you whenever it's convenient for him." He also swore he owed Bart an ass-kicking and he was going to give it to him the next time he came around. Mr. Nicosia, upon hearing his son's tirade, became incensed himself. He angrily told Al that Bart was a decent young man and had his approval to date his only daughter. He ordered his eldest son to treat Bart with respect; as an obedient son, Al never directly confronted Bart while his father was alive.

Friday night couldn't come soon enough for Bart and Gina. Suppressing their fiery passion, they first went to a party at the house of one of her classmates in Douglaston. Just as it had on previous occasions, when Gina caressed the back of his neck and nestled her body in close to his while they were dancing, the chemistry between them precipitated an overwhelming physical and emotional arousal. It had bubbled over a year earlier, and now it was exploding. The difference this time was they both knew and agreed on the boundary.

Leaving the party early, Bart found a secluded place to park. The anticipation had been building all week, so when they were finally alone their passion was explosive. They first attacked each other's bodies with a sense of urgency, leaving them breathless. However, amazingly, when the moment arrived to totally surrender to their passion, they both pulled back. An hour later, when they finally surfaced, unfulfilled, they knew the next time Bart better be packing some protection.

On the drive home, Gina surprised Bart. "How long a drive is it from Columbia to DC?"

"Eight or nine hours; why?"

"Well, I was thinking; if I went to Trinity, we might be able to see each other on long weekends."

"Yeah, that's possible. Are you really thinking about going there?"

"I'm not thinking about it anymore, I'm going to do it."

"That's fantastic!"

CHAPTER 14

Bart and I were putting in longer days. Now that we were deep into his and Gina's courtship, it seemed that he didn't want to stop reminiscing. Patty Jo was right; he still had an unshakable love for Gina and he was reliving it through this chronicle. Marie and I were enjoying it, too. Even though she didn't hang around to hear Bart telling his story, at night she would ask me to fill her in on his latest revelation. Our discussion brought back fond memories of our own dating experiences. Invariably Marie would interrupt my report by asking, "Do you remember the time we . . . ?"

Yesterday it seemed as if Bart couldn't wait to tell their story. Today I couldn't wait for him to continue. He picked me up around nine; Marie had already left to play golf. Bart suggested we take a drive up into the hills twenty-five minutes north of Portimão to the ancient Roman hot sulfur springs in the town of Monchique. While exploring this picturesque region of sawtoothed mountains and magnificent vistas, Bart continued recounting the story of his and Gina's love.

■ ■ ■

The six weeks waiting for the end of the semester seemed like an eternity to Bart. Every night he pictured holding Gina in his arms again.

Bart was on the road ten minutes after his last exam. The trip home to the Island convinced him the Ford was not going to make it back for the fall semester. On the drive it used two quarts of oil for every tank of gas; he could no longer get the tired vehicle over 50 miles per hour.

He pulled up in front of Gina's house in a cloud of oily smoke around one on Sunday afternoon with a sense of anticipation and excitement reserved only for a returning lover. With equal anticipation, Gina spent the last few hours constantly checking the street for his arrival. It was only seconds after he shut the car door that she burst out of the house and ran into his arms. As they hugged and kissed on the front lawn, Bart kept looking over her shoulder, anticipating her parents interrupting their passionate embrace. But they discreetly avoided the scene. Finally, after several wonderful moments, she dragged him into the house to greet her parents. They seemed as happy to see Bart as they would for one of their own sons coming home from school. In fact, when John arrived from Baltimore about three hours later he received the same greeting, except for his mother's kisses instead of Gina's. When John asked about Al, his father revealed that his eldest son had decided to spend the summer in Rhode Island with the Patrones. Although neither of them said anything, Bart got the impression that Pietro and Eleonora were not overjoyed with their son's decision.

Over dinner they all heard about John's newfound love of lacrosse and Bart's adventurous drive in the crippled Ford. Finally, the conversation turned to the prom the following weekend.

Stone-faced, Pietro introduced the question Gina had put him up to. "So, what are you planning on using for transportation to take my beautiful daughter to her senior prom?"

Bart stammered, "Uh . . . well . . . I hadn't really thought about it. I guess I could borrow my father's car or maybe one of Gina's friend's dates would take us."

"Why don't you use my Cadillac."

Straight-faced, Gina injected, "Are you serious, Daddy; your new Caddy?"

"Yeah, I'm not going anywhere that night."

Still playing her cards close to the vest, she looked quizzically at Bart. "Gee, what do you think, Bart?"

"My car is a hunk of junk, and my father's Dodge isn't exactly stylish. What the heck, I wouldn't mind arriving at the prom in something classy."

"OK, then it's decided. You'll take my Caddy."

John, unaware of his sister's and father's "conspiracy," appeared stunned. Later, when the three young people were alone, John expressed his surprise over his father's offer, explaining he didn't even let him or Al use it for their proms.

"Apparently," quipped Gina, "he doesn't trust you guys the way he trusts Bart."

"More likely he knows if Bart gets away, he'll have to support you for the rest of his life," countered John.

Fortunately for Bart, on Tuesday he was able to pick up some quick cash caddying at the country club. But nagging him, in the back of his mind, was how he would replace the Ford. He really didn't want to purchase another piece of junk but couldn't see how he had any other choice. His dad had only offered to give him $250 toward a replacement vehicle.

▪ ▪ ▪

The Mary Louis Academy senior prom was held at a beach club in Lido. The band was pretty good, but there were too many chaperones and nuns hanging around, cramping everyone's style. Everybody couldn't wait for the after-parties to start. Bart and Gina first went to an unchaperoned party at the same girl's house, in Jamaica Estates, where they met a year and a half earlier. Gina gleefully retold the story of Bart slapping her on the butt in that very basement.

After the physically constrained atmosphere of the prom, many of the couples were anxious to get romantic. By two o'clock in the morning, with the lights down low and Ray Charles' "I Can't Stop Loving You" playing for the third time, virtually every couple was passionately entwined in each other's arms. For the longest time, Gina and Bart, lost in the euphoria of their love, were oblivious to the activities surrounding them. Finally, around 3:00 a.m. the girl's parents returned from a night in the city. The mood was broken and couples began to discreetly leave by themselves. It was a warm night with the waning crescent moon hanging low in the western sky when Bart finally found a secluded place to park. The unlit neighborhood was sheltered by numerous large trees blocking out the meager moonlight and the glow from a single porch light on the nearest house. The lots were large for Queens, with big lawns and lots of mature shrubs. Parking the car at the end of a dead-end street, Bart scanned the area and assumed their car would go undetected.

Compared to the Ford, the backseat of the Cadillac was like being in a motel room. They started off with the same fervor as in April; this time Bart had protection with him. They had been going at it for about twenty minutes and were stone naked with Bart poised to tear open the Trojan wrapper when all of a sudden there were red and blue flashing lights followed by a blinding light.

"Oh my god!" screamed Gina.

"Shit?!" Bart muttered. "Quick, put your clothes on!" He fumbled for his underpants.

Depending on your viewpoint, the scene was either terrifying or comical. To the horrified and humiliated Gina and Bart, what should they do first, try to cover up or jump over to the front seat. To the cops, paramedics, and firemen, it must have been quite amusing watching the two teenagers scrambling around in the backseat. Minutes later, when Bart and Gina were able to get about half dressed, they were ushered out of the car, frisked, and the car was searched. They found themselves face-to-face with the head of New York City's Organized Crime Task Force. His routine check of the teenagers' IDs revealed Gina was the teenage daughter of Pietro Nicosia. He was both relieved that it was not a homicide and annoyed to have brought so many resources into play for just a couple of love-birds. After releasing the rest of the emergency squad, he addressed the two lovers.

"So, Miss Nicosia, does your father know that you're making out in the backseat of his car?"

"Jesus, no! You're not going to tell him are you? He'll kill us both!"

Holding back his amusement at the irony of the girl's statement, the captain mustered his most serious and official voice. "Look, when one of the homeowners called with the license plate number, we were afraid we were going to find a body in the trunk. If you two promise me that you will never again park in these residential neighborhoods, especially with your father's car, I guess I can keep your little secret. Agreed?"

Relieved, they answered in unison, "Yes, sir."

"Come here, son, I want to talk to you." Escorting him out of Gina's earshot, the captain put his arm around Bart's shoulder, whispering, "Do you know who her father is?"

"Yeah, he's a reputed Mafia guy."

Raising his voice, he said, "Not reputed, he is a dangerous Mafia boss; you'd be smart to stay clear of that family. Understand?"

"If you say so, officer" was Bart's undaunted curt reply.

Shaking his head, the police captain ordered tersely, "Get out of here, kid."

After they were in the car Gina asked, "What did he say to you?"

"He told me to stay away from you."

Gina didn't respond.

CHAPTER 15

The following Saturday Bart picked up a "double-double" at the country club and finished the second double bagger at 4:30. Before he headed into the city to pick up Gina at her part-time waitress job at Cellestino's, he stopped at home to shower and change.

While he was waiting for Gina to shower and change, her

father asked Bart about the Ford. "I'm afraid it's on its last legs," he told him, "but I don't have enough cash right now to get anything better."

"Look," Mr. Nicosia said, "I'm not happy about the two of you gallivanting all over the Island at night in that heap. How much money do you have?"

"My father said he'd give me $250 and I have another $100, but I need some cash for spending money."

"Because I am concerned for my daughter's safety, I have a proposition for you. My brother, Paul, just purchased a new car and would be willing to sell his old 1956 Oldsmobile to you for $400. If you put up the $250, I'll loan you the rest and you can pay it back to me at $15 a week. How does that sound?"

"That's some deal if the Olds is in good shape."

"See for yourself. I'll call him now and you can stop off there on the way out and pick it up. You can use it tonight and take it home for your father to look at. If you are still interested tomorrow, bring me the $250 and we'll sign it over to you. You might even be able to sell the Ford for a few bucks to help pay me off."

It sounded like a pretty good deal to Bart. Pietro was obviously a man of action, since he immediately called Paul. At about the same time, Gina finished her transformation. She didn't seem surprised at what had transpired, leaving Bart to figure Gina must have been putting the bug in her father's ear.

Paul was waiting for them when they arrived at his apartment above the bar. He had Bart park his car in the lot behind the bar and handed him the keys to the Olds. It only had 62,000 miles on it and seemed to be in fantastic shape. The car was a two-tone coupe, white and aqua. The three of them took it for a spin down Queens Boulevard and out on the Expressway. It was a magnificent machine, incredible power and smooth riding. Bart couldn't figure out why Paul was willing to sell it for $400; in his estimation it had to be worth at least $600. Thinking that Pietro had made a mistake on the price, he said to Paul, "So you want $400 for it?"

Paul responded, "If that's what my brother told you, that's what it is."

Interesting, thought Bart, not quite sure what to make of Paul's statement.

Bart felt like a real "hot shit" that night tooling around with his babe in a cherry Olds. The next day Frank LaRocca agreed it was a great deal; in fact, almost too good a deal. Both father and son vacillated about accepting, wondering what kind of debt they were incurring with a reputed mafioso. However, in the end, both Bart and his father rationalized that Pietro's motivation was purely his daughter's safety. Frank was so pleased with the vehicle he agreed to give Bart the whole $400. Years later, Bart found out Pietro had paid his brother an extra $250 out of his own pocket. He often wondered what he and his father would have done if they had known about it at the time.

That was a great summer for Bart and Gina. Their blossoming love affair had them in high spirits for the entire ten weeks they were together. They were still learning about each other, and each revelation seemed to make them fall deeper in love. The last few days before Bart had to leave for football practice were agonizing. They talked about transferring to local colleges and planning to get married. But in the end they both accepted their short-term fate and had a passionate farewell date.

CHAPTER 16

Bart dealt with Columbia's heat and humidity much better his sophomore year. He made the team as a second-string half-back and kick returner. His playing time was mostly limited to third-down passing situations where he would be set out on the flank. He didn't catch a pass until the third game, but that was in a critical situation for a first down. The team had a horrible season, going 1–8–1. However, for Bart, the season was a success. The only game USC won was against the University of Maryland in Hyattsville, and both John and Gina attended the game. Bart caught two passes for a total of thirty-five yards and two first downs, but the best part was that he got to spend two hours with Gina the night before the game.

The team's one tie was against the University of Virginia in Charlottesville. Bart didn't catch a pass but he ran back a kickoff to Virginia's forty-five-yard line. That play gave USC the field position they needed for their tying field-goal drive. Gina and John also went to the game. Friday night he got to see Gina for three hours.

During their short visit together in Charlottesville the big topic of conversation was Al. Although the details at that time were sketchy, John revealed Al had been arrested for dealing drugs. He had been suspended from both the football team and URI. He was currently out on bail and living with his cousin in Providence. Gina expressed her opinion Al was set up, and her brother would never get involved with drugs. As she was telling them this, John was rolling his eyes, as if to say, *Yeah right, little sister, you're so naïve.* Six months after Al's arrest, when the state's key witness recanted his story, resulting in the charges being dropped, Gina felt vindicated. She never even wanted to hear the story of how, after he recanted, the witness suddenly left Rhode Island for parts unknown or that key evidence disappeared from the police property room.

John told Bart the complete story several years later. Apparently Al was getting marijuana, LSD, and amphetamines through his cousin Raf Junior. Al had an exclusive on the college campuses in and around Providence. He was pulling down several thousand dollars a week for himself and his cousin. He was fingered as the supplier when police raided a raucous frat party and found several students puffing on weed. Police raided Al's apartment on Monday but they only found a couple of $5 bags of pot and a handful of amphetamines. It had been a very good weekend for sales and he was not due to be restocked until Tuesday.

Although Al didn't do time, the fact he didn't rat on his cousin earned him the reputation of someone who could be trusted. He left school and Rhode Island, returning home. His relationship with his father was strained because Pietro hated drugs. Then, all of a sudden in the spring of 1964, Al joined the army and volunteered for the Army Rangers. In June of 1965 Specialist Al Nicosia received orders for Saigon. Although the US Army had military advisors embedded with the Army of the Republic of Vietnam since 1959, they only numbered about 20,000 by 1965. Many of those were communications specialists, but Al was not a communications specialist; he was a trained killer. Based upon stories he later told the boys back in New York, he was embedded in an ARVN unit hunting and eliminating Vietcong in the jungles, swamps, and villages many miles from Saigon. Apparently, Al loved his job a little too much. About nine months into his tour, he was quietly reassigned to Fort Benning in Georgia. Then a few months later he received a "for the good of the service" discharge. Although he never fully explained the reasons for his early release under less than honorable conditions, rumors among the wiseguys hinted it had something to do with his overzealous pursuit and elimination of insurgents. Whatever the truth was, it enhanced Al's image as being ruthless and being someone you didn't want to piss off.

As confirmation of the rumors about Al's discharge, Bart told me a story from Al's bachelor party.

"We all had been sitting around drinking at his uncle's bar for a few hours; even his cousin Paulie was there. There must have been eight or ten guys besides Al, John, Paulie, and me. Everybody was telling stories about Al and his many exploits. When there was a lull in the revelry, Paulie says, 'Al, tell us about killing gooks again.'

"Al in a uninterested air replied, 'Nah, Paulie, these guys don't want to hear my war stories.'

"'Sure we do,' was the resounding reply from his buddies.

"'Yeah, come on, I love to hear the part where you slit those gooks' throats and burned down their hooch,' responded Paulie.

"'No, not tonight!' Al barked. Then he immediately changed the subject.

"I don't have any specifics about what Al did in Southeast Asia, but I do know he had a real penchant for killing things. After he was discharged, he would drive upstate to go deer, turkey, and black bear hunting. He never brought anything home to eat or mount, but he had pictures of himself with almost every kill he made. Later on, when he had lots of money, he would go on exotic hunting trips. He had pictures of himself with nearly every conceivable dangerous large game on the planet. I've seen photos of him with dead grizzlies, alligator, moose, water buffalo, and wild boar. He particularly loved hunting bears in Alaska. He said it gave him the ultimate high to know one false move and he would be the quarry.

"There were also rumors he continued to enjoy slitting the throats of his adversaries. Over the years, there have been several guys with mob connections that turned up dead with their throats slit. At least two of those were known to have pissed off Little Nicky. But in every case, Al had a rock-solid alibi."

CHAPTER 17

Bart was in a European history class on November 22, 1963, when the news of JFK's assignation spread like wildfire throughout the campus. The distressing news precipitated one incident which really pissed him off and almost got him thrown out of school. A redneck in Bart's class, on learning that John F. Kennedy had been shot, announced, "We finally got that nigger-lovin' Yankee." After a heated discussion and some pushing and shoving, Bart punched him out and broke his jaw. The only reason Bart was not thrown out of school was that all the witnesses swore the other guy threw the first punch. When the administration assessed all the potential divisive publicity, they quietly made a deal not to throw either of them out if they swore not to talk about it again.

Friday night Gina called Bart in tears. "I need you to come up here, I can't stand it. He was the President. Why would anybody want to kill him? They're cancelling all the classes next week and I want to go home early."

"Sorry, I wish I could; they've cancelled our classes too, but the Clemson game was moved to Thanksgiving Day."

"You've got to come and get me. I can't stand it and I don't want to be in DC when his body gets back here. You were going to pick me up on Tuesday anyway," she begged.

"That was before they moved the game to next Thursday," Bart said sternly. "I'm already in trouble with the coaching staff for decking some guy the other day. If I blow off practices and the Clemson game, I'll lose my scholarship."

"You and your football; what's more important to you—me or that stupid game?"

"That's not a fair question. It's not the football game, it's the scholarship. God, can't you see past today? We have a long future together; without a degree it will be a miserable one."

"You can still get your degree. We can both go to St. John's; then we will be able to see each other every day. Wouldn't that be . . ."

Cutting her off, Bart interjected, "I'm sorry, Gina. I just can't leave right now with the game on Thursday. I won't even be able to come home for Thanksgiving."

"You bastard!" she screamed, slamming down the phone.

Bart got stinking drunk that night.

Fortunately, John was able to leave school early and pick up Gina. On the drive home he was partially successful in persuading his sister Bart had done the right thing by fulfilling his football obligation. Nevertheless, it was not the last time the couple would clash over Bart's choice of priorities.

■ ■ ■

Following their Thanksgiving spat, Bart made a concerted effort to get up to DC once a month. His Friday classes were over before noon and his first Monday class wasn't until 1:00 p.m. so he could be in DC before midnight, giving them almost forty-eight hours before he had to drive back. Gina had it all worked out. On Friday evening she would get a ride out to a cheap motel on US Route 301 in Upper Marlboro, Maryland, rent a room with cash, and wait for Bart to show up.

Periodically, Gina would accompany her roommate home to North Carolina, making it convenient for Bart to meet her there. Between these weekend rendezvous and the long Christmas break, the couple did spend a lot of time together over the winter. Their best rendezvous came over spring break.

Bart's roommate's family had a beach house near Myrtle Beach. David Tanner's father gave him permission to use it over spring break. Patty Jo took the train down to Baltimore and hooked up with John. The two of them picked up Gina in Al's old '57 Chevy convertible. The three of them met Bart, David, and David's girlfriend at the beach house on Good Friday evening. The next seven days ushered in a whole new relationship for Bart and Gina. The house had five bedrooms, so each couple could enjoy their intimate moments in private. The area itself was still relatively undeveloped with the nearest neighbor a quarter of a mile down the beach. Myrtle Beach's spring weather was perfect with daytime highs in the 70s and night temperatures dropping into the 40s. The lovers would sunbathe during the day and snuggle in bed or in front of the fireplace at night. With the absence of time pressures and fears of getting caught, they experienced an exhilarating sense of liberation and intimacy they would remember as one of the happiest times of their lives.

■ ■ ■

The summer of 1964 started out better than the previous year. The two lovers were now soul mates, with the awkwardness of their early days well behind them. Bart continued to caddy at the country club and Gina picked up spending money working at Cellestino's. They saw each other three or four nights a week, and at least once a week Bart had dinner with her family. Fortunately for the two lovers, Al was still off doing his army thing.

Then just before the Fourth of July, Gina invited Bart on her family's annual vacation to the Patrones'. Gina's father had bought a forty-two-foot yacht that spring. He planned on taking his new toy across Long Island Sound to the Patrones' beach house on Narragansett. Reluctantly Bart declined, believing he couldn't afford losing out on the busiest golf weekend of the year. Again, Gina was pissed with Bart's decision; she couldn't understand how he would choose working over being with her. "Damn it," she exclaimed, "that's the second time you chose your stupid sports stuff over me. If the money is so important to you, I'll give you the hundred bucks out of my own paycheck."

"It's not just this weekend's money, Gina. If I blow off my regulars, they may find another caddy. Then I'll be screwed for the rest of the summer."

"You always have an excuse. I'm not in the mood to go out tonight, take me home."

By the time she got back home from the holiday weekend in Rhode Island, it was as if their tiff never happened.

Just before Bart left for the start of fall practices, he and Gina had begun talking about getting engaged. Their wedding plans had even progressed to the point of discussing where they might live after they married. Although there was much they did not agree upon, one thing was certain: they both wanted to finish college before they got married.

■ ■ ■

The fall semester of 1964 seemed agonizingly long for both of them. At the University of South Carolina, the heat and humidity was oppressive well into October; and Bart had a difficult time dealing with it. His performance suffered and his playing time dwindled. He didn't catch a pass until the fourth game of the season. Gina was not able to attend any of his games, making it a long three months for both of them.

Gina's school year also started off on a disappointing note. She and her freshman-year roommate planned on rooming together again; but just prior to the start of school, Gina received a letter from her friend saying she had gotten pregnant and would not be returning to Trinity. Gina wound up with a transfer student as a roommate. The new girl, from Gladwyne on the Philadelphia Main Line, was not Gina's type. Gina had been around some spoiled rich girls in high school, but living with one turned out to be a lot different. From the first day the new girl complained about everything, from the location of their room to the thickness of the mattress. It didn't take Gina long to realize the two of them were not compatible. Nothing was ever good enough for her spoiled roommate. Gina started calling her roommate "The Princess," in reference to the children's tale "The Princess and the Pea." To make matters worse, her roommate treated everyone like they were her servants. Of course, Gina would not put up with that kind of disrespect, telling her off on the spot and causing the girl to brood for days on end. Unlike her relationship with her freshman-year roommate, Gina and The Princess hardly ever hung out together. Gina tried to change rooms, but there was nothing available until the spring semester. The constant agitation and frequent confrontations, exacerbated by not seeing Bart, resulted in a surprising change in Gina's behavior and personality. She began to lose interest in her studies; as a result, her grades dropped off dramatically. She was always tired, yet she had a difficult time sleeping. Those friends who knew her from the previous year described her as irritable and withdrawn.

When Bart finally was able to make it to DC, he was astonished by the change in his lover. Her letters and occasional phone calls revealed her troubles with her roommate, but he passed it off as a temporary thing. Arriving on Friday evening, he was not prepared for the distressed Gina waiting for him in the motel. She had lost ten pounds; her hair was short and straight and it looked as if she hadn't slept in days. Instead of the joyful reception he anticipated, what he got was an annoyed "What took you so long?" He was about to shoot back with a wisecrack when Gina suddenly broke into tears; for the next two hours she unloaded all her frustrations and fears on Bart.

She started with a blow-by-blow description of her confrontations with her roommate but soon revealed her innermost fears. It was like being caught without oars in a class-four rapid on a kayak. She was throwing things at Bart so fast and furiously, he didn't have time to digest one thought before she hit him with another. Finally, after a couple of hours, she fell asleep sobbing and exhausted. In spite of his long drive, Bart couldn't sleep; he quietly lay in the room trying to sort out the plethora of troubles Gina had hurled his way. Besides the roommate problem, she disclosed her fears about getting pregnant or about her father and brother getting arrested or, worse, killed, and finally her confused feelings about her father's involvement in organized crime. The rest of the stuff she had conveyed seemed to Bart to be normal issues for a college student; heck, he worried about most of the same things. Even at this point in their relationship, Bart believed it was his responsibility to fix everything for Gina. He figured that her first problem would resolve itself. When he took into account Christmas break, there were only a few weeks left in the semester; then Gina could have her new roommate. He wasn't sure why suddenly the pregnancy issue was such a big deal. It must have something to do with her former roommate, but they had a pact they would not let her get pregnant; besides, he always used protection. The only other thing he could do was suggest they stop being intimate. He finally settled on them reaffirming their pact. The family issue was a whole different story. The only thing he could do was what he and John had discussed several times—move as far away from her father and brother as possible.

Finally, around three o'clock he fell asleep. When he awoke, it was just getting light out and Gina was sitting in the chair next to the bed staring at him. She was wearing nothing but one of his shirts.

"It's about time you woke up, sleepyhead. Don't you realize you're in a room with a horny coed?"

"Did I miss something or am I dreaming?"

Without responding, she stripped off the shirt and jumped back into bed. An hour later, with both of them totally spent, she got up and proclaimed, "I'm starving, let's take a shower and go to breakfast."

The rest of the weekend transpired without any repeats of Friday night's emotional outburst. Bart brought up a few of the issues but she immediately brushed them off as no longer important. She did mention one new issue; she was worried about her mother. She told Bart that over Thanksgiving her mother didn't seem to be her normal energetic and enthusiastic self.

■ ■ ■

Gina's concerns for her mother were confirmed while she was still home for winter break. Just after New Year's, Eleonora requested Gina accompany her to a gynecologist appointment. The forty-two-year-old had been experiencing chronic pelvic pain and prolonged heavy bleeding. Her regular doctor had referred her to this specialist. After the specialist gave her a complete exam and reviewed X-rays, he informed mother and daughter that Eleonora had a condition called endometriosis. In this condition, endometrial cells grow outside of the uterus, attaching themselves to other organs in the pelvic cavity. He recommended a total hysterectomy be performed as soon as possible. Eleonora was relieved it wasn't a cancerous growth, but Gina was distraught. She went to the library and got as much information as she could about the condition, hysterectomies, and the recovery process.

Within two days of the diagnosis, Gina announced she was taking a leave of absence from school. She planned on remaining at home to take care of her mother. Gina was not going to allow her mother to do any strenuous activity for four months, not cook, clean, or any of the other chores that were part of her normal routine. Everybody — her mother, father, brother, and boyfriend — tried to talk her out of such a drastic measure, but she would not listen to anyone. Her father even offered to hire a nurse and a live-in housekeeper instead of Gina leaving college. However, Gina was adamant; she wasn't going to trust her mother's recuperation to anyone but herself.

CHAPTER 18

Many mothers and daughters often find themselves at odds with one another during the teenager's high school years. That never happened with Gina and Eleonora Nicosia. Mother and daughter always had a special bond and understanding. It wasn't like Eleonora was her daughter's best friend; their relationship was one of love and mutual respect.

Gina never knew any of her grandparents. Eleonora's mother and father returned to Italy before she married Pietro. Both her father's parents died when he was a teenager. Eleonora rarely spoke of her parents, but when she did it was with indifference. Her coldness was probably the result of her parent's apparent apathy to Eleonora's refusal to return with them to Italy. Although their daughter was still not fifteen years old, neither parent expressed any concerns about leaving her behind. During the first few years after they left, Eleonora wrote to them in Italian, but she never received a reply. Occasionally, when the Nicosias were on their annual vacation to the Patrones' in Rhode Island, Gina would listen as her mother and Aunt Agnese talked about their parents. The only emotion the sisters expressed was their regret for not having any happy memories of their parents.

Maybe it was this void in Eleonora's life that gave her a special understanding of what children need from their parents. Her children, and even Bart, could feel the deep interest she had in their lives. It was not a meddling interest but an appreciative and accepting understanding. They all knew she loved them, and that she would, in her own way, and in her own time, do anything to make them happy. It was probably these same traits that Pietro saw in her when he was first introduced to her by his future brother-in-law, Raf Patrone. Pietro Nicosia was twenty and Eleonora was fifteen years old. When they first met he had been on his own, living in the streets since he was thirteen. He was already running with a crew that included Albert Anastasia, Joe Leucchi, and Raf Patrone.

Growing up, Gina spent hours in the kitchen with her mother rather than outside with her friends. During those times mother and daughter talked about everything from school, to friends, to cooking, to what it was like being a mother. It was an easy conversation. Gina never felt like her mother was grilling her about her friends or how she was spending her time. She always felt at ease discussing with her mother subjects that would make most other teenagers uncomfortable. For her part, Eleonora had a way of giving advice without it seeming like she was telling her daughter what to do or being judgmental. So after the initial worry and stress of the operation, the time that mother and daughter had together was enjoyable.

One afternoon in late March, while Eleonora was chopping fresh spinach and Gina was pounding breast filets for chicken piccata, the conversation came around to the family.

Their discussion meandered to different uncles and aunts, with Gina asking how they were related. Since Eleonora only had one sister and Pietro one brother, Gina was curious how so many people could possibly be blood relatives. In many cases, Eleonora's answer was they were really "distant cousins" somehow connected through her or her husband's parents' siblings. But in many cases her answer was they were close business associates of Gina's father. Finally, Gina got up the nerve to ask the $64,000 question: "Is Daddy in the Mafia?"

Gina watched as a look she had never seen before came over her mother's face. Then in a frosty tone she demanded, "What brought this up, Gina?"

Instantly regretting her insolent query she stammered, "Uh . . . well, I, um . . . sometimes read stuff in the papers and, uh . . . hear people talking; they say Daddy is connected with the mob. I assume, since we are Italian, when they say 'mob,' they mean Mafia."

Visibly annoyed, her mother tersely replied, "I don't even know if there is such a thing as the Mafia, but let me tell you about your father. He was orphaned at thirteen and lived on the streets taking care of his younger brother, your Uncle Paul.

I don't know what he did to keep a roof over their heads or fill their stomachs, and frankly I don't care. When my parents went back to Italy, I moved in with my sister and her husband, Uncle Raf. When they moved to New England, your father asked me to marry him; and he supported both me and his brother. In those days, it was not easy for an uneducated Italian to make a living in the United States. Most of the people with money and power didn't think that we 'guineas' were good for anything but low-paid manual labor. Your father only went through eighth grade, but he was smarter than most of those people with college degrees. He knew, in spite of their education and breeding, they had the same vices as the rest of us. He exploited those weaknesses by providing them with the things they couldn't get in their neighborhoods. He was wise enough to know their power and money not only shielded them from the law but, as long as he gave them exactly what they thought they wanted, it also shielded him. There were other people who were envious of the living your father was making, supplying the privileged, and they would occasionally try to hurt him in order to steal his business. If he defended himself and his family from those attackers, I personally do not see any evil in that. Your father is not a cruel or violent man. Have you ever seen him hit me or your brothers? Did he ever raise a hand to you? I don't even recall him raising his voice to you. He loves all of us and would do anything to protect us. Now, you can either pursue this line of questioning directly with him, or you can drop it and accept him for who he is — a kind and loving father."

Gina stood there, meat mallet in her hand, tears welling in her eyes, ashamed she had questioned her father's respectability. A few minutes later her mother inquired, "Is it Bart who's filling your head with this stuff?"

Her voice faltering, Gina responded with shame, "No . . . he's never said anything . . . but I've heard other people say stuff about Daddy." She wanted to tell her mother about the incident after her senior prom and everything the police captain said to them, but she thought better of it.

CHAPTER 19

Bart was so excited the day he returned home for summer vacation. He couldn't wait to see Gina again and to hold her in his arms. He had called from Maryland to tell her he would probably be there in six hours; yet when he arrived, she was not anxiously waiting for him. He rushed into the house without knocking and found her vacuuming the living room. Since she did not notice him enter, he quietly came up behind her and put his arms around her. At first she was startled, but slowly she turned, saying, "Oh, you finally got here."

"Glad to see you, too. How's your mother doing?"

Undaunted by Bart's sarcasm, Gina's casual retort was, "Much better. Are you staying for dinner?"

"I was hoping to just say a quick hello to your parents . . . then perhaps you and I could drive out to Jones Beach for a hot dog on the boardwalk and some quiet time in the dunes."

"My mother and I made cioppino, expecting you to stay for dinner. Maybe we can go to the beach after dinner."

"Jeez Gina, you know the parking lots close at dark. By the time we get there it we'll only have an hour alone."

"Well, then we can go tomorrow."

"It's not the same. You want to wait until tomorrow to be alone with me?"

"I didn't say that."

"Well, what are you saying?"

"I had plans for dinner. Don't you care that my mother and I worked hard to please you?"

Bart gritted his teeth and held back what he was thinking, *You want to please me, let's get a hot dog and snuggle up in the dunes.* At the same instant Mrs. Nicosia walked into the room.

"Sorry to eavesdrop, but I overheard your dilemma. I agree with Bart, you two haven't seen each other in almost two months. You should be alone. Look it's only four o'clock. I can have dinner ready by five. I'll try to get in touch with Pietro, maybe he can be home by then. If not, you two eat and go out; that's what young lovers are supposed to do."

Bart looked at Gina; her facial expression was one of consternation. She hesitated then replied, "OK, Mom, if it's OK with you and Daddy." It was now obvious to Bart the four months Gina spent back at home didn't do much to improve her emotional state. He understood the concern for her mother's health had taken a toll on Gina's psyche, but now Eleonora appeared to be fully recuperated.

After dinner, while they were driving to Jones Beach on Meadowbrook Parkway, Bart got his second indication everything was not normal with Gina. Previous summer vacations were a relatively spontaneous time for the couple. This was partly the result of Bart's caddying being unpredictable, but also because they both needed the escape from the rigors of school. Except for their regular Saturday night date and an occasional Sunday dinner with her family, he would just generally call and say, "I'm coming over." She always sounded delighted when he called. Then, when he arrived, they would decide what to do and where to go.

This year Bart was offered an accounting internship at Long Island Lighting Company. Although he thought he would miss being outdoors for the summer, he was looking forward to what he assumed would be a more predictable schedule and a chance for some valuable business experience in his major. He didn't know where he was going to work or what his hours would be, but he was scheduled to report to the personnel office at LILCO's Hicksville facility on Monday morning. When he mentioned this to Gina, she became upset. "I thought this summer job was going to give us the opportunity to see each other on a regular basis. I was planning on taking some summer courses at St. John's. How am I supposed to schedule my summer classes when I don't know where you are going to be or what your schedule is?"

"Easy, Gina, I'm sure I'll find out on Monday when I report to the personnel office."

"I hope this isn't going to be a problem."

Bart was perplexed with her making a big deal over a temporary uncertainty. Looking for something to change her mood, he offered, "Well, the best part about this job is I'll have weekends off. We've never had that before."

That was all Gina needed to hear; she calmed down and immediately began talking about what they would do on weekends. After a couple of minutes of excited chatter about all the things they could plan, she exclaimed, "Oh my god! You can come with us to Rhode Island this Fourth of July! You're finally going to get to really know my family!"

Oh boy, Bart thought to himself.

When they arrived at Jones Beach's Parking Field 5, Bart retrieved two blankets from the trunk.

Gina looked at him strangely and asked, "What are those for?"

Bewildered, Bart replied, "Did I miss something or did we not eat dinner early so we could get lost in the dunes?"

"Oh yeah" was Gina's uninspiring reply.

He was unable to contain his annoyance any longer; the irritation dripped from his words. "I just love your newfound enthusiasm."

Gina ignored his wisecrack, but it had the desired effect. She casually took hold of his hand, entwining their fingers.

It was a weekday, still very early in the season, and a cool 70 degrees, leaving the dunes virtually empty. Much to his delight, after they pulled the top blanket over themselves, it didn't take Gina long to warm up.

The ride back was very different from the ride out. Now Gina seemed to be her old self, telling charming stories about her experiences with her mother over the last few months, asking him questions about spring practice, his courses, David and Joe Z. On the drive home from Gina's house, he reflected on her mood swings, but eventually blew them off as temporary.

While Bart worked at LILCO, Gina took courses at St. John's University. The two six-week summer sessions enabled her to make up for her lost spring semester. Bart's learning curve as a vacation replacement resulted in his having to occasionally work late in order to keep up with the work. Between Gina's course load and Bart's overtime they soon discovered that getting together during the week was difficult. Fortunately, they did have weekends all to themselves, except that Gina had to study.

As the Fourth of July approached, a slight glitch appeared in the plan for Bart to join Gina's family on the Rhode Island trip. The plan was for everyone to meet at Port Washington Marina on Thursday, July 2. With the fourth falling on Saturday, LILCO employees also had off Friday the third. Knowing this, Bart and Gina figured he would request Thursday afternoon off so he could meet her family's 1:00 p.m. cast-off for the seven-hour crossing to Narragansett.

Weeks in advance, Bart checked with the summer intern coordinator, receiving a positive response to his request. But when the time actually came, he was heavily involved in the company's annual physical inventory that began on June 27.

Being a summer intern meant getting all the crappy jobs. Taking physical inventory is one of the crappiest, so it was no surprise Bart found himself assigned to the most difficult and time-consuming locations, the Hicksville yard and warehouse. All the actual counting was completed before the weekend was over, but Bart was then assigned to the warehouse supervisor to assist in reconciling the thousands of parts in the huge storeroom. The warehouse supervisor was a crusty, middle-aged Italian by the name of Angelo D'Augustino. At first Angie appeared to have little use for Bart, but after Bart discovered several transposed part numbers on inventory tickets, the old hand started to warm up to the "college kid," as he constantly referred to Bart. By Tuesday he was using Bart, instead of his regular staff, to verify counts and to keep a running record of new withdrawals.

By 9:00 a.m. on Thursday, the warehouse inventory had still not been reconciled. Bart went to Angelo and told him about his agreement with the summer intern coordinator. Angelo glared at him. "That doesn't mean anything unless she plans on coming down here and taking your place." By ten Bart started to get a feeling the reconciliation was not going to be completed in time for him to make the one o'clock cast-off. When Bart finally was alone in the office with Angelo, he worked up the nerve to ask him again if he could leave at noon.

Angie responded, "What have you got going, college boy, a hot date or something?"

Bart explained he was supposed to meet his girlfriend's family at the marina in Port Washington for a weekend trip across the sound to Rhode Island.

"I need you here 'til we figure this out. They're just going to have to wait for you or leave you behind," snarled Bart's supervisor.

At 11:30 the phone rang; Angie answered it. Bart heard him tell the caller, "Hang on, I'll see if I can find him." He put the caller on hold and turned to Bart, "It must be your girlfriend checking up to see if you are going to make it."

Bart took the phone and explained to Gina he didn't know when he would be done; that if they had to, they should leave without him. She was furious, going on and on about not being able to depend on him; just like after the Kennedy assassination, he was always too busy with his stuff to care about her. Finally Bart told her not to worry, if they had to leave without him, he would drive to Rhode Island that night.

Out of the corner of his eye, Bart could see Angie watching him with a Cheshire cat grin on his face. Bart hung up and went back to work without saying a word.

About fifteen minutes later Bart found a posting error. The inventory ticket read 995 but the number that had been posted was 945. He had found two-thirds of the "missing" inventory.

Angelo was ecstatic, exclaiming, "Good work, college boy, you've finally earned your pay."

At 12:10 they had not made any further progress on the missing inventory.

Unexpectedly, Angie's curiosity got the best of him. "So what's your girlfriend's name?"

"Gina."

"Geeena." The older man almost savored her name like it was

rich chocolate. "She must be Italian. What's her last name, Lollobrigida?" the older man teased.

"No, Nicosia," Bart abruptly stated.

There were ten seconds of silence before Angelo mused, "I used to know a couple of Nicosias, Pete and Paulie; you don't know if she has any relatives by those names?"

"Yeah, her father's name is Pietro, but I've heard people call him Pete, and she has an Uncle Paul."

Again there was a pregnant pause. "You're shitting me, LaRocca. That's not really her father's name, is it?"

"Why would I make that up?"

"Damn, what are you trying to do, get us both a pair of cement overshoes? Get your ass out of here now! I'll finish this myself."

Speeding to Port Washington, Bart made it to the marina by 1:05; just minutes before the lines were cast off.

Gina was jubilant when she saw Bart hurrying down the dock with his overnight bag. She bounded off the boat and ran into his arms. "I'm so sorry I gave you a hard time; Daddy told me you would be here in time. You must be starving, let's jump on board and get you something to eat." Bart smiled, thinking to himself, *What is it about women that makes them think all they need to do to make men happy is to feed them often and give them an occasional piece of ass?*

True to form, the galley was overstocked with food and drink. The main course was a six-foot hero sandwich stacked with Italian cold cuts. There was also a huge dish of *insalata caprese.* Of course the bar was stocked with enough beer and wine for a month-long voyage.

Pietro was not a particularly accomplished yachtsman, but he was a smart-enough man to know his own limitations, especially when the lives of his family were at stake. He had hired a retired captain from an Italian cruise line to coach him through the voyage. Although Pietro was at the helm, the debonair silver-haired seafarer provided his apprentice with professional guidance during each critical nautical maneuver. The weather was perfect, temperatures in the low 80s, a mild breeze from the west, and a calm sea. The forty-two-foot Hatteras motor yacht was equipped with a large topside deck covered by a vinyl canopy and plenty of room below deck to socialize and party. On board, in addition to Gina, Bart, and her parents, were John and Patty Jo, Paul and his wife Camille and son Paulie, Captain Verona, and two of Pietro's cronies, Vito and Vinnie. Vito and Vinnie pretty much kept to themselves. The motor yacht was equipped with two Mercruiser 454 inboard gas engines that provided a cruising speed of 16 miles per hour. The ninety-mile crossing was accomplished in just over six hours.

CHAPTER 20

Smiling, Bart recalled, "I don't think the image of Raf and his son, Raf Junior, enthusiastically waving to us from the dock just as we cleared the breakwater will ever be erased from my memory." As if he was talking to himself, he continued, "In all my family's get-togethers, I can't recall any of my relatives being so excited to greet one another, no matter how long it had been since they had last seen each other." Then with a wry smile he said, "Say what you like about how ruthless these people could be, but never think for one minute there wasn't an intense love between them."

After securing the vessel, Mr. and Mrs. Nicosia, his brother, and his brother's wife went with the senior Patrone in his Caddy while everyone else, except for Vito and Vinnie, squeezed into a Jeep Wrangler with Junior. That was the last time Bart would see Vito and Vinnie until Sunday morning when they all boarded the yacht for the return trip.

It was a short five-minute drive to the Patrones' huge house on three beachfront acres. During the voyage, Bart wondered where everyone was going to sleep, but as soon as he saw the three-story, turn-of-the-century Kennedy-style complex with the wraparound porch, his concerns subsided. The place had to be over 5,000 square feet, with six bedrooms in the main house and an apartment with two more bedrooms above the four-car detached garage. Gina and Patty Jo slept with Gina's twin cousins, Alessandra and Carla, in a huge bedroom that took up half of the third floor. Pietro and Eleonora were on the second floor across the hall from their hosts. Captain Verona took up the third bedroom on the second floor. Paul and his wife were in another third-floor bedroom. John, Bart, and Paulie were housed in the apartment above the garage. Raf Junior returned each night to his apartment in Newport.

After the guests were shown to their rooms and had a chance to wash up, a buffet-style dinner awaited them. It didn't take Bart long to realize why this annual get-together was so important to Gina. The eating, drinking, and side-splitting storytelling went on for hours. It was almost midnight when Pietro and Raf announced the guys better get some sleep because at 7:00 a.m. they were all going fishing.

When the rising sun burst through the garage apartment's windows, Bart thought they had overslept. He immediately jumped out of bed and woke John. John was a little smarter and looked at his watch before he reacted. "Damn," growled John, "it's only 5:30." He pulled the sheets over his head and went back to sleep. By the time Bart had relieved himself of the half-dozen beers he had consumed some six hours earlier, he was wide awake, though sporting a ginormous headache. By the time he worked his way to the main house, Raf and Pietro were already sitting at the kitchen table sipping black coffee.

"Need a couple of aspirin?" quipped Raf.

"Yeah, that would be great, and some orange juice if you got it," groaned Bart.

As his host got up to accommodate his young guest, Pietro asked, "So how'd you get away so quickly after you were pretty sure you weren't going to make it?"

"I'm not sure," replied Bart. "But I suspect it had something to do with your name."

Just then, Raf returned with the aspirin and orange juice. Bart eagerly washed down the aspirin and sighed as if he was disappointed that there wasn't instant relief from his agony. Raf gave him a second to recoup then asked, "What's this guy's name?"

"Angelo D'Augustino," responded Bart.

Raf and Pietro glanced each other, grinning. "Little guy, fair skin with big blue eyes and long eye lashes?" Raf inquired.

"Yeah, that's a pretty good description. You know him?" Bart asked apprehensively.

Again, the two older men looked at each other, smiling.

"Yup, we go back a long way. We used to call him Angie," Pietro answered.

■ ■ ■

It was 6:45 when Raf pulled the Wrangler out of the driveway with Pietro, Paul, Paulie, John, and Bart. Junior was waiting for them when they pulled into the marina parking lot. Raf Junior directed them to a forty-foot fishing charter named *Esmeralda*. The boat had a captain and a two-man crew already prepared to shove off. Again, the weather was perfect. It was still a little chilly, but the sun was rising quickly and provided some warmth. As the captain gunned the engine and guided it into the rising sun, the two-man crew began cutting bait and preparing lines.

While they were cruising to their fishing spot some twenty miles off shore, Bart asked Pietro, "Why are we using a charter instead of your vessel?" Pietro's answer was "Oh, this captain owes Raf a favor and he knows where the fish are."

They sailed southeast for almost an hour. When they were about a mile off the coast of Block Island, the captain slowed the vessel and the two crew members began setting four lines, two straight off the back and one off each side. The three young men and Paul took the rods first, and the captain began a moderate troll in a north-to-south run. The first strike took about fifteen minutes, and it was Paulie's rod, which was almost stripped out of his hands. One of the crew had the others quickly reel in their lines so as to not get tangled in Paulie's.

Paulie was so excited he began yelling, "I got 'em, I got 'em;

boy, it's a big one." His father made his way to his son's side and tried to calm him down. But Paulie continued to shout, "Dad, I got 'em, I got 'em, and he's a big one." Paulie was a strong kid, but after about five minutes, he was winded and his arms ached. He then seemed to calm down, realizing he needed all of his strength to land this fish. It took almost twenty minutes before one of the crew was able to gaff the fish and the other to work him into a net. It was a whopper of a striped bass, thirty-six inches nose to tail and over forty-two pounds. Raf proclaimed it was a keeper and would be our Friday night dinner.

We continued trolling for the rest of the morning, catching six more stripers and twelve blue fish. On one strike John had three blues on the same umbrella rig, but Paulie's first catch was the highlight of the day for everyone, especially for Paulie and his father.

It had to be tough on Paul Nicosia to know his only son would never mentally or emotionally progress beyond an early teenager. So triumphs like this, as few and far between as they were, must have been especially satisfying for this loving father.

Paulie couldn't wait to get back to the house to show off his trophy. Upon their arrival, the ladies responded with great enthusiasm to Paulie's catch and his story of battling the sea monster. He was the hero of the day, and for one weekend in July 1965, Paulie Nicosia was probably the happiest person on the planet. All of a sudden this mentally challenged twenty-two-year-old was the center of attention. When he wasn't talking about the fishing trip, he was relentlessly going on about the New York Mets. He wasn't just another Mets fan; he was a walking, talking Mets encyclopedia and promoter. He knew every player's batting average and home runs for this season and last. He knew every pitcher's record, strikeouts and walks. He absolutely believed the Mets were going to win the pennant and the World Series. By Saturday morning his constant babble about the Mets and his struggle with the striper was wearing pretty thin with everyone. Finally, to escape, John borrowed his uncle's Caddy, and the two young couples drove into Newport to tour the mansions and hit some of the local hot spots. John asked Junior if he wanted to come along, but much to Bart's delight, he declined. Bart didn't like Raf Junior. It wasn't anything tangible, Bart just didn't like the way Raf looked at his cousin or the way he hung around Gina whenever Bart wasn't at her side.

All things considered, Bart thought it was a good weekend even though he and Gina hardly had a minute alone. One thing he found interesting was there was hardly any mention of Al.

On Sunday morning, when the group arrived at the marina, Vito and Vinnie were already onboard. Bart wondered what they had been up to all weekend, especially when Vito's first whispered words to Pietro were, "It's done, boss." The "boss" just nodded and immediately proceeded to the helm with Captain Verona.

Approximately an hour into the return voyage, Bart was descending the steps from the bridge when he caught a glimpse of Vito deviously slipping a paper bag overboard. Bart's immediate thought was, *Freakin' pig, why would you pollute this beautiful ocean?* When he looked for the floating debris, there was none; just then Vito became aware of Bart watching him. Recalling that moment, Bart winced. "At the time, I took Vito's fierce look as simply a warning to not tell anyone he threw garbage overboard. It wasn't until Raf Patrone's trial almost eighteen years later I figured out what was probably in the bag and how Vito and Vinnie most likely spent their free time over that Fourth of July weekend."

In the spring of 1982 Raf Senior was on trial for numerous felonies, including two counts of murder. The New England papers contained daily front page reports on the sensational Mafia trial. According to the testimony of one of Patrone's lieutenants turned federal informant, Raf Senior had imported a couple of hit men from New York to kill Bernie Walsh, an Irish mob kingpin who had begun interfering with Patrone's loan-sharking operations in Boston. The body of Walsh, with two bullets in the base of his skull, was found floating in Boston Harbor on Sunday morning, July 5, 1965. Before the trial was over, the seventy-four-year-old

Rafaele Senior died quietly of a heart attack in the apartment of his forty-two-year-old girlfriend. He was survived by his son, Rafaele Junior, and his twin daughters, both now married and anonymously living out of state. His wife, Agnese, had died in 1976 after a long bout with breast cancer.

CHAPTER 21

When Bart returned to work on Monday, he was assigned to the internal audit department. On Tuesday morning he received a telephone call from Angelo requesting they meet after work at Jabby's Bar on Broadway in Hicksville. A lot of the LILCO guys stopped off at Jabby's after work for a beer and a game of shuffleboard. Bart usually stopped once or twice a week for an hour or so but had never noticed Angie there. By the time Bart arrived, Angie was already there, sitting alone at a table, sipping his beer and watching a shuffleboard game. Bart ordered a draft of Pabst.

"So kid, how was your weekend?"

"Fine. Angie, is that why you invited me here, to see if I had a good time?"

"No, I wanted to know what you told those mafiosos about me."

"Nothin'. Mr. Nicosia wanted to know how I finally got away in time to catch the boat and I guess I mentioned your name. Both he and Raf said they knew you from way back. Why, has something happened?"

"Yeah," Angie scoffed. "A brand-new twenty-inch Magnavox color TV in a mahogany cabinet was delivered to my house yesterday."

Ignoring Angie's tone, Bart raised his beer glass in celebration. "Wow, that's great!"

"Like hell it is! I don't want any part of their thievery. Don't you know that these guys don't come by anything legit? Any time they offer you a good deal on something, you can bet your ass that it 'fell off a truck' somewhere. Do you get what I mean, kid?"

"Sure, Angie, but I've been around the family a lot over the last few years; except for the oldest boy, Al, I've never seen or heard of anything illegal."

"Yeah, I know, kid, and neither have the cops. Just because he's never been caught doesn't mean he hasn't broken the law."

After Angelo took a long swig of his beer, he continued, "Let me tell you a story." He took another long guzzle. "My brother and I go back a long way with Pete and Raf. My brother Carl is Pete's age and I am Paul's. We used to all play together before Pete and Paulie's parents were killed. Pete must have been about thirteen and Paulie ten when their parents' vegetable wagon was smashed by a runaway truck. Their father was killed instantly but their mother lasted about two weeks before she died. The boys had no other relatives here in the States so they were sent to an orphanage in upstate New York. It took Pete about six months to run away from the orphanage and back to the old neighborhood. He hooked up with Raf, who was a couple of years older. Raf hung with a gang of mostly orphans or runaways who lived off of petty crimes. They slept in abandoned buildings or down in the subway.

"Within a year or so Raf and Pete were doing small jobs for the local mafiosos. That meant stealing anything off the back of delivery trucks, running numbers, and creating diversions to keep the cops away from whatever the big-time hoodlums were after. My brother and I knew what they were doing but didn't care because they never did anything to hurt us. In fact, Pete used to give us stuff, small stuff, like an apple or a hat; he even gave my brother Carl a pocketknife once. We thought they were pretty cool, staying out all night, going where they wanted anytime they wanted; basically not having to answer to any parents.

"One time, Pete gave Carl a real baseball and bat; boy, did we think we were hot shit. Everybody would ask us to go down to the park to play ball, as long as Carl brought his bat and ball. So one day we're down at the park playing ball and on the next field were some older and bigger guys. They saw our real bat and shiny white ball and stopped their game to come over to watch us play. After a few minutes, three or four of them walked out on the field and stopped our game. The biggest one of the bunch goes up to the pitcher and says, 'Gimme the ball, kid.' Scared out of his wits, Tommy Amaro hands the guy the ball, then the bully turns around and walks to home plate where my brother is batting. He says to Carl, 'Gimme the bat.' Carl says, 'No way. In fact, you give me back the ball.' The guy stares at Carl for a few seconds then hurls the ball right at Carl. It hits him right in the gut, he goes down gasping for air, and the big kid just saunters over and picks up the bat and ball. Then he turns and shouts, 'You faggots aren't good enough to have a real bat and ball yet. Tell you what, I'm going to hold 'em for you until you're good enough to use 'em.' With that, he and his buddies walk back to their field and start playing again with our bat and ball.

"After Carl gets his breath back, he asks us to go after them and retrieve his bat and ball. The other guys are scared shitless and just want to get out of there. Carl looks at me. I'm the youngest and smallest of the whole bunch. He just shakes his head and stomps off, leaving me to quietly sit at a safe distance and keep an eye on our bat and ball.

"About twenty minutes later, Carl comes back with Pete and Raf along with a half dozen of their gang. Pete walks right over to the big bully that threw the ball at Carl. Pete only comes up to the guy's chin. The guy looks down at Pete and says something I couldn't hear. Pete then goes right up in the guy's face and also says something I couldn't hear. I could see the guy nervously shift his weight. Then, the bully backs away, turns and walks to home plate. He takes the bat from his buddy in the batter's box. He then walks over to Carl and hands both to Carl. Carl later told me the guy apologized and asked his forgiveness. Then the big guy and all his buddies left the park."

"Do you know what Pete said?"

"I'm not exactly sure," Angie reflected. "Carl could only make out a few words like 'split your head open' and something about his brains running down his face."

Bart took a swig of his beer. "That's a great story."

Angie just stared at his beer for a long moment; he then looked straight into Bart's eyes and continued, "That story is not the point, LaRocca. It's what happened a few months later that is the point. You see, my brother was now indebted to Pete and he would eventually have to pay for it. About two months later, Pete came to Carl and asked him to hold a bag of stuff for him. It was a blue satin bag. When he shook it, it sounded like marbles. Ever since the incident at the ball field, Pete was Carl's hero. He wouldn't think of not doing him this little favor. Pete told my brother that, for his own good, he shouldn't look in the bag or tell anyone about it. Pete took the bag and hid it in the coal bin in the basement of our tenement. It stayed there for a couple of weeks, and Carl pretty much forgot about it. Then one day the super was working in the basement and stumbled across the bag. When he looked inside, he discovered ten medium-sized diamonds. He took them to the cops, who were soon all over the building questioning everyone. It turned out that a Hasidic jeweler had been rolled and pistol-whipped on West Forty-Seventh Street the night before Pete gave the bag to Carl. Now Carl was not a hardened criminal, so when he was questioned, the cops could tell that he knew something. After hours of intense questioning and threatening, Carl remained adamant he had found the bag in an alley off West Seventeenth Street. After questioning everyone in the building, the cops verified that, at the time of the mugging, Carl was sitting on the stoop with me and several of our friends. The authorities already suspected Pete's and Raf's crew were behind the mugging, but they had no evidence. The cops tried for weeks to get Carl to talk. My father and mother pleaded with him. I knew it was Pete who gave him the bag and that Carl would never squeal on his hero. Finally, the cops charged Carl with receiving stolen property; since he was still only fifteen, he was sentenced to six months in a youth detention center upstate. After he was released, he never came back home. Much to my parents' dismay, he wrote them a letter just before he got out announcing he was going to California. I didn't see him again for the next twenty-five years.

"Until I enlisted in the Army Air Corps about five years later, I would see Pete and Raf around the neighborhood. Their reputations for criminal activity continued to grow and I heard they became 'made men.' Pete eventually rescued his little brother from the orphanage and took care of him until he could fend for himself. Raf was the more violent of the two, and rumors had it that, during Prohibition, the New York families sent him up to Boston to deal with the Irish mob's encroachment into their flow of alcohol from Canada.

"So the point is, my young friend, I don't want his damn color TV. I have it in the back of my pickup for you to take back to him."

"I can't do that, Angie."

"Yes, you can, and when he asks you why, you tell him the story I told you. Then you can see what your future father-in-law is really made of."

Angie helped Bart load the TV in the trunk of the Olds and secured the lid with a rope. Bart decided to deliver it that night. Gina was surprised when he called from Jabby's and told her he was coming over. When he arrived at the Nicosias', Gina and her mother were cleaning up after dinner. John was reading in the backyard and Mr. Nicosia was watching what looked like a brand-new color TV almost identical to the one in Bart's trunk. As usual, Mrs. Nicosia had saved a plate for Bart. You'd think Bart was 6 foot 6 and 300 pounds by the amount of food heaped on the plate, half a roasted chicken, a huge pile of risotto, and a quarter of a head of broccoli. Nobody ever accused Eleonora Nicosia of putting out too little food. Of course, just as she suspected, Bart ate every last morsel.

Gina sat there the entire time he was wolfing down his dinner, telling him about her day and reminiscing about the weekend. Finally, she noticed that Bart was not paying attention; it was apparent his mind was off on another planet. Annoyed, she said, "What did you come here for, just the food?"

"No," Bart sheepishly responded. "I have to talk to your father."

She gave him a quizzical look and whispered, "Oh. Is something wrong?"

"No, I don't think so. I just have to return something to him."

"What?" she asked.

"A TV he gave as a gift to somebody who doesn't want it."

She just looked at him for a few seconds then took his empty plate and utensils and went to the sink to wash them. Bart took the cue and headed to the living room to deliver Angie's message. For his entire thirty-minute drive, Bart rehearsed what he was going to say; but when he walked into the living room, he forgot all the pretty speeches and decided to just lay it on the line.

"I have the TV you sent to Angelo D'Augustino in the trunk of my car; he told me to tell you that he doesn't want anything from you. He says you ruined his family once and he won't let it happen again."

Pietro just stared at Bart with an undaunted look and an air of calm resignation. After what seemed like an eternity to Bart, waiting for whatever came next, his likely future father-in-law spoke in an almost remorseful tone. "That was a long time ago and I understand Angie's continued bitterness. I involved an innocent friend in my foolish act of dishonesty. Although it is no excuse, I never thought Carl would get caught. But when he did, I should have come forward and told the authorities he had nothing to do with it. I could have copped a plea in exchange for Carl's release, but for selfish reasons I didn't do it."

Again there was a long moment of silence and then Pietro continued, "Now you know what kind of man your girlfriend's father is, but that's not her, nor is it John. It is better you find this out now rather than after you're married. Is there anything else you need to know?"

Bart, taking full advantage of Pietro's offer to answer another question, boldly asked, "Are you in the Mafia?"

Pietro smirked. "You've got cojones, kid!" Then his demeanor became stoically serious and he continued, "I will tell you this because I respect your intelligence and discretion; I have had dealings with some people that could be considered involved in organized crime, but for the most part my businesses are legit. If they weren't, I would not be here talking to you; I would already be in jail or dead."

"Angelo says you just haven't been caught yet."

"Angelo is a wise cynic." Then his voice chilled. "So, what do you want from me, kid, to confess I'm a criminal? I'd be a fool to admit that to you or anyone else."

Bart was about to respond when Pietro said, "If you would, just take the TV over to Paul's place. I'll get John to help you."

The interruption was enough to persuade Bart to just drop the issue right there. Bart turned and headed for the back door to get John. As he did, he passed Gina standing against the wall in the dining room with tears streaming down her rosy cheeks. She apparently had been there listening for the entire time. When she saw Bart, she let out a little gasp and bolted for her room. Neither one of them called the other until Friday night.

When Gina finally called on Friday evening, the conversation was almost sanitized. If you listened in, you would have thought it was two business colleagues scheduling a meeting. "Pick me up Saturday at 5:30. We have a lot to discuss."

"OK, anything special you want to do?"

"No, let's just talk and see where it goes."

"Fine, see you at 5:30 tomorrow."

The first half hour of their "meeting" was strained. They had driven out to Roslyn Harbor and were still sitting in the car parked in the marina's parking lot. Finally, Gina broke the ice by announcing, "So, you think my father is a criminal. I suppose you're thinking about ditching me and my family."

"Where is this coming from? I never said I thought he was a criminal; all I did was relay what somebody told me. Your father was the one doing all the talking. If you were there for the whole discussion, you heard the same things I did; you never heard me accuse him of anything."

"But you think he is a mafioso," she came back hotly.

"Again, I never said that. I asked him and he sort of evaded the direct question. I didn't even press him for an answer."

"You're being just as evasive. You really think he is in the Mafia, don't you?" she rebutted.

"OK, I guess I do. So there, I said it; what do you believe?"

"I believe I love my parents and they love me. I don't care if he is or isn't."

They both just sat there for a few minutes staring at the waning sun reflecting off the glasslike water. Bart was first to break the silence. "Does it really make any difference who or what I think your father is? I'm not in love with him, and once we are married we can go and live our own lives and be as far away from all this as we want."

"I hope you don't think that once we are married I am going to just up and leave my family and never see them again."

"Of course not, but we don't have to be intimately involved in their lives nor they in ours. Right?"

Unconvincingly, Gina replied, "I guess so."

Not prepared to press the issue any further, Bart decided to try to change the mood. "Let's drive over to Jericho Turnpike in Mineola and get a couple of White Castles, then we can swing over to Jericho Drive-in. I think that new James Bond movie is playing."

Shaking her head in disbelief, Gina posed, "How can you be hungry after a discussion like this?"

"Easy," Bart joked back, "it's past my dinnertime."

With a half-hearted smile, Gina responded, "You're a piece of work, LaRocca."

As the rest of the summer flew by, the couple avoided any further discussions of the issue although they both thought about it a lot. Bart secretly promised himself that after he and Gina were married, he would try to put as much distance as possible between them and her family. Gina, on the other hand, found it hard to contemplate ever moving away from New York. In fact, in early August she declared she was not going to return to Trinity College. She intended to finish her degree at St. John's so she could be near her parents.

When Bart finished telling me about Angelo and the whole Rhode Island thing I was flabbergasted. "Gina was right; you are a piece of work, LaRocca. Right then, you knew that her father was Mafia and she wasn't going to just walk away from her parents."

"Yeah, I knew he was Mafia, but I really believed that he wanted to keep both John and Gina safe from all that stuff."

"So, you weren't worried?"

"To say I wasn't concerned would be a lie, but I never thought about bolting. Like Pietro said, it wasn't her or John. That sort of told me he intended to keep us clear of his business. Besides, I really was madly in love with her."

Frowning, I replied, "Man, I would have been out of there quicker than you could say arrivederci."

CHAPTER 22

When Bart's roommate, David Tanner, turned twenty-one in March of 1965, he gained access to his trust fund of approximately seven million dollars. Now it wasn't like he could go to the bank and withdraw the seven million, but he did get an annual stipend of over $100,000.

After spring practice, David decided to give up football and begin focusing on a business career. He was third or fourth on the depth chart at quarterback and certainly didn't need the scholarship to pay for school. David was not a spendthrift by any stretch of the imagination, so a hundred grand left him with a lot of money to invest. The first thing he did with his money was to buy a big old house a few blocks from the campus for $20,000.

Bart's status on the team also had declined over the past year as a new crop of sophomores, who were bigger and just as fast as Bart, moved up to the varsity. But he had not given up on getting substantial playing time in the fall.

Over the summer, David had the house renovated into six

apartments. With off-campus housing scarce, he had no trouble renting them. Actually, he only rented four of the apartments. He moved into the biggest one himself and offered one to Bart. The deal he offered to Bart was that he could live there, rent free, if he cut the lawn, took out the garbage, and cleaned all the common areas like the kitchen, living room, and the two full bathrooms. In other words, Bart would be the janitor in exchange for rent.

It was a generous offer, causing Bart to struggle with his decision. After some deliberation, he concluded, during football season, he wouldn't have the time to add janitor duties to his already busy schedule. As inviting as it sounded to live off campus with his buddy, he turned David down. After all, he was on a scholarship that included room and board, and all it required was he stay on the team.

After explaining his thought process to David, his long-time roommate smiled. "That's exactly what my father said when I told him about the deal. He also predicted you would turn me down."

Bart's new roommate was a baseball player who had transferred to USC following his sophomore year at the US Naval Academy. Robert Allen Ryan was the son of Air Force Major General Harlan "Big Cat" Ryan, a Korean War ace and grandson of former Oklahoma Senator Robert Allen Gifford. Robbie, as he liked to be called, was a left-hand pitcher with a blazing fastball and a heinous curve. Bart was only half joking when he remarked that the only thing Robbie relished more than seeing a batter bail out on a called third-strike curve was pissing off his father. Not only did he infuriate his old man when he chose the Naval Academy over the Air Force Academy, but then he heaped insult upon injury by quitting after his second year. Robbie Ryan had reached the conclusion that he was destined to be the next Sandy Koufax and eight more years committed to the armed forces didn't fit into his time table.

The new roommates got along exceptionally well. Bart envied Robbie's laid-back attitude. Ryan was delighted to room with a football player, since they generally attracted more coeds than the baseball players did. When not studying or practicing, the roommates could often be found on the lawn behind the dorm tossing around either a baseball or football.

The 1965 USC football season was a mixed bag for both the team and Bart. The team had a 5-5 record but tied for the championship of the ACC with Duke. Bart, for his part, worked his way up the depth chart during the early practice sessions. Then, during the last heavy scrimmage, before the first game, he severely sprained his right ankle. By the time his ankle could take the strain of a quick cut, a dazzling sophomore receiver had emerged, limiting Bart's playing time. Finally, in the last game against Clemson, the coaching staff played the senior receiver and he caught five passes in the Gamecocks 17-16 victory.

With great excitement Bart went back home for Thanksgiving. He had saved enough class cuts so he could leave the Saturday before Thanksgiving, right after the Clemson game. By 1965 almost all of I-95 had been finished from Virginia to New York. That development, along with his superb-running Olds, had cut the drive down to about fourteen hours. After driving all night he had the windows wide open and the radio as loud as it would go so as not to doze off. Since he hadn't specifically told Gina which day he would get there, he figured she would not be disappointed if he first went home to catch some sleep.

Instead of a short nap, he slept straight through the night. He called her early the next morning, but she had already left for classes. He knew from her letters she had a break from 12:30 to 2:00, when she could generally be found in the cafeteria. Figuring he would surprise her at lunch, he headed into the St. John's Queens campus about 11:30 and was waiting on the steps of the cafeteria building by 12:15.

He first saw his girlfriend when she was about a hundred yards away, walking with another guy. They were having a grand old time, talking and laughing, and what Bart thought was flirting. He immediately put that thought out of his head and waited for

Gina to see him. She didn't notice him until she was almost at the first step. The initial look on her face was one of surprise, but that quickly turned to what Bart took to be guilt. She stopped, seemed to be pondering the situation for a few seconds, and then finally displaying the reaction Bart had expected, she dashed the last few yards to him. But, after witnessing her initial reaction, Bart was only partially listening to Gina's now excited greeting. He was sizing up the guy with whom she had been walking. He was about 5 foot 9, maybe 150 pounds. He had short blond hair, blue eyes, and was exceptionally good-looking. He was decked out in the classic preppy starched button-down long-sleeve pink cotton shirt, chinos, and polished brown penny loafers. The clincher was the blue Polo sweater he had draped over his shoulders. Gina was saying something but Bart wasn't listening; he was focused on the asshole with his girlfriend.

Recognizing Bart was preoccupied, Gina got his attention by grabbing his hand and raising her voice. "Bart, this is my friend Brian. Brian, this is the boyfriend I've been telling you about, Bart LaRocca."

That move not only got Bart's attention but caused Brian to lose his puffed-up demeanor. Quickly recovering, Brian cautiously made a move to shake Bart's hand, but Bart ignored the gesture and, in an intimidating move he had learned from Al, moved menacingly close to him. In a tone that sent chills through Brian's body, Bart growled, "So Brian, you can run along now; I can take it from here."

Brian nervously backed up a few steps. "See you next week, Gina." Then glancing apologetically at Bart, he added, "In history class." Without waiting for a reply, Brian quickly turned and seemed to slink away. By the time he had gone twenty yards, he recognized some other friends and the arrogance returned to his bearing.

Gina was mortified by Bart's attitude. She glared at him. "What was that all about? Why did you treat my friend like shit?"

"Why'd you look so guilty when you saw me?"

"What are you talking about? I was just surprised you were here and that you never told me you were coming so early. That's all."

"Right, that's not the way I saw it."

Gina immediately changed the subject. "When did you get in?"

"Last night," Bart snarled.

Her voice chilled. "And you didn't stop by or call?"

Still in a nasty mood, he couldn't control his abruptness. "Nope, I was too tired to be civil."

Finally sensing that Bart's attitude was not going to quickly improve, Gina's Sicilian temper kicked in. "It sounds like you're still not civil."

Not to be outdone, Bart shot back, "Perhaps you're right. I'm not yet up to seeing my girl flirting with another guy. Maybe I ought to go home for an attitude adjustment." He turned and started walking away. Funny thing, she didn't stop him.

Here were two stubborn lovers. As much as both of them wanted to call the other, neither of them would give in. It wasn't until Tuesday night that John called Bart to ask what was going on. Bart described the whole incident to John, who chided him, "You don't think you overreacted, do you?"

"I don't know. Was she or was she not flirting with that asshole?"

"I wasn't there to judge, but I can tell you she's been up in her room crying her eyes out over you for the last two days. Does that sound like somebody who's no longer in love?"

John had a way of talking sense into Bart. "OK," Bart sheepishly replied, "how do we fix this?"

"I'll talk to her. Maybe I can smooth it over."

Wednesday morning Gina called apologetically. She admitted Brian had been coming on to her and she hadn't discouraged him. Her only explanation was she missed the attention Bart always showed her and Brian was a convenient substitution. Bart, on his part, acknowledged perhaps he had overreacted; his attitude was the result of his overwhelming love for her. Immediately after hanging up, Bart rushed into Middle Village for a tearful face-to-face reconciliation. The best part of a disagreement between two young lovers is making up. Bart and Gina spent the rest of the day and half the night making up for all the time they had been apart.

Perhaps the most interesting outcome of their spat was Gina convinced her disappointed and reluctant parents she should have her first-ever traditional Thanksgiving turkey dinner at Bart's house.

CHAPTER 23

When Bart returned to Columbia, his new roommate, who had also gone home for the holiday, began warning Bart that his father, who was currently assigned to the Pentagon, predicted the US involvement in Vietnam was likely to escalate. US troop deployments had already escalated from 25,000 in February 1965 to over 175,000 by Thanksgiving. General Ryan strongly suggested to his son he sign an early commitment letter to join the Air Force after graduation. His father tried to convince Robbie there was a high probability he would be drafted soon after his graduation. If he waited for that to happen, the demand for officer candidate spots in the Air Force could outstrip the openings. An early commitment would guarantee him a slot in Officer Candidate School during the next summer or fall. Both Bart and Robbie wondered if this wasn't simply a convenient excuse to get his son into a military career. However, they both agreed his father's suggestion to take the Air Force officer qualifying test made absolute sense; both men took the test before Christmas.

By February, it became apparent General Ryan was right. The US was now deploying an additional twenty thousand troops a month to Southeast Asia. To further solidify Robbie's father's suggestion, almost all their college friends who graduated in '64 and '65 and were eligible for the draft had already started serving or had received their draft notices.

Also in February, Robbie's father came down to the university in one final attempt to convince his son to make the commitment to OCS. Robbie agreed, with the stipulation his roommate also be given the same opportunity. After interviewing Bart for two hours and checking Bart's qualifying test scores, the general was able to secure a non-flying slot for his son's roommate.

■ ■ ■

"You what?" Gina gasped at Bart's announcement over the phone that he had signed up for a four-year commitment to the Air Force. "You did that without discussing it with me! You must be out of your mind. So what if you get drafted, it's only a two-year thing."

"You don't understand. I did this for us. I'm going to be an officer; we'll be able to get married. The chances of me being assigned to a duty station where you can join me are real high. More importantly, I won't have to slog through the swamps and jungles of Southeast Asia getting my ass shot at."

"Well, maybe you did the right thing for you; but you could have at least talked to me first. If this is the way you intend on making decisions for us, perhaps this isn't going to be the partnership I expected."

Surprised and exasperated by Gina's reaction, Bart didn't know what to say. Finally, he countered, "I told you I was going to take the test."

"That's a far cry from making a four-year commitment."

Still stumbling to justify his unilateral action, all he could manage was "I'm sorry you feel that way. I thought you would be happy I wouldn't be getting shot at and that we probably will be able to live together while I'm serving."

"I am happy about that stuff, but next time I expect you to talk to me first."

In May, the Air Force sent Bart a letter assigning him to the June 13th Officer Training School class at Lackland Air Force Base in San Antonio.

May graduation at the University of South Carolina was on the same weekend as the Johns Hopkins graduation. Gina was torn between her brother and her boyfriend, but in the end she opted to join her parents and Patty Jo in Baltimore for John's ceremony. His parents and sister Fran were Bart's only guests. Although he understood Gina's dilemma, he couldn't help but wonder if this was retribution for his unilateral decision.

On the drive back to New York Bart made up his mind he and Gina needed to decide where they were headed together. He knew he loved her, but he was still convinced he had to get her away from her family. Besides, if he was right, as an Air Force officer, he and Gina would be able to get married soon and live together, but that would only work if she was willing to follow him wherever he was assigned. This was probably the defining moment of their four-year involvement. Yes, he needed to know whether she loved him enough to be willing to move away from her family. If she wasn't ready to make that leap, their relationship probably wouldn't endure.

Bart had a way of approaching an issue that sounded like criticism. Gina took any difference of opinion as a direct assault, so his initial attempt at reaching an understanding of her commitment to him was doomed from the onset.

Bart tried to convey "I love you and want to spend the rest of my life with you, but there are a few things that we have to work out, such as your willingness to move away from your family."

Gina thought he said, "I think I love you, but before I make a commitment for life I need to know that you are willing to abandon your family."

Gina thought she responded, "I'll do whatever my husband's career requires even if it means moving away from my family, but I need to be part of the decision process and not just be told what we are going to do."

Bart thought she said, "I'm not going anywhere I don't want to go just because of your job." Reflecting on what he perceived as the potentially disastrous direction this discussion was taking, he decided to change tactics. "It's not just my career that motivates me to leave New York. John and I have been talking. He and Patty Jo are definitely leaving because of your family's involvement in organized crime. John thinks that if they stay around, it will somehow have an effect on them. But, more than anything, he doesn't want their children exposed to any of it."

Gina threw up her hands and raised her voice a few octaves. "I don't care what my brother thinks or does. I want my children to know and love their grandparents on both sides of the family."

Bart scoffed, "Even if it is common knowledge that one of them is a criminal?"

"You son of a bitch!" Gina burst into tears.

By now the two lovers were emotionally spent, and they both realized that pursuing the argument at that moment would only exacerbate the situation. "Take me home," she demanded. The ride back to Gina's house followed an eerily familiar script; neither of them dared say anything for fear of reigniting the conflagration.

They didn't see each other for two days, and the subject didn't come up again for almost a week. Finally Gina, obviously having given it considerable thought, declared in what was evidently a prepared speech, "I understand and accept your concerns about having to stay in New York both from a career and family perspective. For the most part I agree with what you are saying; you probably will be the breadwinner in this family and, if and when I do work, my job can be done anywhere, even at home. I can also see the validity of your and John's concerns with the family's involvement in organized crime. On the other hand, if you can accept I love my parents and would never agree to completely estrange myself or my children from them, I believe we could make this relationship work. I am willing to seriously consider getting married; I only expect, in the future, you include me in decisions affecting both our lives."

Bart was flabbergasted; he did not expect this. In fact, he had reached the conclusion their differences were irreconcilable and that before he left for OTS, they would probably break up. It took him a minute to compose himself; then he simply agreed, "That works for me."

They never went home that night, staying at a motel off 25A in Centerport. It was the most liberating and passionate night they had together since Myrtle Beach two years earlier. By the time Bart took Gina home the next day, they had agreed not to make any wedding plans. They would wait until Bart finished OTS and received his first permanent assignment. Oh yeah, they agreed on one more thing. Bart would ask Gina's father for permission to marry his only daughter.

They didn't have to wait long for the discussion to happen. Mr. Nicosia was still at home when they pulled up to the house. He had long ago accepted his only daughter and Bart were probably intimate, but he was still worried when his daughter did not come home at all. Pietro's anxiety subsided when he heard the car door slam and saw Bart and Gina walking up the sidewalk. He immediately put on his suit jacket, kissed his wife good-bye, and headed out the door. As they met on the front stoop, his only slightly irritated comment was "Glad to see you are all right, but you should have called and told your mother you wouldn't be home. She was a wreck all night worrying about you two."

Gina hugged her father and gave him a kiss on the cheek. "Daddy, do you have to leave right now? Bart wants to talk to you."

Scanning the jubilant faces of his daughter and her boyfriend, Pietro sensed the significance of the request. He put his arm around Bart's shoulder. "Let's go to the garage where we can have some privacy."

Why is it that most guys are petrified at the thought of asking a father for their daughter's hand in marriage? In most cases the father is relieved his daughter is finally going to become an "honest" woman. Bart had no reservations about his talk with Pietro Nicosia. Maybe it was the result of the Angelo D'Augustino discussion or maybe it even preceded that, but whatever the reason, asking Pietro for his only daughter's hand was not a scary event for Bart. Pietro's only comments were "Shit, boy, what took you so long?" and "Now that I am going to be your father-in-law, do you think you could call me Pop or Pete?"

CHAPTER 24

January 23, 2010

I had been thinking about the spectacle of a New York Mafia wedding ever since Bart told me how he and Gina finally reached a consensus to get married. Last night, Marie and I had envisioned a huge guinea wedding for Bart and Gina at someplace like the Waldorf Astoria ballroom. We imagined black Caddy after black Caddy pulling up to the hotel's Park Avenue entrance where uniformed doormen would hold the door and mobsters in $1,000 suits would emerge, along with his lacquer-haired wives. All the while their bodyguards would methodically pace up and down the street with their eyes constantly scanning for any threats. Across the street were several government vehicles, one with two FBI agents and the other with two NYPD plainclothes men from the organized crime unit. A police photographer would take pictures of each vehicle's license plate as it pulled up, with another cameraman snapping pictures of the arrivals as they entered the lavishly decorated lobby.

It was early Saturday afternoon and the midwinter weather on the Algarve coast of Portugal was delightful. Bart and I were washing down our sandwiches with bottles of Sagres and admiring the views of the Atlantic Ocean from the balcony of my villa. "Boy, that must have been quite a shindig when you two got married. How many guests were there?"

"Oh it was small, only a handful of family and friends," replied Bart.

I couldn't contain my surprise. "What'd you do, elope?"

"Well, not exactly. John, Patty Jo, Gina, and I conspired to avoid the inevitable extravaganza the Nicosias were almost obligated to host. It was kind of funny how the whole thing transpired. After OTS, I received orders for Aviano Air Force Base in northeastern Italy. While I was on leave waiting to ship out, the four of us started talking about our wedding plans. None of us wanted to go through the inevitable lavish spectacle and New York media circus that would accompany a Nicosia wedding. So we hatched this plan to have a double wedding in Italy. When we told the Nicosias of our plans, Pete was ecstatic; he wasn't excited about the prospect of a New York spectacle either. Eleonora was a little disappointed, as were my parents. Patty Jo's widowed mother didn't care as long as it didn't cost her anything. Since Aviano is only sixty miles from Venice, the four of us romanticized about having a double wedding there. Gina and I talked with Father Bolling about getting married in Italy. He thought it was doable; he even offered to try to arrange the ceremony in St. Mark's Basilica. That possibility was the clincher for Eleonora and my parents."

"You're putting me on. You guys didn't have a double wedding in Venice?"

"We sure did," chuckled Bart, "on June 17, 1967."

"Don't tell me anymore," I protested. "Marie's got to hear this whole story straight from you."

Bart thought about that for a minute and then said, "OK, I'll tell you what we can do. Tomorrow we'll leave early for Seville; it's about a two-hour drive. I can give you both all the sordid details on the ride there and back. Pack an overnight bag in case we decide to spend the night. Anyway, you can't go back to the States without seeing Seville. It will be fun. In the meantime, let me bring you up to date on Al's exploits during this time."

▪ ▪ ▪

Just before Bart came home for spring break, the Nicosias got word that Al had been reassigned to Fort Benning, Georgia, and had been restricted to his barracks pending an official inquiry. In a telephone conversation with his parents, the only thing he would say was that he had a disagreement with his superior in Vietnam. A couple of weeks before Bart was scheduled to report to Lackland AFB, Al returned home as a civilian. He really didn't say anything to his brother or sister about what happened, but John was aware of a heated exchange between his father and brother. Following the talk, Pete appeared upset for several days. Shortly afterward, Al moved out of the house and rented an apartment in Hempstead. It wasn't until Al's bachelor party several years later that Bart learned about his overzealous search-and-destroy missions, which probably resulted in Al's "for the good of the service" discharge and the quarrel between father and son .

In the fall Al registered at Hofstra. He took a few courses but never did finish up his degree. Both John and Bart suspected that his real purpose for returning to college was to peddle drugs to the students.

According to John, his brother was livid when he learned Gina and Bart were engaged. John relayed to Bart that his brother proclaimed, "Out of all the assholes in the world she had to pick him? He's like a bad case of herpes, he just keeps showing up whenever you least expect it."

He was even more pissed when he found out Patty Jo was looking for a nursing job in Baltimore so she could be near John in the fall. John had decided to continue at Johns Hopkins in pursuit of his doctorate in medicine. It must have seemed to Al the whole world had turned against him. The army thought he was unfit to serve, his father was pissed at him, his sister was marrying a guy he despised, and his brother was moving in with a girl that had humiliated him.

It was about this time Al started doing his best to undermine Bart's character with Gina. In fact, I was part of one such incident; although at the time I didn't realize it. There were about a half dozen of us from high school who were scheduled to enter the military that summer. Bart was the first one scheduled to report so we all got together on the Thursday night before he had to leave for San Antonio. We hit all our old haunts, the Chop House in Garden City, Ryan's in Roslyn Harbor, and Ted's in Mineola, where most of us had our first illegal beer. About 1:00 a.m., after leaving the Chop House, we headed over to Hempstead and were planning on hitting Tiny's favorite pub, the Flamingo Lounge. On the way we passed by a joint with one of those flashing red neon signs announcing topless dancers. I don't remember who was driving the lead car, but he swung a U-turn and stopped across the street from the flashing sign. Titty bars were not a common sight on Long Island back in the '60s; most of us had never been to one before. When the waitress brought us our beers and said they were $10 each, our enthusiasm for staying and watching the entertainment vanished. The dancers were OK, but in spite of all the alcohol we had already consumed, it was not our thing. We weren't there ten minutes when a guy, a real greaseball, strutted over to Bart. "Don't I know you from somewhere?"

Bart looked the guy up and down then replied, "I don't think so. Did you go to the University of South Carolina?"

Guido, clearly racking his feeble brain, just stood there for a minute eyeing Bart, then he sneered, "Yeah, I remember you, college boy, you're the asshole who is going out with Al's sister. We went to a Mets game together a couple of years ago."

Clearly feeling the influence of several hours of drinking, Bart couldn't contain his sarcasm. "Sure, now I remember. Aren't you the one who got drunk and puked all over the guys sitting in front of you?"

"Whoa, we've got a smart-ass," snapped back Guido. "Why don't you and your faggy friends finish your beers and get the fuck out of here before somebody gets hurt."

Hearing this, Tiny was ready to kick some ass, but Bart pulled him aside and warned him the guy was probably packing a gun. We were out of there in two minutes. As you would expect, the scuzzball told Al he saw his future brother-in-law at the topless bar. The next time Al was at Sunday dinner with his family he smugly announced to Gina in front of the whole family, "Sal DiBenedetto tells me, before he left for the Air Force, your fiancé and his buddies liked to hang out in a topless bar over in Hempstead."

John reported that Gina seemed miffed but did not respond. Al's revelation must have had the desired effect, however, because Gina appeared moody for the next couple of days.

CHAPTER 25

Even though Bart arrived early Sunday morning, Marie and I were already anxiously pacing our living room. Marie was out the front door and down the steps to Bart's car before he had a chance to shut off the engine. Bart, sensing Marie's enthusiasm, didn't waste any time getting back to the events leading up to his and Gina's wedding.

■ ■ ■

Except for the heat and dust of San Antonio, Basic Officer Training School was a cakewalk for Bart. The physical and academic curriculum was not difficult for someone who just completed four years of playing a major college sport and attending classes. Since every waking moment was planned it left little time for him to miss Gina. The first sixty days flew by, but the last month seemed to drag, and the week prior to receiving his official orders for his first assignment was interminable.

During those twelve weeks of school, Bart wrote Gina two letters a week. She, on the other hand, wrote him almost every day. It was a result of reading the plans that Gina and her mother were concocting that first convinced Bart a New York wedding was going to be a media circus. After much trepidation he came up with the idea of getting married wherever he was stationed, rather than in New York. He had no idea how he was going to convince his fiancée to forgo the elaborate ceremony she and her mother were envisioning. Bart was convinced the New York media would really play up the wedding of the daughter of a major Mafia figure. He could almost see the headlines in the society section of the *Post*: Mafia Princess Weds Ex-Football Player. He would bet that his family's name and pictures would be plastered all over the pages. Oh, how his parents would love that!

Bart was thrilled when Gina wrote to say she had purchased airline tickets to attend his graduation. He was equally elated when he received orders for his first permanent assignment, which ordered him to report to the 40th Tactical Group at Aviano Air Base, Italy. Upon getting his official orders, he rushed to the base library where he discovered Aviano AB was in the small town of Pordenone at the foot of the Carnic Alps less than two hours from Venice. *Bingo!* He thought, *Venice, how could any Italian bride not want to get married in Venice?*

Gina was as excited as Bart about *their* assignment, though when he mentioned the idea of getting married in Venice, she wasn't as enthralled. Besides her own childhood dreams of an elegant affair in her family's parish church, she feared her parents' disappointment at not having their only daughter married in front of all their relatives and friends. Bart decided not to push the issue until he had a chance to discuss the idea with John.

The couple's return to New York coincided with John's trip back to the City to help Patty Jo pack and move her personal belongings to Baltimore for her new nursing position at Baltimore City Hospital. John had already rented a townhouse in Dundalk and had only three days before he needed to be back for classes. On Saturday morning John and Bart rented a U-Haul and started packing the few household items Patty Jo could call her own. Gina helped Patty Jo pack up her clothes and personal items. With the four of them working at it, they were done by late in the afternoon. John suggested they all go out to dinner to celebrate both Patty Jo's and Bart's new careers.

Over dinner Bart floated by his idea of getting married in Venice as a way around the inevitable media circus. When he had finished, the other couple looked at each other for a long moment and John said to Patty Jo, "Are you thinking what I'm thinking?"

"Definitely," replied Patty Jo.

"What?" asked Gina.

"You want to tell her, or should I?" asked John.

"I'll do it," said Patty Jo.

"We've been talking about getting married by a justice of the peace in Maryland just so we can avoid the circus that would surround a wedding in New York. We know how disappointed your parents would be, but we can't handle the kind of scene a New York wedding would create."

Gina was stunned. "No, you weren't!"

"Oh yeah," answered John. "In fact, when I just heard Bart's idea, I was pretty sure Patty Jo was thinking the same thing. Right, sweetheart?"

"Absolutely," Patty Jo responded.

Gina just looked back and forth at the three of them like she was waiting for one of them to break out in laughter and declare it was all a joke. When no one cracked, she declared, "Mom and Dad will never go for it."

Reaching across the table, John clasped Gina's hand, "Maybe not, sis, but it is worth a try."

For the next half hour the three conspirators went through all the reasons why a double wedding in Venice made sense. By the time they had paid the bill, Gina was on board. Now all they had to do was sell the parents on their plan, and they only had the next day to do it as a "team."

■ ■ ■

Having all three of her children in New York for the first time in years revitalized Eleonora Nicosia, even if it was for only a few days. She was planning one of her now-rare Sunday feasts with antipasto, a meat dish, pasta, salad, and dessert. Since John had classes on Monday morning, he didn't want to get back to Baltimore too late. Eleonora was happy to accommodate her son by planning the meal for early afternoon.

Al was in an unusually pleasant mood. He was extremely civil to Bart and Patty Jo. He congratulated Bart on the engagement to his sister and asked him numerous questions about OTS. At dinner, much to Bart's surprise, Al even suggested that he would like to visit them in Italy. That gave the conspirators the opening they needed.

John took the lead, announcing, "Funny you should bring that up; you can all come to our double wedding in Venice."

At first, no one reacted to John's invitation. Finally, Al was the first to react. "You're kidding, aren't you?"

Gina now chimed in, "No, we've been seriously talking about it. What you think, Ma?"

Eleonora winced. "Oh honey, why would you want to do that?"

Glancing at her mother apologetically, Gina somehow found the gumption to respond, "Doesn't it sound like a uniquely romantic experience none of us will ever forget?"

Sensing his sister's faltering conviction, John chimed in, "How many families have the opportunity for a double wedding, much less in Italy?" After a brief hesitation, he added solemnly, "Patty Jo and I were going to get married by a justice of the peace in Maryland in order to avoid the New York media, but when this idea came up, we jumped all over it."

Realizing that Pete hadn't reacted yet, everybody looked at him. He silently glanced at each of them, one at a time, letting the anticipation build. Finally, he spoke up. "I like it. Unlike all the previous extravagant weddings we've attended which were more for the guests than the bride and groom, this one would be for them. Eleonora, think about what you were planning; it would turn into a media circus. If John and Patty Jo are intent on getting married at the same time, it would become a media orgy. None of us, especially the kids, would enjoy it. I like the idea of having a small, intimate affair away from the scrutiny of the New York media. Bart being stationed in Italy is a great excuse to have it there."

Eleonora looked at Patty Jo and asked, "What does your mother think about this idea?"

"I haven't told her about it yet, Mrs. Nicosia. I doubt that it makes any difference to her as long as she doesn't have to pay for it," Patty Jo asserted.

Swallowing her reservations, Eleonora smiled faintly. "Well then, if that's what you all want, how can I object; after all, it is your wedding."

Throughout the whole discussion, Al never said a word; he just sat there intently listening. After dinner, the guys accompanied

Mr. Nicosia out to the garage so he could have one of his cigars. On the way out Al turned to his brother and future brother-in-law and whispered, "I could learn a thing or two from you guys about manipulating the old man and old lady. Every time I make a suggestion to do something different, I get my head handed to me."

Smiling, Bart thought to himself, *That's probably because most of your ideas are illegal.*

A week later Patty Jo finally told her mother, over the phone, about her wedding plans. The widow's reaction was exactly as Patty Jo had predicted. Bart's parents were delighted when he and Gina told them a few days later.

After mass on Sunday, Frank and Margaret LaRocca stopped by the rectory to congratulate Reverend Bolling on recently being awarded the honorary title of monsignor. As usual, the priest asked about his favorite sprinter. When they told him of their son's new assignment in Italy and his wedding plans in Venice, the priest indicated that he had a contact at St. Mark's Basilica. He suggested that if Bart and Gina were interested, he might be able to arrange for them to have their ceremony in one of the most magnificent churches in the world.

It didn't take Bart and Gina long to drop by Blessed Sacrament's rectory to pursue Father Bolling's offer. The priest was so pleased to see Bart again he gave him a sincere hug. Bart introduced Gina to his athletic mentor. After expressing his joy at meeting Bart's future bride and extolling Bart's virtues as a youth, the priest, smiling faintly, addressed Bart. "We haven't seen much of you here at Blessed Sacrament since you went off to college. I suppose when you're back on the Island you go to Sunday mass at Gina's parish."

Bart cringed. Ever since he started caddying on Sunday mornings, he had only been to Sunday Mass a handful of times. So, with a smattering of guilt, he only responded with a muted, "Yup."

The astute priest, sensing Bart was uncomfortable, changed the subject. He told them that the previous year on a trip to the Vatican he became acquainted with a priest who was in charge of St. Mark's Sacristy of the Basilica. The other priest explained that on rare occasions and for unique pastoral circumstances, he had the authority to grant special events such as weddings at St. Mark's.

Understanding the Church's mechanisms, Monsignor Bolling added he suspected a modest donation to the preservation of the basilica constituted "unique pastoral circumstances." He then went on to suggest if Gina and Bart's families were interested in offering such a gift, he would be happy to try to make the arrangements. Gina assured the priest she would have her father contact him for further advice and guidance. Just before they left, the monsignor made one last appeal. "I hope the two of you will leave enough room in your lives for God and the Church."

"We'll try, father," Bart replied unconvincingly.

Within the month a date was set for the double wedding of Gina Maria Nicosia to F. Bart LaRocca and Patty Jo Koenig to John Nicosia at St. Mark's Basilica on June 17, 1967. Pietro Nicosia subsequently made a gift to the Sacristy of the Basilica for 3,125,000 Italian liras, which was approximately $5,000.

CHAPTER 26

Second Lieutenant Bart LaRocca arrived at Aviano Air Base on October 1, 1966. His assignment was in Base Services; his initial primary duties entailed management and oversight of Visiting Officers Quarters and transient housing. Other than dealing with an occasional discontented senior officer, it was a relatively easy first assignment. He had plenty of free time to gather information for the wedding. His brief trips to Venice and St. Mark's confirmed it was a great venue for the wedding. He was able to locate a realtor who showed him numerous large villas that could be rented, but it was Pete who finally found the perfect location for both the reception and guest accommodations.

From the onset, Gina's father was excited about the wedding

plans. Eleonora, on the other hand, remained cool to the idea. Gina was concerned about her mother's lack of enthusiasm, but her father predicted that, after she had seen Italy during their planned Thanksgiving visit, his wife would love the idea.

Not surprisingly, Pete Nicosia knew a few people who were familiar with the Venice area. After consulting with his private sources, he booked three rooms at a boutique hotel on the Lido. Initially built as a sixteenth century casino for the Venetian aristocracy, it had been recently renovated and made into a hotel. Many of its common areas still contained features from the original structure, including marble columns, fireplaces, and wood-beamed ceilings.

Bart eagerly met Gina, her parents, and John and Patty Jo at Venice's Marco Polo Airport on Sunday morning. He had made arrangements for a water taxi to transport them to their hotel on the Lido.

It was on the morning of their second day, when the vaporetto dropped them off at Piazza San Marco, that Eleonora first showed some enthusiasm for holding the wedding away from New York. Her sister, who had taken several vacations in Europe, had been telling her for years that she would love Italy. Now, standing in front of the basilica, she began to understand what her older sister had been trying to tell her. Being a typical New Yorker who had never traveled too far from the city, Eleonora's concept of a cathedral was the monochromatic, neo-Gothic design of St. Patrick's marble façade. Standing in the center of Venice's most famous piazza, she could hardly believe what she was seeing. St. Mark's was a smorgasbord of architectural styles and colors. It was almost too much for Eleonora to absorb between the many arches, terraces, sculptures, open towers, and spires. She was mesmerized by the beauty, variety, and complexity of the exterior. Giddy with enthusiasm, she turned to Gina. "I can't wait to see what the inside is like." Entering the beautifully decorated atrium, she continued to be awed by its golden mosaics. She was in such amazement that Pietro had to take his wife's arm and guide her into the interior of the basilica. As he gently escorted Eleonora out of the atrium and into the interior, he whispered to his wife, "Are you feeling a little better about this idea?"

Energized, Eleonora replied, "Oh, my God, I had no idea that anything could be so beautiful! How could I not be overjoyed at having my children's nuptials here?"

It took the family over an hour to tour the basilica's many chapels and to view the many iconic masterpieces adorning its interior.

Over lunch at a small trattoria near the entrance to Piazza San Marco, the whole group was enthusiastically describing their favorite parts of the tour when three women walked in. One of the women hesitated, staring directly at the visitors from the US. She then said something to her companions and headed straight for Bart. Bart and John, in the midst of an animated conversation, didn't notice the woman until she was at their table. The attractive blonde, her eyes focused directly on Bart, proclaimed in a sultry southern accent, "Lieutenant LaRocca, fancy meeting you here!"

Startled, Bart hesitated before managing an awkward "Lieutenant Rice . . . what a surprise." Collecting his poise, Bart said to Gina, who was seated to his left, "Honey, this is one of the officers from the base, Lieutenant Betty Rice. Betty happens to also be a graduate of the University of South Carolina. Lieutenant Rice, this is my fiancée, Gina Nicosia, and her family."

The female officer eyed Gina inquisitively, giving her a less than enthusiastic "Nice to meet you, Gina."

Gina's look was slightly more hostile and the tone of her voice left no doubt she was not happy to meet Lieutenant Rice, "So, I guess you weren't aware that Bart and I are getting married here in a few months."

Pete, always the astute peacemaker, quickly intervened in what had the potential of becoming an ugly scene. "Lieutenant, I'm Gina's father, Pete, may I call you Betty?" But without waiting for an answer, he continued, "Why don't you and your friends join us for lunch?"

Lieutenant Rice, feeling uncomfortable from Gina's obvious

rebuff, replied, "Thank you, Pete, but I wouldn't want to intrude on a family get-together."

"Don't be ridiculous," Pete said convincingly, "we are a fun-loving family; the more the merrier. Besides, we Americans have to stick together over here." With that he stood up and turned to the empty table behind him, commandeering three more chairs.

Before he had finished strategically placing the chairs around their table, Lieutenant Rice motioned the other two women over, introducing them as Captains Lora Fagan and Donna McCoy, both nurses on the base. As soon as the two nurses discovered that Patty Jo was a nurse and John was attending medical school, the tension on that side of the table melted away. However, between Gina and Betty no truce was eminent.

Gina, disappointed by her father's invitation, continued with her initial acrimonious tone, "So, did you and Bart know each other in college?"

Undaunted, Betty mustered up her best scornful southern accent. "Heavens no, darlin'; I wouldn't have been caught dead with a Yankee in those days, even one that was a big football star like Bart. We just met a few weeks ago at the officers' club."

Bart, appearing oblivious to the hostility, cut in, "We both work in Services, I'm in housing and Lieutenant Rice runs the commissary." Gina gave him an annoyed look that implied *Shut up!* The two women continued on as if he wasn't there. An hour later, when they parted company, Bart wasn't sure what had just happened, but he didn't think Gina and Lieutenant Rice were now friends.

Later that afternoon, the future wedding party met with Padre LoGalbo, the priest who oversaw the sacristy of the basilica. The young priest was very gracious, explaining the process for hosting a wedding at the basilica. He spent almost two hours with them, taking them back through the many side chapels so that they could choose the one that would be used for the ceremony. After much debate, Gina and Patty Jo settled on St. Peter's Chapel. Before they left the basilica, the priest gave them a copy of the documents required for US citizens who marry in Italy.

The next day Bart gave them a five-hour tour of the city. They walked the same narrow passages that Venetians and their visitors had for over a millennium, stopping in the abundant boutiques and shops lining the canals and alleys. Each couple went on a romantic gondola ride along the Grand Canal. Between the exchange rate and the competition, it was easy to find what Patty Jo classified as a "steal." By the time their five days had ended, everyone returned to the States with at least one pair of Italian shoes and a leather jacket. Eleonora probably spent more money on clothes and knickknacks then she normally would in a year.

One day, while the rest of the family made a side trip to Padova, Bart took Gina to Aviano Air Base. The two-hour train ride from Venice to Pordenone took them through typically rural post-World War II Italy. They saw latticed hillside vineyards and crossed dirt roads leading to dilapidated villages which hadn't changed in hundreds of years. They saw peasants pulling carts filled with vegetables, and in contrast saw huge castles on the mountaintops. But the area was changing fast; besides the American air base, the city now housed Italy's 132 Armored Brigade, and it was the headquarters of Zanussi, the second largest home appliance manufacturer in Europe.

Unlike traditional military family housing, Aviano's housing was not located on base but spread throughout the local Italian communities. The only restriction to off-base housing was that it had to be within thirty minutes of the front gate. After a day of viewing the currently available apartments, the couple decided they needed to rent a unit big enough for guests and, perhaps, even their first child. With that settled, it was up to Bart to locate a three-bedroom unit and furnish it by June. Meanwhile he would stay in temporary housing.

On the train back to Venice, out of the blue, Gina asked, "So tell me about Lieutenant Betty Rice."

"There's nothing to tell," replied Bart. "We met once at the officers' club and I occasionally see her at headquarters."

"OK, make sure it stays that way!" demanded Gina.

"Jeez, Gina, do you think with you moving here in a few

months I'd be screwing around with someone on base?" Bart responded with annoyance.

"No, not intentionally, but Lieutenant Mint Julep has designs on you" was Gina's acerbic reply.

Sighing, Bart decided to let the matter drop.

Although they did not spend a lot of time at their hotel, everyone found it intimate and restful. With its floral courtyard and beam and white stucco exterior, it was more like a large country home surrounded by an arboretum than a hotel. It had its own rustic bar and restaurant along with adequate banquet facilities. Only minutes from the canals and alleyways of Venice and Marco Polo Airport, it felt as if they were many miles out in the country. All in all, it was an ideal location for the wedding reception and for guest lodging. Pete began negotiating with the owner. By the time they left for the airport all the details had been worked out and Mr. Nicosia had made a $2,000 deposit. The owner agreed to set aside five suites and twenty other rooms for June 14th through 17th. In addition he reserved the banquet facility for the 17th.

CHAPTER 27

January 24, 2010
Seville, Spain

The last time Marie and I traveled around Europe we had to contend with border crossings at every country. One of the really good things about the current European Union is that you hardly notice when you cross the border from Portugal to Spain. On the other hand, one of the bad things about the EU is you hardly notice when you cross the border from Portugal to Spain. The other really good thing is you there is only one currency on the continent.

I was surprised to discover metropolitan Seville had a population of over a half-million and just like any other large metropolis it is plagued by congested traffic and never-ending buildings. Bart found a parking spot not far from the city center and its magnificent cathedral. The city sits on the Rio Guadalquivir, which is its access to the sea and was its source of riches from the New World during the fifteenth through eighteenth centuries. As was now his custom, Bart acted as our tour guide on a walking tour of the central city. We started with the massive Cathedral of Seville and its magnificent 320-foot-tall bell tower. We then made our way to the Reales Alcázar, originally built as a fortress for the Moorish caliphs in AD 712. Over the next thousand years, it was enlarged and embellished by a succession of Moorish and Christian rulers. Throughout our tour we were amazed by the intermixing of Arab and Gothic architecture.

We were walking west on Calle Virgenes when suddenly Bart's tone abruptly transformed from a light-hearted tour guide to someone who had something serious to convey. "In a few blocks we are going to get to Barrio Santa Cruz and the reason I suggested we come to Seville today. First, let me give you a brief history of the barrio. For hundreds of years, during the Moors' occupation of the region, Seville had a vibrant and prosperous Jewish population, many of them living in this neighborhood. However, following the defeat of the Moors, anti-Jewish riots and massacres became commonplace across Spain. The reason I am boring you with all this history is the ancestors of my college roommate, David Tanner, fled to Germany from this barrio during one of those massacres in the late fourteenth century. Then in 1492, Ferdinand II of Aragon and Isabella I of Castile issued the Alhambra Decree, expelling all Jews from Spain. Surprisingly, it wasn't until 1968 the decree was lifted. Today, David is one of a handful of investors revitalizing the barrio. He actually maintains a house here. In fact, he is here this week, and I thought you might like to meet him."

"So, you and David have remained in contact all these years?"

"Well, not all the time, but like John, David and I have a process for keeping in touch. But more importantly, he was extremely helpful in providing me the means to disappear.

"After college David was able to get into the Army National Guard and stay in South Carolina, where he used his inheritance to amass a huge real estate development empire. Initially he concentrated around Myrtle Beach and Hilton Head, but eventually he expanded into the Caribbean and today he has worldwide interests. Forbes estimates he is worth somewhere between $800 million and $1 billion.

"Anyway, I'm not sure I could just disappear today; 9/11 changed all of that. But I do know I would not have been able to vanish for all these years without someone like David and a couple of other good friends providing the expertise and occasional assistance.

"It takes three critical things to successfully disappear alive. First, you need a lot of money; second, a new bulletproof identity; and third, a way of getting to your money without triggering a link between who you were and who you are. David was central in two of the three."

As we stopped to peek through the wrought iron gates of a magnificent fifteenth-century townhouse and its wonderful garden, the air was filled with the aroma of jasmine and orange. For the moment it was as if we were transported to a different era. We all stood there silently for a few moments, captivated by the charm of this fascinating neighborhood that must have seen so much sorrow over the centuries.

Bart broke the mood in a whisper reminiscent of someone talking in church: "Come on, David's place is just around the corner." He led us out of the narrow shaded alley we had been meandering down and into a cul-de-sac with three large houses. He headed for the one in the middle, a large three-story with a rooftop garden. It was whitewashed stucco with yellow trim. The outside wall was broken up by only a large arched portico with two huge wooden slat doors. Each door had a iron knocker in the shape of a life-size hand protruding through a small porthole. Bart ignored the door knocker and pressed a button on the inside of the doorjamb. He then stepped back and looked up, smiling at a small camera mounted just above the arch. It took almost a minute before the massive doors began to creak open. Bart was greeted by an imposing man who made a quick scan of the courtyard before he fully opened the doors and let the three visitors inside. *"Buenos días, Señor LaRocca; le espera el Señor Tanner."*

Bart replied, *"Estoy feliz a verte otra vez, Azzan. Este es el Señor y la Señora Stanfield."*

Azzan nodded his acknowledgment and proceeded to check the courtyard one more time before he closed up and locked the entry. He then led us through a stunning open-air courtyard adorned with tropical flowers and plants. The centerpiece of the courtyard was a fountain featuring an eight-foot statue of Neptune. The workmanship was exquisite. The house was adorned with hand-painted Spanish tiles and the second and third floor balconies were protected with ornate wrought iron railings.

From the roof we were greeted with "What took you so long? I was expecting you an hour ago."

Looking up, he saw his friend and smiled. "Why the hurry? Won't Sarah let you start drinking until the guests arrive?"

"Just get your butt up here."

We traversed large terra-cotta tiles through one of the three open atrium doors into a wonderful open area. This level was subdivided into three sections, a sort of family room with dark leather couches and chairs facing a rock fireplace, a large kitchen, and a dining area.

The far wall in the dining room led to a staircase and the second level. Azzan led us down a narrow hall to another staircase at the opposite end. We passed what appeared to be three bedrooms and a bath. These stairs emptied onto the rooftop terrace where David was anxiously waiting. Like the garden around the corner, David's terrace seemed to transport us from a twenty-first-century city to a romantic villa hundreds of years in the past. There were two round planters, one containing a mature orange tree and the other a lemon tree. Lining three walls were rectangular planters with a wide variety of ferns, plants, and flowers. Across half the back brick wall was a large veranda covered in green-and-white-striped canvas containing a wet bar. In the center of the terrace was a large round fire pit surrounded by thick cushioned chairs. On the other half of the back wall two colorful stained-glass atrium doors concealed some type of enclosure. We later discovered that it was another guest suite.

David was waiting for us behind the bar. "OK, Bart was right, my wife won't let me start drinking until 5:00 p.m. except when we have guests. So, can I make you a Bloody Mary or a tequila sunrise?"

David Tanner was almost exactly as I had envisioned him, six feet tall and thin with a full head of slightly curly brown hair and sparkling blue eyes. His handshake was firm, but not so firm it took your attention away from the sincerity of his greeting. He didn't exude money or class, but his persona definitely assured you he was a person of prominence. After a few moments of small talk, mostly about our stay in Portugal, Bart injected, "So I was telling Chuck and Marie how indispensable your guidance has been in my disappearance and my ability to remain incognito for all these years."

"Bart gives me too much credit. While I may have provided him with a few suggestions and introduced him to some people, it was his ingenuity and tenacity that put all the pieces together and made it happen. Heck, half the time I didn't even know why he was probing the areas we talked about." David continued with a mischievous grin, "Granted, if it wasn't for my financial recommendations he would probably still be in Myrtle Beach living off Social Security!"

"Stick it," Bart shot back. "No wonder they ran your ancestors out of this country. If they were anything like you, they pissed off all their friends."

They both laughed. Then David said, "Friends, you want to talk about friends. Who was it that got Chuck and Marie's home phone number?"

"OK, OK, I admit it," replied Bart. "Without you as a friend, I wouldn't have a lot of friends left."

In between Bart and David's verbal jousts, Marie and I were held spellbound by the two friends as they recounted some episodes of their fifty-year relationship. Fortunately, I had brought a spiral notepad in which I later recorded over thirty pages of notes.

We never did find out exactly how he did it, since neither of us saw Bart give him the car keys, but about 4:00 p.m. Azzan informed us our overnight bags were now in one of the bedrooms on the second floor. That must have seemed like a good segue for David because he asked us if we had decided whether to return to New York for a few days.

"Is there anything about us you don't know?" Marie asked him.

"Probably" was David's grinning reply, "but it couldn't be important."

"We really haven't reached a conclusion yet," I said. "On one hand, we would like to be home for our granddaughter's sixteenth birthday next weekend, but on the other, neither of us is looking forward to the hassle of two more transatlantic flights."

"Well, maybe I can make the trips a little easier for you. I have to fly to Israel on Tuesday, but on Thursday I am meeting my wife Sarah in New York; then we will both be flying back here for the month of February. Bart probably didn't tell you I have my own private jet that eliminates many of the inconveniences associated with transatlantic flights. Since my plane is capable of landing at almost any airport, I can drop you off and pick you up again in Westhampton at Francis Gabreski Airport."

When we immediately jumped at the offer, David made arrangements to pick us up at Faro Airport on Thursday.

The sun had drifted almost to roof top level when David suggested we all take a siesta to prepare for an exciting evening of heavy-duty tapas bar–hopping.

We must have consumed more alcohol than we realized; Marie and I both fell asleep for almost two hours. We awoke after 7:00 p.m.; Bart and David were waiting for us when we returned to the terrace. After a mild ribbing about what Marie and I were doing in the room for so long, David led us down to the courtyard where Azzan and another younger, even more physical man, were waiting. David introduced the new man as Eitan. He then informed us Azzan and Eitan were part of his security detail and, at the insistence of his board of directors, accompanied him when he traveled out of the United States. Later Bart told us the two men were both former members of one of the Israeli intelligence organizations. The reason for David's security detail resulted from his 2006 kidnapping by a Hamas splinter group. Fortunately, Israeli intelligence received a tip as to where David was being held and were able to rescue him. Following the successful operation, resulting in the capture of four kidnappers and the killing of two others, David made an offer to the leader of the operations, Azzan, to head his security. To his surprise, Azzan accepted. David, however, was never really sure whether the Mossad was just using it as a cover for their agents.

With Azzan and Eitan scoping out every street, alley, and bar before we entered, the four of us spent a wonderful evening sampling the wine and tapas menus of what seemed like half the joints in Seville. We ended up the evening at a flamingo ballroom watching some of the most moving and beautiful dancing performances imaginable.

CHAPTER 28

On our drive back to Albufeira, Bart finished the story of the double wedding in Venice.

With Patty Jo totally immersed in her new job, Gina and her mother planned the whole wedding. The only part Patty Jo got involved in was the choice and fitting of her wedding dress. Mrs. Nicosia was able to get one of her childhood friends, an accomplished seamstress, to make both dresses. The brides decided they would be each be the other's maid of honor and to have only two bridesmaids and two ushers. Gina's two cousins from Rhode Island would be the bridesmaids while Al and Robbie Ryan would be the ushers. Bart had first asked David Tanner to be an usher, but David did not feel comfortable actively participating in a Christian ceremony. Of course, John and Bart were to be each other's best man.

By Christmas the girls had a preliminary invitation list prepared. When Bart first saw the list he was livid; the Nicosias' guest list totaled almost 150 while Patty Jo's and Bart's list contained only 42. Even though Pete was paying for the whole thing and had the right to invite anyone he wanted, Bart remembered they all agreed that it would be a small wedding. In Bart's mind, 182 guests was not a small wedding. Annoyed, he immediately put in an overseas telephone call to Gina.

As usual, when the telephone operator announced, "I have a person-to-person call for Gina Nicosia from Aviano Air Base in Italy," her voice literally bubbled over with excitement. "This is Gina Nicosia." She patiently waited while there was some clicking in the background as the final connections were made. Finally, Bart's irritated voice literally exploded through the receiver. "Gina, it's Bart. I just got the guest list; I thought this was supposed to be a small affair."

Ignoring her fiancé's caustic greeting, Gina responded enthusiastically, "Bart, I'm so happy you called. I've been waiting all week to hear your voice."

Her greeting had its desired effect. Bart was thrown off course. He quickly realized he needed to backpedal and start all over. "Uh, yeah, it's great to hear your voice too. I'm sorry I started out so confrontational. How are you doing? How's the planning coming? Is everyone getting excited about the wedding? "

Maintaining her upbeat attitude, she matter-of-factly responded, "I've been fine. Mom's really getting into this thing. We are almost done with all the plans and yes, it will be a small wedding and reception."

Attempting to make a point without sounding critical, all he could manage was "I wouldn't call 140 people from your side small."

Still unfazed by his insinuation, Gina let out an abbreviated laugh.

"Something funny?"

Coolly, she replied, "We knew this would be your reaction, but don't worry. Daddy assures me that no more than a few dozen will actually show up. Hell, half his guests would never get back into the States if they left. The reason for inviting all his associates is out of respect and for the loot."

Bart was bewildered. "What are you talking about, what loot?"

"It's another one of those Italian things. The few who come will give us a couple of hundred bucks; the ones that send regrets will probably give at least a hundred. From the 150 names we will probably make over twenty grand."

Bart was astounded. "Twenty grand!"

Gina let that sink in a little longer before adding, "Trust us, honey, there will only be between forty and fifty people on my family's list that will make the trek to Italy, and those from my side who do come will be *very* generous." She then changed the subject by asking him how his job was coming.

That was the last conversation Bart and Gina had on the invitation list until all the RSVPs were in; the final tally was 43 guests: 3 from Patty Jo's side, 15 from Bart's, and 25 from Gina and John's. Just as Gina had predicted, after the wedding, when they opened up all the envelopes the gifts totaled over $21,000. John and Patty Jo received almost an identical amount. Ninety percent came from people on the Nicosia list.

The last time the couple saw each other before the wedding was during her spring break when she flew over to help Bart make a final decision on a place to live. The house-hunting part went smoothly, and they quickly agreed on renting a three-bedroom house halfway between Aviano and the ski resort Piancavallo. The couple was in high spirits on the evening they signed the lease. It even got better when, over dinner that night, Bart presented Gina with a half-carat engagement ring. Gina had originally told Bart not to spend any money on a ring, but when he presented it to her, she was ecstatic.

The problem did not surface until the next day when Bart announced he needed to add a few people from the base to the invitation list.

"No problem," replied Gina, "Just give me a list of names and addresses."

Having anticipated this reaction, Bart had the list already done. They were sitting in the parking lot of a restaurant at the ski resort in Piancavallo; Gina was about to put it in her pocketbook without looking at it when she had a change of heart and took a quick peek. Bart could see the blood rush into her face as she now focused her attention on the list.

"You want to invite that bitch to our wedding! Are you crazy?"

"Calm down, honey," Bart apologetically pleaded. "I didn't tell you, Betty has been my boss since New Year's. I have to invite her." As soon as the words left his mouth, he knew he had made a fatal mistake.

"Oh, so now it's Betty, not Lieutenant Rice anymore?" With that, she took off her engagement ring and threw it out the window.

"Christ, what are you insinuating?" Without skipping a beat, his aggravation really kicked in. "If I had anything going on with her would I still be here planning our wedding and our living arrangements?" The more he thought about Gina's reaction, the more pissed off he got, especially since she didn't show any indication of apologizing. His next move was a calculated risk; he opened his car door, turned and angrily barked, "I'm going inside for a beer and lunch. You can sit here and believe whatever you want about my fidelity or you can get your crazy guinea ass out of the car and find that engagement ring. After you've found it, I would be glad to buy you a glass of wine and lunch." Slamming the car door he stomped into the restaurant. Fifteen minutes later Gina came into the restaurant's bar wearing the ring and sporting dark streaks where the tears had caused her eye makeup to run. Standing next to him at the bar, she looked into his eyes and, touching his hand, said with the utmost sincerity, "I don't know what got into me. I'm sorry I doubted you. Will you forgive me?"

"Yeah, but please, Betty has been promoted to captain and is now my boss. I'll be working with her for a while; I don't need to be worrying that you're thinking it's anything more than a professional relationship."

Glancing at him apologetically, she said, "I'll do my best to contain my jealousy that another women will get to see you as much as I do." Then, with an angelic expression she added, "By the way, I seem to remember an incident a few years ago where the situation was reversed."

■ ■ ■

Gina, John, and Patty Jo arrived for the wedding on Sunday, June 11th. Bart had moved into their house on the 1st, so they all stayed there. The rest of their immediate families arrived on Wednesday. The remaining guests began arriving on Thursday.

Wednesday night Bart and Gina hosted a barbecue for their immediate families at their new house. Of all the events of the week, perhaps this was the most enjoyable. Everyone was over-flowing with enthusiasm, and there was none of the formality and pressure that would accompany the rest of the proceedings.

Bart hired one of the off-duty Air Force photographers to record the entire week and Mr. Nicosia, through his Italian connections, found an incredible organist and young mezzo-soprano to perform at the mass. With the backdrop of St. Mark's complimented by the beautifully performed hymns, there was never a better venue for a wedding. But that wasn't what became forever emblazoned in everyone's memories; it was the incredible innocence and beauty of the two brides in their matching wedding gowns walking down the aisle. It was quite a sight seeing Gina at the side of her still-handsome father and Patty Jo clutching the arm of the only man, besides her soon-to-be-husband, whom she loved and trusted, Bart LaRocca.

One of the more surprising outcomes of the event was the instant attraction of Al and Captain Betty Rice. When Captain Rice was met at the door of the chapel by usher Al Nicosia, she was instantly aroused by what appeared to be a suave Latin with a New York swagger. To Al, Captain Rice, decked out in her mess dress uniform adorned with a half dozen colorful ribbons and silver captain's bars, presented the ultimate challenge. During the mass and ceremony neither of them paid much attention to the proceedings. At first each of them tried to keep it to subtle glances, but by the time the wedding vows were being taken, they had abandoned any attempt at subtlety. Neither of them could wait for the wedding ceremony to be over and for the cocktail hour to begin. David Tanner described the interaction between Al and Betty as "eye fucking."

After the ceremony, the two newly married couples along with the rest of wedding party and immediate family members made their way to the specially decorated gondolas that would take them to the Rialto Bridge for photographs. The rest of the guests were transported via water taxis to the Lido hotel for cocktails in the courtyard.

Wedding receptions are generally all the same, only the names and locations change. This one just might have been different. It wasn't just the location or the fact it was a double wedding. It was the intimacy. It was more like a family celebration.

For Al and Betty Rice it was foreplay. They danced virtually every dance together, and although they were officially seated at different tables, Al never got more than a few feet away from his prey. For her part, Betty made it easy for Al; she drank too much and ate too little. As a result her inhibitions were somewhere on another continent. She was all over him, flaunting her sexuality without regard for who took any notice. It was obvious the two newly married couples weren't the only ones who were getting laid that night.

Just before the cake was to be cut, Al sauntered over to Bart and said, "Hey, brother-in-law, I'm thinking about hanging around Italy for a few more days. Would it be all right if I shacked up at your place while you're on your honeymoon?"

What could he say, it was the happiest day of his life; how could he turn down a request from his new brother-in-law? "Sure, just clean up after yourself before you leave." Bart gave him the keys but had an uneasy feeling as he did so.

While the newlyweds were making their rounds of the guests, Bart found himself, for just a moment, alone with Betty. In order to relieve some of his uneasiness he whispered to her, "Be careful with Al, he is a dangerous man."

Betty in her alcohol-induced euphoria coyly replied, "Oh, I hope so."

Bart, sensing she did not quite understand what he meant by dangerous, responded, "Seriously, Betty, he has been known to physically hurt people."

This time, in spite of her inebriation, she too got serious. "Don't worry, Bart; I am fully capable of defending myself."

"OK, OK," Bart answered, and let it drop.

Gina and Bart chose Positano for their honeymoon; John and Patty Jo rented a car and traveled all over Tuscany and down to Rome.

CHAPTER 29

The newlyweds returned home a week later to find Al already gone, and the house showed few signs anyone had been there over the previous week. It was a few days later when Bart threw out the garbage he noticed the empty liquor and beer bottles. Gina got her first indication Al had used the house when she found the unmistakable captain's cap from a women's Air Force summer dress uniform in the guest bedroom. If the guest bedroom furniture hadn't been delivered after she had arrived in Italy, she might have thought Bart and Captain Mint Julep had gotten it on together. In fact, when she recalled the electricity that had been passing between her brother and Captain Rice, she was elated; now she would probably never have to worry about this rival again.

Bart returned to work to find his boss's behavior to be curious. Although she asked him how the honeymoon was, she didn't seem to be listening to his response. On top of that, she appeared to avoid any discussions concerning the wedding or reception. Intrigued, Bart asked Gina if she had spoken to Al. She said yes and then added, "It was weird; I asked him about what he did after the reception and he said he just toured around the area for a few days and then flew back to New York."

"That is strange," replied Bart, and he told her about the bottles he found in the trash. Gina then told Bart about the cap in the guest bedroom.

"Has Captain Rice said anything to you?" asked Gina.

"No, in fact, she seems to be avoiding the whole subject of the wedding."

After a few thoughtful moments Gina finally offered, "Well, perhaps that situation did not go as well as it appeared it would." That was the last time the couple spoke about the incident, but it wasn't the last time Bart would have the discussion.

By early fall the newlyweds had settled into a very comfortable routine. Gina was substitute teaching at the base elementary school. With the escalation of the Vietnam War, Air Force promotion time lines were accelerated. Bart received his first lieutenant's silver bar in early October. During the previous promotion cycle, Betty Rice's promotion to captain came with a new assignment to redistribution and marketing and one of the first things she did was get Bart transferred to her unit.

France pulled out of NATO in early 1967; by the end of the year all NATO facilities in France were closed. This caused a domino effect on people and equipment. Military units were reassigned, and all equipment that still had a useful life and was not to be taken with them had to be redistributed to other bases, sold in nonmilitary outlets, or otherwise disposed of. Captain Rice became the focal point for the excess equipment in the Mediterranean arena; she assigned First Lieutenant LaRocca to head up the disposal and redistribution of nonstrategic equipment.

It was in their new roles that they came to travel together to

Ramstein Air Base in Germany for a meeting of all Air Force redistribution and marketing officers from all over Europe. Ever since the wedding, Captain Rice had maintained a cordial but distant relationship with Bart. He knew it was at her request he got his new job, but he also felt that since the wedding she was avoiding any personal interaction with him. On their second night at Ramstein, she suggested they go out to dinner alone in Kaiserslautern. Even though they only talked business for the first half hour, for the first time in months, Captain Rice seemed to put aside her professional demeanor and present a warm and casual mind-set. Finally, as they started their second glass of Riesling she blurted out, "I should have listened to you; your brother-in-law was a brutal pig. Not at first, but later when I was at my most vulnerable."

"I'm sorry to hear that Betty, but it doesn't surprise me. What did he do, hit you?"

She sighed and said in a sad hushed tone, "I wish he had. No, it was much more demeaning than that. Look, Bart I haven't told anyone what he did so, if I tell you, you have to swear you won't tell a soul." Before Bart could respond she added, "I know you, LaRocca, you're probably already trying to figure out how you are going to get back at him on my behalf; but you have to promise me you will let me deal with it in my own way."

Reluctantly Bart agreed, and Captain Betty Rice divulged the most agonizing and humiliating experience of her twenty-six-year life.

Captain Rice had driven to the wedding with four other Air Force guests — her boss, Lieutenant Colonel William Hearst and his wife, and Bart's two best friends at Aviano, Lieutenants Terry Moaks and Frank Morgan. By the end of the reception, her Air Force comrades, recognizing that she was totally blitzed, convinced her to let them take her back to base instead of, as Al suggested, spend the rest of the night with him "doing the town." However, before they whisked her off, she gave Al her phone number, telling him, if he was interested, she would give him a tour of the region.

He called the next afternoon, surprising her by announcing he was staying at Bart and Gina's for a few days. She told him she needed to go into the office Monday morning but she would pick him up for lunch. They had lunch at a quaint little trattoria in Piancavallo, downing a bottle of Alto Livenza. It didn't take long for the lusting to start all over again. Fortunately for them, they were not the only couple in the trattoria having a steamy interlude; so their below-the-table antics went unnoticed. By midafternoon they were at Bart's house with enough wine and booze to keep them in orbit for a few days.

An hour later, Betty had switched to vodka tonics and was again all over Al like a bitch in heat. Al, attempting to make this an event he would remember, stuck with wine; but by this point he had finished a whole bottle himself. Their clothes started coming off in the living room and they left a trail of discarded garments down the hallway and up the stairs to the guest bedroom, where they threw themselves on the brand-new mattress with reckless abandon. It wasn't long before they both sensed that after two days of foreplay, it was time to finish it off. With Al in the dominant position, they both fell into a rhythm of controlled gyrations. Then Al started to increase the tempo and ferocity.

Betty, in spite of the booze, recognized they were quickly approaching the point of no return and realized Al didn't have on a condom. In spite of her huffing and puffing, she whispered as softly as she could, "Al, hadn't you better put on some protection?"

Al had already reached his point of no return; he rose up on his arms and shoulders without stopping the pounding of his loins and half-mockingly responded, "I don't go swimming with a raincoat on."

Not expecting that kind of reaction, Betty, momentarily stunned, froze. Then recovering her composure, she tried to push him off, "Well, then you're done, buster!"

Al continued to pound away, pushing down on her chest with both his hands. "Like hell I am," snarled the now-incensed aggressor; with that he wrapped one of his huge hands around her neck and began to squeeze. She tried her best defensive tactics, but he was too big and strong for her. It didn't take long for the loss of air and blood from his choke hold to render Betty semiconscious; all the while he continued to ram himself in and out of her. In her clouded state, Betty had no concept of how long his attack went on. She knew he had reached his conclusion when she felt him relax and brusquely roll off. He then did something which woke her up at night in a sweat for years to come. He slapped her on the side of her butt and said, "Now wasn't that exactly what you wanted, cunt; if you're lucky, in a few months you'll be carrying a little *paisan* of your own." Angrily Betty started to get up, but Al said, "Where do you think you're going, I'm not finished with you yet." He grabbed her on the arm with one hand and with the other he grabbed her crotch. When she tried to pull away, he clamped down on her crotch with such force that she let out a muted shriek. He eased up. "That's only a sample of what's in store for you if you don't make me a very satisfied man tonight."

Finally, recognizing that she was no match for this brute, and remembering Bart's warning, she resigned herself to escape the night with as little physical damage as possible. He used her for another three hours, making her do things that she wouldn't even relate to Bart. As dusk approached, Al finally declared, "OK, captain, it's time for you to go off duty. If you know what's good for you and your career, you'll keep this little incident to yourself."

Captain Betty Rice returned to her apartment and cried for thirty-six hours, knowing Al was right; if she accused him of rape, there was little chance of him being convicted of rape in the dual male-dominated societies of Italy and the military. No matter what the outcome of her charge, it was fairly certain the ugly incident would follow her for the rest of her career and in all likelihood impede her ability to advance. Except for Bart LaRocca, she never told anybody what happened. In fact, she never even told Bart that two months later she went to Stockholm for an abortion.

CHAPTER 30

The LaRoccas' two and a half years at Aviano seemed to go by at supersonic speed. For the first year the couple toured Europe whenever Bart could wrap a day or two of leave around the weekend. In April of 1968 Gina found out she was pregnant. The couple was so excited; they both still wanted a large family and now they were on their way. Once the baby started moving, Bart couldn't wait to get home from work to feel Gina's stomach.

Peter Francis LaRocca was born on November 18, 1968, at the base hospital at Aviano. The seven-pound two-ounce boy, with a full head of jet-black hair, reluctantly entered the world a week late at 1:18 a.m. after putting his mother through almost thirteen hours of grueling labor. It's interesting how cultural conventions change in such a relatively short time. At the time Gina gave birth, it was standard practice not to allow the father in the delivery room; yet, less than twenty years later, an expectant father was often required to act as a coach in the delivery room. Many years later Bart, reflecting on this change, was glad he was not witness to the love of his life going through such excruciating pain. For him, seeing his sweetheart's drained and exhausted body shortly after delivery was distressing enough. After he recovered from the shock of seeing Gina in her post-delivery state, he was amazed at how she could instantly forget about her thirteen-hour ordeal simply by holding the result of that suffering. Like his wife, the first time he held his beautiful son in his arms, he forgot all about Gina's ordeal.

Eleonora Nicosia was already halfway across the Atlantic when Gina finally delivered Peter. She was at the base hospital by early afternoon and cooking dinner for Bart that very night. When Bart asked her how long she expected to stay, her response was "Until I am convinced Gina can handle my first grandchild." Gina was home in two days and, for the first time in her life, delighted not to be the center of her mother's attention. Her father arrived a week later. Bart, not that he minded, thought the proud first-time grandparents would stay forever. Finally, two weeks later they reluctantly returned to New York.

Before they left, the subject of Peter's christening came up. During the conversation as to when and where to have it, Bart realized both his wife and in-laws assumed Al would be the godfather. In his mind, Al Nicosia was the last person on earth that Bart wanted to give the guiding spiritual responsibility for his son. His assumption was John would be Peter's godfather and his sister Fran the godmother. When he mentioned his choices to Gina, she was uneasy. She relayed a conversation she had with her mother. Eleonora described the excitement Al displayed at being a first-time uncle and of becoming Peter's godfather. Gina also parroted her parent's opinion that Al, as the oldest immediate male family member, was the only logical choice to be Peter's godfather. She also correctly predicted that, should they ask John to stand up for Peter, he would turn it down, deferring to his older brother.

For days Bart struggled with the decision; finally he called John to get his advice. John was adamant his brother was the only acceptable choice. What Bart did not know was Gina had already told her parents of his preference. Although Pete had some appreciation for Bart's position, he could not let his eldest son be disrespected by having his younger brother chosen for what was in the Italian culture a significant honor. On his return to the States Pietro immediately instructed John that, if he was asked, he should defer to his older brother. Bart continued to labor with the decision up to Christmas, trying to decide if he should tell Gina about Al's brutal assault on Betty Rice in their guest room. But in the end, his promise to Betty seemed more important than the choice of what was becoming more and more just a ceremonial role. During their Christmas telephone call from the family gathering in New York, Gina formally asked Al to be Peter's godfather. Because the conventional wisdom was the newborn should be freed from original sin as soon as possible and newborns should not travel on jet planes, the baptism was scheduled for a church in Pordenone in February.

Al was on his best behavior during his stay for the christening. Only Fran, John, and Patty Jo stayed at the house. Al, Gina's parents, and Bart's parents rented hotel rooms in Pordenone. Following the ceremony, Gina and her mother prepared a wonderful veal parmesan and pasta dinner. After dinner, braving the 20-degree temperatures, the men moved out on the deck for cigars and cognac.

Halfway through their second snifter, Al pulled Bart aside and said, "Look, I know you didn't want me as your son's godfather, but I was the right choice. I am anxious to take an interest in my nephew's upbringing and personal development."

Bart without hesitation caustically replied, "That's what I am afraid of."

Al gave him a strange look, wondering if Bart knew about the incident with Captain Rice or whether it was just their old dislike for one another rearing its ugly head. Deciding to ignore his brother-in-law's acerbic comment, Al smiled faintly and said, "You won't regret agreeing to this."

Barely able to contain his loathing Bart responded, "I hope not."

CHAPTER 31

Following Peter's birth, Gina and Bart were perhaps the happiest and most fulfilled of all their married life. Bart's job allowed him to be home for dinner most nights, and Gina loved being a wife and mother. They talked about having another baby; however, looming in the background was the prospect of what would happen when Bart's tour was up. When Bart received orders for Tan Son Nhut Air Base in South Vietnam, the couple decided they did not want a child born during Bart's absence.

Thinking about the possibility of going to a war zone and

actually getting orders to report to one are two different things for both the serviceman and for his family. Gina was devastated, not just because her husband was going to be in harm's way, but also because she would not see him for a year. Based on the scuttlebutt from returning airmen, Bart had little fear about being in the middle of an active conflict. Compared to some of the other bases in Vietnam that were regularly under mortar attacks and small arms fire, Tan Son Nhut Air Base was relatively safe. The thought of being separated from Gina and not being able to be there to hear his son's first words or take his first steps disheartened him. Knowing Al would have almost unfettered access to Peter made him downright depressed.

After Bart called Gina about his orders, it took her less than an hour to call her parents and ask them if it was all right for her and Peter to stay at their house while Bart was away. It took her mother less than two seconds to say yes. She didn't even hesitate to ask her husband. In fact, based upon the conversation that followed, Bart suspected his in-laws had already discussed the possibility and were ready to initiate actions to redecorate Al and John's old room into a nursery.

Within a week Gina, Peter and Bart were on a plane headed for New York. Landing at JFK was bittersweet. On one hand they were both glad to be back home; on the other hand it meant they were one step closer to being apart. Bart was scheduled to be on a plane to Southeast Asia a few days before their second anniversary. Gina, Bart, and Peter spent their first week at the Nicosias' in a dizzying parade of relatives and friends who had never seen little Peter. The following week the couple slept at Bart's parents' house, which was a welcome break from the confusion and noise of the Nicosias'. But that only lasted a few days. By Thursday Bart's relatives started dropping by, and on Saturday there were over twenty-five of Bart's relatives at the house for a barbecue. Fortunately, when they returned to Gina's house the following week, things were relatively peaceful. At the start, thirty days' leave seems like a lot of time; however, before they knew it, their time together was up.

■ ■ ■

There has always been a stage on which emotional farewells between soldiers heading off to war and their loved ones played out. For millennium the difficulty of travel demanded it be wherever the departing soldier lived; it has only been in the last couple of hundred years the stage shifted to more centralized embarkation sites like ports and train stations. The Vietnam War was the first conflict where much of the drama played out in airports.

Gina insisted on driving Bart alone to JFK for their tearful good-bye, but as she found out, they were not alone. During their last hour together the couple witnessed scores of other couples in the same poignant circumstances, but there were an equal number of lucky ones there to meet the returning warriors. She couldn't stop herself from staring at the lucky ones even though she felt as if she was an interloper. She was particularly intrigued with the reaction of the loved ones whose returning warrior happened to be one of those that had suffered an obvious wound. She wondered if they would have any different emotions if their loved one had returned unscathed.

These thoughts drove Gina to consider what her own feelings might be when Bart came back under either circumstance. Then, what if he didn't come back, what would she feel? She was jolted back to the present when the first boarding announcement for Bart's flight came over the loud speakers. That night, in her first letter to Bart, she described how she felt as if she was no longer in her own body. She described feeling as if she was someone else watching the two of them bid farewell. She didn't feel as if she was reunited with her body until after she got into her car.

CHAPTER 32

Southeast Asia has two seasons, hot and humid and rainy, hot and humid. Until he arrived in South Vietnam, Bart thought he was acclimated to hot and humid climates from his four years in South Carolina. Not so; except for a few days a year, Columbia was never as consistently oppressive with heat and humidity as South Vietnam. Although he did not keep track of it scientifically, he figured it rained at least a brief period every day during his first three months in the country. It wasn't just an occasional sprinkle either; it came down in buckets.

Bart had hardly settled into his new assignment at Tan Son Nhut AB when his CO asked him to take a sixty-day temporary duty (TDY) to Phan Rang AB about two hundred miles up the coast. The base had been without a finance officer for the last month and the permanent replacement was not due in from the States for another six weeks.

It was a short one-hour flight on the C-123 to Phan Rang AB; but it was light years away from the headquarters mentality of Tan Son Nhut. After his first week, Bart reached the conclusion that, in spite of its lousy reputation, the organization had some really good and dedicated NCOs and airmen. In Bart's judgment, there were a few things that could be quickly done to vastly improve the service performance of the finance organization.

Two weeks after Bart took over there was a marked improvement in the internal workings of the finance organization. The number of crises was cut in half. The new permanent CO did not arrive for another six weeks, resulting in Bart's TDY being extended an extra month. By the time the new CO of finance arrived on base, the department was almost completely turned around and the base executive officer sent Bart back to Tan Son Nhut with rave reviews.

Bart's last Friday night at Phan Rang developed into an exciting reunion. He was having dinner at the officers' club with a few of the friends he had made during his short stint when in walked a new group of F-100 pilots. This was a common occurrence at Phan Rang; fighter pilots were constantly rotating in and out of the base. Bart hardly paid any attention to the flyboys until they were all seated at a table and ordering drinks; then he heard it, a laugh he'd never forgotten. Sure enough, when he gave the newcomers a good look, there was Robbie Ryan's all-American face beaming with his effervescent smile. They hadn't been in touch since the wedding. Bart knew that Robbie had completed F-100 flight training, and somebody had told Bart they thought they saw him in Da Nang.

Figuring he would surprise Robbie, he quietly excused himself from his buddies and stealthily made his way around and behind Robbie's chair. Robbie realized someone was behind him by the way his fellow pilots were staring over his head, but before he could turn and look, Bart announced in his best deep voice, "So, asshole, I hear you've been messing with my wife."

Never at a loss for words, Lieutenant Ryan replied, "Yup, right after I finished with your mother."

You could have heard a pin drop in the room as Robbie's fellow pilots anxiously waited for the fight to break out. To their surprise, Robbie jumped to his feet, turned, and gave his antagonist a big hug and kissed him right on the mouth. When the two former college roommates were done with their exuberant greeting and updating each other on why they were at Phan Rang, they each made introductions around both tables. That started a night of drinking Bart never tried to duplicate again. By the end of the evening both airmen were so shit-faced, they passed out and didn't remember how they got back to their rooms. Neither of them could keep any solid food down until the following night. But by Monday Lieutenant Ryan was flying cover for ground forces again and Lieutenant LaRocca was on his way back to Tan Son Nhut Air Base.

It wasn't until the forced solitude caused by the noise of the C-123's engines that Bart recalled what Robbie revealed to him after they both had downed way too many boilermakers. Robbie confirmed this was his second tour in 'Nam, the first one having been completed six months earlier. He then volunteered for a second tour because, and this was a little fuzzy for Bart, he needed to get back to his girl. Could that be right? Did Robbie tell him he had a Vietnamese girlfriend?

CHAPTER 33

January 28, 2010

As we had agreed, Marie and I met David Tanner's corporate jet on Thursday in the executive terminal at Faro International Airport for our six-hour flight back to Long Island. What a difference. Instead of an hour and a half at the airport at both ends and a two-hour ride in a limo from JFK to Westhampton, our corporate ride cost us fifteen minutes at each end and a ten-minute cab ride from Francis Gabreski Airport to our home. The food was really good, and it was all we could eat and drink.

We spent a wonderful week with our family. At our grand-daughter's birthday party Marie turned to me and declared, "I am so glad we were able to make it back for this. I really missed the kids and grandchildren; I don't think I want to go back with you. Can you go by yourself?"

Wanting to continue to be perceived as an understanding and loving husband, I reluctantly replied, "Sure babe, if that's what you want."

So on the 7th of February I boarded the Tanners' Falcon 2000 jet alone. Sarah Tanner was disappointed she would not have Marie as a female companion during the long flight. However, she did manage to talk my ear off, anxious to hear all about my family and telling me the story of David's and her courtship.

■ ■ ■

David and Sarah had known each other since they were young children. Sarah was the daughter of Ben Cohen, David's father's New York attorney. Growing up, their fathers used business meetings to bring their families together. David, who was five years older than Sarah, never thought of Sarah as anything other than a cute little girl. It wasn't until Ben Cohen's funeral in 1969 that David became aware Sarah had morphed into a beautiful and intelligent young woman. At the time of her father's death, she was in her sophomore year at Columbia. She, on the other hand had a crush on David since she was eleven years old. When David showed up at the funeral the day after her father's passing, Sarah wasn't sure if David would return after the shivah. She broke tradition and actually invited him to visit her and her mother at their home in four days. David was delighted to have an opportunity to reconnect with Sarah and her mother; not to mention he was awestruck by how incredibly beautiful and intriguing she had become.

Following their second meeting, David invited Sarah to dinner whenever he was in New York on business. They saw each other numerous times over the next three years and developed an ever-escalating bond. Following Sarah's graduation from NYU with an MBA, she persuaded David to hire her as an intern at one of his commercial real estate ventures headquartered in Boca Raton. Two years later they were married at his oceanfront mansion in Palm Beach. The couple had two children, a boy and a girl. Their son worked for the State Department and their daughter managed the family trust.

■ ■ ■

About two hours into the flight, David received a call from Bart; and after a brief discussion, David turned to me and said, "If you have no objections, Bart and I think it would be fun for you to stay with us in Seville. We have plenty of room and Sarah would love the company." I agreed, and we changed destinations from Faro to Seville.

I discovered the Tanners owned more than the villa Marie and I had visited; they also owned the buildings on either side. One of them was leased as a single unit on an annual basis, and the other was divided into six apartments, four of which were short-term vacation rentals. While David was in the city, his security detail occupied the two ground floor units closest to the main house. One of the apartments had an access door to David's courtyard. David put Bart and me up in two apartments on the second floor.

It was almost midnight when we arrived in Seville; Bart was waiting for us with a nightcap. Sarah and I had knocked off a bottle of Pinot Grigio on the flight, so I declined, but I was still wide awake. For me it was only 5:00 p.m. New York time and I could tell Bart wasn't ready to sleep. There was something that had been bugging me since before I flew back to New York. I took the opportunity to ask Bart, "What did Robbie Ryan mean when he said 'he needed to get back to his girl'?"

Bart got this strange look on his face and without his usual fervor described the events that culminated his tour in Vietnam.

After returning to Tan Son Nhut AB from Phan Rang, Bart tried several times to call Robbie but never got through. Finally, almost a month later, Robbie called him. He apologized for not getting back to Bart sooner, and explained the Vietcong had stepped up their attacks on convoys and his squadron was hardly getting enough downtime to eat and sleep. He finally had a few days of R&R and hoped Bart could meet him in Saigon. It was easy for Bart to get R&R himself; his boss, Colonel Trucks, was always telling him to take some time off and get into Saigon. Frankly, Bart was afraid to go into the capital, not because he feared the sporadic attacks by the Vietcong, but because of the many cheap temptations that were so prevalent in this thriving metropolis of 4.5 million people. In spite of his apprehension, Bart agreed to meet Robbie at the Rex Hotel for three days of R&R. After he hung up, he thought to himself, *There would be no rest and relaxation in this R&R; it would probably be more like raunchy and ruination.*

Robbie was already waiting at the hotel when Bart arrived, but he wasn't alone. Sitting with him was another American, and the two of them were having a good time.

Robbie saw Bart entering the bar and jumped up to greet him. "Really glad you could get away to spend time with us," Robbie declared. "Bart, this is Major John Slaughter, US Army. John, this is Lieutenant Bart LaRocca, my asshole roommate from college."

Bart took Major Slaughter's outstretched hand; he was surprised when he got it back without anything being broken. John

Slaughter could have been the model for a comic book superhero. He was 6 foot 4, 235 pounds of nothing but muscle and bone, and all of it in the right places. His head and face reminded Bart of the baseball card photo of one of his favorite Yankees from the great 1950s teams, Hank Bauer. Slaughter had the same square jaw, high cheek bones, pronounced brow, and slightly receding crew cut as the former Yankee right-fielder and ex-Marine. His eyes were steely gray, and they seemed to peer right into your soul, just like Pietro's.

"What do you fly, LaRocca?" asked Major Slaughter.

"A 100-key Olivetti calculator; I'm in finance," Bart replied in a tone that was slightly apologetic.

"Well, we need those too," replied Slaughter. "Without the money we couldn't buy booze or broads over here."

"Here, here," chimed in Robbie Ryan. "In fact it looks like we need some more beer right now." Ryan did an about-face and headed for the bar.

"How do you know Robbie?" Bart asked Major Slaughter.

"Well, your buddy has saved my ass on at least three occasions. My job is to escort convoys. During my first tour, your buddy saved my platoon twice up on the coastal highway near Da Nang. This time I'm down here on Highway 1 around Xuan Loc Province. Your buddy's F-100 ground support squadron was originally out of Da Nang AB but recently it was redeployed to Phan Rang. Then again just last week after the Huey assigned as our cover was badly hit and had to return to base. I thought we were going to be overrun. But, suddenly, out of nowhere, comes Ryan with two other F-100s. They dropped six 500-pound bombs right on the forward edge of the enemy's lines. Those VC that survived began hightailing it south, but Ryan and his buddies swung around and incinerated most of the retreating enemy with six tanks of napalm. Not satisfied, Ryan made another run, strafing the few lucky ones that escaped the inferno with 20-mm cannon fire. When I found out it was Ryan again, I just had to meet him; so here we are."

"Wow, that's one hell of a story; I don't know how either of you guys can do what you do. I'm not sure that I wouldn't shit my pants if I were in the same situation."

"I doubt it," replied Slaughter. "I'm a pretty good judge of character, and I'd bet my life you would do whatever you had to do in order to keep yourself and your troops from getting killed." Major Slaughter hesitated for a moment, checked to see that Robbie was still at the bar getting drinks, then quietly said with sincere concern, "I'm worried about the lieutenant. He just told me he shacked up with some Vietnamese broad during his first tour at Da Nang. This time he is having her brought down to Phan Rang so they can play house again. Do you know anything about this?"

"Nope," replied Bart. "Last time we were out drinking, he said something about having a girlfriend, but I had no idea he was living with her."

"Shit," said the major. "The only way a Vietnamese would shack up with an American was if he bought her from a pimp or she is a VC spy. We need to get this guy's head screwed on straight."

Just then Robbie returned with the beers.

Two beers later Bart said, "I'm hungry, let's get something to eat."

"Do you like Vietnamese food?" asked Major Slaughter.

"Don't know, never really had any. I've been eating exclusively at either the mess hall or the officers' club. Hell, the only time I've left Tan Son Nhut was to fly to Phan Rang. Why don't you old-timers show me the ropes?"

They took Bart to a *pho* restaurant. Major Slaughter ordered *pho ga*, chicken and rice noodle soup, and several different kinds of *cuon*, spring rolls, for Bart. In addition, Bart sampled the more sophisticated meals Robbie and Major Slaughter had ordered for themselves. It didn't take Bart long to become a big fan of Vietnamese food.

After dinner Bart's buddies took him on a wild-eyed tour of the city. They rode on cyclos down Saigon's colorful neon-lit streets. The city exuded energy, not all of it good. It both seduced and disgusted you with its sordid reality of life. Its impoverished inhabitants cooked, ate, drank, washed, slept, and deposited all their bodily secretions in its streets and alleys. Drugs and prostitution were everywhere. In contrast, the rich and powerful lived a life of opulence in secure walled mansions and chauffeured automobiles. Bart wondered what it had been like before American GIs flooded the city. Did this thriving black market, selling everything from Zippos to Levi's and Bud, already exist and only the product changed to satisfy the latest influx of rich foreigners? Did the constantly blaring American rock music replace constantly blaring French cabaret music?

Both Robbie and Slaughter knew where all the best bars were in the Ton Dan section; the ones owned by the wives of South Vietnamese Army officers or by the few American civilians. In one bar-hotel on Rue Catinat, Robbie was instantly recognized when they walked in. On seeing Robbie, the madam, an unusually tall women of obvious French-Vietnamese ancestry, scurried to the front door and broadcast, "Lieutenant Ryan, have you worn out my girl already and you're coming back for a new one?"

"No, Anh and I are doing fine. I'm just here with my buddy, showing him the sights."

Turning to Bart, the gregarious madam announced, "Welcome, Lieutenant Ryan's buddy, five dollars will get you a lot more than a look."

"No thanks," replied Bart, "I've taken a vow of celibacy." Turning to Ryan, Bart said, "I've seen enough, and I'm tired. Let's go back to the Hotel Rex."

On the walk back to the hotel, Robbie said to Slaughter, "You have a vehicle, right?"

"No, but I can get one."

"Good, tomorrow let's blow this town and drive down to the beach at Vung Tau."

"Sounds good to me," replied the major. "Are you in, LaRocca?"

"Beach it is," responded Bart.

Eighty miles south on the South China Sea, Vung Tau had been a long-time beach resort for Saigon residents. During the war, it was home to the Royal Australian Army and also to some US support units. The breathtaking beauty of the Vung Tau Peninsula provided a sharp contrast to the horror of the Vietnam War and the circus atmosphere of Saigon. It was a classic beach party with plenty of food, beer, and music. Like most of 'Nam, where you found foreign military installations, women and drugs were plentiful and cheap. The three comrades got rooms right on the beach and settled in for what Bart hoped would be a relaxing but uneventful thirty-six hours.

It took Major Slaughter about an hour to hook up with an Australian army nurse from the Aussie medical facility in town. It was the last time they saw him until it was time to leave on Sunday. Bart was surprised when Robbie said to him, "If you want to get yourself a honey, go right ahead, but I've got all the woman I want waiting for me back in Phan Rang."

"Yeah, tell me about this Anh," Bart said.

"Not much to tell, old buddy. You obviously figured out she was working at that whorehouse, and I bought her freedom. She is a good kid about seventeen years old; her family was among the hundreds of thousands of Catholics who fled the north when the Communists took over in 1954. They moved into a little village just over the border until her father was executed by the Vietcong.

"Her mother, in order to survive and provide for her family, moved Anh and her brother to Da Nang, where her mother worked as a prostitute to feed her kids. By the time Anh was fifteen she had run away to Saigon, where she too began working in the brothels. When I first met her, while on R&R, it was not for paid sex. We met at a *pho* restaurant. She was so worldly, yet underneath she seemed so sweet and innocent. I was fascinated; we met for lunch every day while I was on R&R. Afterwards we would walk around town and talk.

"I never figured out she sold herself to GIs for a living. Hell, I didn't even screw her that time. I came back two months later and found her again at the same restaurant. It was then she told me what she did for a living. I had to rescue her. By then, I had been in country long enough to know you could buy a whore's freedom for the right price. Without telling her, I went to the whorehouse and paid $500 for her freedom. I moved her back to Da Nang, rented a place big enough for her, her mother, and brother. Over time she fell in love with me, and when I wasn't on duty, I sort of moved in."

Bart just stared at Robbie for a few moments, trying to absorb what he had just heard, then he responded, "Are you nuts? I can understand you feeling sorry for some young girl and buying her freedom, but living with her. That's crazy!"

"Maybe it is; but if you could have seen her, you might have done the same thing. She couldn't have been more than fifteen when I met her, and she had been working at that place for only a few months. You may find this hard to believe; but in spite of fucking a couple of hundred GIs, she still was innocent. She was only doing it to support her mother and younger brother. I knew that if I could get her away from Saigon, give her family a place to live and enough money to buy food, she could live a decent life. When I first I moved her back to Da Nang, I stopped by once a week to make sure they had enough to eat and that no one was harassing them.

"Then, after a few months, it just happened. I didn't want to fall in love with her, no more than you wanted to fall in love with a Mafia princess, but I did; and I can't help it anymore. I figured after my tour was up and I went back to the States I would forget about her, but I didn't. As soon as I could, I volunteered for another tour. When they moved our squadron down to Phan Rang, I had to figure out how to get them there. It is all done now, except for the brother who ran away or was taken away by the Vietcong. This time we are going to have kids together."

"Holy shit, Rob, what does your father make of all this?"

"I haven't told my parents. If they knew, they would disown me, especially the general. No matter what happens, you can never tell them."

"Robbie, if the general ever asks me, I'm not going to lie."

"Fair enough," replied Lieutenant Ryan.

The intense discussion abruptly ended when they stumbled across a house with a half dozen GIs milling around on the front porch. This was a strange sight; the place was unlike any other place in town. It definitely wasn't a bar or whorehouse, and it wasn't like any of the other hotels. Bart stopped and asked one of the Americans what the attraction was. He was told that it was a servicemen's home run by an American couple referred to as Mom and Pop Gifford. Bart was intrigued and went inside to check it out. Inside he ran into Dan Gifford. The Giffords had been in Vung Tau since the fall of 1967; they had become local legends, both for the GIs on R&R and the Vietnamese people on the southeast coast. In addition to their "home away from home" for the American military, they ran a foster home for abandoned Amerasian babies. They were partnered with an incredible Vietnamese couple who actually ran the orphanage. At the time Bart and Robbie were there, the couple had eight children of their own and six more orphans. Bart and Robbie were both so impressed with the couple and their mission, they each gave Dan $100 for the foster home.

Bart never forgot the passion the Giffords displayed for both the servicemen's home and the foster home. Having just come from the cruel reality of Saigon, where Amerasian children as young as five years old wandered the streets and alleys eating out of garbage piles and were constantly under threat of molestation, Bart found the near normalcy of the Giffords' foster home to be refreshing. For the next six years, in order to quell the pangs of remorse he felt for the pain and anguish he witnessed in Vietnam, he sent a check to the Giffords.

The first time Gina noticed the $100 check, she asked him about it. Bart never talked much about Vietnam, preferring to attempt to put that year and its memories of distant explosions and flag-draped coffins out of his mind. Gina was always miffed by his reluctance to share his experiences with her; but, as her brother Al had warned her, "Some guys can't deal with war." So until she saw the check, she never pressed the issue. Reluctantly, after two years removed from the turmoil of Southeast Asia, Bart was able to reveal to his wife some of his experiences, both pleasant and unpleasant. One story he did cover was the R&R to Saigon and Vung Tau; he told it with such vivid detail that Gina was mesmerized by his words. The only thing Bart left out was his subsequent meeting with Robbie and his Vietnamese family just before he rotated back to the states.

Gina was so moved by the plight of Amerasian babies she conveyed the story to her brother Al, telling him how proud she was Bart felt compelled to send money to the orphanage. Al, always the cynic and never passing up the opportunity to disparage his brother-in-law, responded, "Good intentions, my ass, he probably has a kid of his own in that orphanage. Every GI that ever went on R&R left his wad in one of those bar girls. Hell, I probably have a half-dozen little half-breeds running around 'Nam."

Gina was taken aback by her brother's admission and his accusation that Bart was of the same inclination. Although she didn't say anything to Bart, she never forgot the implications of Al's accusation.

■ ■ ■

Near the end of his tour, on the pretense of following up on the progress of the finance organization, Bart was able to wangle a short TDY to Phan Rang Air Base. His real objective was to see Lieutenant Ryan one more time before he left the theater. While at the base Lieutenant Ryan excitedly invited Bart to meet his "family," as he called them. Reluctantly, Bart accepted the invitation to a home-cooked Vietnamese meal. They picked up one of those three-wheel taxis outside the base and headed down to an ancient little village about ten clicks south of Phan Rang. Arriving at this quaint little town known for its ceramics, Bart was amazed at how peaceful and serene it was. Robbie had rented a modest house for Anh and her mother. It was a single-story building with wood plank walls covered in mud and rice straw. The windows around the walls were open and the roof was covered with yin and yang tile. It had the traditional symmetrical design with the customary odd number of rooms. The central compartment consisted of two rooms, a kitchen with a woodburning hearth, and a separate eating-common area. On two sides of the main compartment were bedrooms; the larger one on the right where Robbie and Anh slept, and two smaller ones on the opposite side for Anh's mother and her still-missing brother.

Just as his friend promised, Anh was a beautiful young girl who was now noticeably pregnant. She wore pink traditional Vietnamese pajamas. She was tall for a Southeast Asian woman, just over five feet. Before she started showing, it was obvious, she had a body that turned heads. Her mother, who Robbie introduced as Pham Thi Ly, was six inches shorter and, although she probably wasn't forty years old, looked sixty. She also wore the traditional black silk pajamas with a white top. Ly prepared a wonderful meal of pork and shrimp with lots of rice and different vegetables she had grown in the small garden on the side of the house. Ly did all the food preparation, while Anh hovered around Robbie like he was a rock star.

Robbie Ryan was always a shutterbug. Bart recalled that at Gina's and his wedding Robbie had taken dozens of pictures. That day in Hoi An town was similar; he insisted on taking several shots of Bart with Anh, and Anh with her mother. He even convinced a passing GI to take shots of the four of them together. Bart enjoyed his visit. Maybe it was due to a year of nothing but constant reminders of the anomaly of war, whereas this one day felt normal and serene with a family atmosphere.

Bart returned to Phan Rang by himself. While riding back to the base he reached four conclusions: first, Robbie was hopelessly in love with Anh and in all probability would try to extend his tour; second, Anh knew she had a good thing in Lieutenant Ryan and would do anything to keep him interested; third, Ly Pham was not all that happy with her daughter shacking up with an American, much less with the prospect of her having an Amerasian baby. His final conclusion was the one that disturbed Bart the most and was probably the reason Ly was not happy with her daughter's arrangement. Eventually, when his buddy couldn't extend his tour any further, Robbie would come to his senses and return to the States, leaving them all behind.

CHAPTER 34

It didn't take long for Gina and her parents to get into a comfortable routine during Bart's year in 'Nam. Pietro commented he couldn't remember Eleonora being so happy since Gina was a small child. She was born to manage a household and raise children.

On nice days, after they had finished their household chores, mother and daughter would take Peter in the baby carriage to Juniper Valley Park. In the heat of summer, Gina would occasionally drive them to Coney Island. They still had a very comfortable relationship; Gina felt she could confide her deepest thoughts, fears, and aspirations to her mother.

■ ■ ■

By 1969 Al Nicosia had become a "made man." He ran a small crew out of Hempstead. Although his father disliked the whole drug business, he put up little objection when it was suggested his eldest son be tapped to run the Leucchi family's drug and gambling operations in Nassau County. Al was very successful, doubling the volume every year. He did it with a combination of innate understanding of human nature, particularly for guys of his own generation, and a brutal reputation among other gangsters. In most cases, when he decided to move into a new territory, the incumbents joined his outfit, moved their operation, or disappeared.

In contrast to his reputation on the streets of Long Island, Al

Nicosia was the paragon of an uncle. He usually stopped by his parents' house twice a week for dinner, and on most occasions, he brought something for little Peter and frequently for his sister.

When they were alone, his sister would ask him what it was like in Vietnam; he would tell her horror stories that always made her uncomfortable. She would read parts of Bart's letters to her brother and he would interject his interpretation of what Bart was thinking and feeling. He always used these opportunities to plant seeds of mistrust in Gina's mind. After each of these discussions, she swore to herself she would not confide in or listen to her brother again; but she continued to do it throughout Bart's tour.

Al truly loved his nephew. He could talk and play with Peter for hours. He took him for walks in the park and told him stories from his own childhood. When he left him, he couldn't wait to see him again. Whenever Peter saw his uncle coming, he got all excited and begged to be picked up. Unlike Bart, Al was there when Peter took his first step and uttered his first words. They developed a bond that was in one way beautiful and in another tragic; a bond Bart found, when he returned home, disturbing and of which he was forever jealous.

Pete Nicosia was as loving a grandfather as he was a father. He, too, couldn't wait to get home to hold his grandson. His favorite thing was to see and hear his grandson laugh. He would do or say anything to get the child to react to his antics. He discovered Peter was especially susceptible to any strange noise he made with his mouth. He would put his index finger on the inside of his mouth and make a popping sound with his cheek; he would make his lips in the shape of an O, tighten his cheeks, and snap them with his middle finger, making a loud sound similar to pouring liquid out of a bottle. His namesake never tired of these frolics, urging Grandpa to do it again. These moments were an escape for the mobster, who was embroiled in a very difficult and dangerous time. Santo Leucchi, the head of the family, had been diagnosed with a brain tumor, leaving him unable to provide any leadership. Pete had always shunned the limelight and despised the hard-core crimes such as drugs, extortion, and murder for hire, preferring what he commonly referred to as "soft" rackets such as gambling, prostitution, construction schemes, and hijackings. As one of the top leaders of the family and the oldest friend of Santo, he found himself in the uncomfortable position of sharing leadership with two others of Santo's top henchmen, Dominic DiMarco and Frankie Bono. Pete had the backing of the heads of the other four New York families, but he didn't want the top position. He also knew the reason the other Mafia heads wanted him as boss. They believed he was the one least likely to start a war when they divided up Leucchi's rackets. On the other hand, he didn't like where his other two rivals wanted to take the family. They were convinced the future of the family lay in the drug trade, while Pete was convinced it was in gambling meccas like Las Vegas. His dream was to use the family's political influence to convince the New Jersey legislature to approve gambling in Atlantic City. For him it was a game of give-and-take; he would not oppose Dominic and Frankie's advances into drug relationships with Colombians as long as they supported his investments in Vegas and Atlantic City.

In early 1970 Pete was invited to a secret meeting with the heads of the other four families at Bonavita's Restaurant in Brooklyn. He sensed the objectives of the meeting were to peel away the lucrative pieces of the Leucchi Empire, leaving him as head of a much-weakened family. He even thought they would offer to eliminate his rivals in order to avoid an all-out war. As if by divine intervention, the day before the meeting was to take place the head of the most powerful family suddenly died of a heart attack. A week later, Santo Leucchi expired from his brain tumor. Their deaths threw the Italian underworld into chaos, unleashing years of violence and territorial encroachment. During the ensuing three years, the federal government finally got its act together and aggressively prosecuted one crime boss after another. It was a tribute to Pietro Nicosia's brilliance and cunning that he was the only living crime boss scheduled to be in the meeting at Bonavita's who was not convicted of a crime.

In addition, his two rivals for the top spot of the Leucchi Family were arrested, convicted, and incarcerated. That left Pietro Nicosia in a perfect position to succeed in his dream of a major stake in Las Vegas, and three years later in succeeding at getting the state of New Jersey to approve gambling in Atlantic City.

CHAPTER 35

Bart's year in Vietnam was enough to convince him a career in the military was not to his liking. Two months before his Vietnam tour was up, Bart informed the Air Force of his intention to leave the service. After a brief counseling session by a retention officer, the Air Force agreed to transfer him to inactive reserve status.

As he got nearer to the end of his tour, his letters to Gina got more frequent and his tone became anxious. Gina couldn't understand the fearful nature of his psyche that never had been in Bart's nature. He wrote continually about his son not knowing who he was. He wondered how he would adjust to the "real world" and, what seemed to be his biggest fear of all, whether he had changed so much that she wouldn't love him anymore. She tried, in her letters, to reassure her husband he and their son would soon reconnect, he would readjust to the "real world," and nothing could ever change her love for him. In spite of her reassurances, Bart's apprehension continued up until his last letter when suddenly the euphoria of actually getting on a plane to return to the States trumped his paranoia.

Gina confided to her mother Bart's fears. Eleonora, in her most understanding style, recommended Gina meet her husband's plane at JFK alone and suggested the two of them take some time together to get reacquainted. The evening Gina met Bart's plane felt to both of them like their wedding day, exciting, scary, and much anticipated. As excited as they were to finally be together again, the first minutes were extremely awkward. If they each said it once they must have said it a dozen times: "God, I missed you."

While they were on their way to baggage claim, Bart asked, "Is there a reason you didn't bring Peter?"

Gina, smiling faintly, replied, "I thought we could use some time alone getting to know each other again; is that OK with you?"

"As anxious as I am to see Peter, being alone with you has some very attractive aspects to it."

"My, how diplomatic you've become. One of those attractions would be getting me alone in a hotel room, would it?"

Coyly, Bart replied, "Oh, what an interesting idea! Now that you mentioned it, how about we drive out to Centerport and get a room in the motel at the marina?"

"Boy, you must think I've become an easy make. At least you could buy me dinner first."

"Pardon me, madam, would you like to go to dinner before I ravage your body?"

"That's better, now I feel like a lady!"

The Thatched Cottage Restaurant was less than two hundred yards from the motel. Drinks, appetizers, dinner, dessert, and after-dinner liquors lasted for over two hours. When they emerged from the restaurant it was almost as if they hadn't been separated for a year.

The passion that night was akin to those days and nights from years earlier. In all probability it was also the night Gina got pregnant again. Gina gently woke Bart at 7:00 a.m. the next morning by nuzzling her buttocks up against him. Fast on the uptake, Bart was ready for action before he even opened his eyes. A few minutes later, Gina lay naked across Bart's chest; he was gently running his fingers through her hair. In an almost pathetic tone he whispered, "I can't believe I survived a whole year without you." Gina let out a deep sigh and tears ran down her cheeks.

While Gina was slowly nibbling on a bagel and he was ravenously devouring his, he took enough time between bites to declare, "They didn't have anything like this in Vietnam either." Almost without hesitation, he declared, "Now I'm anxious to meet my son again."

Peter was happy to see his mother but the man with her had little appeal for the eighteen-month-old. Over the next month, father and son were continuously in each other's company, but in spite of their hours together, Peter still seemed to prefer his grandfather's attention over this new guy. It wasn't until they were living in a place of their own for a few months that Bart felt he was Peter's favorite male.

CHAPTER 36

Bart had started to accumulate addresses of Fortune 500 companies two weeks after he returned from visiting Robbie in Phan Rang. A week before the end of his tour in 'Nam, he began sending out résumés. He was rewarded with six interviews and three job offers; all three offers were within the first six weeks of his return home. He chose International Packaging Company (IPC) for its operations accounting training program and because the position was in Baltimore where John and Patty Jo were living.

Fortunately, Gina was with her sister-in-law when the cramping and bleeding started. She had experienced minor cramping and bleeding during her first pregnancy so she wasn't concerned this time. Patty Jo, on the other hand, was not so cavalier about the situation. She believed her mother-in-law's endometriosis, which was known to cause ectopic pregnancies, could be an affliction inherited by Gina. Initially, she did not say anything to Gina or Bart. However, she did mention it to John, who also became concerned. Over the next several days, the medical couple took turns checking in on Gina. When the cramping and bleeding persisted, John convinced his sister to make an early appointment with her obstetrician.

Patty Jo and John's doggedness may have saved Gina's life.

During the examination, her obstetrician suspected she had a tubal pregnancy. Further examination and testing confirmed the unfortunate condition that demanded immediate surgery to remove the ten-week-old fetus along with Gina's fallopian tube. The surgery was performed just in time to avoid a ruptured fallopian tube and serious complications for Gina. Although the necessity to abort the fetus was saddening for Gina and Bart, the appreciation of just how close Gina had come to a life-threatening situation provided the couple with sufficient reason to be thankful. Examination of the surgically removed tube confirmed endometriosis was the cause of the ectopic pregnancy.

Several weeks later John was offered, and accepted, an internship at Yale New Haven Hospital in Connecticut. It was a huge loss for Gina and Bart when their best friends moved from Baltimore.

■ ■ ■

Bart was one of the fortunate ones whose military discharge timing was perfect. In the first three years of the 1970s, American industries were adding management talent at an incredible rate. Most large companies had fantastic training programs for new talent. If you were a college graduate and had gained the maturity of several years in the military, you were golden. Just a few years later, after the disastrous withdrawal from Vietnam, the job market was flooded with ex-military college graduates. Then by the late '70s the MBAs became the darlings of the blue chips.

In his first years with IPC, Bart's strategy for getting ahead was to take the jobs no one else wanted, providing there was a promotion and a raise that came with it. His first job after the twelve-month training program in Baltimore was at a small plastic film plant in Scranton, Pennsylvania, right in the heart of one of the most economically depressed regions on the East Coast. It was perceived as such an undesirable location that when his boss, the plant controller, left a year later, the company could not get anyone else to relocate there. By default, Bart became the plant controller, giving him the distinction of progressing from trainee to controller two years faster than anyone else in the company's history.

Gina liked Scranton, or more precisely Clarks Summit, where they purchased their first home. For northeastern Pennsylvania, Clarks Summit was an upscale community of mostly white collar executives or entrepreneurs. She had no trouble finding excellent doctors and a dentist right in Clarks Summit. Shopping was close, with a major mall only a few miles away.

Compared to buying a home in the greater New York area, Clarks Summit gave the young couple a lot more for their money. The couple was able to purchase a ten-year-old, three-bedroom house, on a half acre for half of what it would cost on Long Island. Peter had plenty of children his own age in the neighborhood. In some respects, Scranton reminded them of the area near Pordenone, Italy. They were of similar size, had comparable weather, were both in hilly terrains, and were both struggling economically.

The young family of three lived a relatively happy and comfortable life, although Gina occasionally complained Bart worked too many long hours. He did find time on weekends for the three of them to take day trips. The area was dotted with many lakes, although it was not the same as Long Island's ocean beaches. A hot summer day on Lake Wallenpaupek almost felt like old times, except now, instead of finding an isolated spot in the dunes, they scouted out a safe place for Peter to swim and play. In spite of Gina's previous difficulties, the couple was anxious to have another child. Walt Disney's 7:00 p.m. Sunday television show played heavily into their plan. They made a point of finishing dinner before seven, giving Peter his bath, and setting the young boy up in the den to watch his favorite program. As soon as their son was engrossed in the television program, Bart and Gina would sneak up to their bedroom for their baby-making exercises. Usually, before Disney was over little Peter was fast asleep on the couch and his parents were huffing and puffing away down the hall. The third year into their lives in Clarks Summit Gina got pregnant again. This time she and her obstetrician were vigilant for signs of another ectopic conception. Sure enough, a blood test in her sixth week revealed it was not a uterine pregnancy. Unfortunately, medical solutions did not become widely available until the 1990s. Besides aborting the pregnancy, the standard surgical procedure was performed, rendering Gina incapable of conceiving another child.

■ ■ ■

Reacting to the growing tide of environmental activism toward the ever-mounting rivers of garbage going to landfill, IPC developed a plan to get into the resource recovery business. Finally in 1974 after many false starts, they came up with a process they believed could successfully and efficiently recover a profitable stream of salable materials from municipal waste. In fact, their plan was so well-thought-out and logical, they were able to sell the concept to the city of Milwaukee. The city agreed on a contract to pay IPC for recycling their municipal waste. IPC established a new division with the catchy name of Eco-cycle. After signing the Milwaukee contract, a public relations campaign was launched touting Eco-cycle's mission to eventually recycle the nation's garbage.

The company again found it difficult to find an accountant who was anxious to risk his career in an unproven and unglamorous situation. The position was a promotion for Bart and located in a metropolitan area a lot more attractive than Scranton. He figured he was trading a less appealing industry for a better place to live, more money, and, assuming the venture was successful, a ground-floor opportunity in a brand-new venture. Gina was not initially excited about moving so far away from her family. To Bart's surprise, Pietro convinced his daughter the move was important to Bart's career. He then said something that, for just a brief moment, caused Bart to question whether this was the right move for him: "Uncle Frankie has some friends in the garbage business in Milwaukee; he tells me it's a nice town. Maybe the winters are too long but the people are real friendly. Besides, your mother and I will come to visit."

CHAPTER 37

Pietro was right. Wisconsin had to be right at the top of the list of places with the nicest, friendliest people on the planet. Maybe it was the agonizingly long winters, with weeks on end of zero temperatures or below, compelling the inhabitants to cherish the companionship of their fellow frostbitten cheeseheads. Perhaps it all started with Friday nights, when virtually every neighborhood bar in Milwaukee had an all-you-can-eat fish fare. Of course, the fact Wisconsin has the highest per capita consumption of brandy in the world certainly helps to foster lively get-togethers. Brandy was not the only alcoholic beverage to be coveted by Wisconsinites; at one time Milwaukee brewed more beer than any other city in the world. It was the home of some of the grand old brands of American beer, with Miller, Schlitz, Pabst, and Blatz originating in the city.

The moving van was still in the driveway of their new Waukesha four-bedroom colonial when the Welcome Wagon ladies arrived at the door. As New Yorkers, both Gina and Bart were leery of these way-too-friendly strangers offering free stuff and providing a host of local information. It didn't take Gina long to determine almost all the ladies in the neighborhood were as friendly and helpful as the two Welcome Wagon greeters. In less than a month she had half a dozen new friends, all with young children about Peter's age. It was a fantastic place for young families, with lots of activities and parties for both parents and children. Even during the coldest winter months, there were impromptu ice skating and sleigh riding outings. Gina joined a Monday morning ladies bowling league and convinced Bart they should participate in a Friday night couples league. There were always neighbors' teenage daughters available for sitting so Bart and Gina had plenty of opportunities to get out without Peter. Bart took Peter to Milwaukee Brewers' games whenever the Yankees were in town, and father and son fished at a small lake a few miles away.

■ ■ ■

The signing of the contract between IPC and the city of Milwaukee was a big deal not just locally but nationally. As the first partnership between a major city and a public company attempting to recycle 100 percent of the community's municipal refuse, it was hailed as a major step forward in the battle to deal with the ever-mounting tide of trash generated by the American consumer.

IPC's process was to pulverize the garbage with two massive shredding machines. Then the much smaller particles could be sorted. The next operation separated out the combustibles using huge air cyclones. This was followed by large magnets to remove the ferrous metals and electromagnets to sort out the aluminum. The last material to be recycled was glass via a water flotation device. Theoretically this left only a small percentage of refuse requiring landfill. Of course, the success of the whole project depended on the value of the recovered materials.

Concurrent to the signing of the contract with the city of Milwaukee, Eco-cycle signed five other contracts. The first contract was with the local electric company to purchase the combustibles as a fuel substitute for coal. The second was with the city to purchase the ground-up glass as an additive in the asphalt used for paving roads. The third contract was with a metal recycler for the purchase of the reclaimed metal and aluminum. The one catch in the deal with the city was that Eco-cycle would be responsible for all the garbage eighteen months before the plant was ready to begin operations.

This little nuance in the deal resulted in Eco-cycle requiring a significant amount of landfill space until the plant actually was capable of recycling. Thus the last two contracts were for landfill of the garbage. One landfill contract was with American Waste Industries, which dominated the garbage collection and landfill business east of the Mississippi and was rumored to have mob connections; the other contract was with a small privately owned company, Brown & Sons. Ferris Brown owned the last operating landfill within fifty miles of Milwaukee which wasn't controlled by American Waste Industries. Over the previous ten years, AWI had purchased all its competitors except for the one "stubborn old codger," Ferris Brown.

During the eighteen months the plant was being built, besides monitoring the prime contractor's construction accounting, Bart's primary responsibilities were to oversee deliveries to the landfill and to approve payments to landfill operators. Although all of the project's heavy-duty public relations were initially handled by corporate headquarters in Connecticut, Bart became the local spokesperson and tour guide when no one from corporate was in Milwaukee.

One of the perks of being part of a high-profile project is entertaining and being entertained. There were times when it was appropriate for Bart to bring along Gina for dinner, especially if a visiting dignitary had brought his spouse with him. Gina was a big hit at these events. She still had an innocent sexy beauty that charmed the male guests but did not make their spouses feel threatened. There were a handful of wonderful restaurants in Milwaukee the couple enjoyed and guests always found superb. Of course, the city was famous for its German restaurants, Carl Ratzsch's, Mader's, and John Earnst's. A dinner at any one of the three was never a letdown for Bart's guests. Occasionally, Bart hosted a dinner at one of his and Gina's non-German favorites, Alito's or Sal's Steak House. Both were owned by the same Italian family and run by the patriarch, Salvatore "Sal" Alito.

Sal Alito spent most nights at one or both of his restaurants making sure the food was up to his expectations; plus he loved schmoozing with the guests. He was a diminutive dynamo who, although he in his sixties, still had jet-black hair and an eye for the ladies. It must have been Sal's astute eye for beautiful and intriguing women that brought him over to Bart and Gina's table at Alito's where they were hosting a dinner for a visiting dignitary and his wife.

Sal started with his standard dinner guest greeting: "Has everything been to your satisfaction?" When everyone acknowledged their approval, he focused in on Gina. "Didn't I see you here last week?"

"Oh, yes," she replied. "We come to one of your places whenever we get a chance."

"You mean you prefer our simple Italian-American fare over our more famous German competitors?"

Grinning, Bart chimed in, "You need to ask? Couldn't you tell by her accent that she's an Italian from New York?"

"I detected a slight accent and the features were definitely Mediterranean, but I didn't want to appear presumptuous. Although I should have known a woman so beautiful could only be Italian. She even reminds me of my daughter Regina."

In spite of Bart having given his credit card to the waiter, Sal returned with the receipt for Bart to sign. While Bart was adding the tip to the credit card invoice, Sal with a wry grin remarked, "You didn't mention that you're a *paisan*, too, Mr. LaRocca."

Preoccupied with the bill, Bart just sort of grunted, "Yup."

Undeterred by Bart's lack of enthusiasm, the restaurant owner turned his attention to Gina. "Say, when's your birthday?"

When Gina informed him it was the following month, the sly old fox replied, "Hey, come back on your birthday, the meals and drinks are on me."

That got Bart's attention; he jumped on the offer. "Thanks Sal, we just might do that!"

Sal Alito extended a handshake to Bart. "If you decide to honor us on such an important event, give me a call so I can save a good table for you."

Bart firmly clasped his host's outstretched hand. "OK, Mr. Alito, you can expect a call a few days beforehand."

Bart called Alito's about a week before Gina's birthday and asked for Sal. The restaurant owner seemed genuinely pleased when Bart accepted his invitation to celebrate his wife's thirty-first birthday at Alito's. Before they hung up, Sal Alito promised Bart he would make sure Gina's birthday dinner was unforgettable.

When the couple arrived for Gina's birthday dinner, the hostess asked them to wait while she went to get Mr. Alito. Sal was on the other side of the dining room; but when he was told the LaRoccas had arrived, he hustled to the front entrance. He greeted the couple enthusiastically, kissing Gina on the cheek and hugging Bart. Not accustomed to such an emotional and personal greeting Bart slightly pulled away, whereupon Sal whispered, "Relax, *paisan*, we're family and that's the way Italian families greet each other."

Their host led them to the back of the dining room to the entrance of a private room. He opened the door and quickly ushered them in to a room decorated with ribbons, balloons, and a hanging banner declaring, "Happy Birthday, Gina." To their astonishment, waiting for the couple to arrive was a room full of people, not just the few friends they had made during their short time in the city, but Gina's parents, John and Patty Jo, Al, the Patrones, and even their son, all gleefully bellowing, "SURPRISE!"

It was an unforgettable evening for Gina, having her entire family to celebrate her birthday. For Bart, it was an epiphany. First, he realized Sal Alito had expertly orchestrated the evening and his assertion that "we're family" was not a metaphor. In order for Sal to be able to arrange a visit by one of the most powerful mobsters from New York, it meant he himself was a significant player. Secondly, there was a comment by Al that made Bart realize something he thought had been an isolated incident was actually a calculated attempt to draw him into the fold. Al's words were "You've got a good gig here, LaRocca, but you're not smart enough to take advantage of it."

Later, reflecting on Al's poignant words, Bart concluded his brother-in-law was referring to a proposal made to him by the controller of AWI. In less than two months Eco-cycle would become responsible for the city's garbage disposal. It would be an additional eighteen months before the plant would begin recycling. During that time Bart was to be in control of over 1,000 tons a day in need of disposal. The landfill contracts with AWI and Brown & Sons gave IPC substantial leeway in deciding how much each company would receive. IPC's contract with AWI guaranteed they would receive a minimum of 51 percent of the landfill volume while Brown & Sons' contract guaranteed them only 10 percent. That left 39 percent, worth over $150,000 in landfill fees, to IPC's discretion, and Bart was the day-to-day decision maker.

Several weeks before Gina's birthday party, AWI's controller offered Bart $10,000 to make sure AWI received 90 percent of the refuse going to landfill. Since that was within the terms of both landfill contracts, it would have been easy for Bart to accept the offer. But he flatly turned it down. A week later AWI's general manager invited Bart out to lunch and asked him, "How much would it take to get you to direct 90 percent to us?" Insulted by the thought they believed he could be bought, Bart left the restaurant before the lunch was served.

The week following the birthday dinner, Bart was again approached by AWI's general manager, who inquired, "How much?" More determined than ever not to be sucked into what he considered a death spiral, Bart angrily turned him down. That was the last time anyone from AWI approached him, but it was not the last he heard on the subject.

A month later the vice president and general manager of IPC's Resource Recovery Sector stopped by Bart's temporary office trailer. Up to that point the executive, when he was in town, had hardly said hello to Bart, preferring to spend his time with the prime contractor on the construction project. But this day he invited Bart to lunch, just the two of them. Over lunch the vice president told Bart he wanted him to direct a minimum of 90 percent of the refuse to AWI. When Bart argued it was in IPC's best interest to make sure Brown & Sons had enough volume to stay in business and remain independent from AWI, the executive's response was "Fuck Ferris Brown; let him and his sons scrounge up enough commercial waste to stay independent."

Figuring AWI had found a new partner, Bart's ornery streak kicked in. He slowly ramped up AWI's percentage but never let it get over 70 percent. Funny thing was nobody ever pushed him to up it the last 20 percent.

Starting up the new operation required hiring approximately thirty employees, twenty-five hourly workers for the plant and five administrative people for the truck scales and office. Bart was given sole authority to hire the administrative staff. His only directive from the corporate vice president of employee relations was "Make sure they are all lookers. We may be in the garbage business but we want that unpleasantness forgotten when people walk into our admin building." That's exactly what Bart did; in fact, he did such a good job the Milwaukee DPW dubbed the staff "LaRocca's harem."

The first time Gina stopped by the office after the new staff was in place, she was taken aback. She had no idea her husband spent his days among such beauties. While questioning him about them, she learned there wasn't a happily married one among the group. She also sensed they seemed uncomfortable when introduced to her. Whether founded or not, she reached the conclusion they all had secret designs on her husband. After that day, she never quite felt comfortable when Bart called to say he would be working late.

CHAPTER 38

During their two years in Milwaukee, three important events took place. First, Bart's reputation as a sound financial manager was solidified. Second, shortly after the birthday celebration, Pietro Nicosia was indicted by New York state authorities on extortion charges. The indictment weighed heavily on Gina; not being close enough to provide support to her parents left her with a sense of guilt for abandoning them at a critical time. Her guilt translated into a tension between her and Bart. More and more, the couple found themselves bickering over meaningless issues; and Gina discovered she could escape by having a few drinks with her friends. Lastly, their years in Milwaukee validated Bart's concerns about Gina's family connections, culminating with an event that caused Bart to request a hasty transfer out of Milwaukee. This incident also renewed Al's open hostility toward his brother-in-law.

The event occurred a few weeks before the resource recovery plant's grand opening. The grand opening was a big deal for IPC, the city of Milwaukee, and especially the staff of the new facility. The ribbon-cutting ceremony was to be attended by the mayor, the chairman and president of IPC, and numerous other dignitaries. But even before the opening ceremonies, Bart needed to prepare for an event he believed was critical to his career. He was given the opportunity to make a presentation and give a tour to IPC's operating committee. This group of senior executives met monthly to review the company's financial results and to discuss and decide on most of the important strategic issues.

The operating committee's schedule called for them to arrive at Eco-cycle's administration building for a lunch Bart arranged to have catered. Lunch was to be followed with a short presentation by Eco-cycle's director of operations and Bart; finally, the committee members would be escorted on a tour of the plant. As a surprise for the committee, the Eco-cycle management team decided to actually run several tons of garbage through the process during the committee's tour. The week prior to the meeting was an exciting and tense time for the staff. The plant manager and all the engineers were performing final shakedowns on the equipment; Bart was finalizing the detailed schedule and arranging the logistics.

On the Thursday prior to the tour, while Bart was rechecking all the details for the umpteenth time, he received a call from Bob, the local controller of American Waste Industries. In his usual monotone voice Bob started by asking the same question he had been asking for the last few months: "How quickly do you think the volume going to landfill will drop off?"

Bart responded, as he had every other time Bob had asked

the question, "Hell, I don't know yet; why don't we wait until we run some real volume through the plant before we start making those kinds of projections?"

Since Bob already knew Bart's answer, he was ready with the real reason he called. "Say, we've got some guys from AWI's Chicago office coming to town next week. Can you get them a tour of the facility?"

"Sure," replied Bart, "any day but Monday."

"Oh, that's a problem," replied Bob. "They're only going to be in town on Monday."

"You're right, that's a problem. I have IPC's operating committee here sometime in the late morning and the plant will be off-limits until they are gone."

Annoyed, Bob mumbled something Bart couldn't understand; then he hung up. Bart didn't give it another thought until Bob's boss, AWI's Milwaukee-area general manager, called a half hour later. The GM was more aggressive, almost demanding the tour; Bart held his ground. Again, when he hung up, Bart thought it was a dead issue until he received the third call.

This time it was Sal Alito. "Hey Bart, what's this I hear you won't give some of *our friends* a tour?"

"Not true," replied Bart, and he went through the whole scenario for Sal.

When Bart was done, Sal scoffed, "Come on, you can work 'em in as a favor to me. After all they're our friends and you don't want to snub your nose at them again."

Astonished by the implications of Sal's words, he could feel the anger well up inside him. Bart, raising his voice, was unable to hide his antagonism. "Look, Mr. Alito, like I told the guys from AWI, I'll give them a tour any other day, any time of day, but just not Monday. And I still resent their assumption that I could be bought. End of discussion." Livid, Bart slammed down the receiver. A few seconds later, Bart LaRocca realized rebuking and hanging up on a man like Salvatore Alito was probably not the smartest thing to do.

When he got home that night, the probability turned to certainty. Gina, almost imperceptibly slurring her words, greeted him with "What did you do now to piss off my brother Al? He said you better call him as soon as you got in."

"Screw him," Bart muttered, heading straight to the refrigerator for a beer. He was right in the middle of choking down his dinner while trying to explain to Gina why he was so pissed when the phone rang.

It was Al and he was irate. "What the fuck were you thinking? Just because you got away with rejecting our friends once doesn't mean you can disrespect a man like Sal Alito. He's going to have your ass if you don't crawl on your knees and beg his forgiveness. Then if he doesn't cut your balls off, you better figure out how to give our friends from Chicago a tour."

Bart was not in the mood to mince his words. Just before he slammed down the phone, Bart LaRocca maliciously told his brother-in-law, "Fuck you." Returning to the table, he sarcastically said to Gina, "Not a bad day, I got to hang up on two mafiosi and it's not even 7:00 p.m."

Following a sleepless night, first thing the next morning Bart was in the plant manager's office explaining the whole story, including Gina's family background. When he was done with the story, his boss was clearly agitated and definitively told him, "I don't have time for this now, LaRocca. I've got the biggest dog and pony show of my career on Monday, and I need to make sure the horses don't shit all over the paying customers. You just make sure your goombahs don't get in the way."

Paranoid, Bart did two things before he drove home that evening. First, he walked out to the plant and located the plant engineer. He found him performing a shakedown run on one of the air cyclones. Bart pulled him aside and said, "Look, Jim, you may have already thought of this, but if you haven't, I would suggest you have your guys check through the two truckloads of trash that are coming in on Monday morning for the demo. We wouldn't want something dangerous or ugly to show up on the conveyor belt while the big boys are here."

Jim smiled at Bart and said, "OK, what's up, old buddy?"

"It wouldn't be out of the question for a propane tank or a dead body to wind up in a garbage truck."

"Good thinking; I'll have my guys sort through the piles before they hit the conveyor belt. I'll also station a guy on either side of the belt just before it dumps the stuff into the shredder. You look stressed, buddy; is there something specific you're worried about?"

Bart frowned thoughtfully. "I don't know. I just don't want something to sabotage our big show."

The second thing Bart did before he drove home was to check the engine and the underside of the car before starting it up.

This time, when he walked in the door, Gina was smiling. "I know you told me my father has enough of his own troubles and not to bother him with this, but I called him anyway. I didn't even have to tell him why I was calling, he knew. Before I could say anything he told me we should be careful with our telephone conversation because the government was probably listening. He went on to say he was aware of your present situation. He said you need to learn a little more diplomacy when dealing with certain people, but he understood your dilemma. He assured me the situation has been defused and we should have a nice weekend. So there, in spite of what you think about my family, Daddy is still a good guy who is on your side."

Not wanting to get into any further discussion on the subject, Bart assured her, "You're right, honey, your father has always been great to me. Thanks for taking care of this for me." Then he went to the refrigerator for a beer.

On Monday everything went right on script. The operating committee was blown away by the demonstration as over ten tons of trash was processed during their tour. As they watched from the control room, six tons of combustibles, two tons of ferrous metal, a half ton of aluminum, and one ton of glass, sand, and other various granulates were successfully recovered from the garbage stream. It was an impressive demonstration. No one, except Bart, noticed the propane cylinder being removed from the conveyor belt just before it was to fall into the shredder.

During the tour and demonstration, Bart made sure he was paired with the senior vice president of finance, Bud Huffman. The VP of finance had made it a tradition to meet all newly promoted controllers, so he and Bart had met several years earlier. To Bart's surprise, Bud remembered their meeting. In fact, he had followed Bart's short career. After the demonstration, while walking back to the admin building, Bart worked up the balls to ask Bud if he could talk to him in private. In Bart's office, with the door closed, Bart bared his soul to the man who would either be the savior or assassin of his career.

Halfway into explaining his dilemma, Bart could tell the VP was fully engaged in the situation. His facial expression went from passive to concerned, but he did not interrupt Bart's story. Finally, when Bart was done and after several moments of what must have been serious contemplation, Bud Huffman stood up and offered Bart his hand to shake. Bart, thinking he was going to get an "adios, amigo" handshake, reluctantly complied. To Bart's surprise, the senior vice president of a major corporation said to the mere plant controller, "Young man, telling me this took more balls and integrity than I've seen in a long time. As long as I'm around IPC, your future is assured. Although right now, like your father-in-law, I'm not impressed with your diplomatic skills. All that being said, it's obvious IPC shouldn't leave you exposed to any further situations where your wife's family connections could put you and the company at risk. Why don't you let me use your office to make a few phone calls; I'm sure we can find a position in another division where your skills are needed."

By Thursday Bart was on a plane headed to an interview at a folding carton manufacturing plant in Charlotte, North Carolina. Bart started his new plant controller's job in Charlotte the following Monday. Gina took Peter back to New York for the summer and Bart began scouting for houses the first week on the job. Gina made her first visit to Charlotte near the end of July after Bart had whittled down the choices to just a handful.

Not only was Gina unhappy about leaving her friends and

activities in Milwaukee, she was initially dejected about moving to the South. First, if she had to move, she wanted it to be closer to her parents to provide emotional support during her father's trial. Secondarily, as a lifelong northerner, she had many preconceived notions about the South and southerners. Sure, she had liked the beaches, but the ocean was almost two hundred miles away from Charlotte. Although the population had more than doubled in the previous twenty years, in the late 1970s Charlotte was a fairly small city of less than 300,000. It still retained a lot of its rural southern flavor without the character and charm of either Charleston or Savannah. It did have a few really nice new neighborhoods that offered lots of house for the money, but the shopping was still limited and the selections were narrow. She was particularly unhappy with the availability of ethnic food choices at the supermarkets and restaurants. There didn't appear to be a good pizza or bagel place within a couple of hundred miles. She hated Carolina barbecue, pulled pork, grits, collard greens, Dr. Pepper, and country music. It seemed as if the radio stations were laden with preachers telling their listeners they were damned to hell if they didn't become born again. Worst of all was the combination of oppressive heat and humidity in the summer. It could get hot and humid in New York while Baltimore was stifling; but during Gina's first house-hunting visit, Charlotte's weather was brutal. Though the temperature hovered in the mid-90s, the humidity made it feel like 100 degrees. After long exhausting days slogging in and out of used houses and model homes, they would have both loved a cool dip in the motel's pool, but even that was disappointing. The water temperature was 84 degrees and Gina described her first plunge as "like swimming in everybody else's bath water."

By the middle of their second week of house-hunting, Gina told Bart in an annoyed voice, "There are lots of nice neighborhoods and houses. You pick one out, but don't expect me to like it here." The next day she flew back to New York. She and Peter didn't return until the closing of their new house at the end of

September. Bart bought a new home in the town of Mint Hill, about fifteen miles from downtown Charlotte. The house backed up to a private country club with an eighteen-hole golf course, tennis courts, and an Olympic-size swimming pool.

CHAPTER 39

February 11, 2010

I had only been in Seville for four days without Marie, but I missed her immensely. It wasn't the same spending the whole day listening to Bart relive his and Gina's lives and not being able to retell it over cocktails and dinner to my attentive partner. Bart's mood began changing as we got deeper into the Milwaukee saga. Early on, Bart took immense pleasure in reliving their romance. However, now as he described the events in Milwaukee and Gina's dissatisfaction with their move to Charlotte; it appeared to me it was getting excruciatingly painful for Bart. On several occasions I saw his eyes well up with tears, and he could hardly force the words out of his larynx. Bart's sour mood was beginning to affect me; my only escape from his sullenness and my loneliness was an occasional dinner with David and Sarah. In spite, or perhaps as a result, of their incredible wealth, they were a private and unpretentious couple. However, after a few cocktails, I could occasionally prod them into telling me about their fascinating lives. Over the course of these discussions, David also revealed an incident or provided an insight that would add to my understanding of Bart and his relationship with Gina. Several of his stories began to shed some light on how and when Bart and Gina's marriage began to visibly deteriorate.

■ ■ ■

On several occasions David had invited Bart and Gina to spend time with him and his fiancée in Palm Beach. David couldn't wait to introduce his new love to Bart and to show Sarah his perception of his ideal couple. Each time, Bart gave him some lame excuse as to why they couldn't make it. Finally, David called Bart announcing he and Sarah would be in Charlotte on business. David was working a deal to develop a golf resort on Charlotte's south side. If things still looked promising on Friday, he planned on staying the weekend so they could meet with potential financing partners on Monday.

The two couples met for dinner on Friday evening at an Italian restaurant. David was surprised Gina had not insisted they come over to their house for one of her famous Italian dinners. Every other time David had visited the couple; no matter where they lived, Gina refused to let him take them out to dinner. It seemed to be a matter of her Italian pride that declared, "You can't buy a better meal than I can make for you," and to his recollection she was always right. Yet this time, when meeting their long-time friend's future wife, Gina never offered to make them dinner.

Their weekend together was pleasant but not exceptional. Bart seemed genuinely pleased to see his old roommate and to meet Sarah, but Gina seemed uncharacteristically preoccupied. Bart, not Gina, invited the couple over to the house for a barbecue on Sunday afternoon. In her own environment Gina seemed more at ease. However, David suspected she was half-sloshed when he and Sarah arrived. In fact, she continued to put down gin and tonics most of the afternoon.

Driving back to their hotel, Sarah could sense David's uneasiness. Hoping she had found the right words, she warily said, "You seem a little pensive." Not getting an immediate reply, she continued, "You obviously came away with the same sense as I did. This is not the same 'ideal marriage' you always described to me."

David had been struggling with the same issue for the last several hours. "Well, at one time I believed it was. Either I was wrong or something has happened to cause a strain on their relationship. That makes me really sad. I love both of them like my brother and sister; I wish I could do something to change whatever is tearing them apart."

After a few minutes, Sarah asked, "Did Bart give you a clue as to their problem?"

Reflecting on their talks, David responded, "The only thing he told me was Gina hated Charlotte and wanted to get back up north."

"Yeah, after she asked me how I liked the South she didn't mince any words when she told me how much she hated it here."

The couples did not see each other again until the week of David and Sarah's wedding. In the interim, David learned about Gina's father's legal problems. According to news reports, state charges against Pietro (aka Pete) Nicosia and two other Mafia kingpins had been dropped; but promptly after leaving the court-house, they were re-arrested on federal racketeering charges. David reached the conclusion Gina's family issues were behind the strain in his friends' marriage.

During the wedding reception at the Tanners' Palm Beach mansion, it was again apparent Gina had developed a penchant for booze. Less than an hour and a half into the affair, Bart suddenly disappeared with his wife and returned a half hour later alone. David, concerned, asked Bart if Gina had gotten ill. Bart's caustic response was "Yeah, she must have gotten into a bad batch of vodka." The next day while flying to their honeymoon in Barbados, David reflected on Bart's words and was deeply troubled by his friends' state of affairs. Thirty years later and cognizant of all that had transpired in the intervening years, David Tanner described the situation as "a loose stitch on a knit sweater being snagged by life's obstacles until so much was unraveled it was easier to throw it out than to try to mend it."

■ ■ ■

One night over dinner we were having an interesting discussion concerning the effect Gina's family connections had on their marriage. I asked David if he knew the reason behind Bart's hasty departure from Milwaukee. "Oh yeah," and then asked, "Did Bart ever tell you the follow-up to that incident?"

"No," I said curiously, "there's a follow-up?'

"Yup, and it's a beauty!"

"Tell me about it," I anxiously begged.

"About a year after Bart transferred out of Eco-cycle, he got a call from his corporate savior, Bud Huffman. Bud started out by saying, 'LaRocca, I hope you didn't leave us with a problem in Milwaukee.'

"Thinking he was referring to a financial issue, Bart answered without hesitation, 'The books were clean when I left. Heck, we just had an internal audit of the construction accounts two months before I left and you know there is virtually no inventory to screw up.'

"'I'm not talking about the books, it's the women!'

"Stunned, Bart thought about it for a moment. 'Why don't you just come out and tell me what the problem is?'

"Bud proceeded to detail a civil lawsuit filed by one of the female accounting clerks Bart had hired by the name of Janet Haliburton. Although the suit did not name Bart as an offending party, in Janet's deposition she claimed she and Bart had a consensual affair. Hearing rumors of the affair, Bart's replacement, Doug Clinton, tried to pressure Janet into sleeping with him. When Janet refused, Doug built a case to fire her. Thereupon, Janet got herself an attorney and sued for sexual harassment and unjustified termination.

"When Bud Huffman finished filling Bart in on the situation, Bart adamantly told the senior VP, 'Although Janet and I got along real well, we never even went to lunch or dinner alone. I was very careful that another employee, customer, or vendor always joined us. I never proposed or inferred I wanted to have sex with her and she never tried to seduce me. In short, the two of us having an affair, consenting or not, is a lie.'

"'So what's her motivation? She's not accusing you of sexual harassment. Why even bring up your name in this thing?'

"'I have no idea. Who is her attorney?'

"Scanning through the folder on his desk, Bud replied, 'Uh, yeah, here it is . . . Attorney Bruce Cutter.'

"Bart exploded, 'Son of a bitch! I know that shyster. He's Sal

Alito's mouthpiece. I met him several times; Sal introduced me to him and told me if I ever needed a good lawyer, Bruce was the guy. He even went as far as to tell me he used him for all his sensitive cases. The funny thing is Sal knows I know Bruce is his guy. I'm willing to bet my left nut Sal is providing the legal representation to Janet and somehow convinced Janet to drop that little tidbit into her deposition. In fact, now that I think about it, Sal was one of Janet's references on her application. If I recall correctly, he told me Janet and his daughter, Regina, went to high school together.'

"After a brief pause, Bart added, 'This must be Sal's way of getting even for my disrespect of him. Maybe Janet's accusations against Doug are true, but throwing in an affair with me is Sal's payment for providing free legal council to her. His real objective is, at a minimum, to embarrass me; but more probably, to hurt my career and perhaps my marriage. Look, can you send me a copy of Janet's deposition?'

"'Sure; I'll FedEx it tonight,' Bud responded. 'If it makes any difference, I believe you, and you don't have to worry about this being damaging as long as there continues to be no compensation claimed for the alleged affair with you.'

"'Fair enough, but I still would like to figure out how to refute her claim that we had an affair.'

"The next morning Bart received the deposition. In reading it he noticed there was four specific dates and times Janet claimed she had consensual sex with him. Now Janet was the hottest of the office staff, divorced with a six-year-old daughter. She was five feet four inches of perfectly proportioned womanhood. Her strawberry blonde hair did a nice job of framing a face reminiscent of some movie starlet whose name you forgot. If Bart was going to have an affair with anyone he worked with, Janet was first on his list. But he was too scared, knowing if he started up with this beauty, he probably couldn't stop. Running each of the dates through his memory, he tried to put them into perspective. What had been going on at work, at home and in the world on those days? One date, November 13, kept bouncing around like a racquetball in his memory, but he just couldn't quite catch up with it, so he went back to his budget preparation.

"Just before lunch, while he and the general manager were reviewing next year's sales projections, it hit him. 'Holy shit, that's it!' he exclaimed out loud. Surprised and confounded, the GM just stared at Bart with a look of amusement. Realizing he had announced his elation out loud, he smiled at his boss and said, 'Sorry, I just figured out something that might save my ass. Can we break for lunch? I have to make a few calls.'

"'Fine,' replied the GM. 'Let's get back together at two.'

"Checking his watch, he made a beeline for his office. He wanted to catch the general ledger clerk at Eco-cycle before she went to lunch.

"When Diane Orback answered the phone, she was delighted to hear Bart on the other end. Diane was an innocent twenty-two-year-old junior college accounting graduate and this was her first job. 'Boy, it's good to hear your voice, Mr. LaRocca. You have no idea what a zoo this place has been since you left.'

"'I heard,' Bart replied. 'How are you taking this whole thing?'

"'You mean Janet getting fired then claiming it was because she rejected Mr. Clinton's advances? You know we haven't seen Mr. Clinton at the office in a couple of weeks,' Diane offered.

"'Really, you've heard all about this then?' Bart half asked and half stated.

"'Oh, yeah, I had to give a deposition. You know, I sort of witnessed him harassing her. He didn't know I was still in the office, but I had to come back for my car keys and heard him tell her she drove him crazy and he just had to . . . you know . . . have her; but he didn't use those words, he used the f-word.'

"Bart prodded her. 'Did you ever talk to her about it?'

"'Not until after she was fired and sued. I ran into her when a date took me to Alito's. She was working as the hostess. Even though there was a waiting list, she got us a table right away. We didn't talk much, but she did say Mr. Clinton was harassing her; when she wouldn't do it with him, he fired her. I told her what I had overheard and promised to tell somebody. That's how I got to give my deposition; I called the corporate confidential hotline and told them what I heard.'

"'Good for you, Diane . . . How did Janet seem?'

"'She seemed OK. She told me she was making a lot of money under the table. She said if I talk to you to tell you to check the dates carefully. Do you know what she was talking about?'

"'I think so, Diane, that's why I called. Can you do a favor for me and look up these dates in my expense report file?'

"'Sure, Mr. LaRocca, anything for you.'

"Bart gave her the four dates and told her if she found expense reports with corresponding dates to make copies of everything, including the receipts, and FedEx them to him.

"The next morning he received a package with the expense reports for the weeks that included the dates Janet claimed she and Bart had sex. Just as Bart had suspected, on November 13, 1976, he had taken the director of sanitation for the city of Milwaukee out to dinner at Mader's. He thought he recalled, on that afternoon, he and the director were reviewing the tonnage projections for the following year in the city's offices. The time stamp on the cash register receipt was 9:47 p.m. Janet's declaration claimed they were together from 6:00 to 9:30 p.m. Further scrutiny revealed all three of the other dates could also be challenged by receipts with date and time stamps contradicting her claims of rendezvous with her boss.

"Bart LaRocca finally was sure he knew what had happened. While Janet's claim that Doug Clinton had used his position to sexually harass her was probably valid, she was not willingly claiming she had an affair with Bart; somebody else was pulling the strings. If she really was trying to hurt her former boss, she would not have picked dates she knew could refute her claims. On top of that, she would not have given Diane the clue to unravel the allegation. Now that he had evidence Sal Alito was behind the allegations, what was he going to do about it? Janet Haliburton had walked down a dangerous path. She had let the mob believe she had done what they asked, and she had probably taken money and favors for the deed. If Sal found out all the dates could be refuted, he would know Janet had conned him into thinking she did his bidding. Bart decided to send copies to Bud Huffman with a note requesting that he not use the information unless it made a difference in the company's liability. That was the last Bart heard about the incident from the company; he never told anyone else about either the allegations or his vindication, not even Gina. Months later, out of curiosity, he checked on Janet and found that she was still working for Sal."

CHAPTER 40

Having heard David's revelation on Sarah's and his experiences with Bart and Gina's relationship following their move to Charlotte, I anxiously anticipated Bart providing me with some of his insight. I also was aware he and Peter started drifting apart at some point. On several occasions over the last few weeks I thought the topic was going to naturally present itself, but every time he appeared to be on the brink of unburdening himself, he pulled back. When it became apparent to me he was avoiding these obviously painful experiences I decided to come right out and confront him. Picking the right moment, I cautiously said, "I get the impression that the move to Charlotte turned out to be a problem for the three of you. Am I right?"

It took Bart a few seconds to decide whether he was ready to unburden himself. Grimacing, he replied, "In retrospect, Gina and I could have dealt with that situation much better. It probably all started the summer she and Peter spent in New York waiting for the house to be ready. Perhaps I could have been more insistent that she stay in Charlotte; but then again, I'm not sure she would have listened to me. She was worried about her father's legal issues and she hated North Carolina. I on the other hand didn't want to acknowledge that my father-in-law was being prosecuted. I threw myself into my work and to make matters worse, I started classes at UNCC for my master's degree.

Poor Peter, at ten years old, was pretty much left on his own. Gina and I started bickering, at first over stupid stuff like me working to much or she'd make some comment about 'this redneck hick town.' But it quickly escalated to me complaining about her drinking or whether or not she should go to New York to be at her father's trial. She would generally retaliate by saying something about my being self-absorbed in my career and ungrateful for all her parents did for us. Once we got on the subject of her family, things would get pretty ugly. Of course, as much as we tried to shield Peter from our verbal clashes, he knew what was going on. Peter adored his grandfather and Uncle Al. I suppose when I would get really pissed and tell Gina I didn't want our son exposed to her mobster relatives, he got really confused. Hell, I was a lot older than him when I found out about Pietro's mob connection, and I still courted his daughter. Anyway, it got to the point where Gina wouldn't even tell me she was going to drive up to New York and take Peter with her for a week or longer. Frankly, even though I didn't like the idea of Peter's exposure to all that, I was so involved in work and school I actually enjoyed the time alone.

"The one thing Peter and I always enjoyed doing together was playing catch in the backyard or tossing the football around in the street. Even that changed while we were in Charlotte. All his friends were playing soccer but spring soccer conflicted with baseball, so Peter quit baseball and joined a soccer team. Peter was a natural at the sport. He was fast and agile. It didn't take him long to master the dribbling and kicking. I didn't know jack about soccer, so after the first couple of times he tried to kick the ball around with me, he gave up.

"I'm sure that's when I really started losing Peter and gave Al the opportunity to creep into his life again. He already had a strong bond with his uncle from the year I was in 'Nam. Even after I came home and we moved all over the place, Al never missed sending him fantastic presents for his birthdays and Christmas. In fact, he generally made our present pale in comparison.

"During one of their trips to New York, Al took Peter to his gun club out on the Island. I knew nothing about this venture until that fall when Peter asked me if I would get him a .22 rifle for Christmas. When I told him I didn't want any guns in the house, he said, 'Uncle Al warned me you would say that. Uncle Al says real men own guns, that you're a wuss, that's why you joined the Air Force.'

"I was livid, not just at Al but at Gina for letting Al take our son shooting. We had a big argument that got pretty ugly. Peter couldn't help but hear our tirades. We lashed out at each other; as usual, I said some things about her family and her drinking that I probably shouldn't have. She lambasted me for not taking more of an interest in my son. It was probably at that point Peter decided he had to choose sides, and he chose the Nicosias.

"It was shortly after that incident when we started to get reports from Peter's school —his grades were slipping and he had gotten into a couple of fights. The private school Peter was attending had little tolerance for persistent troublemakers or students who didn't appear to try. Fortunately, Peter still had a fear of incurring the disappointment and wrath of his parents. It only took one meeting between the vice principal, Peter, and Gina and me to jolt him back into line. Unfortunately, it wouldn't be too many more years before he didn't seem to care anymore about parental authority.

"By the time Peter reached his teenage years, he and I had few interests in common. We pretty much went our separate ways."

I listened to Bart ramble on about his relationship (or lack of) with his son for over two more hours. When he seemed to have exhausted most of his frustrations I surprised him with "So, what should you have done differently?"

He gaped at me for a few seconds. I could feel his aggravation building. Finally he burst out, "Hell, Chuck, don't you think I've asked myself that question thousands of time over the last forty years? Frankly, there's only one answer, I fucked up. I was the adult; I should have seen the whole thing evolving. I should have found more time to spend with both of them."

"Did you ever have a talk with Peter and tell him what kind of a man his Uncle Al was?"

"I tried, not then, he was too young to understand; but later when he was about fifteen. You know what he said to me?" Without waiting for my response, he continued, "Peter said to me, with ice dripping from his words, 'You've never liked Uncle Al, and as far as I know, he's never been convicted of any of the stuff you mentioned. I learned in school that you're innocent until proven guilty.'

"You let him get away with that?"

"No, but at that point his mind was made up and nothing I could say would change it."

CHAPTER 41

It was not quite two years after they arrived in Charlotte when Gina gave her husband an ultimatum: he should find a job closer to New York. She needed to visit her mother more frequently while her father served out his four-year sentence on a federal racketeering conviction.

Thinking maybe this could be the channel to relieve whatever had come between the two of them and perhaps even result a reduction of her drinking, Bart aggressively politicked for a position at IPC's corporate headquarters in Connecticut. Bart being one of IPC's most highly regarded plant controllers, the company was more than willing to accommodate Bart's overtures and bring to their corporate environment an experienced hands-on operations accountant.

Except for the increased cost of housing and Bart trading his ten-minute commute to work for a forty-five-minute commute, the entire family seemed happy with the move. Bart discovered his operations expertise was highly regarded at corporate. Gina was able to regularly visit her mother and periodically take her mother to visit Pietro at the medium-security facility in Otisville,

New York. Initially, even Peter seemed happy, although that turned out to be short-lived. Peter developed the kind of antagonistic attitude toward authority that does not go over well with school officials. Although his grades remained exceptional, he was constantly challenging authority and alienating his junior high schoolteachers. His soccer coach benched him, even though he was one of the better players on the team; Bart and Gina were summoned to the school on several occasions. Rather than serve as positive lessons, these incidents reinforced his resentment toward authority.

The first time Peter told his father he hated him and wished he was dead, Bart laughed. He sarcastically replied that if he expressed those feelings to his uncle, Al could possibly make his wish come true.

On one occasion when Peter called and "told" his father he was staying at a friend's house overnight, Bart reacted in what Gina termed as "predictably irate." His response to being told by his fifteen-year-old child that *HE* had decided to stay overnight was swift and firm: "Young man, you don't tell your parents what you are going to do, you ask permission to do it." Displaying the one thing he did have in common with his father, Peter's comeback was swift and lethal — "Go fuck yourself, old man" — and he immediately hung up.

Outraged by his son's defiant expletive, Bart slammed down the phone and headed for the front door.

As he was dashing out the door, Gina nervously shouted after him, "What did he say?"

Over his shoulder Bart angrily yelled, "That little shit told me to eff myself. He's not going to get away with that!"

Fearful for her son, Gina pleaded, "Don't hurt him, he's only a kid!"

The whole neighborhood heard the tires on Bart's Chevy station wagon squeal as he stomped down on the accelerator a microsecond after aggressively shifting the automatic transmission from reverse to drive and fishtailed down Eastgate Lane.

Bart was almost rational when he pulled up in front of Billy

Lynch's house. Billy played on the soccer team with Peter. Both Bart and Gina liked his parents. In the past, the LaRoccas had no trouble allowing their son to stay over at the Lynches', or for Billy to sleep over at their house. If one of Billy's parents had called to suggest Peter stay over or if Peter himself had asked permission, the whole incident would never have happened. Not intending to offend the Lynches, Bart had decided on the ten-minute drive to calmly collect his son and return home before venting his anger and disappointment in the boy.

One can only imagine what Peter LaRocca thought his father would do after he told him to have sex with himself, but it became obvious he had not carefully thought out what the worst case scenario could be. Bart was getting out of his car in the Lynches' driveway when Peter bolted out the back door and began racing for the woods that were about fifty yards from the Lynches' house. This desperate reflex action was prompted by his mother's frantic telephone call warning him his father was heading that way and was pissed. Bart gave a halfhearted chase but had no intention of chasing a scared teenager through the dense trees and underbrush.

The first time the phone rang at 7:15 p.m. Bart answered and the caller hung up. The second time at 7:50 he answered with "Don't hang up, let's talk." The caller hung up again. The next time at 8:45, Bart told Gina to answer it. Mother and son talked for a few minutes, and she finally told him his father wasn't "violently pissed off any more." Peter, with a sheepish grin on his face, walked in the door at 9:15.

His mother ran to him and hugged him hard. Transferring her gaze between the two of them, she said, "You two should talk, but you have to promise me you won't start yelling at each other."

Bart nodded his agreement; then he and Peter cautiously walked down the stairs into their finished basement.

There was a brief moment of awkward silence. Bart originally had planned not to start the reconciliation chat until Peter apologized. When Peter just nervously sat there without saying a word, Bart decided to unleash his prepared speech. "Look," he began, "a fifteen-year-old telling his father to go fuck himself is not the best solution to a disagreement. A couple of years from now, when you have the wherewithal to support yourself, it might make more sense. In the meantime, unless you plan on running away, you are living in this house; and during that time, your mother and I would appreciate the courtesy of being consulted on matters rather than being told what you plan on doing. Is that understood?"

"Yeah" was his son's meek response.

"Do you have anything you want to say?" asked Bart.

"I have just one question."

"Shoot."

Peter fought to conceal his smirk. "Were you going to kick the crap out of me if you had caught me?"

Bart let out a hearty laugh. "Definitely when I first hung up, you were mincemeat. By the time I got over to the Lynches', I had calmed down. Unless you had done something very stupid, I wouldn't have become physical."

No longer capable of concealing his grin but with a hint of humility Peter inquired, "You sure looked pissed . . . is there anything left over from dinner?"

"Not so fast, young man; before you eat, I still need an apology and an agreement between us. You understand that your mother and I are to be consulted, not told, about what you want to do."

"Do you really need me to tell you I'm sorry? Isn't the fact I came home enough?"

"Not really; why can't you just say the words?"

"OK, if that will make you happy. I'm sorry."

"Sorry for what?"

"For not asking your approval and for cursing at you."

"There, was that so hard?"

The teenager never answered and Bart decided not to press it any further.

■ ■ ■

A year later it was his mother who had the opportunity to test her patience with their only child. By now Gina had been substitute teaching in the Danbury Public Schools. The principal of the high school had discovered Gina could walk into any classroom and any subject and hit the ground running. Returning teachers would say their classes didn't skip a beat when Gina filled in for them.

Being a typical teenager, Peter was not pleased when his mother got the call to substitute at his school. It was even worse when it was for more than a day or two. Although their paths rarely crossed in the school, she occasionally would wind up teaching one of his classes. He was always embarrassed when one of his friends asked him if Mrs. Nicosia was any relation. However, when one of the guys would say she was "hot," he would get a strange feeling of both pride and anger. On the other hand, the girls loved Mrs. Nicosia, and that had a very positive effect on Peter's social life.

Gina really loved getting back into teaching even if it wasn't in her own classroom. The random nature of the assignments still gave her the opportunity to visit her mother a few times a month and to also make the trek to Otisville to visit Pietro. She felt good about herself and cut way back on her drinking. She and Bart even resumed regular sex, something that had been a once-in-a-blue-moon occurrence since the move to Charlotte.

After several week-long assignments, Gina got to know many of the teachers; and they treated her like any other staff teacher. A few of them had Peter in their classes and would occasionally express their disappointment in her son's efforts. They claimed, and his standardized test scores verified, he had the ability to do better than his B average. This seemed to be a recurring theme. Even the soccer coach asserted Peter had the talent to be an all-state midfielder but he just didn't seem to have the drive. The thing was he liked to hang out on the fringe of the counterculture group. It wasn't that he was hardcore, but he was one of the alienated ones who pretty much rejected the values of mainstream suburbia. They liked to think they had their own value system but were not quite prepared to totally reject everything middle-class America had to offer the contemporary teenager. For example, Peter refused to wear shirts with a Polo logo or pants with a Dockers label; on the other hand he and his friends were very conscious of the model car the family drove. Bart referred to him as a "new-age hippie" who in time would rejoin the mainstream.

On one of those rare non-teaching days, while Gina was doing her regular thorough job of house cleaning, she happened to stumbled upon Peter's stash of condoms and *Penthouse* magazines. They were hidden in the box spring lining of his bed. The idea her baby was now into sex surprised and upset her so much she later claimed it was like someone kicked her in the gut. Not knowing what to do or say, she ignored Peter when he came home from school. She called Bart at work and asked him to meet her for dinner at Mangifico's Restaurant. When Bart asked what the occasion was, she only responded, "We have to talk about Peter."

When Bart arrived at Mangifico's, Gina was already halfway through a carafe of Sangiovese. By then, the wine and the realization that her boy was growing up faster than she needed had made her sullen. As usual, Bart didn't pick up on her mood until after he had declared, "Wow, this is great to have a romantic date in the middle of the week!"

Thinking he was being flippant, Gina sternly replied, "This isn't a date. We have to talk about *your* son."

Recognizing the deadly "your son" and now feeling his wife's vibes, Bart immediately changed his demeanor. "OK, tell me about it," he said in his most somber tone.

When Gina finished her emotional tale of discovering her son was no longer an innocent child, she announced in no uncertain terms, "You've got to talk to him."

"And what do you expect me to say?" asked Bart, sounding perplexed.

"Well, you need to tell him about respecting girls and the dangers of having sex."

"Look, honey, we already had the birds and bees discussion two years ago. His reaction was to tell me he already took enough biology to understand how and where babies come from. As far as respecting girls, the fact you found his condoms tells me he respects them and himself enough to wear protection. He is sixteen years old, not much younger than you and I when we first started having sex; or have you forgotten that little bit of history?"

"Yeah, but we were in love; you didn't have a bunch of nude pictures hidden under your bed, did you?"

"First off, while I may not have had my own copies of *Playboy*, I sure as hell saw almost every centerfold from about the time I was twelve until we got married. And yes, we were deeply in love when we first made love, but as long as it's consensual, does it really make a difference?"

"Considering the fact I suspect you screwed half the girls on Long Island and more than your share of coeds, I don't know why I thought you would be as concerned as I am."

Completely taken aback by his wife's accusations, Bart just sat there, flabbergasted. Considering his options, Bart knew the best course of action was to ignore the dig and change the conversation back to Peter. But, true to his nature, he just couldn't let it die. When he replied to Gina's allegation, it was in his best sarcastic and condescending intonation. "If you think I am such a Don Juan, why'd you stop your accusations with college?"

Without any hesitation at all, Gina responded matter-of-factly, "Well now that you mention it, rumor has it you were screwing Little Miss Mint Julep in Italy and were doing two or three at a time in Milwaukee."

"Where do you get this shit from, your asshole of a brother, Al?"

Ignoring his acerbic question, Gina replied, "It doesn't matter where I got it from, I just hear things."

"Yeah well, those allegations aren't true." Changing the subject before he revealed several confidences, Bart ended the discussion by telling his miffed wife, "Look, I'll talk to Peter about the stuff you stumbled across, but I am going to use the opportunity to tell him how glad I was you didn't find any drugs. It's time I had that conversation with him although I will be speaking from ignorance." Bart finished his dinner, but Gina hardly touched hers.

When Bart told Peter his mother had stumbled upon his stash while she was vacuuming, he was startled by the boy's reaction.

"Stumbled upon while vacuuming? That's a load of crap! She was snooping around my room just like she always does when I'm at school."

"I don't believe that's the case, but no matter; she knows you have it and she is upset. On the other hand I am pleased she didn't find any drugs. Is it because you don't do drugs or because you have a safer spot to hide them?"

"I don't do drugs; that stuff is for losers."

"OK then, I guess this conversation is over . . . unless there is something you want to talk about."

"Nope" was his son's response.

Unfortunately, by his own definition, Peter became a loser less than two years later.

CHAPTER 42

Shortly before Pete Nicosia was released from federal prison, he was diagnosed with terminal liver cancer. The specific diagnosis was hepatocellular carcinoma. His doctors speculated it was the long-term effect of hepatitis B contracted when he was twelve years old. Having just spent four years away from his family, Pete was not about to let doctors squirrel him away in some hospital room. In the two months he was able to still get around, he called in favors from decades of making accommodations. By the time he had become bedridden, an almost perfect replica of a small private hospital ward was fashioned out of the family dining room. The living room became a waiting room, and the front porch was the nurse's station with all the electronic gizmos and medical devices. Over his wife's objection, Pietro arranged for 24/7 nursing assistance and daily visits from his doctor. Periodically, a specialist would accompany his regular doctor.

During the five weeks the legendary mafioso languished at home, he successfully negotiated continuing control of most of the family's lucrative rackets for his son Al. It was a tribute to the old man's reputation and negotiating skill that he was able to obtain such a favorable result for his son. Even though it was common knowledge that Al was one of the best earners in the New York mob, he was far too visible for the other bosses. For the previous five years, Al Nicosia had been showing up in the society columns of New York papers. If he wasn't pictured on the arm of a famous starlet at some opening night gala, it was rumored he was the new beau of one of New York's many glamorous heiresses.

The press's fascination with Al Nicosia began after he was arrested and put on trial for bribing a Suffolk County official over a landfill contract. Since the only money that changed hands was $100,000 in cash, there was no clear electronic or paperwork trail leading back to Al. The state's only evidence was the statement of an inebriated official at a Southampton bar telling some friends how he came by a new Mercedes Benz and a condo down the street on his $30,000-a-year salary.

Interestingly, it was Al's attorney who threw the media spotlight on the handsome, smooth-talking gangster. He declared on the courthouse steps following Al's arraignment, "Either the state's witness is mistaken or has been persuaded by the prosecution to identify my client as the landfill company's employee who bribed him."

Whereupon Al Nicosia, dressed in his $700 Italian silk suit, smiled into the cameras and asked the New York citizenry, with the same charm he used to seduce dozens of young women over the years, "Do I look like a garbage man?"

Those few words and the resulting media coverage were enough to launch the public's fixation with the narcissistic gangster. When under cross-examination the county official failed to identify Al Nicosia as the person who paid him the bribe, the trial was over and New York had a new favorite mafioso.

The second reason Pete's wheeling and dealing for his son was so impressive was the other Mafia leaders all feared Alfonse. It was common knowledge among the young Turks that Al Nicosia was the most ruthless gangster since the 1950s. Legends surrounding his brutality in Vietnam and his dealings with rivals on Long Island had been surfacing for years. But, in an historic meeting with the heads of two of the five families, Alfonse Nicosia swore, on his mother's life, he would not seek to disturb the current leadership and balance of power in the New York Cosa Nostra.

■ ■ ■

Gina did not deal well with her father's illness. Every chance she got, she would make the two-hour drive to Queens. In the beginning, there were days she was so distraught Eleonora would tell her to go home or call Al and ask him to take her daughter someplace. It didn't take her brother long to find a sure-fire diversion for his sister. He would take her to Atlantic City. Not surprisingly, Al bragged he and Donald Trump were acquaintances. As far as Gina was concerned, her brother's relationship with The Donald, not how much she lost, got her exclusive treatment at Trump Plaza. Similar to her brother's fascination with media attention, Gina's addiction to gambling happened like a bolt of lightning. One day she had never bet on anything, the next day you couldn't pry her away from the slot machines with a crowbar. After their first trip to Trump Plaza, Al wasn't sure whether Gina drove down to the Middle Village to visit her father or to get him to take her to Atlantic City. Al always gave her a couple of C-notes to blow.

Shortly after he found out about his father's condition, John flew back from Arizona to confer with his father's doctors and to help with the plans for the infirmary. Before returning home, he told his father he would be back in a few weeks. Pietro, however, told him to stay in Phoenix and save as many of his patient's lives as he could. Pietro then said, "I'll send for you when I need you again." On the way to LaGuardia Airport, John silently wept.

Three months later, Dr. John Nicosia received the call he had been dreading since his return from New York. His brother Al caught him just before he was scheduled to perform an angioplasty. Al's only words were "Dad asked me to tell you he needs you now." Knowing his mind could easily be distracted by his father's impending fate, Dr. Nicosia switched roles with his assisting physician. After the successful opening and stenting of the artery, John called Patty Jo to tell her to begin packing for the fateful trip back east.

Al, Gina, Bart, and Peter were already there when John and Patty Jo arrived. Their father had been transitioning in and out of consciousness; but when he heard John's voice, it was like someone had given him a shot of adrenalin. He smiled at each of them and said, "Thank you for all the years of joy you have given me. Please don't mourn over me. I have been extremely fortunate and have lived happily much longer than I deserve. I've already spoken to your mother, and she understands this is the end. Within the next day or two I will die. Please do nothing to revive me or keep me hanging on. It is time for me to go; I have made peace with myself and with God. Now, please go to the kitchen and come back with a plate of pasta so that we can have our last supper together."

■ ■ ■

Mafia wakes and funerals are spectacles, especially if the deceased was a boss. When the departed is one of the best-liked and most-respected bosses in decades, it's like a state funeral. Lines began forming a half hour before the viewing was to commence and, instead of thinning out, they became longer as the evening progressed. Although Pietro Nicosia's open casket revealed his cancer had consumed over fifty pounds of his once-powerful body, his gaunt facial features were clearly recognizable. The general mood in the large room where his body was laid out was somber and respectful, almost as if the mourners were afraid of offending him. That mood sort of moved like an uneasy breeze down the line of mourners standing in the foyer and out through the main entrance into the parking lot. At 8:30 p.m. on the first night of his showing, several hundred mourners still waited to pay their respects.

You can tell how important a Mafia kingpin was by two bellwethers; first, by the number and size of the flower arrangements at the funeral parlor, and second, by the number of black Cadillacs and Lincolns in the funeral procession. At Pietro's wake the owner of the parlor had to set aside an overflow room to display all the flower arrangements. Not counting the hearse and the two cars for family, the funeral procession had twenty-five black Cadillacs and Lincolns.

Bart was astounded by the hierarchical dynamics first at the wake and then two days later at the cemetery. During the wake, the focus of attention was on Pietro and Eleonora; but immediately following the lowering of the casket, the focus became Alfonse. There was a very clear changing of the guard that day, and that change was readily apparent on Alfonse Nicosia's face. Watching his brother-in-law as the who's who of La Cosa Nostra filed by, first grasping the hand of the departed don's widow then kissing the new don on the cheek, Bart could not help picture a neon sign on Al's forehead flashing "I'm the Boss."

CHAPTER 43

February 13, 2010

It was the end of another week in Seville, and while going over some earlier notes, I had come across what I thought was an important loose end. First thing on Saturday morning I broached the issue. "You once relayed a story to me from Al's bachelor party, yet we've never talked about his marriage or any of the movie stars or heiresses he dated. The only thing you've told me about was the Captain Rice incident."

"Oh . . . yeah," replied Bart, "I forgot about Little Nicky's marriages. About a year after I got back from 'Nam and Al was maybe twenty-seven or twenty-eight years old, he met a college junior from the horse country of Virginia who was attending C.W. Post College in Brookville. Even at that age, Al was still a regular at all the college parties. That was the height of the drug craze on campuses and Al was the Willy Wonka of pot and smack on Long Island. Anyway, this naïve kid, Dede Wilson, was a recreational pot smoker. Dede was really a good-looking girl and the type Al liked to show off to his wiseguy buddies. He would showcase her at the Copa or some other nightclub on Saturday nights to impress her and the other young Turks.

"She had never met anyone like Al Nicosia before. He was older, incredibly handsome, had lots of money, and knew how to show a girl a good time. They dated on and off through most of her junior and senior years. Near the end of her senior year, they got really serious; and during spring break, she brought him home to meet her folks.

"Dede's father, not the country bumpkin Al had expected, took an instant dislike for this slick New Yorker. He had the local sheriff check Al Nicosia out with the NYPD. When the word came back both Al and his father were Mafia, Mr. Wilson asked Al to leave and forbade his daughter to see him again. Having learned in college this wasn't the 1800s and fathers could no longer tell their twenty-one-year-old daughters with whom to associate, Dede stubbornly continued to see Al and even succeeded in convincing him they should get married after she graduated.

"Mr. Wilson was so infuriated when Dede told him she and the gangster were going to get married whether he liked it or not, he refused to attend the wedding. One of Dede's brothers, a very large farm boy, decided he was going to make a visit to New York and convince this greaseball he should forget he ever met his little sister. After Al and his crew dangled the red-neck out his hotel window by his feet, he sheepishly returned to the Shenandoah Valley and the family cut off all ties with their prodigal daughter.

"It didn't take Dede long after Al and she tied the knot to real-ize Al was not the devoted husband she had been brought up to expect. About the third time his *goumada* called asking for Al, she got suspicious. When she talked to the wives of some of Al's friends, she learned that having a mistress was the wiseguy equivalent of playing on a softball team. At the advice of the other wives, she tried to ignore his infidelity. After all, he was still a good lover and never gave her any shit about how much money she spent.

"It wasn't until she went to the doctor for what she thought was a yeast infection that she learned she had contracted chlamydia. It had progressed to the point where she probably was going to be sterile. She confronted her husband with the diagnosis. She told him she knew about his *goumada* and if he didn't give her up, she would leave him. Al slapped her around a couple of times then laughed and announced, 'If that's what you want, bitch, get out.' Realizing she had no place to go, she stayed but escaped into heroin. Less than a year later her body was discovered in a sleazy motel room on Route 25A, the apparent victim of a drug overdose. When Al informed her family their daughter had died, her father replied, 'We have no daughter.'"

"Oh, what a ghastly story. Al Nicosia is really a heartless prick!"

Bart pursed his lips and nodded. "That might be an under-statement. Let me tell you about his other wife. You'll like this one because Al was the one who got burnt.

"About ten years later, Al started hanging around movie types. He started by dating a couple of the soap opera girls; then he worked his way up to one of the gals that starred in a sitcom filmed in New York. Her name was Julie Newman; she played the dumb blonde secretary in that office sitcom popular in the late 1980s. The two of them were a hot item for a few months, regularly showing up in the society pages of the *Times* and even once in *People* magazine. On one of their frequent junkets to Vegas, after a few days of nonstop drinking and gambling, they decided to get married.

"Al was head over heels for this broad; she, on the other hand, wakes up and must have said to herself, 'What the fuck have I done?' The first chance she gets, she signs a movie contract, gets herself written off the sitcom, and moves to an apartment in Los Angeles. She knows Al would never leave New York and his ego wouldn't allow him to accept her being seen with other guys. Slyly, she makes sure the tabloids pick up on her dates with some big-name hunks. Pissed off, Al flies to LA to kick the crap out of his wife and drag her back to New York. The thing is, Julie is not, in real life, the same dumb blonde she played on television. When he shows up at her apartment, she is ready for him. She lets him hit her once in the face, blooding her nose and splitting her lip, and shouting, 'If I ever find out you have been with another guy I'll kill you myself!'

"Satisfied that she has all the evidence she needs, she falls to the floor and skillfully pulls a small can of pepper spray out of her back pocket. She slowly gets to her feet, concealing the pepper spray, and as her irate husband comes after her again, she nails him in the eyes with the spray. Not finished yet, she then retrieves a two-quart cast-iron pot off the kitchen counter and smacks him on the head, knocking him out cold. She binds his hands and feet with duct tape and calmly calls 911 to report the attack. Her cunning didn't stop there; she also had hidden cameras installed in the apartment and the whole incident was recorded.

"The cops cart off the domestic abuser and lock him up. Before Al can get one of his connections to bail him out, Julie's lawyer puts up the money. Figuring his wife has had a change of heart, he accompanies her attorney out of county lockup. Instead of being taken back to Julie's apartment, they wind up at the attorney's lavish office. In a safely sequestered glass-enclosed conference room, Julie's attorney shows Al a videotape of the incident.

When the 45-second video is over, the slick lawyer slowly shuts off the tape player, giving Al the opportunity to absorb his damning attack and then the humiliating retaliation by his wife.

"'Mr. Nicosia,' the attorney begins, 'I know you are a powerful man, and you have at your disposal the means to make things very uncomfortable, if not dangerous, for my client; but you are also a smart man. This tape clearly shows you attacking your wife and inflicting pain and suffering upon her person, not to mention the verbal threat to kill her. It also shows that this little 115-pound woman proceeded to, pardon the expression, kick your ass. Now, I have been authorized by my client to make the domestic assault charges go away and, more importantly, insure that no one from the New York media ever gets to see this video . . . if you will cooperate.'

"Recognizing that he had been played, an uneasy smirk slowly worked its way to the left corner of his mouth. 'Ohhh-K, what does the bitch want?'

"'First, in exchange for making the charges go away and storing this tape so that no one will ever see it, she wants your promise that you will never try to see her again or send your associates to harm her. Then, she wants a divorce, quick, easy, with no alimony or strings. *Capisci?*'

"Resigned that for once he didn't hold the winning hand, Al responded, 'I gotta hand it to the broad, she played this one perfectly. Yeah, I agree to her conditions.'"

When Bart was finished I laughed out loud at Julie's ingenuity and audacity. "How the heck did you find out about this incident?"

"Obviously I didn't hear about it from Al. About fifteen years ago, I was over in Hong Kong negotiating an agreement with a Chinese paper company and ran into Julie. She was there making one of those martial arts movies, and we were both staying at the Mandarin Oriental Hotel. Anyway, I recognized her in the lobby and approached her. To my surprise, she not only remembered me but seemed glad to see me again. We had drinks, which led to dinner which led to after-dinner drinks. It was a fun night. After about the third martini we both started telling Al stories. When she told me this one, I laughed so hard, I almost pissed my pants."

CHAPTER 44

The day Peter went off to SUNY Purchase, Bart and Gina's marriage effectively ended. They cohabitated for a couple of more years, but it was an accommodation rather than a union. It wasn't like they had violent arguments or hated each other; it was more like neither one of them had the energy to try to make it work. Nowhere was this more apparent than with lovemaking. It was almost like a contest as to who was going to make the first move. On one of those rare occasions when one of them surrendered to their carnal instincts and made an advance, the other would usually receive it eagerly and the experience was generally pleasant if not fulfilling.

The worst part was they could not have a dispassionate discussion on what was bothering them. Any negative comment, whether meant to be constructive or not, usually resulted in the other party becoming defensive and ultimately withdrawn. As a result, they were never capable of getting to the root cause of their relationship issues. Bart knew several classmates from both high school and college and two drinking buddies from the Air Force who were either psychiatrists or psychologists and found them to have no more relationship savvy than anyone else. In spite of these personal experiences, Gina was able to convince him into a series of sessions with a marriage counselor. However, driving home after their eighth $100 per hour session, they jointly reached the conclusion that it wasn't helping.

■ ■ ■

Peter loved college, not the studies, only the social life. The reason he picked SUNY Purchase was because it was far enough away from his parents and just outside New York City in Westchester County. His attraction to New York revolved around an obsession for pot which he developed during senior year in high school. It was through his Uncle Al, a regular drug user himself, that Peter was able to get his hands on all the marijuana he wanted at wholesale prices. Once a month he stopped by his uncle's, picking up enough stuff for his own use with plenty left over to sell in the dorm. Even though he was pocketing a couple of hundred dollars a month, he didn't think of himself as a drug dealer since it was only pot.

Over the summer between his freshman and sophomore year, Al used his influence to get Peter a job collecting tolls at Southampton's magnificent Cooper's Beach. During the twelve weeks he stayed in the Hamptons, he had almost exclusive use of his uncle's six-bedroom house in Sag Harbor. Between the house and his never-ending supply of party enhancers, Peter was, arguably, the most sought-after friend on the east end. It was over that summer he added cocaine, heroin, and untaxed cigarettes from North Carolina to his "product portfolio."

Peter finished his sophomore year at SUNY Purchase. Over that second summer in the Hamptons, the very successful part-time drug dealer realized he had adequate clientele who were year-round residents or winter weekend escapees from the city to make a lucrative living all year-round.

■ ■ ■

Perhaps because their home lives were so empty, Bart and Gina flourished away from each other. Gina loved teaching, even though she didn't have a permanent position. She was so in demand as a substitute teacher she could almost pick and choose the days she worked and classes she taught. Before taking a day off, whether personal or sick, dozens of teachers throughout the district checked with Gina to make sure she was available. This gave her ultimate flexibility. If she chose, she could make herself unavailable for several days and hop on down to see her mother or maybe even get Al to take her to Trump Plaza. Gambling had become Gina's recreational outlet. On one of her trips to Atlantic City, she wound up sitting next to a sixty-five-year-old retired navy nurse, Ida Smith. By the time the day was over, they each had a new friend. Over the next two years, Ida introduced Gina to Milford and Hartford jai alai, bingo at the Mashantucket Pequot Reservation, and finally she talked Gina into persuading Al to take them both to Las Vegas for three days. Between her work, her gambling, and her visits with her mother, she and Bart were more like roommates than a couple. Their occasional brief encounters were not unpleasant. Every once in a while they even found themselves in bed together. Even though Bart despised her gambling, she was not using the household account to fund it.

Her father had been one of those rare breeds of gangster that used some of his ill-gotten monies to make legitimate investments. For over thirty-five years, the savvy businessman provided capital to local entrepreneurs. He owned pieces of dozens of successful local companies and left these investments totally legitimate and beyond the reach of his Mafia associates. In those weeks before his death, Pietro Nicosia sold back his share in every single business, in some cases receiving ten times what he had invested. When he was done, he had enough to provide for Eleonora's needs and still establish a substantial trust fund for each of his children. Between Gina's trust and her teaching, she was pretty much financially independent.

Meanwhile, Bart continued his steady rise through the ranks of IPC. Raises every year and promotions every other year had gotten him to a position by 1988 where he had few financial worries. With Peter no longer in college, Gina financially independent, and a mortgage payment less than 15 percent of his monthly salary, he could virtually do whatever he wanted, whenever he wanted. His job generally required he make regular trips to the company's plants and mills. This routine of eight or ten days on the road each month was another factor in providing both spouses with the space they needed to live virtually independent lives.

It was during these trips Bart became attracted to a co-worker, a thirty-five-year-old, single manager of human resources. She was unlike anyone of the opposite sex Bart had ever met. At first, her independence and self-assurance reminded him of Captain Betty Rice; but upon further scrutiny, he concluded Betty was never as uninhibited as Bridgitte Rouseau. Born in New Orleans of a French Creole father and an immigrant Irish mother, the recalcitrant teenager ran away from home when she was sixteen and made her way to Boston. She got a job as a waitress in Cambridge and soon was the focus of every Harvard undergraduate who frequented the greasy spoon where she worked. The horny academics soon discovered this luscious redhead with eyes the color of emeralds had a venomous tongue for any of them who assumed she would be a pushover for their Harvard pedigree. Mornings she took classes to obtain her high school diploma. At age twenty, at the urging of the Harvard graduate student she was living with, she began taking college courses at Bunker Hill Community College. By the time Bridgitte was twenty-six, she had a four-year degree in business administration from the University of Massachusetts in Boston and two years' experience as a benefits coordinator at an envelope factory in Somerville.

When Bart met Bridgitte, her nearly twenty-year journey from a teenage runaway to a successful middle manager of a major corporation had provided her with confidence and a lust for life most men found both captivating on one hand and intimidating on the other. At first, Bart's reaction to her was the same as most of the guys, cautious; but after attending a few of the same meetings and traveling together, he decided he liked the way she thought and expressed her views without fear of rejection. Thereafter, when Bart needed advice or assistance with a human resource issue, he would generally go first to Bridgitte. For her part, it was pretty obvious by her enthusiastic reaction she liked it when Bart called or dropped by her office.

CHAPTER 45

Call it what you like: fate, destiny, or luck that prompted a new general manager of a division in Lexington, Kentucky, to request Bart LaRocca and Bridgitte Rouseau assist him to assess his organization. When they arrived at the facility and asked the GM why he had specifically requested them, he responded, "Because both of you have the reputation to tell it like you see it; and frankly, I have plenty of managers working for me that will only tell me what they think I want to hear."

On weeknights when the University of Kentucky's basketball team was not playing at Rupp Arena, the Hyatt Regency Hotel at Lexington Center can be quite dull. On Bart and Bridgitte's first night alone in the city, the Lexington Center was virtually empty. After a very nice steak dinner together at the Peppercorn Restaurant, Bridgitte decided to cruise the shops that made up much of Lexington Center. Bart went back to the sports bar at the Hyatt to watch whatever college basketball games were on its six big-screen televisions.

Bart was on his second goblet of Wild Turkey when Bridgitte sauntered into the bar and climbed on a bar stool right next to him.

Without even a greeting, she scoffed, "Christ, for a hick town they sure have some expensive stores in this place."

Smirking, Bart swiveled in her direction. "I take it that means you didn't buy anything."

Bridgitte responded with "the laugh." It was referred to as "the laugh" by most of the guys at corporate because it was neither feminine nor masculine; yet it had characteristics of both. It was short, throaty and sensual. You would have thought she had just heard a dirty joke or an off-color remark. Bart had only heard it a couple of times but each time his reaction was the same, *Damn that's sexy.*

At that moment, the bartender wandered down their way, Bridgitte ordered a B&B on the rocks, Bart another Wild Turkey.

Before she let him get away, Bridgitte instructed the bartender,

"We'll be moving over to that table in the corner. Would you please have our drinks brought to us over there?" She stood up and without even looking in his direction said, "Coming?" Bart watched her leave. He didn't follow until she had reached the table and turned in his direction with an inquiring gaze.

Although they had worked in the same office for over a year, neither of them really knew much about the other. Bart knew Bridgitte was single and surmised from previous discussions she lived alone. All she knew about him was he was married and had a grown son; so they had plenty to talk about.

It was nearly midnight before they were both talked out and decided to call it a night. Their rooms were across the hall from each other so they took the elevator together up to the fifteenth floor. In the hall they said good night and went into their own rooms, but neither of them would sleep well that night. They both felt a strong attraction and sensed the other felt the same way. Bridgitte had learned that Bart was in a dying marriage but, sadly, still in love with his wife. Bart was intrigued with Bridgitte but couldn't figure her out. She seemed to be attracted to older men but never seemed willing to make a long-term commitment. He speculated she might be using older men as mentors; upon getting what she wanted, she moved on.

The next morning, over breakfast, neither of them mentioned anything about the previous evening. Their interviews with the management team and meetings with the GM were especially hectic and tense. Conclusions had to be reached about people and departments which would have a profound effect on the lives of the 283 employees of the division. Lunch was brought into to the conference room and their only breaks were to use the bathroom. By the time they had presented their conclusions to the GM, it was nearly 7:00 p.m. They were both physically and emotionally spent.

On the way to the Hyatt Bridgitte remarked, "That was the shits. We just helped decide 32 people are going to lose their jobs. At an average of four people per family, it means that over 120 people will be affected. I don't even think I can eat now."

Bart cleared his throat. "Funny you should mention that. I was just thinking about going to hit the hotel's health club to work off some stress. When I've exhausted myself, I was going to soak away the day's drudge in the pool, hot tub and sauna; then I might consider eating . . . or drinking."

"I don't work out but I'll meet you at the pool in an hour, if that's all right with you?"

Bart grinned. "Now that's something for me to look forward to."

When Bart arrived at the pool an hour later, Bridgitte was just finishing a lap at the far end. He dove in and swam underwater half its fifty-foot length, surfacing and finishing the lap with a breast stroke. As he slowly made his way the last few yards, he could see Bridgitte waiting for him with a relaxed smile on her face. "Been here long?" he asked as he floated the last few feet.

"Long enough to shed some of the tension from this afternoon," she replied as she pulled herself out of the pool.

Not bad, he thought. This was the first time he had a glimpse of Bridgitte's physique without her usual long dresses or skirts and loose-fitting tops. It was not well-toned but it was firm and nicely proportioned. The best part was the way all the parts moved in a sensual rhythm that seemed to be inviting his lustful survey.

"How about you, did your workout have its desired effect?"

"Oh yeah, I feel better, too. I watched your last lap; you have a nice smooth rhythm. Did you ever swim competitively?"

"No, but I did work as a lifeguard at a pool the summer before running away from home."

They talked, swam, and joked for a few minutes and then Bart suggested they move to the hot tub. They were the only ones at the pool, and their voices echoed off the glass walls and cedar ceiling until Bart turned on the jets in the hot tub. As they sat there in the 104-degree bubbling caldron, the rest of their day's tensions melted away. Their conversation had no direction except to provide a few additional tidbits about each other. Finally, after about fifteen minutes Bridgitte announced she'd had enough.

She climbed out and dove back into the 20-degree-cooler pool water. Bart followed suit and they raced the length of the pool.

Reaching the far side, Bridgitte did something that caught Bart completely by surprise. She reached out for his hand and, grasping it tightly, pulled him in close to her. She looked him straight in the eyes and declared, "I like you, Bart LaRocca. Why don't we go to my room and order room service?"

Bart stared at her, trying to determine just how serious she was. "Are you sure?" he asked. "I got the impression you and I shared the same philosophy — don't get too involved with anyone at work."

"No, I'm not sure — and yes — I feel the same about co-workers — but let's do it anyway." She then lifted herself out of the pool, inquiring for the second time in two nights, "Coming?" This time Bart didn't hesitate.

Wrapping themselves with towels, they made a dash to the elevator. Before they had reached the fifteenth floor, it was clear to both of them room service was not high on their priority list. The door to Bridgitte's room was hardly closed when they were in each other's arms. Bart hadn't felt this surge of raw passion in years. It was exhilarating. Bridgitte's voraciousness was unlike anything Bart had ever encountered. Her lips, tongue, and hands explored every erogenous zone on his body, some of which he hadn't even known existed. But her most amazing skill was how she used the rest of her body to engulf him and almost absorb him into herself. For Bart this was the coup de grâce for his marital fidelity. He fumbled to get her bathing suit off so he could feel her skin against his.

"Easy, big boy," she whispered, "let me help you." Stepping away, she deftly removed the last vestiges of mystery from her body. "Lie on the bed," she instructed.

Bart frowned but complied. "Yes, ma'am."

Those were the last intelligibly words heard in the room until Bridgitte rolled on her back panting. "Now wasn't that worth violating a few principles?"

Bart, equally fulfilled, could only manage, "Man, that was incredible." His rapture had been so consuming he had no idea whether she had reached an orgasm.

As they sat naked on the bed, he apologetically asked her if she had climaxed. Bridgette shot him a devilish look. "Don't worry about that, I enjoyed every second . . . now I'm ready for room service before we start round two."

Bridgitte called down to the kitchen and ordered two turkey sandwiches and two Heinekens. While they were waiting for the delivery of their dinner, they showered and put on the terrycloth robes from the closet. If they didn't know room service would arrive shortly, they probably would have gone at it again in the shower. Room service arrived just as Bridgitte finished drying her hair.

If there had been a world record for devouring turkey sandwiches, Bart and Bridgitte broke it that night. Bart didn't think it was possible, but the second time was better than the first; mainly because this time he maintained some semblance of control. This time he took the lead and the dominant position. Having earlier cleared weeks of pent-up desire, he could control his passion long enough to provide sustained pleasure to his partner. This time he knew Bridgitte had reached her climax.

Later as they lay in bed, Bart was outwardly sullen, if not pensive. Sensing his uneasiness, the intuitive Bridgitte asked, "Something bothering you?"

Bart took a long few seconds to answer. "I don't know — I guess I feel sad."

"Of course you do. How long has it been since you had sex with anyone other than your wife?"

"I haven't made love with anyone other than Gina since my freshman year in college."

"Well, that says it all. First off, we didn't make love tonight; we fucked. And for the first time in a long time, you enjoyed the hell out of the act itself. What you are experiencing, my dear boy, is guilt, not sadness. You'll get over it." Reflecting for a few moments she then continued, "Not since your freshman year in college? Not even when you were alone in Italy for those few months, or in Vietnam? Hell, everybody got laid in 'Nam!"

"Nope, not in Italy, Vietnam, or even Milwaukee where everybody thinks I was screwing my staff."

"Christ, you're practically a virgin. No wonder they refer to you as the Boy Scout at the office."

"Who refers to me as that?"

"Everybody."

"Why, they don't know me from jack."

"They've observed you enough to know you have integrity and you make decisions based upon facts and principles, not on how it is going to affect you personally. You come to work, earn your badges through hard work, and do what you think is best for the company. In short, you're perceived as being nonpolitical."

"That's bullshit! I'm as political as anyone."

"Sure you are, but for a different purpose. You're political in order to get the things done that you believe will benefit the company, not your own career."

CHAPTER 46

In the weeks and months that followed Bart's first marital infidelity, he finally came to grips with the fact his marriage was over. Bart began sleeping in Peter's old bedroom. To his surprise, Gina did not even comment on this new development. When he came home from work and she was not visiting her mother, dinner was still waiting for him. They would keep each other informed when they were not going to be home for dinner, but unless it was a trip that lasted a few days, details of their whereabouts were not offered or requested. In short, they were amiable platonic roommates.

Although the significance of Bridgitte's comment — "We didn't make love tonight; we fucked" — eluded him for some time, he eventually came to understand the subtlety of her statement.

When he and Bridgitte had sex, it was an amazing but exclusively physical event. He became incredibly aroused and found he was able to go at it several times, something he hadn't been able or inclined to do for years, and each time being as good as the last. But it was not the same as when he and Gina made love while they were dating or during the first few years of their marriage. Fucking Bridgitte was an extraordinary physical high; making love to Gina was a physical and emotional nirvana, a state he doubted he could ever achieve again with anyone other than his first love.

In the summer of 1989 Bart was offered the position of vice president of finance and CFO of IPC's specialty paper subsidiary located in Holyoke, Massachusetts. Confidentially, he was told by the division's new president that the $130 million company was a candidate for divesture but it needed to be spruced up before it being put up for sale. Besides a hefty raise to take the position, he was given a contract that included both a severance package, should his services not be wanted by a new owner, plus an incentive bonus if the unit was sold for more than its book value. Of course it meant he would have to move to the Springfield, Massachusetts, area.

When he told Gina about his new opportunity, she was visibly happy for him and asked, "You're going to take the job; aren't you?"

"Well, it means moving to the Springfield area."

"I figured that," she replied. "It fits right into my plans. I've been holding off telling you I decided I want to work full-time."

"That's great!" Bart responded enthusiastically.

"Hold on; you haven't heard my entire plan. As we've discussed a lot, in order to get my permanent teacher's certification in Connecticut, I will have to go back to school and get a master's degree. However, I am grandfathered in New York with permanent certification; so I've been thinking of moving back with my mother and finding a teaching position in the City. Besides getting a permanent job, I see that Mom is beginning to deteriorate physically and mentally. Frankly, she needs me more than you do, so I've decided to move down with her."

It was the matter-of-fact tone in which she said it that jolted Bart. He just gaped at his wife.

Not realizing how stunned he was, Gina scoffed, "So, say something. Are you surprised? Do you even care?"

Struggling with several emotions, he wasn't sure what he felt. It wasn't as if he hadn't considered them separating, he just never could admit it was over. He finally managed, "Do you want a divorce?"

Momentarily hesitating, Gina replied, "Well, we've already tried counseling. What do you want?"

"To be honest with you, I always figured something would happen to put us back on the right track. As it turned out, what's happened is we are not only on different tracks but going in different directions."

She pressed him for an answer. "So, let me see if I understand what you're saying. You're content to just go on like this until some 'serendipitous event' fixes everything?"

Bart just stared at her.

Gina waited a few seconds then asked with an apprehensive sigh, "Do you still love me?"

"Sort of."

Ridicule crept into her voice. "Wow! That's reassuring. Don't you even want to know if I still love you?"

Bart smiled faintly. "Of course I want to know."

She sighed. "Not enough to go on with this charade much longer. Let's be realistic, nothing is going to change. Eventually we are going to have to deal with it."

Bart wanted to ask her if there was someone else but was afraid of both her answer and inevitable comeback question. Confused by his emotions, Bart searched for a way to postpone the decision. All he could muster up was "I think I need some time to absorb this new development. Can we forgo any decision on a divorce for now?"

Gina, herself anxious to avoid an all-out confrontation, said, "OK, but we'll have to deal with this again in a few weeks."

■ ■ ■

It didn't dawn on Bart until the middle of August that when Gina suddenly announced she had landed a teaching job in Elmhurst she must have started her job search in New York prior to his new job opportunity. The weekend before Labor Day, two of Al's crew showed up with a small panel truck to move Gina's personal items. Bart conveniently spent the weekend on Block Island with Bridgitte.

Things moved fast for the separated couple as both of them threw themselves into their new jobs. During one of their infrequent telephone calls, the couple decided to file for divorce. Within a month, Bart received notice of divorce proceedings from Gina's attorney. Bart signed the papers that split all their assets right down the middle and did not include any alimony payments. Bart did agree to continue to pay for Peter's college and expenses.

On his ride home from signing the divorce papers, Bart had an uneasy, empty feeling in the pit of his stomach. He realized he still loved Gina but no longer had the will to do anything about it.

Given the uncertain tenure of his new position, rather than sink his portion of the net gain on the sale of the house into another house, he decided to invest in a real estate development deal David Tanner was starting on Hilton Head Island. Besides, at the time, having zero debt seemed an attractive concept.

■ ■ ■

The following February, Frank LaRocca suffered a heart attack and was dead before he hit the ground. Gina attended both the wake and funeral; it was the first time the couple had seen each other since signing the papers ending their twenty-four-year marriage. It was during those ceremonies Gina met Bridgitte for the first time. Bart introduced her as "my friend" but it was obvious that they were more than friends. The encounter produced surprising emotional responses on both their parts. Although she masked her jealously pretty well, it was obvious to Bart that Gina hadn't come to grips with the prospect of him having a new lover. Bart, sensing Gina's emotion, felt as if he was caught red-handed in an illicit affair.

Ironically, before the end of the year, the tables were reversed when Eleonora Nicosia developed an abdominal aortic aneurysm that burst, causing a massive internal loss of blood. Gina returned home from work to find her mother lying on the kitchen floor, already dead. Both John and Gina were pleased that Bart attended their mother's wake and funeral. On the other hand, Al did his best to avoid Bart. He even went so far as to not acknowledge him when Bart approached the siblings as they greeted mourners and accepted condolences at the wake. Both Gina and John went out of their way to personally invite Bart back to the house for the catered lunch after the burial. It was at the luncheon Gina introduced Bart to someone she referred to as "my friend Kyle." Bart thought, and John later confirmed, Kyle was the same guy he had seen her with many years earlier outside the cafeteria at St. John's.

Bart was driving home on the Hutchinson River Parkway, trying to sort out his feeling about Gina and Kyle, when he suddenly became aware of the flashing red-and-blue lights on an unmarked Crown Vic right on his tail. Knowing he had not been speeding, he ignored the lights for a mile. Finally, the unmarked Crown Vic gave a short chirp on its siren. Bart put on his flashers and pulled up onto the next wide grassy area. To his surprise, the driver of the Crown Vic was not in uniform; he was dressed in a gray pinstriped business suit and striped tie. Bart rolled down his window as the muscular man with a military-style haircut, appearing to be in his midthirties, carefully approached his vehicle. Holding his wallet out in front of him so Bart could see the glimmer of a badge, he announced, "Special Agent Sam Sardo of the FBI. If you can spare a few minutes, Mr. LaRocca, I'd like to talk to you."

"What's this about, Special Agent Sardo?"

"Your brother-in-law, Al Nicosia."

"You mean my ex-brother-in-law, Little Nicky."

"Well, I've never heard him referred to as that but if that's what you call Al Nicosia, yeah him."

"I don't know what we could possibly have to talk about. Until today, I hadn't seen Little Nicky in over a year and even then we never got along. However, I could use a cup of coffee."

"OK, follow me off the next exit, I'll lead you to a Starbucks where we can talk."

Bart followed Special Agent Sardo off the Hutch at the next exit and into a Starbucks.

Agent Sardo bought them each a coffee and the two men settled at a small round table.

"I suppose you can guess I followed you from Mrs. Nicosia's services . . . can I call you Bart?"

"Sure, call me anything you like except a member of Little Nicky's crew."

"That's what I want to talk to you about. We know you have never had any dealings with organized crime, except for your marriage to Gina Nicosia. In fact, we are pretty sure you and Little Nicky, as you call him, don't like each other very much. "

"Don't like each other . . . that's cute . . . I hate the son-of-a-bitch and he would probably like nothing better than to pound my face into oblivion."

"Maybe we can help each other," Agent Sardo declared.

Bart grimaced and his voice went up several octaves. "Like how! I know nothing about his operation, and now that Gina and I are divorced I doubt I'll have much contact with the asshole."

Agent Sardo glanced around the room hoping no one was paying too much attention after Bart's outburst. Leaning forward he almost whispered, "Well, perhaps your son will tell you something that would be of interest to the FBI. Should that occur, we would really appreciate if you give us a call."

Flabbergasted, Bart bellowed, "What the fuck are you implying . . . you can't be seriously suggesting Peter is involved with Al's crew?"

Sardo again scanned the room. "Easy, Mr. LaRocca, I'm not implying anything, just suggesting I will listen to anything you may deem of interest to your government as it relates to Al Nicosia."

"Bullshit, you attempted to get me to believe my son is involved with Al's criminal empire." Bart's irritation was now in full bloom. "Well, thanks for your generous offer; I'll keep it in mind. As for my son, I'm not big on innuendo. If you've got something concrete to discuss, I'll be all ears. Bart hesitated for a moment. "Well, do you have some evidence my son is involved in a crime?"

"Not at this time," Agent Sardo said sheepishly.

Bart stood up. "Thought not. Now, if you'll excuse me, I have a long drive back to Springfield." He didn't wait for a reply. Leaving his coffee on the table, Bart tramped out the door.

Two things resulted from Bart's meeting with Agent Sardo. First, Bart became concerned about his son. He called Peter and bluntly asked him if he was doing business with his uncle. Peter's response was an unapologetic "That's none of your business." Second, Agent Sardo began referring to Al Nicosia as aka Little Nicky. It didn't take long for law enforcement to regularly refer to him as Little Nicky and eventually this moniker made its way into the media. Rumor has it the first time Al Nicosia saw it in print, he did $10,000 worth of damage to his kitchen.

CHAPTER 47

Eighteen months into Bart's new job in Holyoke, the team his boss had assembled began showing marked progress. In the first six months, a three-year strategic plan had been developed to streamline the division and significantly improve profitability and cash flow.

When the actual results of the first year of the plan exceeded IPC's expectations, the company decided to sell the division. To their delight, several parties immediately expressed an interest.

The most serious suitor was a large mid-Atlantic–based private equity firm, Mason-Dixon Investments, LLC. Their strategy was to invest in mature industries that were highly fragmented then, through strategic acquisitions and sound business practices, transform their new investment into the dominant player in the industry. As soon as the principals at Mason-Dixon saw the strategic plan and the first year's progress, they were convinced IPC's Specialty Papers was the right fit.

A deal was completed in less than six months for almost twice what IPC had projected just two years earlier. Bart received his bonus the week after the deal closed and promptly signed it over to Mason-Dixon Investment, LLC, for an equity position in their new affiliate.

The day it became evident the sale of the company was imminent, Mason-Dixon's managing director suggested the senior management team find a new name. They decided on Custom Specialties International, Incorporated, or CSI.

CSI and Mason-Dixon Investments were a perfect marriage. The management team at CSI was driven by an intense desire to turn the company into the dominant player in their market with world-class business practices. Mason-Dixon Investment's expectations were exactly the same for its portfolio companies; they were willing to make investments in people, equipment, and additional synergistic acquisitions in order to achieve superior returns. They provided generous equity positions to the management team.

For two years CSI went on a dizzying ride of reinventing itself through a combination of organizational redesign, systems implementation, product and equipment rationalization, and quality improvements. At the end of those two harrowing years, CSI was a very different company than the one Mason-Dixon had acquired. Mason-Dixon was now ready to make the additional investments in order to dominate the market.

In preparation for negotiations of its first acquisition, a Barcelona-based paper company, Bart enrolled in an intense Berlitz

Spanish language course to facilitate the negotiations and perform due diligence.

Over the next several years, CSI more than doubled its revenue and tripled its profits through two strategic acquisitions and the synergies that followed. Within five years Mason-Dixon was ready to cash in on its investment.

After the managing director of Mason-Dixon Investments casually let it slip at an international packaging trade show that CSI might be available, inquiries soon followed. By the mid-1990s Finnish paper companies were aggressively pursuing international acquisitions, and two of the biggest were among the first to call.

It didn't take long for negotiations to start moving fast. More detailed historical financials and the most recent strategic plans were presented. The questions were never-ending. Bart described the Finnish company's analysts as "potato chip people"; they couldn't stop at just one question. When he gave them an answer, they immediately had two more queries. Having spent the last five years typically putting in sixty-hour weeks, it was almost too much for Bart when the six months of intense information exchange, negotiations, and due diligence actually increased his hours. The one thing that kept Bart and the rest of the senior executives plodding through the minutia and drudgery was the pot of gold at the end of the rainbow. The six senior executives of CSI all had substantial financial incentives to see a deal go through. Besides an equity interest, they all had a very generous golden parachute.

During due diligence, it became obvious to Bart the new owners intended on bringing in their own CFO. This realization was almost a relief to the physically and emotionally drained fifty-three-year-old financial executive. The prospect of an extended, stress-free sabbatical seemed like an acceptable reward for his seven years of sweat equity.

The deal was completed on January 30, 1997. Bart was asked to stay on through the end of the year as a consultant.

CHAPTER 48

The Merriam-Webster Dictionary defines *transference* as the redirection of feeling and desires, especially of those unconsciously retained from childhood, toward a new object. More often than not, the phenomena are associated with a psychoanalyst conducting therapy; however, there are numerous examples of its occurrence in everyday life, and under many instances it is not a psychologically harmful issue.

It was Dr. John Nicosia who first described the condition to Bart as a means of explaining Gina's blind devotion to her eldest brother, Al. Though not a psychiatrist, John hypothesized Gina was subconsciously attributing her father's traits to her eldest brother. Pietro doted over his only daughter, and she in return adored her father. Rather than the friendship that existed between mother and daughter, Gina's relationship with her father was much more complicated. As a child, Gina viewed her father as the one person who validated her worth. Besides being her white knight, he could fix or make anything happen; and he was always there to encourage, support, and applaud her efforts. There was a time when Bart was able to assume that role in her life; but as their relationship waned and her father's legal and health issues consumed much of his energy, Gina experienced a void she first filled with booze and later gambling. But even those emotional crutches left her, much of the time, with a feeling of isolation.

After her move back to Queens, Al became the lightning rod for her incessant search for a new champion. She was willing to overlook her brother's well-publicized transgressions with the law, just as she did with her father. Al, for his part, was as eager to assume this role as he was to take his father's place in *La Famiglia*.

■ ■ ■

Peter LaRocca thrived in the Hamptons. His drug-peddling connections made him think he could parlay that franchise into real estate. After studying for six months under the tutorage of a small successful broker, he was able to pass the state exam and get his license. For several years his efforts only resulted in a handful of sales. Still, it gave him a legitimate source of income. Between the two cash flows, Peter was able to buy a small two-bedroom fixer-upper in East Hampton. Finally settled into a community, and in spite of his drug peddling, he worked hard at becoming part of the community. He signed on as an apprentice volunteer fireman. The chief of East Hampton's Volunteer Fire Department was a retired captain from the New York City Fire Department. Peter showed such an intense desire to learn all he could about firefighting the chief took him under his wing. He found numerous opportunities for the eager young apprentice to attend training courses all over the New York metropolitan area. Within a year, Peter LaRocca was one of the most capable firefighters on the South Fork.

Peter's newfound skills did not go unnoticed by his Uncle Al. Whenever Peter visited his mother in Queens, Al magically showed up. Just as he did when his nephew was a child, he always had some goodies to hand out. His favorite gifts were tickets to events, Mets, Knicks, and Jets games, and rock concerts. Sometimes Al would also attend and bring his cousin Paulie along, but most of the time he just handed them to his only nephew to do with as he pleased. On those occasions when they were together, Al questioned Peter about his new firefighting passion; he made sure he acknowledged what a unique and valuable skill his nephew had obtained. Always the clever opportunist, Al waited until the right moment to take advantage of his nephew's talents. During the winter of 1995, on one of their trips to the Garden for a Knicks game, Peter mentioned he would love to get his hands on $10,000 so he could buy into a new yuppie bistro several of his clients were developing in Sag Harbor. A few days later Peter received a call from his uncle inviting him out to dinner. Always up for a free meal, Peter enthusiastically accepted.

They met at a small restaurant run by the granddaughter of a post-WWII refugee from the same small mountain village in

Sicily as the Nicosias' ancestors. As soon as they gave their order to the waiter, Al got right to his objective, presenting Peter with an opportunity to make an easy ten grand. According to Al, all Peter had to do was solve a problem for one of Al's business associates by using his knowledge as a fireman. Al claimed he had no direct knowledge of the details, but one of the family's long-time friends, Frankie DelMonico, could fill Peter in. Frankie pretty much ran the garbage collection and landfill operation on Long Island for the mob. At seventy, Frankie was still a bull of a man. By using the strong-armed tactics he learned from the Mustachio Petes of the 1930s, he pioneered the mob's forays into the garbage business during the 1950s. He was so good at what he did, Al gave his father's friend of four decades a free hand to run the racket as he pleased. In return, Frankie made sure Al was well-rewarded. A meeting between Peter and Frankie was arranged for the following evening.

Not being a virgin to the illegal activities of the mob, Peter was not surprised when Frankie explained he wanted him to torch an old building. Playing to Peter's ego, the older man told him he was his first choice for the venture because with his skills it would be easy for him make it look like an accident. After the accident, the building's owner would then be able to collect the insurance money and afford to redevelop the property. Everybody would win — Frankie, the building's owner, and Peter. The only loser on the deal would be the insurance company, but as Frankie said, "What the hell, that's why you buy insurance and why the insurance companies charge such exorbitant rates." It seemed like a slam dunk to Peter. With his skills, he could make it look like the fire was accidently started by either some homeless drunk, a bunch of druggies, or neighborhood kids.

The building, on the waterfront in Brooklyn, was a perfect first try for Peter. It had been vacant for almost a decade. The razor-wire-topped cyclone fence around the property had been breached numerous times over the years and the site was a known winter haven for the local homeless. The project, as Peter called it, went off without a hitch and he had his buy-in on the bistro before the week was over. Peter figured his share was only a small sliver of the entire take for the mob. For torching the building Frankie was paid $50,000 upfront by the owner.

The insurance policy had been written to cover cleanup of the site in case of disaster. The reason the building had been vacant for so many years was because of the large amount of asbestos it contained inside. Due to the stringent environmental regulations enacted in the late '70s and '80s, the asbestos had to be removed before anything else could be done to the site. Hazardous waste removal and disposal was one of the more expensive propositions a building owner faced. The estimate was a staggering $450,000. It was no wonder the building's owner was willing to fork up fifty grand for a solution, whether legal or not, that would get the cleanup and demolition covered by insurance.

Not surprisingly, the only viable bid for the cleanup and disposal came from a company run by Frankie DelMonico. In order to sell Al on the profitability of the venture, Frankie calculated he could, for a few grand, buy off the environmental inspectors as his crews skirted the regulations. His estimate to complete the cleanup and illegally dump the waste offshore was for less than $100,000. The icing on the cake was once the site was cleaned up, it could be sold or redeveloped by the current owner. In either case, Frankie was guaranteed a cut of the sale price or an exclusive on any concrete work required for redevelopment. Talk about a win-win proposition!

CHAPTER 49

February 14, 2010

I could sense Bart was starting to feel cooped up; we had been constant companions since Thursday. We were both staying at the Tanners' villa in Barrio Santa Cruz while they were on a business trip to South Africa. Being alone together, in the same residence, had given me the opportunity to push him with fourteen-hour days to finish his incredible story. Sometimes I wanted to shake him and shout, *Let's get to the attack and your disappearance!* Then I'd think, *No, there is still so much I don't understand; Peter's and Gina's deaths . . . he still hasn't explained where all his money comes from or how he managed to execute a plan that has kept him hidden for almost a decade.*

Finally Sunday afternoon Bart couldn't stand it anymore. He walked to the edge of the terrace, surveyed the city, and declared, "I've got to get out of here. Except for my morning runs, we've been holed up in this place for three and a half days. I know you're anxious to get back to Marie, but can't we continue this while we're fishing?"

"Fine, as long as we keep moving forward with your story."

Bart smiled. "Good, I know a Brit who lives about an hour and a half up the Rio Guadalquivir. He's a big-time freshwater fisherman. I'll call him and see if he is available; if he is, we can probably stay overnight in his guest house. It will be a fun drive and tomorrow morning we'll hit the water early, catch a mess of carp or barbel and still be back for dinner. How does that sound?"

"Sounds great; but what's a barbel?"

"It's like a carp, but it only gets to about thirty or forty pounds and is one heck of a fighter."

"Only thirty or forty pounds! How big are the carp?"

"I've caught a sixty-five-pounder."

That piqued my interest. "Let's go."

We quickly packed overnight bags and walked over to the garage where Bart always parked his SUV. I actually thought maybe Bart would finally have to take me to his place to pick up fishing gear. After all these weeks, I still had no idea where he had been living; but I was pretty sure it wasn't back in the Algarve or here at David's. I had picked up on a few of Sarah's inadvertent comments leading me to believe Bart had a place near Seville. But no luck, he already had his fishing gear in the Range Rover.

On the drive Bart called his buddy, Dennis Forsythe. Bart said Dennis was the retired security-head for a UK conglomerate.

Since his retirement, he had been working as an independent hunting and fishing guide. Dennis was at home but he was already booked to take some clients up to lake country early the next morning. When we arrived at Dennis's hunting and fishing lodge, he already had started grilling our dinner. Over dinner he told us where the hot fishing spots were.

The next morning when I awoke at around 7:00 a.m., Dennis was gone and Bart had all our gear ready to go. We fished until midafternoon, catching a half dozen carp and three barbel. We released all but one fifteen-pound barbell. Bart filleted it and put it in Dennis's freezer in payment for his hospitality.

While we were fishing, Bart began relating his account of how he acquired enough money to disappear. It was a fascinating story of hard work, savvy investing, luck, and associations with well-connected friends.

■ ■ ■

Bart had started investing small amounts in the stock market shortly after he and Gina moved to Connecticut. Over the next five years, he probably put about $25,000 in the market. When he liquidated the account and split it with Gina as part of their divorce settlement, it had grown to only $30,000. Based upon those lackluster returns, for the next four years Bart avoided any further investments in the stock market. Beginning with his share of the equity from the Connecticut house, Bart's investment comfort zone revolved around David Tanner and his real estate empire. Each year, with his ex-roommate's encouragement, Bart used his bonus money to buy a stake in one of David's projects. By 1998, after he invested almost his entire payout from the sale of CSI and his inheritance from his mother's estate, he had over one million dollars invested in various Tanner ventures.

In 1992, out of the blue, a brilliant young broker named John Fee, from a Boston boutique investment firm, called Bart at work and began a dialogue on investing in the stock market. Although Bart initially blew him off, John continued to call every few months with opportunities. Finally, in February of 1993

John's persistence paid off when Bart agreed to invest $5,000 in Time Warner, Inc., which John claimed was poised to become an entertainment and media giant. Periodically, John continued to call with ideas. Most of the time Bart declined to take his advice. Every once in a while Bart would halfheartedly agree to put up a few grand on one of John's recommendations. Over the years John's advice turned out to be dazzling, especially Time Warner and the first dot com company John recommended, Yahoo. He also had some real losers, too, but Bart's initial investments were never greater than $5,000 so his downside was always minimal.

In the fall of 1999 when Bart made his decision to get revenge on his brother-in-law, he knew that being able to successfully disappear for an extended period of time required him to have an untraceable financial stockpile. So he began selling off his equity holdings. By some incredible consequence of luck, his timing could not have been better. By late March of 2000 the dot com crash had pretty much decimated the stock market, but Bart was fully liquidated and had squirreled away $1.5 million in after-tax gains.

When Bart first told me about his stock market success I was amazed at his timing and luck. On the other hand, I knew that getting the cash was only half the battle. While Bart was again basking in his good fortune I think I surprised him by saying, "It's one thing to have a lot of money, but it's another to be able to move it to your new identities undetected," I declared. "And don't give me that standard bunk about Cayman Island bank accounts. By the year 2000, in order to avoid blacklisting by the Organization for Economic Cooperation and Development, the Caymans had agreed to information exchange with other OECD members."

He looked at me, noticeably impressed. "You're right, and David Tanner warned me it would be a problem. He suggested I set up a series of international business companies in the Caribbean and Central America, and bank accounts on the island of Dominica. It wasn't until after 9/11 the Caribbean island nation tightened its banking regulations to comply with international anti-money-laundering laws. By the time Dominica made those changes, I had already converted most of my assets into bearer shares, and the remaining bank accounts were in the names of my two new identities. It turned out to be an exceptional scheme that has worked perfectly for a decade. But I never would have been able to pull it off without two new impeccable identities and a vehicle to move the money undetected from my US accounts."

"Are you finally ready to reveal those to me?"

"Yup, first let me take you through the most brilliant part of the plan, and the one I figured out on my own. You'll love this, because it came about as a result of a relationship I developed on the golf course with another unusual character."

CHAPTER 50

Shortly after Bart accepted the job in Holyoke and moved to the Springfield area, he joined a country club, Quaker Farms. During his years at CSI, his rounds of golf were negligible but he did find time to take lessons, practice, and occasionally have beers with the guys at the nineteenth hole. By the time of his retirement from CSI, Bart had made quite a few new acquaintances. Quaker Farms was basically a working man's club with only a handful of retirees who played in the mornings during the week. There was one group of entrepreneurs who usually managed to find time to play at 1:00 p.m. on weekdays. One of the regulars in the group became the inspiration for Bart's successful money laundering scheme. His name was Donatello Serafina.

Although Bart had known Don for several years, he wasn't particularly fond of him; by all accounts, the feeling was mutual. Don appeared to be everything Bart had learned to despise, and it started with his name, Don Serafina. He looked like he could be the don of the local Mafia. He was flashy; he wore a heavy gold necklace and a gold Rolex watch. On his other wrist he sported a bracelet that looked like gold nuggets. To Bart's amusement, during the winter, he wore a knee-length fur coat; and on special occasions, he drove a 1984 Jaguar.

Don, for his part, had stereotyped Bart as an arrogant executive who was clueless as to how the real world worked. On the surface they were probably both right about the other. But as they discovered after playing together for a few months, they had more in common than they first believed. They both graduated from college with accounting degrees; they both opted to forego the CPA route. At one time or another they both attempted to distance themselves from their family's Mafia ties, and they both had impeccable integrity. But the thing that originally drew them together was they were the only two Yankee fans at the nineteenth hole during all the televised Yankee-Red Sox games.

Don's father, Renzo Serafina, had been a member of the local DeLuca crime organization. In fact, one of Don's earliest memories was of his father going to jail over some sort of a stolen car ring. His dad apparently refused to roll on the bosses, so he took the full brunt of the DA's wrath and was given the maximum five-year sentence. Though he loved his father, Don wanted nothing to do with the business. He put himself through Baystate College and after graduation landed a job with the city of Springfield's controller's department. He wasn't on the job a year when a low-level associate of the DeLuca organization approached Don with a scheme for payouts on phony contracts. The associate, Vito Sicilliano, already had a manager in the purchasing department lined up to enter the bogus contracts; all Don had to do was make sure the checks went through without any questions. For his assistance Don's cut was 20 percent. Without revealing any details, Don asked his father about Vito's connections. His father verified Vito was not a made-man nor was he a regular member of a crew. Taking the risk this was not a sanctioned mob operation, Don reported the attempted bribe to his superiors. A sting operation was arranged with the DA's office where Don, wearing a wire, demanded Vito fill him in on the details of the scheme before he would agree to participate. Vito was so proud of his scheme, he and the purchasing manager laid it out for law enforcement to record. Not satisfied with charges of attempted bribery and conspiracy to commit fraud, the DA's office convinced Don to go along with the scheme and let the first check go through to be cashed by Vito. The arrests took place in a McDonald's parking lot on State Street as Vito Sicilliano passed envelopes with cash to Don Serafina and the purchasing manager.

The arrests were front page news in the *Union News* and *Springfield Republican* as well as the lead story on all the local TV news reports. Even though the operation was off the record and no real mob skin was lost, several members of the DeLuca administration were so furious they demanded Don Serafina be whacked. It was only as the result of Renzo's many years of faithful service to the mob that Bruno DeLuca begrudgingly gave Don a pass. Renzo took the message from Bruno back to his eldest son: "You fuck up again, and even God won't be able to save you." Thereafter, he was referred to as "that *gavone* Serafina" by the local wiseguys. Don quit his city job and spent the next fifteen years flitting from one occupation to another, just trying to make a living. He owned a bar, started a restaurant, owned a residential remodeling business, built houses, and had an income tax service. His stress was so intense he almost ate and drank himself to death. He ballooned from 180 pounds to 275 pounds and suffered from high blood pressure and ulcers. His wife, Carmelita, the daughter of another mobster, divorced him.

Then on one fateful February night in 1984, while driving home on Columbus Avenue after closing his bar in Agawam, Don was approaching the block where Bruno DeLuca's restaurant, La Fortuna, was located. He thought he recognized Bruno himself coming out the front door heading for his car parked in the adjacent lot. At about the same instant, a vehicle with its lights off pulled out in front of Don, cutting him off. For Don, everything seemed to go into slow motion as the vehicle slowly made its way toward Bruno and suddenly, out of the side window, a gun emerged. Bruno, always on the alert, also saw the weapon and reacted by diving to the pavement. There followed two muzzle flashes and the corresponding pop, pop of a small caliber revolver. Meanwhile, Don instinctively floored his car and slammed into the rear bumper of the assailants' vehicle. The impact was enough to jar the revolver out of the assassin's hand, sending it careening back down the street and under a parked car. Seeing Don's actions, Bruno, despite having taken a bullet, was able to pull his own weapon and returned fire at his attackers. The driver of the attacking vehicle, after recovering from the impact, floored his accelerator, sped up Columbus Avenue and entered I-91 at the State Street entrance.

By the time the police arrived, several of DeLuca's button men had surrounded their boss and, on Bruno's orders, had pulled Don out of the wreckage of his car. Don was bleeding from his forehead, where it had impacted the windshield. He was doubled over in pain, as a result of cracked ribs from colliding with the steering wheel. Bruno's wound was a through-and-through on his left bicep, requiring only stitches and a few days in a sling. Don's head wound required fifteen stitches and he had three cracked ribs. His vehicle was totaled. The next day when Don Serafina returned home from the hospital, he discovered a brand-new Jaguar XJ Series III sitting in his driveway with a note reading "Compliments of Mr. Bruno DeLuca."

It didn't take the Springfield police long to find the gun that was jolted out of the shooter's hand. It took almost less time, after the fingerprints were identified, for Bruno to have the name of the shooter. Not that he needed it; the forensic evidence only confirmed the word on the street that the shooter was a young tough guy from West Springfield who didn't appreciate having to kick up 50 percent of his drug earnings to the organization. He and his brother had recently complained to one of Bruno's capos they thought 50 percent was too steep. The capo told them if they didn't like it, they could take up their beef with the boss, which they did, but not in a traditional sit-down. After the botched hit, the brothers ran, and ran far and fast. Predictably, without a well-thought-out plan, they couldn't run fast enough or far enough. Three days later, the Florida state police found their car halfway submerged in the swamp off South Dixie Highway ten miles south of Florida City. Both brothers had been shot in the back of the head.

As an additional reward for his quick action and unselfish disregard for his own safety, Bruno DeLuca designated Don Serafina under his personal protection. As word of Don's heroics spread, his life changed again, forever. From that day forward all the local wiseguys called him Don, and when they saw him at a bar or restaurant, they bought him drinks. Legitimate business deals came his way without him even trying. It got so bad Don almost felt dirty himself. Finally, after two years of this celebrity treatment, Don went to Bruno DeLuca and asked him to remove the protected designation. Bruno said the best he could do was to make sure everyone knew that Don was his own man and didn't want any special favors. That seemed to work for a while, but Don Serafina always retained a connected aura about him. Over the years he learned to live with this and even occasionally used it to his advantage. The whole incident revitalized Don's personal life. He began regular workouts at the gym; he lost sixty-five pounds and all his physical maladies magically disappeared.

■ ■ ■

The first time Bart realized Don Serafina might not be a typical greaseball hustler was during the final round of the club championship. He and Don were both paired in the third flight and after the first two rounds were tied for the lead. After twelve holes on the final day, they were still only separated by one stroke and Don had the advantage. Teeing off on the short par four, Don pulled his drive left into the pine trees, about eighty yards short of the green. Bart's ball was lying in the middle of the fairway only sixty yards from the pin. Don made a remarkable low punch shot out of the trees to the edge of the green. Bart hit a half sand wedge to within eight feet of the pin. Don then chipped up within eighteen inches and made the putt for what appeared to be a remarkable par. Bart's birdie putt rimmed out and he tapped it in for a par. *Shit*, thought Bart, *that was my chance to get even.* As they were walking to the fourteenth tee, Don announced, "I had a six."

"Six!" Bart exclaimed. "What happened?"

Don in a disgusted tone replied, "As I was taking my practice swing, I hit the pine needles near the ball and it moved. That's a two-stroke penalty."

That day, Bart's opinion of Don Serafina began to change. Bart had heard that golf was a sport where another man's true character always came out. He now had a real-life example and one self-administered penalty that cost Don Serafina the championship of the third flight by one stroke.

Bart wasn't sure how it happened, but one day while he and Don were walking to their nearly identical drives on the par five fourth hole, they agreed to play as partners in the upcoming member-member tournament. Their partnership in the tournament turned out to be the beginning of a wonderful friendship, a rewarding business relationship for Bart, and the foundation for him to move his stock market gains offshore.

CHAPTER 51

Don Serafina was one of the first individuals to own cash machines in Massachusetts. Beginning in the late 1980s, Don owned a check-cashing business he ran out of several local convenience stores around Springfield. In the 1990s automated tellers were beginning to become popular. As soon as Massachusetts authorized the ownership of cash machines by nonbanks and allowed their placement virtually anywhere, Don launched his most brilliant and successful commercial enterprise.

By mid-1995 Don had over fifty machines in various gas stations and convenience stores all over the metropolitan Springfield area and had the opportunity to add three machines a month if he could find some reliable help to assist him. He turned to Bart to pick up the management of his existing locations so he could focus on adding new locations. Bart was initially reluctant to take on a regular job, but Don was very persuasive when he wanted to be. Don walked him through the economics of the business and had him tag along for a week during his cash restocking rounds.

The user of the cash machine paid a two-dollar fee for each transaction, whether the withdrawal was for $10 or $100. Don worked out a lease-purchase agreement with the manufacturer of the cash machines allowing him pay off each machine in less than eighteen months. Don had a rule that if after six months a location wasn't doing four hundred transactions per month, he would pull it and set it up in a new location. After bank processing charges, fees paid to the location owner, and the maintenance contract, Don was averaging almost $20,000 per month. Don had approximately $250,000 in cash tied up in the machines. He spent five hours each morning restocking machines with cash, leaving him all afternoon to play golf. The processing bank provided an online statement on each machine, including how much cash was left in it. From this detail it was easy to schedule daily cash requirements and his restocking route. The Nevada processing bank made automatic daily collections from the users' banks and deposited the funds, less their fee, in Don's account.

It was a pretty straightforward enterprise except it could be dangerous. Whoever did the restocking usually drove around to known locations with at least $20,000 in cash. Some of those locations were in particularly dangerous neighborhoods. Fortunately, on any given day, only the restocker knew his route and timing; but every machine was generally replenished at least twice a week. The risk was someone could stake out a location for a couple of days waiting for Don to restock the machine with cash. Given his background, Don was a pretty savvy and cool businessman. In order not to draw attention to himself, he made his rounds in what appeared to be a beat-up 1984 Oldsmobile Cutlass, but it was really a mechanically perfect vehicle capable of 0–60 in six seconds. Sitting between his legs, next to his .357

Magnum, was a brown paper bag stuffed with five-, ten-, and twenty-dollar bills. Before he stopped at one of his locations, he always drove around the block a couple of times scouting for suspicious vehicles or individuals. His antenna was always up, even when he wasn't carrying a wad of cash.

Don offered Bart a deal to take over the restocking of his paid-off machines, for which Bart would receive forty cents per transaction. Doing the math, Bart figured that for less than twenty hours a week, he could pocket over five grand a month . . . not bad for a part-time retirement job. The only catch was he had to get a concealed weapon license and learn how to shoot a revolver, something he was not too keen on. It didn't take him long to learn the safest time to refill the machines was when most of the drunks and druggies were sleeping it off, between 6:00 a.m. and noon.

During the two years Bart worked for Don, he slowly took on the responsibility for fifty machines, although Don would have liked him to take on seventy-five or eighty. Bart's reluctance to assume more responsibility forced Don to find another golfing buddy to pick up the slack.

Besides golf, Don Serafina's other passion was gambling. He had been going to Vegas several times a year until the Mashantucket Pequot Indians opened Foxwoods Casino in Connecticut. Thereafter, Don became an almost weekly player at the nearby Indian casino. During one of his trips, he met a Chinese businessman and equally passionate gambler named Li Ng. The two became quite friendly and began coordinating their trips to Foxwoods so they could play the $100 blackjack tables together. One day, Li presented Don with a unique business proposition. Lee and his backers in Shanghai were in the process of signing contracts with several Boston-area high tech companies to supply temporary assembly line workers. Lee had access to hundreds of Chinese, Vietnamese, and Cambodian immigrants, both legal and illegal, who were willing to work for cash on a week-to-week basis. Don's part in the deal was to provide Li with the cash he needed on Friday to pay off the workers. The hiring companies would wire transfer their payment to Shanghai on Friday afternoon and the Chinese, in turn, would wire transfer Don's loan money, plus 2 percent interest, to his bank account on Monday. In all likelihood Li and his partners were charging the US companies a hefty premium over what they were paying their temps; but for the companies this was still a significant savings versus hiring permanent employees. Suspicious, Bart asked Don why the Chinese would borrow money from him at many times the bank rate. Don's response was it had something to do with the availability of US dollars to the Chinese. Having done some business in China himself, Bart was aware the average nonstrategic Chinese business enterprise had difficulty getting US dollars to pay their foreign debts. That left an offshore service business, like a temporary employment agency, scratching for US dollars. With virtually no collateral to secure a bank loan in the US, Don's Chinese clients found his loans a quick and easy solution to bridge the gap between Thursday and Monday. This explanation alleviated Bart's suspicions.

On a normal week, Don advanced Li $40,000. It was the same $40,000, over and over again, fifty-two weeks a year. His annual interest was more than the perpetual $40,000 he had on loan. Don's comment to Bart, when he told him the details of his arrangement with the Chinese, was "My father would roll over in his grave if he knew I was getting more than 100 percent interest without being considered a loan shark."

CHAPTER 52

After the initial recruitment by his Uncle Al and Frankie Del-Monico, Peter's contact for arson-related jobs was always Frankie. His uncle never again brought up the subject, except to periodically indicate Frankie had good things to say about his skills. Eventually Peter's fee was increased to $25,000 a job. Not yet thirty years old, he was living large in the Hamptons. His weekend summer bashes in the Hamptons were talked about all over Manhattan on Mondays. If you were young, spent summers in the Hamptons, and didn't get invited to one of Peter LaRocca's events, you were a nobody.

By 1997 Peter LaRocca was the go-to guy for all the New York families' arson needs. Besides the original scheme for Frankie DelMonico, he was subcontracted for jobs up and down the East Coast. Originally each job gave him an emotional rush. Now those feelings were fading, and he began worrying about getting caught. His real estate business was doing well, and with the money he had socked away from both the drug sales and arson scheme, he felt he could live very comfortably going legit.

Out of nowhere, Peter called his father and invited him to the first Yankee-Red Sox series of the season to be played at Yankee Stadium. Bart couldn't believe it. Was he finally going to reconnect with his son? He couldn't wait for the day to come; he hardly slept the night before thinking about all the things he wanted to say in hopes of making up for all those lost years. The drive from Springfield to the Bronx seemed to take forever.

They met an hour and a half before the scheduled Saturday afternoon game so they could do the whole fan thing: walk through Monument Park, watch batting practice, get a couple of autographs, and have hot dogs and beer together over lunch. The weather was perfect, Peter was incredibly demonstrative, and the Yankees won. For the first time in years, Bart felt Peter seemed at peace with himself.

In August Bart reciprocated. He invited Peter to a weekend series between the two rivals, this time at Fenway. Bart paid a small fortune for box-seat tickets for the three-game series. He also reserved each of them a room at the Copley Plaza Hotel for two nights. In spite of the fact the Red Sox took two out of three games, father and son again had a wonderful time. They drank beers and laughed at the Bull and Finch Pub, had ice cream cones in Feneuil Market, consumed more bear, and listened to Irish folk music at the Black Rose. Peter insisted on treating for dinner at Mamma Maria's in the North End. They spent hours talking about their dysfunctional past, even breaking out in laughter over the times Peter told his father to "go fuck himself" and when Gina discovered his condoms and Penthouse magazines. Peter became interested in his father's new career in the ATM business. The more they talked about it, the more Peter became intrigued and excited with the possibilities of establishing his own ATM operation in the Hamptons. They talked for hours about a marketing plan, concluding it might be slow during the winter, but summers would be phenomenal. Instead of gas stations and convenience stores being the primary locations, both of them felt bars and motels would probably get the most action. The whole subject seemed to energize him. Promising to free himself from a few commitments over the next couple of months, he got his father to agree to help him set up the business.

When Peter returned to the Hamptons, he began slowly extricating himself from his drug sales, telling his uncle he thought local law enforcement was beginning to get suspicious, and at the same time he informed his Uncle Al he would this would be his last torch job. To Peter's surprise Al did not try to talk him out of his plans.

It was as a result of one of those out-of-town contracts for the Bosco crime family in Philadelphia that the whole insurance conspiracy began to unravel. While investigating an arson case in Philadelphia, an insurance adjuster noticed an eerie similarity between that case and two other cases, one in the Bronx and another in Newark. The investigator did not identify anything suspicious until the building owner began to redevelop the property. Curiously, all three unconnected parties used the same Brooklyn environmental firm to do the site cleanup. This coincidence prompted him to dig deeper; and the deeper he dug, the more coincidences he discovered. He found three other fires covered by other insurance companies that had many of the same characteristics: recently insured with environmental site cleanup clauses, fires apparently started by some kind of trespasser, the same site cleanup company, and the same redevelopment contractor. Recognizing their investigator may have stumbled upon a dangerous interstate insurance scam, the insurance company turned their findings over to the FBI. It didn't take the FBI long to recognize the unmistakable fingerprint of a lucrative mob scheme. Using their most successful process for ferreting out mob scams by following the money, it soon became apparent Frankie DelMonico was right in the middle of the operation. Without too much effort, the FBI was able to identify the environmental inspectors that were on the take and with a little pressure were able to get them to accept a generous plea in exchange for their testimony. Frankie, however, being a cautious gangster had maintained sufficient buffers between himself and the inspectors to be able to avoid any direct connection. After a visit from the FBI, one of the property owners panicked and demanded a meeting with Frankie, whereupon the owner suddenly vanished.

Federal prosecutors figured they had enough evidence for a RICO indictment on Frankie, six of his underlings, and the property owners; but they wanted undisputed direct evidence of Frankie's involvement. They also wanted Al Nicosia and the "torch." They decided to set up a sting operation using an undercover agent posing as the owner of a defunct and long-time vacant printing plant on the Brooklyn waterfront.

The undercover agent, at a bar known to be a mob hangout, put on a very convincing drunken tirade about being tired of sitting on his vacant building. Frankie, having already solved the problem of his one skittish owner and not knowing the corrupt inspectors had been flipped by the Feds, agreed to meet with the potential new client. Fearing their plant would be searched for concealed cameras and microphones, the Feds employed the newest parabolic microphone from a panel truck parked in an adjoining lot. Although there was significant background noise, technicians were able to isolate the voices of Frankie, his Brooklyn representative, Carmine Nunzi, and the planted warehouse owner.

Unfortunately, Frankie was too smart to spell out exactly what was going to happen for his $65,000 consulting fee. He just suggested that if the property owner was able to up his insurance coverage to include site cleanup, his problem could be resolved by the end of the year. A week later, with a new policy in force, the undercover agent paid $65,000 to Frankie's representative. Agents concealed in a Brooklyn Union Gas panel truck immediately began their round-the-clock surveillance of the property.

It only took a couple of nights for their vigilance to be rewarded. Near midnight a darkly clad figure was spotted and photographed stealthily surveying the perimeter fence. He carefully made his way halfway around the perimeter before he discovered the small opening. The Feds had cut a hole in the cyclone fence, which made it appear as if there were regular intruders to the property. Once inside the fence it took him another five minutes to find the stacked pallets that gave him access to the portico roof. Again the pallets had been skillfully placed and stacked to look as if intruders had established their entry point. Once on the roof a broken window was clearly visible. The intruder was photographed climbing through the window. Since he was not observed with any gear or paraphernalia, agents correctly assumed this was only a scouting mission. Through the window the surveillance team could just barely make out the muted glow of the intruder's flashlight. Once he was inside the building, the Feds were pretty confident he would quickly discover the telltale evidence of intruders they planted. Agents had planted an old mattress, spent needles, used condoms, and empty beer and liquor bottles in one of the large rooms. The area appeared to reveal regular use by local druggies.

Twenty minutes later, as the intruder climbed back out the window, an agent with an early version of a night vision–enabled digital SLR camera was able to capture a recognizable photo of the suspect. By the next morning, the surveillance team had identified the intruder as Peter LaRocca, nephew of one of the most powerful men in organized crime. A court order authorized phone taps on the suspect's home and mobile phones along with round-the-clock surveillance. Agent Sam Sardo suggested he be allowed to talk to Bart LaRocca about their suspicions, hoping that Bart would be able to convince his son to turn state's evidence. However, Sam's bosses rejected his suggestion. The lead prosecutor did not want to take the chance either Bart or Peter would warn Frankie and Al. Besides, he believed Peter would be more likely to flip on his uncle if he was caught in the act.

Three nights later, under a new moon and within minutes of the start of Monday Night Football, Peter, this time carrying a gym bag, made his way through the fence. He climbed the pallets and crawled through the broken window. Slowly making his way back to the "party room," he warily surveyed his surroundings one more time. He did not notice the two agents perched behind some empty 55-gallon drums on the far side of the large open room. As he began unpacking his tool kit, the beam from his flashlight illuminated the layers of dust and dirt on the concrete floor. Interestingly, there were only a handful of footprints on the floor. *Curious*, he thought, *you'd think if kids were partying here, the floor would be loaded with footprints, but it's not. In fact, I'd suspect that the footprints would be mostly from sneakers, but they're not, they're from flat-soled shoes.* He stood up, scanned his flashlight around the building one more time looking for something else out of order. When he got to the drums, he stopped. There it was; *I don't remember those from my first visit! In fact, there doesn't seem to be any dust on them! Fuck, this must be a setup!* He continued to pan the room with his light, looking for something else out of order. His flashlight beam revealed two sets of flat-soled shoe prints leading to the back side of the drums. For the first time since the day he told his father to go fuck himself, Peter LaRocca was scared shitless. Fighting off the primeval instinct to turn and run, he forced himself to remain calm and find a means of escape. He quickly concluded his only chance was to create a diversion, but first he had to make it look as if he suspected nothing and continue to execute his original plan.

During his first scouting visit to the old printing plant, Peter stumbled across and confiscated an empty toluene can. Toluene was the universal solvent used in the printing industry prior to the introduction of water-based inks. He had refilled the empty can with toluene. His plan had been to litter the area with a combination of empty and full Sterno cans and one well-used pot for cooking crack cocaine. He would leave the opened can of toluene next to the mattress and then dump out the contents of one can of Sterno on the old mattress and light it. Peter figured investigators would conclude the partiers had found the can of toluene and discovered that sniffing it was a quick high. They would also reach the conclusion that, while they were cooking the coke, the toluene fumes were accidently ignited by the Sterno flames. He assumed it wouldn't be too much of a stretch for them to reason the fire was an accident and the partiers were lucky to escape with their lives.

Turning his back to the barrels, he went down on one knee, placed his flashlight on the floor and began quickly removing the pot and can of toluene from the gym bag. At the same time Peter fixed his exit route in his mind and quickly pulled a MSA full-face respirator over his head. He then poured the toluene into the pot and lit one of the Sterno cans. This was to be his diversion; to unprotected eyes and lungs, toluene vapors cause almost immediate eye and lung irritation. At that instant, the two federal agents hiding behind the barrels watched Peter's ghostly image through their night vision goggles. Their instructions were to try to catch the arsonist in the act and alive. Assuming the professional arsonist would set up some kind of delayed ignition, they waited one moment too long. Holding the handle of the pot in his right hand, he straightened up and spun, like a discus thrower. With the same fluid motion, he kicked the lit Sterno can toward the barrels and flung the toluene after the Sterno can. The light from the ignition of the toluene exploded through the agents' night vision goggles, temporarily blinding both men while the vapors from the toluene sucked most of the air out of their lungs. Their survival instincts instantly kicked in, and they began blindly running away from the inferno. Peter had already begun his retreat in the opposite direction toward his exit. With his adrenalin pumping, he barely heard the panicky cries and gagging coming from behind him. The agent who was guarding the exit also had on night vision goggles. He, too, was temporarily blinded, giving Peter the few seconds he needed to bolt past him and out the window. By the time the agent had recovered, Peter had jumped off the second-story roof. The agent's only hope of catching the arsonist was if the backup team was now in place outside the building. When he reached the edge of the roof and looked down, he realized no reinforcements would be necessary. The perp, on his desperate leap off the roof, had impaled himself on an old rusted signpost. The metal post penetrated his groin and severed the femoral artery. Within minutes, as the FBI agents helplessly watched, Gina and Bart LaRocca's only child bled to death.

CHAPTER 53

Shortly after midnight, Bart LaRocca was reclining on the leather sofa in the living room of his rented two-bedroom apartment in West Springfield. Alternating between states of restless sleep and exhausted consciousness, he knew he should summon up the energy to make it into the bedroom. The seven and one-half minute overtime period of the Monday Night Football game between the Green Bay Packers and the Minnesota Vikings had ended a few minutes earlier, and the talking heads were wrapping it up. At first he wasn't sure if the ringing sound was from the television or his phone. He ignored the first few rings. Finally, annoyed, he got up and walked to the kitchen to pick up the receiver. Standing beside the kitchen table he growled into the speaker, "What could be so important at this hour of the night?"

"Mr. LaRocca, this is Special Agent Sam Sardo of the FBI. We met a few years ago after your mother-in-law's funeral."

Knowing it can't be good news when the FBI calls at one o'clock in the morning, lucidity instantly returned to Bart's brain.

Agent Sardo continued, "I know it's late, but I didn't think it was appropriate for this to wait until the morning. Normally we would address this sort of thing in person; but as I said, I am three and a half hours away and I wanted you to hear this news directly from me."

Remembering the last thing Agent Sardo had brought up during their first meeting was his concern about Peter, an alarm went off in Bart's head, followed by an almost inaudible sigh.

Sensing that his listener had just transitioned into alarmed mode, Agent Sardo continued, "There is no easy way to relay this news . . . Peter was involved in a fatal incident earlier this evening." Hesitating briefly to give Bart a chance to absorb the horrible news, the FBI agent chose his words carefully. "I'm sure you have many questions about what transpired this evening. Unfortunately, at this point, I am not at liberty to divulge all the details. What I can tell you is that we have had Peter under surveillance for a week or so in connection with a series of arson fires on the East Coast. This evening, while staking out what we believed to be his next target, we observed Peter entering an abandoned building. When our team attempted to apprehend Peter, he fled. During the pursuit, he apparently tried to escape by jumping off a second-floor roof and, unfortunately, was critically injured. I'm deeply sorry, Mr. LaRocca. This is not what the FBI had in mind. It was our intent to safely apprehend Peter. We have reason to believe he was not acting on his own, and he was just a hired torch. We had hoped that, once caught, he would see it was in his best interest to give up the people who hired him."

As Agent Sardo spoke, Bart felt as if he was standing on an underground subway platform with a train speeding into the station. There seemed to be a wave of pressure building in his head and a sound, nothing specific, just noise. The noise continued to build, until his knees began to buckle. He caught himself just in time and was able to drop on to one of the kitchen chairs. As his body slumped onto the chair, this normally stoic man let out a gut-wrenching cry. "Nooooo!"

The FBI agent could almost feel Bart's pain resonate through the phone. He started to ask, "Mr. LaRocca, are you . . . ?" But he never got to finish his sentence because Bart, through a super-human effort, had already regained enough composure to ask, "Does his mother know?"

"Not yet, Mr. LaRocca . . . we called you first, assuming you might want to break the news to her yourself."

"Has the news been released to the press yet?"

"Not yet; there is a press conference scheduled for 9:00 a.m. announcing that a serial arsonist was critically injured while attempting to elude capture. Right now both police and fire investigators are on site and there are TV news helicopters and ground crews all around the perimeter of the site, but all they know so far is that it is a large warehouse fire. The location is in Brooklyn, so it wouldn't surprise me if your brother-in-law finds out some of the details before the official announcement."

"OK, I'll be down there as soon as I can. Can we meet around 5:00 a.m. somewhere in Queens?"

"Yeah, there's a twenty-four-hour diner on the corner of Queens Boulevard and Fifty-Third Avenue in Elmhurst."

They exchanged cell phone numbers and agreed to meet at five.

▪ ▪ ▪

After he hung up, Bart felt dizzy; he sat on the couch for a few minutes alternating between light-headedness and nausea. It took him several minutes to find enough composure to start thinking about what he needed to do. He robotically made a pot of strong coffee for his three-hour drive. He then headed for the shower with a thousand thoughts running through his head. Forcing his mind to run likely scenarios of what was to transpire over the next several days, he concluded he needed to pack a suitcase with at least a week's worth of dark clothes. Bart made a mental note to call Don Serafina so Don could schedule someone to cover his cash machines.

On a long lonely drive, it's really curious how the mind migrates from one subject to the next. You never know how one thought will suddenly trigger a jump to a completely different and seemingly unrelated topic. That night, as Bart took the cutoff from I-91 toward the Wibur Cross Parkway, he had already rambled through several different topics, including what he was going to say to Gina and why Agent Sardo mentioned Little Nicky would probably learn about Peter's death before the press conference. At that moment, he had transitioned to the last couple of times he and Peter had been together.

Damn it, Bart thought, *finally after over a decade of friction, it seemed as if we were going to bond again.* Then his thoughts made another one of those inexplicable leaps across the chasm to another tragic father and son relationship.

Five years earlier, when the CSI management team was on a strategic planning meeting at Hilton Head Island, Bart ran into General Harlan Ryan and his wife Rita. After a long ten-hour day cooped up in the hotel's conference room, nobody was in the mood to get in the car and drive to dinner. Within walking distance of where they were staying was an above-average seafood restaurant called Alexander's. As it was an off-season week night, the party of seven had no trouble getting a table at the back of the room.

During cocktails and hors d'oeuvres, the strategic arguments from earlier in the day continued unabashed. Bart, bored with any further business discussions, excused himself and wandered out on the patio. Standing on the deck watching the sun sink into the huge pine trees that dominated the island, he heard a strangely familiar voice. It had a powerfully authoritative resonance with a hint of a southern accent. Bart turned to see if he recognized the speaker. Sitting at one of the outside tables was an elderly couple, probably in their late seventies. Instantaneously, Bart made the assessment the man was retired military. He had the classic look of an officer, tall, still in good shape, close-cropped hair with conservative but expensive clothes; and they were on Hilton Head Island, a favorite retirement location of senior officers. The woman was still stunning. Even in her sitting position, Bart could tell she, too, was in excellent physical condition and decked out in the kind of expensive attire a senior officer's wife would wear.

Without appearing to be focusing on the couple, Bart slowly made his way to an empty table next to them. So as to not appear to simply be eavesdropping, he ordered a beer. The discussion was partly a mild argument and partly a lecture by the old man. After listening for a few minutes, Bart continued to have the sensation this was a voice he had heard before. Every few seconds he would steal a glance, trying to place him. Finally the man was saying something like "If we don't do this soon, we'll be out of luck." Bingo! A light went off in Bart's head. *Son of a bitch*, he thought, *that's Robbie's father, General Harlan Ryan.*

Sensing a lull in the conversation, Bart interrupted, "Excuse me, sir, you wouldn't happen to be General Harlan Ryan, would you?"

"Yes, I am; and who would you be?"

"Bart LaRocca, sir."

"Robbie's roommate from USC," enthusiastically exclaimed the woman.

"That's right, Mrs. Ryan," Bart replied while catching a glimpse of a pained expression on the general's face. "I haven't heard from Robbie since Vietnam. What's he up to?"

While the general remained stoically silent, Mrs. Ryan, in a saddened voice, replied, "I guess you haven't heard . . . Robbie was killed in Vietnam in 1974."

Stunned, Bart barely found the voice to choke out, "I'm so sorry, Mr. and Mrs. Ryan . . . I had no idea. I always assumed after his second tour he caught a three-year assignment back in the States and the war was over before he got new orders."

Finally, the general spoke. "That's what a smart officer would have done, but not my idiot son."

"Harlan!" Mrs. Ryan exclaimed in an exasperated tone.

"Yeah, I know, Rita, but that doesn't mean that what he did wasn't stupid and the cause of his own demise." Without hesitation the general looked up at Bart and said, "Sit down, LaRocca, and let me tell you about your ex-roommate." Apparently not wanting to torture herself with the story again, Rita excused herself and headed for the ladies' room. For the next fifteen minutes a stoic General Harlan Ryan related the tragic story.

Robbie's Vietnamese girlfriend, Anh, gave birth to a healthy baby boy just a few months before his tour was up. Robbie reluctantly returned to the States for a tour at MacDill Air Force Base near Tampa. Immediately upon his return, he volunteered for another tour in Southeast Asia. When, after a year, he didn't receive new orders for Vietnam, he resigned his commission. The general was furious; it was his influence that kept Captain Ryan from getting new orders to the SEA theater. He never had considered his son was so much in love he would throw away everything to be with his new family. Even after a desperate, last-minute visit by his mother and father, Robbie wouldn't relent. So in mid-1973 Robbie Ryan returned to Phan Rang as a civilian. He quickly got work as a civilian contractor, air-ferrying cargo between major cities. He moved his family to Saigon and was doing fine until it became obvious the United States was going to pull out and the North Vietnamese would overrun the South. Robbie desperately tried to get his family to the States, but there were thousands of more influential Vietnamese that couldn't get officially relocated. About a month before the fall of Saigon, things were getting pretty dicey around the city. Vietcong and North Vietnamese sympathizers wreaked havoc on those perceived as American accomplices. One night an unidentified assailant tossed a hand grenade into Robbie and Anh's small house. When the rubble was searched, Robbie and Anh's bodies were identified. There was no sign of their son or Anh's mother, who was still living with them. In the chaos that preceded the American evacuation and the subsequent purge by the North Vietnamese, all traces of the grandmother and child were lost.

■ ■ ■

After apparently crying her eyes out one more time over the loss of her only son, Rita Ryan returned near the end of her husband's story. For his part, the only emotion the general displayed was anger, not at the people that killed his son, but at his son.

A few moments of profound silence followed the conclusion of General Ryan's story. It was finally broken by Mrs. Ryan. "It's so good to meet a friend of Robbie's; it helps me to remember all the good times we had together."

Encouraged by her positive twist to an otherwise heartrending evening, Bart offered, "I'm sure you are aware Vietnam is beginning to open up to western visitors. Have you ever considered trying to find your grandson?"

"Are you shitting me, LaRocca?" the general growled. "Do you think I give a crap about some half-breed abomination from my ungrateful son?"

For the first time that night Rita Ryan asserted herself with her domineering husband. "You may not care, Harlan, but I do. If I ever get an opportunity to locate my grandson, I will jump at the chance; and if you won't join me in that search, you can go to hell!"

CHAPTER 54

Bart pulled into the small parking lot of the Empire Diner at five minutes to five. This was it; in a few minutes he would know whether this was some kind of an unfortunate mistake or wretched reality. Agent Sardo and another man were already seated at a booth at the far end of the diner. Based upon their attire and grooming, it was obvious to the other five patrons on the other end of the diner these were two law enforcement officers. On the other hand, they must have figured that Bart, with his nervous and somewhat disheveled appearance, was either an undercover cop or a snitch. Both men already had half-finished cups of black coffee in front of them.

When he saw Bart, Agent Sardo slid out of the booth and stood to shake his hand. The other agent remained seated and waited for Sardo to introduce them. Bart ignored the agent's hand and stared pleadingly at Sardo.

Awkwardly Sardo withdrew his hand and almost in a soft self-conscious voice said, "Mr. LaRocca, I am so sorry we are meeting under these circumstances. As I told you earlier tonight, the bureau had every intention of apprehending Peter unharmed."

"Thanks, Sardo, so much for intentions."

After a prolonged and uncomfortable pause, Agent Sardo introduced the new man in the booth. "Bart, this is Special Agent Trent Eastland. Agent Eastland heads up the task force that's looking into the series of arson fires."

Eastland held out his hand. Bart ignored it and sat down. "I think I need a cup of coffee and something to soak up the acid in my stomach," he mumbled.

Sardo motioned for the waitress, who scurried over with a fresh cup and a pot of coffee. When she arrived, she put the cup in front of Bart and poured.

"Will you get me a toasted English muffin, please?" Bart asked.

"You got it, big boy," replied the perky middle-aged redhead with a still eye-catching body. "Anything for you two sweethearts?" she asked Sardo and Eastland.

"No thanks," they replied in unison.

When she left, Agent Eastland began in a soft almost-whisper, "Sam filled me in on what he told you. Look, we would like to tell you more, but we are still trying to sort out all the facts, and there are issues here the government can't afford to have leaked out just yet. I can add to what Sam already told you that we believe this whole series of arson fires was an organized scheme to defraud insurance companies out of millions of dollars in claims. In fact, the task force believes some New York–based organized crime figures were behind the whole thing.

"In addition, I almost lost three agents tonight trying to apprehend your son. The fire department is still trying to contain the fire Peter started in attempting to escape."

"This is crazy! You're telling me my son is an arsonist for the mob and he tried to kill three agents last night?"

"Unfortunately, we believe that's the case," replied Agent Eastland. After a brief hesitation, he continued, "If there is anything your son relayed to you that might help us in our investigation, your government would be very grateful."

"I bet it would," snapped back Bart. Looking straight at Agent Sardo he asked, "Did you suspect this stuff the first time we met?"

"No, we had no inkling of the arson thing until about six months ago."

"So, what was that all about back then?"

"Well, there were some unconfirmed reports Peter was dealing drugs to some of those rich socialites out in the Hamptons."

Scrunching up his face muscles Bart snarled, "Unconfirmed?"

Agent Sardo shifted uncomfortably in his seat. "At the time there was no direct evidence that he was, and it was so small time; nobody ever seriously investigated it."

"Is that still unconfirmed?"

"The task force is searching his house as we speak. So far they have uncovered a small quantity of cocaine and other drugs."

Visibly shaken by this whole episode, Bart just sat there for a few moments, nervously staring at his hands. He slowly raised his head, revealing the moisture in his eyes. Fighting to keep his emotions out of his voice, Bart managed to tell the agents without his voice cracking, "I can't add anything to your investigation. Until earlier this year, Peter and I really didn't see each other or talk on the phone. I thought recently perhaps things were changing and there was a chance for me to become part of his life again, but obviously there were things he could never reveal to me." Hesitating briefly, the distraught father let out a muffled sigh and continued, "I'm guessing the bureau believes my brother-in-law, Al Nicosia, is somehow involved in this scheme, right?"

Sardo gave Eastland a quick glance. "We can't confirm or deny your supposition, but if you have any evidence supporting that theory, we'd be grateful."

"I have nothing. Look, Agent Sardo, were you planning on coming with me to break the news to Gina?"

"If that's what you want."

"No, I'd rather do this myself; although it might get dicey if Al's already there."

"I'll tell you what, we'll follow you over there."

As Bart pulled up to the house that Gina and his two brother-in-laws had inherited after their mother died, he saw the two goons standing on the front lawn. *So, Little Nicky knows . . . I hope I can keep my cool with that son of a bitch*, he thought. He was hardly out of the car when the bigger of the two goons yelled, "Get back in the car, LaRocca. Al will call you when Gina is ready to see you."

Not even hesitating, Bart continued to head for the front door. "Are you speaking for Gina or Little Nicky?"

Ignoring Bart's question, one of the thugs blocked the sidewalk. "Get back in the car or there will be more than one funeral this week."

Bart attempted to fake right and go left, but the second goon, surprisingly agile, grabbed him by the shoulders and shoved him back. Bart stumbled backward and almost went down. He caught himself with some of the same agility that had made him a good receiver thirty years earlier. He tried a new tactic. "Look, if Gina tells me she doesn't want to see me, I'll go quietly. How's that?"

"That's not going to happen, asshole; now this is your last chance to get out of here in one piece."

The two FBI agents were parked in plain view at the corner. They were just about to hit the lights and intervene when Al came out the front door. "What the fuck is all the commotion about out here?" Then he saw Bart. "Oh, look who showed up, if it isn't the grieving father who didn't have any use for his kid for the last ten years. You're not wanted here, LaRocca. I'll call ya when everything is arranged."

"Don't be an asshole, Al. I'm his father, and I'm here to see his mother. Now unless Gina said she didn't want to see me, I'm going in to talk to her."

"I swear, LaRocca, one of these days I'm going to kick your ass all over this town."

Bart played his trump card. "So tell me, Al, was it you that got Peter involved in this debacle?"

Little Nicky took two quick steps toward his brother-in-law, then, from years of looking over his shoulder, he saw the unmistakable government-issued Crown Vic at the corner. Stopping in his tracks, he growled, "Fuck you, LaRocca, I loved that kid as if he was my own."

"That doesn't answer the question."

Changing the subject, Al barked, "The only reason I'm not going to beat the living shit out of you now is because of Gina. I better not find out you upset her anymore than she already is." With that Al Nicosia let the aluminum storm door slam behind him and marched to his car. On his way to the car he said to his two goons, "Stay here and keep an eye on my sister and make sure those assholes from the press don't bother her."

Without even ringing the bell or knocking, Bart opened the front door. He could hear Gina sobbing before he got out of the foyer. He found her sprawled on the living room couch with her head buried in her hands. The sobs were coming in short gasps. Bart slowly moved toward her, trying to decide how to make himself known. Before he could make a decision, Gina somehow sensed his presence. She looked up and through tear-stained eyes she recognized him. Choking her words, she pleaded, "Oh Bart, tell me it's not true . . . Peter can't be dead."

Reaching out with his arms, Bart gently took her hands, raising her from the couch. He wrapped his arms around her and pulled her in close to him. He wasn't sure what to say, so he said nothing; he just held her cheek against his chest and gently stroked the back of her head. Gina started sobbing again. He could feel her body pulsating with every pathetic whimper. God, how he always loved this woman; it hurt him to the core to feel her pain. At that moment, Bart LaRocca felt an overwhelming emptiness. How could he have let the only women he ever truly loved get away and their only child come under the destructive influence of his brother-in-law? After what seemed like an eternity to Bart, Gina finally broke off their clench. She looked him in the face and said, "What did we do so wrong to cause our boy to end up like this?"

Forcing himself not to scream at the top of his lungs, *It was your fucking brother, Al; he's the one who did this to our son*, he somehow managed to reply, "I don't know."

Half expecting Gina to say something that would put the blame on him, he was surprised when she finally said, "The last time Peter was here he told me what a good time you two had in Boston and that you were going to help him get into the automated teller machine business. I thought everything was going great; I was even considering calling you this week and inviting you to have Thanksgiving dinner with us."

"Gina, I talked to two FBI agents before I came over here. What did Al tell you?"

"He didn't have any details except that Peter died in a fire."

Bart began telling her what he had learned from the FBI. When he was done Gina was crying again. She looked at Bart. "I just don't understand it. He was a fireman, for God's sake; he loved his job of saving people and property . . . why would he start fires? It can't be for money. He sold plenty of expensive houses and he knew that if he needed money, I'd give it to him. Besides, he didn't associate with the kind of people who would . . . ," and then she stopped. Aghast she pleaded with Bart, "No, it can't be; he loved Peter like a son. He wouldn't do anything that could harm him . . . would he?"

Bart didn't respond immediately, so Gina pressed him again. "Is Al responsible for this?"

"I don't know for sure, but it wouldn't surprise me."

Gina began weeping uncontrollably. Bart moved toward her, putting his arms around her again and holding her tightly. Neither of them spoke for a long time. Finally Bart apologetically said, "Somebody has to identify the body. I can do it alone, if you're not up to it now. But at some point today we have to talk about arrangements for the wake and funeral."

Choking back her sighs, Gina mumbled, "Yeah, you go; I don't think I could look at his body right now. If you want, you can also make all the arrangements. I just don't want it turned into a spectacle; arrange something quick and private, OK?"

"All right, I'll call you later." Putting his arm around his grieving ex-wife, he kissed her on the cheek.

"Thank you, Bart," Gina whispered. Just before he reached the front door, Gina called out to him, "Would you mind if we had him interred with my parents at St. John's Cemetery?"

"If that's what you want, I can do that."

CHAPTER 55

Identifying a loved one in a morgue, especially your child, has to be one of the worst feelings a human being can experience. Seeing a deceased loved one is always devastating, but the helplessness one feels in the clinical coldness emanating from the sanitized stainless steel viewing room slaps you upside the head, screaming, "Gone forever!"

Driving back to Middle Village, Bart used the time to call Don Serafina, his sister Fran, and finally, John Nicosia. He arranged to stay at Fran's for the next several days. When Bart called John's cell phone, he heard the standard message that Dr. John Nicosia was currently unavailable and for patients to call his office, or dial 911 for an emergency. Bart left his normal brief message: "It's Bart, call me back."

John didn't return the call until Bart was driving to the same Metropolitan Avenue funeral parlor the Nicosias used for both Pietro's and Eleonora's funeral arrangements. Bart sat in the parking lot of the funeral home for almost a half hour talking with John. He could always depend upon John to be a calming influence along with giving him honest feedback and reasonable suggestions, but not this day. The call opened the floodgates of exasperation brought on by the last fifteen years of family strife and heightened by the stark reality of Peter lying on a slab at the morgue. For the first time since his grandmother died thirty-seven years earlier, Bart LaRocca sobbed.

After achieving a little relief from his emotional release, he finally anxiously inquired, "So when are you coming?"

"I just completed two valve replacements and need to stick around until Wednesday morning. Patty Jo and I will catch the one o'clock flight; it gets into LaGuardia at about 9:00 p.m. Do you want to pick us up at the airport?"

"Yeah, I can do that. By the way, John, I'm convinced Al had his hand in this thing Peter was involved in."

"Damn, don't think that, Bart; Al always loved Peter like a son. Hell, I think Peter was the only one Al ever loved besides himself. What did you tell Gina?"

"I told her the FBI thinks organized crime was behind the arson scheme. I believe she has the same suspicions I do but she will probably never accept it as a fact."

■ ■ ■

The arrangements Bart made were simple and dignified: a private viewing on Thursday at the funeral home attended by a few dozen family and friends, followed by a family memorial service Friday morning in the chapel of the funeral home and a ceremonial placing of Peter's ashes in the family mausoleum at St. John's Cemetery. The actual ashes would be interned a few weeks later. After the ceremony at the cemetery they gathered one last time for a buffet lunch at a nearby Italian restaurant. Bart and Al managed to ignore each other, but to everyone except Gina, who once again had found her solace in tranquilizers and vodka, the tension between them was obvious.

Disturbed by Bart's insinuation Al was somehow responsible for Peter's involvement in the arson spree, John confronted his brother out in the garage on Thursday night. Al expressed outright indignation at his brother's suggestion; he categorically denied knowledge or involvement in any arson scheme. Always able to read his brother's body language, John came away from the discussion convinced Al was lying. Equally disturbing to John was his sister's state of mind. Not only had she reverted back to her reliance on drugs and alcohol, she seemed to have given up any hope for the future. Patty Jo, always the optimist, expressed her opinion it was just a temporary phase and over time Gina would emerge a stronger person than before the tragedy. John prayed she was right, but remained doubtful and concerned for his sister's mental and physical well-being.

CHAPTER 56

February 15, 2010

Ever since I arrived back in Seville, Bart had been bragging about the Carnival of Cádiz. On Monday I asked him what time we were leaving on Fat Tuesday for the festival. Completely caught off guard by my inquiry, he just stared at me for a moment, trying to figure out if I was serious. When I didn't follow up with another comment that let him off the hook, he finally replied, "Uh . . . let me check the train schedules and see if there are any hotel rooms left."

Within an hour, using the Tanners' local travel contacts, he was able to get us on a 7:55 a.m. train to Cádiz. David's connections also secured us hotel rooms for Tuesday night at a brand-new four-star hotel, Spa Senator Cádiz, located only a half block from the port.

Like they say about the opera, "You don't have to speak Italian to understand what's happening on stage." It was the same for me at the Carnival de Cádiz. My two years of high school Spanish and the last few weeks in Seville gave me only enough understanding of conversational Spanish to order in a restaurant and understand a fraction of what was going on around me. Even so, the carnival's festivities were not lost on me. The carnival was known worldwide for its acerbic criticisms, stinging sarcasm, and the irreverence of its parody. The locals relished the uproariously funny skits. They were especially fond of the *chirigotas* who train for the whole year to sing in the streets about politics, contemporary news events, and classical everyday situations. The atmosphere and celebrations turned out to be very different from my limited knowledge of pre-Lenten carnivals in Rio de Janeiro and New Orleans. Rather than the spectacular and sensuous, if not raunchy, atmosphere I expected, the Carnival de Cádiz distinguished itself by the cleverness and imagination of the witty and satirical compositions taking place all over the city. For me it was an amusing and entertaining trip.

When the time came to make our way to the rail station for the 8:00 p.m. train back to Seville, I kicked myself for not having challenged Bart a few days earlier. My last-minute prodding of Bart only gave us the opportunity to participate in the last day of the four-day event. My other regret was Marie hadn't been here to share it with us.

Riding on the train back to Seville, Bart began revealing the events following Peter's funeral.

■ ■ ■

Two weeks after the official internment of Peter's ashes, Bart left for Myrtle Beach. David Tanner, who had attended the memorial service, offered Bart one of his real estate company's beach-front high-rise condos. Since Bart didn't know when he would be returning to Springfield, he suggested Don Serafina find a permanent replacement for him.

Bart stayed on the Grand Strand until the end of February, playing golf and fishing the inland waterway. Bart always considered Myrtle Beach a great place to visit and over the years often fantasized about living there. But after two months of resort golf and the never-ending strip malls, he realized it was just that, a great place to visit. It was time to return home; but instead of driving back home on the always-congested I-95, Bart decided to head west on US 74 to Charlotte.

Arriving at the South Park Suites on Wednesday, February 25, 1998, Bart was astonished by the changes in Charlotte since he had lived and worked there in the late 1970s. During the last twenty years the population of the Queen City had more than doubled; and it was now, after New York City, the second largest financial center in the United States. It had transformed itself from a sleepy little backwater town to a modern, world-class metropolis with two professional sports franchises, NASCAR headquarters, and an international airport.

After checking into his suite, he had the sudden compulsion to take a ride out to The Pines Country Club. He wondered if the club was still the same friendly, unpretentious place he remembered from when he and Gina lived in Charlotte. *Only one way to find out*, he thought, *take a shower and drive over there.*

Bart arrived at the Pines lounge around 6:00 p.m. Even though it was a Wednesday night, there were over thirty people either at the bar drinking or at the tables eating dinner. He wasn't sure what kind of reception he would get since it was a private club and he hadn't been a member for almost twenty years. Scanning the room for someone he might remember, his attention was drawn to several tables near the windows overlooking the eighteenth green. To his delight he recognized three of the couples; the guys, all Canadians, were former hockey players for the Charlotte Checkers before the ECHL disbanded in 1977. While he was struggling to remember their names, one of the wives recognized Bart and pointed him out to the others. Rising from the table, one of the former hockey players snaked his way through the maze of people and tables to Bart. In his late forties, the ex-defenseman was still an impressive physical specimen. A tad over 6 feet 2 inches and probably 220 pounds, he still moved with grace and fluidity. "LaRocca, isn't it?" he asked, extending a hand.

"Yeah, I remember you, hockey player from Canada, right? Uh . . . Doug, is that right?"

"Yup, Doug Carbone; what are you doing back here . . . you on business?"

"No, I was just passing through on my way back home to Massachusetts. Figured I'd see how the club was doing. Looks like things haven't changed much in the last twenty years. You guys are all sitting in the same spot as I left you."

"Hell no. A lot's changed, but come sit with us. I'll buy you a drink and we'll fill you in."

Doug reintroduced Bart around the table; they all remembered him and Gina. There was Tim Buckley, better known as "Boomer," and his wife Carole; "The Rocket," real name Tom Richards, and his wife Terry; and finally Doug's girlfriend Nicole. Also at the table were two couples Bart didn't recognize, Larry and Denise Cropper and Gary and June Caesar. Carole was the first to ask, "So how's Gina?"

Bart proceeded, as briefly as he could, to tell them about his and Gina's divorce and of Peter's recent tragic death. As it so often happens while unburdening oneself of one's troubles, people discover they are not alone. Doug was also divorced from his wife, and the Richards had lost a daughter to a drug overdose. All three of the hockey players struggled after the ECHL went bankrupt in 1977. Rocket started his own construction business and struggled for many years to make ends meet. Boomer went into sales, bouncing from one company to another until just recently he landed the position of regional sales manager for Titleist Golf Equipment. Doug returned to Toronto and joined the Royal Canadian Mounted Police. He worked his way up to the rank of inspector in the criminal investigations unit. He eventually was forced to take disability retirement as a result of injuries suffered in a shootout with an IRA fugitive.

Before the evening was over, his Canadian friends had introduced him around the lounge to probably twenty people, half of whom he remembered from his years as a member. Cropper and Caesar, both retired, invited Bart to play as their guest the next morning. Just like at Quaker Farms, there was a group of about twenty guys that regularly played on Tuesdays, Thursdays, and Fridays. Doug also invited Bart to play as a guest on Saturday in another group that included Boomer and Rocket.

February and early March are usually still cold and damp in Charlotte, but that year the weather was spectacular with full sunshine and temperatures rising to the mid-60s by the early afternoon. Bart was in heaven playing a course he had always loved and with guys that seemed to embrace him as if he had never left. Saturday after golf, while having drinks in the lounge with perhaps seventy-five boisterous golfers watching a North Carolina versus Duke basketball game, he made up his mind he was going to move back to Charlotte.

On Sunday and Monday Bart scouted out apartments; he found exactly what he wanted less than four miles from The Pines. On Tuesday he drove the thirteen hours back to Springfield, stopping only for gas and two meals. It took him another two weeks to wrap things up in Massachusetts with Don Serafina, pack his clothes, a few kitchen items, a couple of pieces of furniture and arrange for a U-Haul truck. He towed his car behind the U-Haul. By April 1st he was satisfactorily settled into his new two-bedroom apartment in Charlotte, and he was again a member at The Pines Golf and Country Club.

CHAPTER 57

Bart started scouting out the automated teller situation on his drive up from Myrtle Beach. Stopping for gas at the last South Carolina exit on I-77, he noticed it did not have a cash machine in its convenience store. Before he got back on the interstate, he checked the gas station and convenience store across the street; same situation. During his golfing weekend at The Pines, he stopped at every gas station he passed; conclusion, the Charlotte area seemed ripe for ATMs.

As soon as he was settled in his apartment, he did a broader survey. In less than a week he realized the Charlotte metropolitan area was virtually virgin territory for an independent cash machine business. He immediately hired a local attorney, and member of The Pines, to file the necessary applications for licenses in both North and South Carolina. In June he received all the permits and licenses for South Carolina and immediately contracted with the First National Bank of Nevada for online monitoring, reporting of transactions, and collection from the user's bank accounts. He was able to get the same lease-purchase arrangement as Don Serafina. In July he placed his first two machines just off the interstate in Fort Mill, South Carolina. A week later he received his North Carolina permits and licenses. By December he had fifteen machines in place and was installing a machine a week, with almost half the placements in bars and nightclubs.

His rapid ramp-up was made possible only because of his new golf buddy, Gary Caesar. Gary was a mechanical genius who had recently been laid off by Continental Tire when they closed their Charlotte factory. His severance package had run out six months earlier. When Gary learned of Bart's business plan and requirement for an installer and maintenance man, he anxiously volunteered for the job. After assisting in just two installs by the equipment manufacturer's contract service technician, Gary learned all he needed to know about the machines. The hardest part of the whole setup was getting Bell South to install the dedicated telephone line needed for real-time monitoring.

■ ■ ■

While Bart was getting on with his new life in Charlotte, Gina was struggling with the loss of her only child. Ever since her college days, distressing events had a tendency to provoke rapid mood swings. In most situations it would turn out to be a fleeting emotional roller coaster ride, but occasionally, as with the move to North Carolina in 1979, more serious and longer-term effects would manifest themselves. Peter's death was a devastating experience for everyone that knew him, but for Gina it was an apocalypse. She started drinking again almost immediately upon hearing of Peter's death. By Wednesday, when John and Patty Jo arrived in New York, Gina was virtually incoherent. Following the ceremonies, John stayed in New York for a few extra days. With Al's help, he convinced Gina to attend Alcoholics Anonymous meetings; he even drove her to her first meeting. The AA meetings helped almost immediately, providing her with the support to get and stay sober. John's second recommendation, after he was sure she was sober, was for her to see a psychologist. She attended a couple of sessions but never really connected with the doctor. After he recommended she go on antidepressants, Gina promptly stopped going to him. Shortly thereafter, she also stopped going to AA meetings. For a while, she seemed to be doing well emotionally; but then in November came the first anniversary of Peter's tragic death. It hit her with a one-two punch that drove her back to booze. To add to her grief, a week later would have been Peter's thirtieth birthday. The two events were more than her fragile emotional state could stand. When Bart talked to her, on the anniversary of their son's death, he sensed she had been drinking. When she called him on Peter's birthday, it was obvious to him she was intoxicated. Within a few months she was supplementing the booze with amphetamines, especially when it wasn't convenient to sneak a swig from her flask.

■ ■ ■

One year after moving south, Bart LaRocca had a thriving cash machine business with nearly one hundred ATMs in place. His golf game had improved dramatically. He now sported a single-digit handicap and had made two holes-in-one. When these activities weren't enough to divert his mind from Peter and Gina, he volunteered his time with several nonprofit organizations. During the winter, he volunteered at AARP, preparing free tax returns for seniors. He also had a standing appointment every Monday afternoon advising small business owners for SCORE, the Senior Corps of Retired Executives.

After decades of moving around the world and always feeling like a visitor wherever he lived, Charlotte gave Bart the sense of being home. Charlotte was only ninety miles from Columbia, South Carolina, where he had spent four rewarding years, and a three-and-a-half-hour drive from both Myrtle Beach and Charleston, two of his favorite getaway spots. Furthermore, he thoroughly enjoyed playing golf with the guys at the club.

Probably the one thing that made him the happiest was being able to regularly visit with David Tanner. They invited each other to their clubs' member-guest tournaments; and every chance they had, they met in Myrtle Beach. David, who had maintained an active and influential participation in the University of South Carolina alumni association, periodically dragged Bart to their alma mater's football and basketball games.

David also tried many times to encourage Bart to be more active in his real estate empire. Over the years Bart continued to invest monies in David's projects but never played an active role. By 1998, Bart had hundreds of thousands of dollars tied up in David's enterprises. Finally, David was able to convince his trusted friend to become a corporate officer in several of the companies in which he had a financial stake.

Bart thrived with his diverse and hectic schedule, but he found it increasingly difficult to keep up with restocking his cash machines. Then in early summer, one of Don Serafina's Chinese clients called Bart with a new business proposal. Buoyed by his success with the high tech companies outside Boston, the Asian entrepreneur decided to expand to the Research Triangle Park area near Raleigh. Needing the same kind of local cash source as Don was providing up north, the representative had asked Don if he had any suggestions. Don Serafina confidently recommended Bart.

Already torn between his business obligations, volunteer activities, and active social calendar, Bart knew that if he took on this new opportunity, something would have to give. Not requiring any more income to maintain his current lifestyle but intrigued with the idea of working with the Chinese, he came up with a plan to begin bringing additional partners into the ATM business, just as Don Serafina had done with him. First he asked Gary Caesar if he was interested in enhancing his maintenance deal to include the cash replenishment of fifty machines. He then proposed to Doug Carbone the opportunity to take over the cash replenishment of the remainder of the machines. Both his golfing buddies jumped at the chance to make extra cash for a minimal investment of their time. By September, Bart was providing between $30,000 and $40,000 a week to his new East Asian client and he had dramatically cut down on the time he spent on the cash machine business.

CHAPTER 58

While Bart was experiencing a personal and professional renaissance in the Carolinas, Gina was sinking deeper into an emotional abyss. Sensational revelations about the criminal conspiracy that precipitated Peter's death became weekly media events through the spring of 1998. Each new disclosure was a painful reminder that not only was her only son dead but in all likelihood her brother was the root cause.

By the summer the federal government had garnered what they thought to be enough evidence to indict Frankie DelMonico and a half-dozen other mobsters from New York to Delaware on RICO and other charges for the arson scheme that resulted in Peter LaRocca's death. Prosecutors were convinced at least one of the defendants would give them Al Nicosia and the heads of the other East Coast Mafia families in exchange for witness protection.

In fact, at one point, prosecutors had a statement from Frankie's Brooklyn associate, Carmine "The Fish" Nunzi, which implicated Al Nicosia for recruiting his nephew to be the arsonist. While prosecutors were preparing the case for an indictment of Al Nicosia, The Fish managed to slip out of protective custody. He was able to elude both the authorities and Al's button men for several weeks. Just days before the start of the trial, however, his body was discovered by a homeless person in a dumpster a few blocks from the Cincinnati motel where he had been holed up. His hands were bound behind his back with a nylon cable strap; his feet were bound together with a similar strap. Although his throat had been slit, local authorities listed the cause of death as asphyxiation caused by choking. The choking was apparently caused by the two pieces of anchovy pizza stuffed down his throat prior to the severing of his carotid artery. It was well-known around Brooklyn that Carmine Nunzi had a passion for the thick Sicilian pizza smothered in anchovies and black olives, hence the origin of his nickname The Fish. The word on the street was he couldn't go more than a few days without satisfying this desire. Authorities speculated it was this unusual craving that gave away his location to Little Nicky, who had put the word out to all the major Italian crime families to check local pizzerias for someone ordering this peculiar combination.

In spite of their informant's murder before the tapes of his testimony could be typed for his signature, the US attorney general added Al Nicosia's name to the indictment. Gina had accepted the fact "Uncle" Frankie had been responsible for Peter's demise. Intuitively she knew there was no way Uncle Frankie could involve Peter without her brother's knowledge, but she refused to let her mind go there. The day her brother's arrest was the headline story on all the evening TV news programs Gina realized she could no longer deny his involvement. In response, she sank deeper and deeper into depression and attempted to protect her psyche with increasing levels of prescription drugs and alcohol. To her few close friends it was amazing she continued to get up in the morning and get ready for school. Even more amazing was the fact she was still a good teacher and was able to escape a damaging incident at school.

It all came to a head, however, one rainy afternoon shortly after the beginning of the new 1999 school year. The morning papers had been rife with artist's sketches of the trial and details of the prosecution's case against Al, Frankie, and his co-defendants. The lead prosecutor tried to enter into evidence the recorded statement of Carmine Nunzi implicating Al Nicosia. The defense objected on the grounds it had been a coerced statement from a witness the defense could no longer cross-examine. The judge overruled the objection, and the tape was played in court and a word-for-word account was printed in the paper.

How Gina forced herself to go to school that morning, no one could imagine. When she arrived at school, she succeeded in ignoring the inquisitive glances from some of the other teachers as she picked up her mail in the office. She even successfully paid no attention to the small clusters of students gathered throughout the hallway whispering sneakily as she passed. At lunch she took her normal fortification of pills, but by the last period she was on the verge of losing it. Popping a few more of her favorite uppers just before the class started enabled her to stumble through her lesson plan. When the bell sounded finally ending the school day, Gina hastily convinced another teacher to cover her exit-door monitoring post, and she headed for her car. Disregarding the stream of students and parents in the parking lot, she eagerly retrieved her flask from under the car seat and took a long belt of vodka. Catching her breath, she then fumbled through her purse for another hit of amphetamines, which she threw down with another huge slug of vodka. Then she laid her head back on the headrest, closed her eyes, and waited for the numbing effect of the chemicals to make it all go away. She sat there, polishing off the rest of the flask, with rain beating down and the vehicle's windows almost totally fogged over. Several teachers, noticing the layer of condensation on her car windows, timidly knocked on the window and inquired if she was all right. With some difficulty she feigned a migraine, quelling their display of concern. She knew full well it was more curiosity than genuine worry driving their concern, and they were probably relieved when they really didn't have to get involved. Gina waited until the parking lot was almost empty, then she started the car and tried to make it home.

It was a short fifteen-minute drive from school to Gina's house, but by the time she turned off Woodhaven Boulevard onto Dry Harbor Road, the drugs and alcohol had kicked in. She failed to negotiate the curve at Eighty-Second Avenue and slammed into the retaining wall on the corner. Dazed and confused, she got out of the car, but passed out on the sidewalk. When she awoke, she was in the emergency room with a doctor, a nurse, and a New York city policeman. Other than a bruised knee and chest from hitting the steering wheel and a cut above her eye that required six stitches from when she fell on the sidewalk, she was fine. The doctor had already taken a blood sample which would reveal she was high on amphetamines and just over the legal alcohol limit. She was cited for driving under the influence and ordered to appear in court.

One thing the Nicosias were never short of was a bevy of good lawyers. An old family friend had her plead nolo contendere. As a first-time offender, she was released under the condition she complete a recognized drug and alcohol abuse program. Furthermore, her driver's license was suspended for a year. John and Patty Jo convinced Gina to register in a world-renowned treatment center near Phoenix.

CHAPTER 59

Bart thought he caught a glimpse of a familiar face as he and David Tanner entered the players' and officials' entrance of Williams-Brice Stadium, but she was more than thirty feet away and had just passed through the turnstile of the regular spectator entrance.

David had remained a staunch supporter of the University of South Carolina, serving on its Board of Governors and donating $250,000 for a new state-of-the-art weight room. For his support, each year he was rewarded with field passes to the few games he found the time to attend; and he usually invited Bart. The game, pitting the 1 and 7 Gamecocks against the unbeaten and third-ranked University of Tennessee, was expected to be a blowout; but weatherwise, it was predicted to be a great weekend. They met on Friday morning at the University Club, the school's three-year-old twenty-seven-hole golf facility in Blythewood. Also joining them to make a foursome were Joe Zielinski and another huge ex-linemen from Joe Z's year. Bart hadn't seen

Joe for over twenty years and was surprised how much he had changed. He had lost eighty pounds, but despite the weight loss he had lost much of his former agility. Getting in and out of the golf cart appeared to be a major effort, yet somehow his golf swing remained fluid. Bart and Joe Z played a $20 Nassau against David and the other lineman. David shot his usual 74 but his partner shot a generous 85. Both Bart and Joe Z shot 79s, winning the back nine and eighteen after halving the front.

Friday night they attended a football reunion at a local restaurant. There were about twenty-five former players from the early and mid-1960s that met once a year. Joe Z was one of the organizers of the event. Three hours in a boisterous, smoke-filled private room with two dozen heavy drinkers was not normally on Bart's or David's social calendar. However, as a one-shot deal, it was okay.

As expected, the game was a blowout 49–14, but it was not a total loss. Bart did spot the woman he thought he recognized walking into the stadium. She was seated right next to the university president. Throughout the first half Bart kept sneaking peeks in her direction. She appeared to be about the right age and with the same military-type bearing he remembered. At that distance and with his mental editing to account for thirty years of aging, he was still undecided. At halftime he made his way up into the stands. She did not see him coming until the spectators at the end of the row started standing and he began his sideways shuffle between them and the row in front. She had the same initial reaction as Bart. At first there was an excited surprise, but it was immediately followed by doubt, stemming out of a realization it wasn't possible after all these years. As they got closer, both their doubts faded; she knew from the smile on his face it was her former subordinate in Italy, and he knew it was indeed Betty Rice. It was an exhilarating feeling for both of them to meet after all these years and to almost instantly recognize each other. Though she felt like hugging him, years of military bearing allowed only a broad smile to burst across her face as she excitedly announced, "Bart LaRocca, I hoped one day we would meet again."

"Betty, you have hardly changed. I thought I recognized you as you were entering the stadium but couldn't catch up with you. I am so glad I found you again."

After a brief introduction, the university president, recognizing the intimacy of the moment, excused himself to check on something. During the next fifteen minutes while President Palmetto graciously stayed busy, the old friends gave each other abbreviated updates on their current lives. Betty had retired several years earlier with the rank of major general. Her last assignment was as the United States Air Force's chief materiel officer. She was currently the president of the University of South Carolina-Beaufort, a two-year junior college. However, she was about to become the Dean of the College of Business and Economics at Radford University in southwestern Virginia. Given the success of her Air Force career, Bart was not surprised to also discover she had never married.

When Betty learned Bart and Gina were no longer married, she suggested they have dinner together after the game. Bart had planned on making the two-hour drive back to Charlotte that evening but couldn't pass up the opportunity to renew their friendship.

"Do you remember Anthony's Spaghetti Emporium from your college days?" she asked.

"Of course, back then it had the only authentic Italian food between here and Philadelphia."

"Surprisingly, it is still in the old firehouse on Blanding Street but is now called Villa Testa, and the family still runs it. I ate there a couple of months ago with President Palmetto and the food was magnificent. Don't you think it's appropriate for us to refresh some old memories in an authentic Italian setting?"

"Perfect! Do you want to go right after the game?"

"No, give me the opportunity to go back to my hotel and put on a new face and more appropriate dinner attire. Unless some miracle happens in the second half and this game goes to over-time, I can be ready by 7:00 p.m. It might be tough to get reservations on Saturday night, especially after a game, but President Palmetto is a personal friend of the owners. I'll see if he can pull some strings and get us a table."

Friendships are a little like books; some of them you can read more than once, others you don't even have a desire to pick up again, while still others you may try to rekindle interest in but find they have lost their relevance. Over dinner Betty Rice and Bart LaRocca discovered theirs was a friendship they could both enjoy a second time. Despite their very different lifestyles for the last thirty years, they still related to each other intellectually; and the physical attraction was definitely there. An excited curiosity fueled their dinner conversation. Neither one of them had ever been a prolific conversationalist; especially when it came to talking about themselves or their personal lives, but it felt natural to them to do so that evening. They had moved to the bar around 9:00 p.m. but before the two old friends realized it, there were no other patrons left in the restaurant. Their second bottle of Chianti Classico was long gone and what was left in the cups of espresso, laced with Sambuca, was cold. There was no way Bart was driving back to Charlotte that night, which turned out not to be a disappointment to either of them.

CHAPTER 60

February 18, 2010
Seville, Spain

We were on David's terrace and Bart was in the middle of describing to me how his and Betty's rekindled friendship progressed when the house phone rang three times and stopped. Then after two minutes, it rang again four times and stopped. Bart took out his cell phone, an untraceable prepaid disposable just like the ones he had given Marie and me when we first arrived in

Portugal. He dialed a number and began speaking in Spanish. I couldn't tell who was on the other end, but it was obvious by his body language and tone of voice he was receiving some disturbing news. When he hung up, he turned to me and announced John Nicosia had died the night before. He immediately followed his sad announcement with "I need to think about our options." Then he excused himself and disappeared upstairs to his room. About a half hour later, I heard him on the phone again, then silence, then another phone call. Shortly after I heard him hang up the second time, he returned downstairs.

"OK, I've got it all figured out. I am going to Phoenix to pay my respects. If this works for you, a driver will take both of us to Madrid this afternoon; I've arranged a seat for you on the 6:00 p.m. flight to New York. I am going to fly commercially to Bermuda where David will pick me up with his plane. You can use the return ticket from your original flight here. A car will pick you up at JFK and drive you home."

"That's fine with me. So, have you decided when we are coming back?"

"You're not coming back; next time I'm coming to you. I haven't got it all worked out yet, but it is my objective we get together on Long Island."

▪ ▪ ▪

March 11, 2010
Long Island, NY

Even though it still felt like winter, it was good to be home in the Hamptons. I hadn't heard from Bart for almost three weeks; then, out of the blue, he called. "Hi, it's Carlos; how's everything going? Any problems since I last saw you?"

"No, everything has been real quiet. I had a chance to work on my book. What are you up to, Carlos?"

"Well, I have to be in New York for the next few days and I was thinking about stopping by to see you and Marie, if you're available."

"Great, we'd be disappointed if we found out you were in the area and didn't stop by."

"Good, I'll call when I get into town."

Bart, posing as Carlos, called the next day and suggested we meet at the Starbucks on Montauk Highway in Bridgehampton at 10:00 a.m.

I arrived ten minutes early at Starbucks. To my surprise, at 10:05 Eitan, one of David Tanner's security guys, walked in and ordered a coffee. Ignoring my presence, he got his cup and left. I could see him slowly walking east. I waited thirty seconds and followed him out. I could still see him a block away, window shopping. As I approached, he turned and greeted me; we exchanged small talk and then he suggested I accompany him to his car. He was parked another block east. We got in and he drove east on Montauk Highway. After turning north on Sagg Road he said, "Azzan is making sure no one is following us. If everything is kosher, he'll call and I can take you to Bart."

The call came as we approached Sag Harbor's town center. Apparently getting the all clear, Eitan turned on to Bay Street. A half-mile further he turned again, this time into a cul-de-sac that hid several gated drives. Eitan pulled up to one of the gates, lowered the window and smiled at a video camera mounted into the stone column anchoring the iron gate. The metal wheels on the gate screeched as it opened. The entrance was a hundred-foot-long gravel drive. It ended in a circular drive with an ugly fountain in the center. We stopped between the fountain and the wide concrete front steps. Before I had a chance to get out of the car, Azzan arrived in a Jeep Cherokee.

I did a double take of the man waiting for us on the steps of the generic-looking two-story colonial. I thought it might be Bart; but if it was, he had undergone another amazing physical transformation. Instead of the southern European features and attire I'd been become accustomed to, he now looked the epitome of an English or Ivy League professor. He had on tan slacks and a herringbone blazer covering a classic blue button-down dress shirt; the finishing touch was a royal-blue ascot under his collar, covering the nape of his neck. His head was shaven and most of his tan was gone. But the most drastic changes were on the lower portions of his face. When we were with him in Europe, his smile displayed large, crowded, uncared-for front teeth. Now, as he grinned at my arrival, his teeth were perfect and beautifully white. The most surprising change, however, was the Burl Ives mustache and goatee. Obviously, Bart LaRocca had become quite the chameleon.

A weather front must have been coming across Peconic Bay because the temperature was dropping and the wind had picked up. Reacting to the bone-chilling conditions, our greeting consisted only of a brief hug before we all hustled into the house. The interior of the house was tastefully decorated with minimalistic furnishings. I later learned the house belonged to Sarah Tanner's cousin, who was spending the winter on St. Kitts.

Bart immediately escorted us into the kitchen, where a pot of hot water was already whistling on the stove. He poured the hot water into a porcelain pot that contained a strainer with the tea leaves in it. While we were waiting for the tea to brew, I asked, "So how did it go?"

"Fine," Bart responded. "I spent the first night in Bermuda at the Hamilton Princess waiting for David to arrive. His jet came in the next morning, was refueled, and we immediately took off for Toronto. Waiting for us in Toronto was a dentist friend of David's who joined us on the flight to Phoenix. Going through Bermuda and Canada gave me the opportunity to enter the US with my original Charles Carbone Canadian passport. I am now waiting for it to be renewed with an updated photograph."

"Did you actually attend the wake and funeral?"

"The night before the funeral I had a private viewing with Patty Jo, and I did attend the funeral mass at the church. Patty Jo has become quite the accomplished covert operative. She arranged for me to enter the church with the organist and choir. I spent the entire mass out of sight, up in the choir loft."

"Was Al or the FBI there?"

"Yeah, we saw Little Nicky, but Azzan determined there were

no law enforcement people in attendance or even shadowing Al. Man, has he gotten old-looking. He sure doesn't look like the same old swaggering tough guy he did ten years ago."

"So, if Little Nicky had no idea you were there, why the need for all the clandestine cover this morning?"

"Just precautionary until the US attorney general has the evidence that will hopefully put Little Nicky on death row."

"When do you think we will be ready to start talking to the authorities?"

"Well, I think within the next two weeks I will have given you most of what you need for the book. So you should plan on trying to get something going for the next month. When the time is right, I'd like you to contact Sam Sardo; he is now an assistant US attorney in the criminal division of the Southern District of New York. I always promised Sam, if I ever had anything that could help the FBI nail Little Nicky, I'd contact him."

"OK, I'll wait until we're done and then give him a call and try to arrange a meeting. By the way, how's Patty Jo handling John's death?"

"Not well, she blames herself for his death. He was totally bedridden for the last two years and she was his primary caregiver. When he developed the pneumonia that eventually took him, Patty Jo felt she should have been able to prevent it. As a nurse though, she knew eventually some terminal complication was inevitable. She's had a pretty tough time the last three or four years; now she needs to decide what she wants to do with the rest of her life. Anyway, I convinced her to take a vacation."

"Good, where is she going?"

"Someplace safe."

He said those two words in a tone which I had learned over the last two months meant change the subject, so I did. "How about you? You've been pretty stoic about John's death."

"Yeah, Peter's and Gina's deaths, combined with the fact I've known for several months John's death was inevitable, kind of left me without much emotion. Hell, I loved John like a brother, yet when David gave me the news of his death, I didn't feel any significant new loss. You may remember I had some pretty moody days when we were back in Europe. That was when I found out he had pneumonia; I probably dealt with the emotional loss back then. OK, enough of that disturbing shit; anything else we need to talk about?"

"Just how are we going to continue with the story?"

"Good question. Here's what Azzan and Eitan have suggested; they're going to stay with us for a few days. Azzan suggests we start tomorrow. You drive to East Quay Mall, arriving at 9:15 a.m., park your car in the mall lot and make your way back to the High Street entrance. Eitan will be waiting to pick you up. It's probably an unnecessary precaution; but since David has loaned us his security people, we might as well listen to them."

▪ ▪ ▪

The next morning at exactly 9:15 as I walked out the mall doors onto High Street Eitan pulled up to the curb and I got in the Range Rover. The drive to Sag Harbor was uneventful; five minutes after we arrived at the house, Azzan followed through the automatic gates. Apparently, Bart's presence on Long Island had not been detected. Azzan suggested we go through our security precautions one more day before he and Eitan returned to protecting David.

"Before we get back to the book, I want to finish up on a few details for your meeting with Sam Sardo. Tomorrow, you and I are going to take the eight o'clock Port Jefferson ferry over to Bridgeport. We will board as walk-ons. When we get to Bridgeport, Don Serafina will meet us and drive us to the attorney who has been safeguarding the evidence on Little Nicky. In fact, you may know him. He got his undergraduate degree the year before you from Fairfield University; his name is Bob Byrnes."

"You're kidding? Bob and I were on the same floor in the dorm during my sophomore year. What a coincidence; not only that, over the years we have had several opportunities to refer clients to one another."

"Well good, this part should go smoothly. Just one more little nuance, John never told him what he has been holding for almost forty years. I'm not sure what his reaction is going to be. I'll leave it up to you guys to figure out when it's the appropriate time to transfer the evidence. Seems to me, since Bob's had the evidence all these years, he should probably hold on to it until you've got a deal worked out with the government; but that's up to you."

"Yeah, that probably makes sense. There's no hurry. At this point I'm not sure if I even know all the things from which you need immunity from prosecution."

Bart threw back his head and laughed, "Well then, perhaps we better get on with the story."

CHAPTER 61

During the last eighteen months of the twentieth century, Bart's busy life in Charlotte provided an effective distraction from the heartbreaking events of the previous decade. "Out of sight, out of mind" described his association with Gina. Thanks to Gary and Doug, he now spent little time involved in the ATM business; yet he seemed busier than ever. He really only had two commitments every week; most Mondays he made himself available to counsel small business owners at the SCORE offices in Charlotte and on Thursdays he made a cash delivery to the Chinese in Raleigh. Even those were not firm. It was no big deal if he missed a Monday at SCORE and either Gary or Doug could make the run to Raleigh.

In reality Bart was free to do as he pleased and he did. From February through April 15, he continued to prepare income tax returns two days a week for AARP. His work on the boards of David's real estate companies involved periodic travel to meetings in Florida and the Caribbean. This work schedule still left him plenty of time for golf and fishing junkets with the boys. As a diversion from all this man stuff, he got together with Betty.

They both enjoyed meeting for the weekend at one of the numerous bed and breakfasts along the Blue Ridge Mountain Parkway. Betty had a passion for antiques, and the region was awash with dealers. Bart wasn't particularly excited about picking through rooms and rooms of dusty old stuff, looking for some priceless gem, but he did enjoy wandering around the back roads and quaint little towns in the Virginia and North Carolina mountains. It even gave him a chance to scout out new trout streams for future fishing trips. Betty's other delight was taking cruises. It started when she was stationed in Italy with cruises all over the Mediterranean. Over the years, it became her escape from the pressures of being a woman in command of dozens of resentful male officers. At least once a year, she would take a week and go on one of her escapes. Now that she was retired from the Air Force her motivation was different, but the effect on her psyche at the end of the voyage was the same. She returned relaxed and refreshed. The first time she asked Bart to join her on a week-long Caribbean sailing he only reluctantly agreed. But, to his surprise, he also found the experience to be rejuvenating.

■ ■ ■

In late September of 1999 Bart was on a golf junket to Wild Dunes, just north of Charleston, when John Nicosia called him on his cell phone to tell him about Gina's DUI episode. Though saddened by her unfortunate circumstances, he had finally put all that behind him; so he refused to let himself dwell on it. It wasn't until John called back in early November that Bart gave it much thought. John was not normally someone to ask for anything, but this time he virtually begged Bart to fly out to Phoenix and be there when Gina got out of rehab.

"Did she ask for me?" Bart queried his childhood friend and former brother-in-law.

"Not exactly," John replied. "But she did say she hoped she would have the opportunity to see you again and try to make amends. She now believes a lot of her feelings toward you were the result of emotional issues precipitated by Al exploiting her insecurities."

"I don't know, John," Bart began. "I'm not sure I want to open that door again. Things are going pretty good for me now and I don't really need any complications."

"OK, Bart, I understand your apprehension. Think about it. If you change your mind, Gina will be out of rehab next Sunday. She will be staying at our house for a few weeks. We still have another extra bedroom, and you and I haven't played golf together in a few years."

"OK, I'll give it some thought. Regardless, it's good to hear from you and we do have to play some golf together soon."

■ ■ ■

On Saturday Bart could hardly believe he was on a plane headed for Phoenix and perhaps on a collision course with everything he had worked so hard to forget. As the seat-belt lights came on and the captain announced the plane was beginning its descent into Phoenix's Sky Harbor International Airport, Bart LaRocca again chided himself for letting his dormant feelings for Gina bubble to the surface.

John and Patty Jo were waiting in the baggage claim area when Bart came down the escalator. In spite of his previous qualms about coming, the sight of his two oldest friends sent a blast of excitement and joy through his body. *Why had he waited so long to visit his friends?* John and Patty Jo seemed to have the same reaction. Patty Jo was hardly able to control her exuberance as she hurried across the remaining few feet of terminal to leap into Bart's arms. John, usually as cool as a cucumber, was almost equally as animated, trailing his wife by only a millisecond and throwing his arms around both his wife and his old friend.

On the drive from the airport to their house, Patty Jo surprised Bart by letting it slip Gina was excited about getting out of rehab and seeing Bart again. "Did I misunderstand? Weren't you going to avoid telling her I was coming?"

"Yeah, we tried," Patty Jo said apologetically, "but yesterday she called and asked if we had talked to you recently. When I told her we had spoken on the phone this week, she asked if you knew she was getting out. I'm sorry; but when I told her that you knew, I could sense she desperately wanted to see you. I felt I had to tell her, and I'm glad I did. In spite of her desire to see you, her first reaction was panic. Then, when she had a chance to absorb the news, her mood changed. She became euphoric, declaring, 'If that's the case, I better spruce myself up and figure out what I want to say to him.'"

John was glad Bart had arrived early; it gave him a chance to get him up to speed with the events of Al's trial in New York. John knew Bart did not keep up with the trial even though so much of the testimony revolved around Peter's involvement and the role Al played in recruiting Peter. Bart always told John, "It doesn't matter what happens in court. I know Al was responsible for Peter's involvement."

But when John told him the verdict had come in and Al was the only defendant who was acquitted, Bart lost his temper. He angrily blurted out, "Damn him, he skated again! How many times is he going to escape punishment for the death and destruction he leaves in his wake? Somebody is probably going to have to take him out to put an end to it."

CHAPTER 62

On Sunday they arrived at the clinic just before 10:00 a.m.; Gina was anxiously waiting for them in the lobby. Bart thought he hadn't seen her look this vibrant in decades. She had a glint in her eyes and her body language was energetic yet under control. She greeted all three of them with eager hugs and kisses.

In spite of Gina's initial fervent reaction to Bart, the ride to John's house was awkward for both of them and that feeling carried over through the afternoon and evening. It had been a long time since they'd been together under pleasant circumstances. It almost felt natural for both of them to behave as if they were still lovers, yet there was still an undercurrent of apprehension that this feeling could vanish with one remark.

Coincidentally, the next morning at 7:15 a.m., they found themselves both headed for the front door intending on getting in their morning workout. Ever since he and Gina split up, Bart went on a forty-five-minute run two or three times a week. Gina had vowed that, as soon as she got out of rehab, she would start going on morning walks. From his many years of visits to John's house, Bart had scoped out the neighborhood and discovered a great jogging-walking trail that started just around the corner. He offered to show Gina how to get there. By the time they arrived at the trail, Gina had told Bart how glad she was he had come to her graduation from dependency. Then she began explaining how she allowed alcohol, gambling, and drugs to dominate her life. Of course, Bart already knew because he had been there and watched it happen. But he listened intently, intrigued by the tale from the eyes of the addict. Before they knew it, they had walked for almost forty-five minutes and were now over two miles from the house. By the time they got back, John had left for the office and Patty Jo had fresh bagels and coffee waiting for them.

To everyone's surprise, John came home for lunch and announced he was able to reschedule his calendar so that he had the next two days off. Although it was early November, the daytime temperatures in Phoenix were still warm enough for a swim in the pool. As the two couples lounged in the afternoon sun and frolicked in the pool, John cleverly recounted his memories from their spring break at David Tanner's beach house in Myrtle Beach. At first, Gina and Bart were uncomfortable recalling such a passionate time in their lives. But John was so skillful in his reminiscence it didn't take long for the memories and laughter to melt away the last barriers standing between Gina and Bart. It was later in the evening as the couples walked from their car to the entrance of Macayo's in Scottsdale that Bart's hand inadvertently brushed against Gina's. Almost as if she was expecting it, she instantly entwined her fingers around his, and they walked hand in hand into the restaurant.

It was really strange. Gina did not order an alcoholic drink but she insisted the others have one. John was reluctant, but she vehemently insisted, saying, "Who better to be with to test my will power?" In the car on the way back to the house, she admitted she was tempted, but it was not an agonizing decision. In fact, she claimed without the alcohol, she had a better appreciation for the food.

The next morning they intentionally met at the front door for their morning exercise. During the walk, Bart told Gina he had been seeing Betty Rice for the last year. She was surprised but appeared not to be devastated. He then went on to tell her it was not an exclusive arrangement and they both were seeing other people. Gina seemed to be processing this new information when Bart added, "If you're interested, there is still room in my life for you." They were both surprised by his announcement. He had to do a mental check to make sure he actually said it out loud.

Gina responded by stopping, looking him in the face, and replying, "You surprise me, Bart. Are you sure after all we've been through together, and all the baggage I have, you really want to go down that path again?"

"I'm as surprised as you are I actually said that; and yeah, I am willing to give it a try."

Skeptically staring at her former husband, Gina said warily, "So, what ever happened to that hot chick you were dating? You know the one from work, what was her name?"

"Bridgitte, but that didn't last very long. After I moved up to Springfield, we only saw each other once every couple of weeks. Eventually, she quit her job and moved back to New Orleans. I haven't heard from her in a couple of years. How about you? I seem to recall you had an old college friend you were seeing."

Gina let out a nervous chuckle. "Don't you know that drunks have a hard time maintaining relationships?"

They continued walking until Bart broke the silence. "What are you doing after you leave here?"

"I haven't decided. I'm not really excited about returning to New York just yet; any suggestions?"

"Have you ever been on a cruise?"

"No, have you?"

"A few."

"With a roommate?"

"Does it make a difference if I have?"

"No, just curious about how crowded a stateroom is with two people sleeping in separate bunks."

"Well, if we can get a suite, it's pretty roomy, no matter what the sleeping arrangements are."

"So, are you inviting me on a cruise?"

"Uh . . . yeah; do you want to go?"

"Of course, stupid man, what do you think all this bantering has been about?"

"All right then, let's go down to a travel agency this morning and try to book something."

"So, was it Betty who went with you on a cruise?"

"Would it make a difference if it was?"

"No, just curious as to whom my competition is."

"OK then, she is the one who introduced me to cruising, but in my book, she could never compete with you."

"You sly devil!"

■ ■ ■

After breakfast, Patty Jo gave them the keys to her Lexus and directed Bart to her travel agency. After an hour looking over brochures and checking out cruise lines and ships, the excited couple decided to fly to San Juan, Puerto Rico, and sail off for seven days on Royal Caribbean's *Enchantment of the Seas*. Their itinerary called for them to fly out of Phoenix on Friday and spend two nights at the El San Juan Hotel and Casino before boarding the ship on Sunday. After the cruise, Gina would fly direct from San Juan to New York and Bart to Charlotte. Gina couldn't wait to get back and tell Patty Jo about the trip. When Patty Jo heard the details, her first reaction was "Hell, girl, you need to get some cruise outfits, and we need to get you a makeover, too. You two guys get some tee times for this afternoon and tomorrow; we'll be busy shopping and getting Gina all spruced up."

The last time Gina indulged herself with a clothes shopping spree and a makeover was with her mother before her wedding some thirty-three years earlier. With Patty Jo's enthusiastic encouragement, Gina, as she described it to John and Bart, "went off the deep end" with a suitcase full of new tropical clothes and a complete hair and facial treatment.

Thursday afternoon she held a showing for Bart. He was awestruck. This woman he had known for forty years looked better now than she did when she was forty. When she finished parading in her new outfits, he noticed there was still one more bag of garments she had not pranced in front of him.

"You forgot this bag," he exclaimed.

"Yeah . . . well you're just going to have to wait until I'm sure you deserve to see me in them."

Gina had not asked, nor had they volunteered, anything about Al, but that night over dinner her curiosity finally got the best of her. "So what's going on with Al and the trial?"

Bart and John looked at each other for a moment, then John answered, "Al was acquitted of all charges, but Uncle Frankie got twenty to life."

"Well, Al getting acquitted doesn't surprise me; he's managed to avoid prison for all these years with his cunning and expensive legal representation. But that doesn't mean I don't believe he was involved. We all know Uncle Frankie would never have gotten Peter involved without Al's approval, if not his complicity."

They all sat there silently for a few minutes, and finally Gina added with a welling of tears in her eyes, "You guys are all I have left."

CHAPTER 63

It was still a balmy 84 degrees when the born-again lovers re-trieved their luggage and hailed a cab to their hotel. The ten-min-ute drive from Luis Muñoz Marín International Airport to Isle Verde Beach revealed just a small sampling of this metropolitan area of almost two million people. The El San Juan Hotel and Ca-sino turned out to be a surprising marriage of tropical grandeur and old world charm. Surrounded by fifteen landscaped acres and its own beautiful white sand beach, the El San Juan provided a superbly romantic setting for a second honeymoon. Their one-bedroom suite had a magnificent view of the blue Atlantic.

It was late afternoon by the time the bellboy delivered their luggage to the room. On their way up to the room, they debated what to do for the rest of the day. After tipping the bellboy and closing the door, a strange awkwardness enveloped the room. It was really the first time the ex-lovers had been truly alone since they both moved out of Connecticut. For a brief moment they both pictured a scene where they would leap into each other's arms and plummet into uncontrollable passion, but the years of strife trumped their primitive desires. Gina was the first to break the mood by announcing, "I don't know about you but I sure could use a walk on the beach to work out the kinks from that six-hour flight."

Gina's suggestion let the air out of the awkward moment. Bart breathed a sigh of relief. "That works for me. Do you want to put on one of those great bathing suits you bought in Phoenix?"

Gina responded with a coquettish grin. "Sure, I might feel like showing off the sexy two-piece."

Bart almost drooled.

Isle Verde Beach is a two-mile stretch of white sand and nor-mally gentle surf on a backdrop of luxurious hotels and high-rise residential apartments and condos. Bart and Gina walked for twenty minutes in the late afternoon sun before they turned around and started back to their hotel. By the time they reached the stretch of beach at the El San Juan, they were both ready for a dip in the pool and a cool drink. In spite of the fact their drinks were nonalcoholic, the mood was intoxicating. It didn't take long for them to start cuddling in the pool like two teenagers.

With the same flirtatious grin she had displayed earlier, Gina whispered in Bart's ear, "I'm getting the feeling my plan to seduce you with my new negligee may not be necessary."

"Don't return it yet," Bart lightheartedly advised. "You have a whole week on board the ship to try to duplicate what I hope is about to happen." Then he led his ex-wife out of the pool and up to their room.

It wasn't exactly the Fourth of July fireworks that accompanied their first time, but it was a remarkable event. The years had rewarded them with two qualities that elude most youthful lovers . . . patience and a penchant for the finer details of love-making. It wasn't until almost 8:00 p.m. when they decided to order room service. Gina put on her royal blue satin negligee just before their dinner was delivered, even though the intended effect was no longer there.

The next day the revitalized lovers wandered around old San Juan and the boutiques of El Condado. Dinner was at one of the many wonderful restaurants near their hotel and afterwards they hung out for a brief time in the casino, Gina playing the slots and Bart blackjack. When they finally went to bed that night, they both fell asleep before either of them had an inspiration to initiate lovemaking; their torsos and legs were intertwined. Sunday night, however, Gina's royal blue satin negligee along with the gentle rocking of the ship inspired an encore performance in their stateroom.

Gina loved everything about the cruise. As she told Bart on the second day, "I feel like a princess." The ports were some of the best in the Caribbean: Barbados, St. Lucia, Antigua, St. Martin, and St. Croix. Both of them snorkeled for the first time in the clear aqua waters off Antigua. On St. Lucia they lounged on a secluded cove and drank virgin piña coladas from a thatched hut bar. On Barbados they took an eco-tour to Welshman Hall

Gulley and Harrison's Cave. After docking in Phillipsburg on St. Martin, the couple browsed the duty-free shops. The four-street deep, one-mile long downtown area contained just enough variety to keep them interested until early afternoon when they returned to the ship for an "afternoon delight." After docking at Frederiksted on St. Croix, Bart rented a four-wheel drive vehicle; and the pair toured the St. Croix Heritage Trail, stopping for a swim at Cramer Park.

It was while they sat on the beach, soaking up the warm Caribbean sun, that Gina announced, "I've decided to sell the house and move out of New York. There is nothing left there for me except a brother who I don't care if I ever see again."

Stunned by this pronouncement, Bart could only manage to respond, "Wow! That's a surprise."

"Yeah, the realization surprised me, too. Unfortunately, it came too late for me to save Peter. I know over the years you tried to warn Peter and me about Al, but I was too blinded by family loyalty to listen. Now all I can do is save what is left of my life."

"So what are you going to do? I mean, where are you going to go?"

"I don't know yet, maybe Phoenix. I really love John and Patty Jo, but I am not that fond of the desert. Maybe back to Connecticut, or maybe Florida. Hell, I have the resources to go anywhere I want, and I have no external restrictions."

"So how are you going to make your decision as to where to go?"

"Well, I was thinking I would put the house up for sale and start traveling."

"That sounds like a good plan. Where do you think you want to go first?"

"I don't know; do you have any suggestions?"

"Well, you could come to Charlotte and use that as a home base to check out the Southeast like Asheville, Wilmington, Raleigh, Charleston, and Savannah."

"What about Charlotte? I hear it's come a long way since we last lived there."

"Oh, yeah; Charlotte is now a fine city. It has everything you would want from a big city, except the hassle. The weather is good eight months of the year and when it's not, it's just a short hop to Florida or the Caribbean."

"So, if I go along with your suggestion that your place is a good starting point, we would have to reach an agreement there are no strings . . . I mean . . . we still might not get along or I might still not like North Carolina."

"Yeah, I know. That's OK. Hell, we've both lived alone for a long time now; maybe neither of us can stand a roommate any longer."

Not wanting to delve any deeper into such a sensitive area, Gina ended the discussion by asserting, "All right; let me think about it and I'll let you know before we get back to San Juan."

The next morning, as they were waiting on the Lido deck to disembark, Gina affectionately put her hand on Bart's and matter-of-factly declared, "It will take me a few weeks to get the house ready to put on the market but I think I can be down in Charlotte by Thanksgiving. Does that work for you?"

Bart's eyes lit up. "Sure, that's great. I can't wait to show you how much North Carolina and especially Charlotte have changed."

CHAPTER 64

The day after Bart returned to Charlotte, he received a note from the apartment complex's manager stating:

Mr. LaRocca:
    While you were away, a young man came to the complex several times looking for you. He was adamant about seeing you. On his third visit, I agreed to take his name and telephone number and promised I would give it you on your return.
    Here is the info: Ben Miller 770-555-1010
    Brian

Bart looked up the 770 area code in the front of the phone book and discovered it was for Dallas. Hmm, he thought, I don't know a Ben Miller and I can't think of anyone I know from Dallas. Maybe he wants to buy my ATM business.

Preoccupied with other things, Bart threw the note on his desk and put a telephone call in to Betty Rice. He hadn't talked to Betty prior to his trip to Phoenix. While he was away, she had left several messages on both his home phone and cell phone. He'd been putting off this call, not quite sure what to tell Betty. On one hand she deserved to know he spent a romantic week cruising with his ex-wife in the Caribbean and that Gina was going to stay at his place. On the other hand he was not ready to shut the door on his relationship with Betty without knowing what was going to happen between Gina and him.

He dialed Betty's number, but after the eighth ring, it went to voicemail. He left a brief message saying he had been out of town for a few weeks and was just calling to catch up. He then dialed David Tanner's cell phone.

David answered on the second ring. "Where have you been, old buddy? I tried to reach you all last week but kept getting your voicemail." Kidding around, he added, "Have you been off to some secluded hideaway with some chickie?"

"You got me, old buddy. Gina and I went off on a very romantic Caribbean cruise. So romantic that she's going to be coming to Charlotte to spend a few weeks with me."

There was silence at the other end as David tried to process this surprising news. Finally he exclaimed, "Gina and you; you've got to be joking? A week cruise is one thing, but moving in . . . are you sure you know what you're getting yourself into again?"

"I think so; this time I hope it's different. She finally recognizes her asshole brother for what he is and is determined to get out of New York. She's back there now getting the house ready to put on the market."

"Wow! That's quite a turnaround. I hope it works out."

"Listen, David, to change the subject, do we know a Ben Miller from Dallas?"

"Not that I can recall. Why, what's up?"

"I don't know. He was hanging around my apartment complex while I was gone, apparently trying to talk to me about something personal."

"That's interesting. Well, if you talk to him and need my help, don't hesitate to call."

"No problem. Say, how are Sarah and the kids?"

The two friends talked for another fifteen minutes about family and business before David announced he had a meeting to attend.

About an hour later his phone rang; caller ID indicated that it was Betty. *OK*, he thought, *time to lay it on the line.*

After their normal playful greetings, Betty declared in an inflection denoting more of a question than a statement, "So you must have been off doing something exciting?"

Since he was already prepared to break the news, Bart didn't hesitate. "Gina got out of rehab and John thought my being there would help."

"So did it?"

"Oh yeah, she came out changed but still vulnerable. Having the three of us there for her really helped her transition back to the real world."

"Great, so you stayed with her at John's for two weeks?"

"Well, only one week in Arizona; then we went on a Caribbean cruise."

"Oh . . . that's interesting. The four of you went?"

"Uh no . . . just Gina and me."

"I see, and how did that go?"

"Real well; I think we may have transcended some of our former issues."

"That's nice." Then with a teasing tone, "So are you going to dump me and get back together with your ex-wife?"

"I don't know about that, but Gina is putting her house up for sale and is going to stay with me until she figures out what she wants to do or one of us decides living in the same house isn't going to work any better than the last time."

"Well, that sounds pretty promising. You know, I always figured you two would eventually get back together. What you and I had the last couple of years has been great, but it was never going to go anyplace. I've been single too long and I am not about to give up my independence. So if you and Gina can make this work, no one will be happier for you than me."

"Jeez, you don't know how relieved I am you feel that way. I've always been clueless about women's emotions. Even though I suspected you would feel that way, I was worried I'd lose your friendship."

"Not a chance. No matter what happens we'll always be good friends, and I'll be there if you need me."

They talked for another hour. He told her all about the cruise, sans the lovemaking, and she brought him up to speed on her life.

■ ■ ■

Two days later as Bart was paying bills he noticed the note from the apartment complex manager. Out of curiosity he dialed the Dallas number. On the fourth ring it went to voicemail: "Hey this is Ben, leave a number and I'll call you back."

Bart hesitated, but ultimately decided to leave his unlisted home phone number. At 9:15 that evening Ben called back. Bart recognized the number and answered, "Hello, Mr. Miller, do I know you?"

"Maybe . . . are you the Lieutenant Bart LaRocca of the United States Air Force who was in Vietnam in the early 1970s and once had an address in Middle Village, New York?"

"That's me. Have we met?"

"Perhaps. There is no easy way to say this, but I may be your son."

"Whoa, Ben!" Bart exclaimed. "I had a son, but he died a couple of years ago; his name was Peter."

"Well, I have a photo I believe is of you with my mother when she was pregnant with me. Her name was Pham Thi Anh and my Vietnamese name is Pham Van Minh. I was told my father was an American airman and both my mother and father were killed. My grandmother saved me, but she could hardly feed herself, much less an infant. I was told she tearfully dropped me at an orphanage in Vung Tau. When it became evident the North Vietnamese would take Saigon, the orphanage was able to place me with the Millers in Dallas. I was one of twenty-seven hundred orphans that made it out under Operation Babylift. The only thing, besides me, that survived was a photograph with a handwritten note on the back including your name and an address in New York.

"When I tried to look you up at that address, two really big guys grabbed me and took me to their boss; I think his name was Nicosia. I showed him the picture and told him I thought it was my dead father. He laughed and told me you weren't dead and you were living in Charlotte. In fact, a few days later he called me with your address. You can imagine how excited I was to find out my father may be alive, so I hopped on a plane and camped out at your gate."

"Look, Ben, I am really glad you contacted me, but I am not your father. I know who he was, and he really was killed in Vietnam along with your mother. That photo was indeed taken when your mother was pregnant with you. At the time your father was stationed at Phan Rang Air Base and had a small house a few miles outside the base where your mother and grandmother lived. I visited them once and can tell you that your mother was a wonderful woman. She and your father were very much in love. Your father's name was Robbie Ryan.

"He and I were roommates in college. Your father resigned from the Air Force when he couldn't get another assignment back in Vietnam to be with you and your mom. After his discharge, he made his way back to 'Nam as a civilian; all of you lived near Saigon until a grenade was tossed into the house, killing your mother and father. If you give me a few days, I might be able to put you in touch with some other family members here in the States."

"Wow! I feel as if you just gave me everything I had ever wished for. Thank you, Mr. LaRocca."

"Ben, do you think you could get me a copy of the photo of your mother and me?"

"Sure, Mr. Nicosia had some copies made and he gave me all of the extra ones he didn't keep."

"Really. When did you see Al Nicosia?"

"About two weeks ago."

"OK, thanks. I'll do some checking and perhaps I can find your grandparents."

After hanging up, Bart reflected, with some concern, on what Ben had told him. His brother-in-law had a copy of the picture of Anh and him, and no explanation of the real circumstances surrounding it. Given Al's history of trying to destroy Bart's creditability, he could bet that sooner or later Al would show Gina the picture and spin quite a tale about how normal it was for GIs, even married ones, to have a live-in girlfriend in a war zone. He might even quote some of the statistics about the number of Amerasian children left behind. Now, in hindsight, he could kick himself for not telling Gina about Robbie; in her fragile state she might not give him a chance to explain. Was it already too late? He had to call Gina and tell her even though, at this late date, it would probably sound like a desperate attempt to refute the evidence. Well, at least if she didn't believe his story, he could have her talk to Robbie's parents; they would probably be able to bring some creditability to the photo and his explanation. In fact, he needed to get in touch with them right now and tell them about Ben.

Bart called directory assistance for Hilton Head Island but the Ryans' number, as he suspected, was unlisted. He then called David Tanner. He briefly told him about Ben's call and the photo; he asked David if he could use his contacts on Hilton Head to get the general's telephone number. David was as concerned as Bart about Al having a copy of the picture. Immediately after he hung up from the call to David, Bart dialed Gina's number. After eight rings with no answer, the call went to voicemail. He left a message indicating there was something he needed to talk about with her. He went to sleep without receiving a return call from Gina.

The next morning, David's administrative assistant called with the Ryans' unlisted phone number and both the general's and Mrs. Ryan's cell phone numbers. Reflecting on his chance meeting with the Ryans several years earlier, he decided to call Rita Ryan on her cell phone first. When she did not answer, he left a message with his cell phone number. Rita Ryan called back that afternoon.

Bart recognized the number immediately. "Mrs. Ryan, thank you for calling back. I have something to tell you that I hope you will consider an exciting development."

"Please, Bart, call me Rita. What could be so exciting?"

"Rita, I believe I have been in contact with your grandson."

"Robbie's boy?"

"Yes, we talked on the phone yesterday. I believe he is legit and is now living in the United States."

"Oh my god! I wonder how Harlan is going to react."

"If you don't mind, I've been giving this some thought. They now have DNA testing that can prove beyond a shadow of a doubt whether two people are related. You may want to talk to the young man to have a test done before you tell Harlan. That's just a suggestion."

"Well Bart, I appreciate your concern but I doubt I could pursue this without telling my husband. Regardless of his reaction, I am going to have the DNA test done."

"OK, Rita. The young man's name is Ben Miller. He lives in Dallas and his number is 770-555-1010. Will you let me know how it turns out?"

"Yes, I will. Thank you, Bart."

CHAPTER 65

Gina didn't return his call, so finally around 7:00 p.m. he called again. This time she answered. "Well, if it isn't my ex-husband. What . . . did you run out of whores and decide you'd call me?"

Surprised, Bart thought he detected a slur in Gina's speech. "Gina, have you been drinking?"

Ignoring his question, Gina snarled, "So has your bastard son found you yet?"

"I figured Al wouldn't waste much time spinning a sordid tale out of an unfortunate incident. It's not what you think or what Al told you; he is not my kid."

"Sure, and Bill Clinton didn't have sex with that woman."

"Jeez, Gina, will you let me explain?"

"Please, I saw the picture my brother got from your bastard son, and I remember you used to send donations to an orphanage in Vietnam. So please, for once, own up to your infidelity. You're no better than my brother Al with his lie of not being involved in Peter's arson thing. Both of you can go to hell, there's no one left that I can trust."

"I swear he is not my son; he's Robbie Ryan's. Robbie took me to meet the boy's mother when we were both stationed over there. Robbie took the picture of me and his pregnant girlfriend. They were both killed by a grenade when the child was still an infant. The donations I sent to the orphanage had nothing to do with any of that."

"How convenient the only ones who can testify to your story are dead. I really don't want to listen to you anymore."

Desperate, Bart pleaded, "Gina, don't hang up. If you'd just give me a chance, there are ways to prove he's not my son."

"Save it for someone who cares." Then she hung up.

He tried calling her back, but her phone went right to voice-mail. He tried several more times that night and again three more times the next morning. Finally, in desperation, he called John. After a somewhat disjointed explanation which John believed, he also became extremely concerned about Gina's mental state. John called Gina immediately after hanging up, but Gina didn't answer. He left an urgent message for her to call him. By 10:00 p.m. East Coast time, Gina still had not called back.

Concerned by Bart's comment that he thought Gina had been

drinking, John reluctantly called Al. In order to avoid a heated argument, John did not let on about his conversation with Bart. All he told Al was that he had been trying to contact Gina for a few days but hadn't gotten an answer. He asked Al if he had talked to her. Al played it real cute, and didn't reveal anything that transpired between him and his sister. He claimed he hadn't spoken to Gina in days. John was able to convince Al to go by the house and check on Gina.

When Al arrived at the house, it was totally dark. He was pretty sure Gina was not planning to leave for Charlotte for another week. He hastily rang the bell. Receiving no answer, he figured Gina was sleeping so he used his key to gain entrance. He quietly made his way up the stairs to Gina's bedroom. The bed was still made up. He then checked the other two bedrooms and they were also empty. Fearing that she may have fallen and was unconscious somewhere, he scoured the rest of house; all he found was an empty 1.5 liter vodka bottle on the kitchen table.

Unlike her father, Gina used the garage to keep her car out of the weather. Al decided to check to see if her car was in the garage. He hastened out the back door toward the garage apprehensive as to whether he would feel better if the car was there or not. He was hardly down the back steps when he knew it wasn't good. He could hear the faint sound of an engine idling. Running the rest of the way, he discovered both the overhead and side doors were locked. Smashing the windowpane on the side door, Al was able to undo the lock. As he pulled open the door he was hit by a dense carbon-monoxide fog. Ignoring the toxic fumes and his now-watery eyes, Al rushed around to the driver's side door and yanked it open. As he did, Gina's lifeless body collapsed into his arms. He pulled his sister out of the car and grabbed her under her arms. He dragged her limp body back around the vehicle and out onto the lawn. Checking her pulse, he decided to call 911 first and then try mouth-to-mouth and CPR. Al Nicosia worked on his sister, to no avail, until the emergency response team arrived seven minutes later. After checking a few vital signs and noting her obvious low body temperature, the technicians quickly reached the conclusion Gina had been dead for several hours.

■ ■ ■

Bart LaRocca believed that after Peter's death he couldn't ever feel worse, but he was wrong. Gina's suicide plunged him into an even deeper misery. The thought that he could have and should have done something to avert both their deaths haunted him for the rest of his life.

CHAPTER 66

Since Gina did not leave a suicide note, John, with the help of NYPD, attempted to recreate the events leading up to Gina's death. As the pieces of her last few days on earth were reconstructed, the most likely account went something like this.

After the cruise, Gina arrived back in New York on Sunday, November 14. On Monday morning she met with a realtor friend and agreed that following a few minor repairs she would put the house on the market. On Monday afternoon she called the handyman the family had used for years. Tuesday the handyman came by the house and completed a few of the repairs. Tuesday afternoon she excitedly bought a one-way ticket to Charlotte for two days before Thanksgiving Day, the 24th.

On Wednesday she made a courtesy call to her brother Al, informing him she was selling the house and moving out of New York. Stunned at his sister's surprise announcement, he questioned her as to where she planned on moving. Gina responded she wasn't sure, but she was going to Bart's for Thanksgiving and might stay there for a few weeks. Al was livid. Desperate to prevent his sister from reuniting with the man he had despised for the last forty years, Al Nicosia played his newly dealt trump card. Al rushed over to Gina's. Reluctantly she let him in. Al then told her he finally had proof Bart was the liar and cheat he had been claiming. Gina was still euphoric from the cruise and suspicious of her brother's motives; her first reaction was to throw Al out of the house. But it was all or nothing for Al; if he couldn't convince Gina she was making a big mistake, he would lose the last person for whom he had any real feelings. He pleaded with his sister to allow him to get something out of his car. Reluctantly, she agreed to give him five more minutes.

Al hurried to his car, returning with the photo of Bart and the pregnant Anh. He then relayed the story of Ben Miller trying to locate his father. In Al's version of the story, Ben Miller knew explicitly Bart was his father. How Ben knew this for certain was a little shaky; but all the same, Al's story was good enough to reawaken all the suspicions Gina had harbored for decades. Within minutes, all her old emotions about Peter, her failed marriage, and her meaningless life flooded her psyche; and she began spiraling into anger and depression.

In tears, Gina retreated to her bedroom and bawled her eyes out for over an hour. Finally, not able to stand the emotional pain any longer, and with no booze in the house, she walked down to the nearest bar on Dry Harbor Road to drown her sorrows in vodka martinis. Two hours later the bartender, an old friend from grammar school, cut her off and called her a cab. When she returned home, she stumbled up the stairs to her bed. But unconsciousness eluded her until, in desperation for escape from the emotional pain, she took four sleeping pills.

She awoke the next day around noon and by 3:00 p.m. she had walked to the liquor store and returned with two bottles of Kettle One. Sometime later that afternoon, she checked her voicemail and discovered her lying, cheating ex-husband had left several messages. She thought about calling him back and lambasting him for his deceit but after partially dialing his number she hung up. By 7:00 p.m., when Bart called again, the booze had provided her with the strength to answer and tell him she knew about his secret and that it was now finally over between them. It was their last conversation.

Two hours later, after unplugging her phone and unable to drink any more alcohol without puking, she took two sleeping pills and cried herself to sleep on the living room couch.

Friday the 19th was a gloomy, cold day. Gina awoke in a horribly depressed mood. The last few hours of her restless sleep had been dominated by nightmares of her, Peter, and Bart. It seemed she was always trying to save her only son from some tragic fate while her husband wandered off with some other woman. Early in the afternoon she called for a cab to take her to the family plot at St. John's Cemetery. On the way to the cemetery she had the cabby stop at the florist across the street from St. John's to buy a bouquet of roses. On a standard card that came with the bouquet she wrote simply: "Mom, Dad, Peter, I'm going to be joining you soon." She had the cabby wait while she placed the roses on Peter's grave and then she had him take her home.

After arriving back home, around two in the afternoon, she opened the second bottle of vodka and downed a handful of sleeping pills. Stumbling down the back steps with her car keys, she managed to make it to the garage. After securely shutting and locking both the overhead and side doors, she started the engine. With a few more swigs of vodka, she swallowed the remaining sleeping pills. Authorities estimated there was enough fresh air flow in the old garage to keep the carbon monoxide concentration at somewhere below three thousand parts per million. At this concentration, it was a toss-up as to whether she lost consciousness as a result of the toxin or from the alcohol and sleeping pills. Regardless, she was dead in less than two hours.

CHAPTER 67

Probably for the first time in his life, John Nicosia took charge of a family responsibility by making all the arrangements for his sister's wake and funeral. Al tried to take the lead, but John privately berated his older brother for his part in knowingly creating a situation that probably sent his fragile sister into a death spiral. Besides, John knew if Al were in charge Bart would be prevented from taking any part in the ceremonies. Al was so taken aback by his younger brother's reprimand he begrudgingly agreed to remain in the background. He almost succeeded.

Similar to the proceedings following Peter's death, Gina's wake, funeral mass, and burial were conducted in a low-key manner. There was no public notification announcing the times and places for the events. Her obituary requested that anyone interested in honoring her life should make a donation to the American Cancer Society. Perhaps fifty people were informed of the details of her wake, funeral service, and interment. With John's approval, Bart extended the invitation to the Tanners', Betty Rice, and Don Serafina. David cancelled his schedule for the entire week, reserving a suite at the Hilton near JFK. Betty struggled with her decision to attend or not. She felt an obligation to Bart, but she was not sure how she would react when confronted with her rapist. In the end, she asked him if he would be hurt if she did not attend. When he told her he understood her hesitation, she opted out. Don arrived for the funeral.

All the services were uneventful until the post-funeral reception at Neidermeyer's Restaurant. Bart, unable to avoid the issue any longer, confronted Al by declaring, "If you had any common sense at all, you would have either called me about the allegation that Ben Miller was my son or waited until you were sure your sister was emotionally able to handle it."

"Why would I do that, knowing she was being duped again to move in with you?"

"Maybe for the same reasons I never told Gina why you got kicked out of the army, or that you raped Betty Rice, or how your second wife humiliated you into a divorce. If you cared at all for your sister, you would have realized revealing those kinds of stories wouldn't change what happened but they would destroy Gina's world."

Stunned by his brother's-in-law indictment, Al seemed to be in a catatonic stupor for several seconds. Bart watched as blood filled the capillaries in his archenemy's face and the arteries in his neck pulsed.

With clenched fists and spittle propelling from his mouth, Al Nicosia got right up in Bart's face vowing, in a voice loud enough to be heard by everyone in the private dining room, "You son of a bitch. Your luck has just run out. This time you're going to wish you never heard of me or my family."

Bart, himself now in a bellicose mood, didn't back away. He vociferously retaliated, "Are you stupid? I already wish I had never heard of you. As for your family, I'm not sure there is any blood relationship between you, John, and Gina. Given how different you are from them, I wouldn't be surprised if I found out some derelict left you on the Nicosias' doorstep."

That did it. Al tried to take a swing, but they were too close to each other and Bart had anticipated the move. He shoved Al away before he could get in position to throw a haymaker. John, hearing the shouting, rushed between them. At the same instant David Tanner grabbed Bart's arm, dragging him out of the room, while John and Don Serafina attempted to calm Al down. David, always a cool head, quickly convinced Bart to accompany him back to the Hilton. After a somber and hurried good-bye to John and Patty Jo, Bart told David and Don to meet him outside while he went to the men's room. The restrooms in the building were in the basement. As Bart left the restroom, he was confronted in the narrow corridor leading back to the staircase by Al and two of his henchmen. His only path of escape was blocked. Bart quickly realized his only chance of getting out without serious injuries was to goad Al into a one-on-one showdown.

"What, you're not man enough to take me on alone?"

"I'm not in the mood to screw around with you, LaRocca. Grab him," he ordered his lackeys.

Al's two henchmen charged their prey. Bart got in one punch to the eye of one of them, but the other buckled him over with a shot to his solar plexus. Grabbing Bart by the arms, they held the gasping Bart LaRocca upright so his furious brother-in-law could pound him into oblivion. After Al delivered a furious flurry of blows to Bart's head and midsection, they released their semiconscious victim, who collapsed to the floor. But Al Nicosia was not done yet. He proceeded to kick Bart in the ribs and face until his face looked like a pepperoni pizza and the blows no longer brought a reaction.

Exhausted, Little Nicky and his two cohorts quietly made their way back up the stairs and out into the parking lot. Noticing David Tanner and Don Serafina waiting in Don's Jaguar, Al sauntered over to the vehicle. He went first to the driver's window, motioning Don to roll it down. When Don complied, Al leaned over and menacingly said to Don, "You need to be careful who you stand up for, Serafina. Bruno DeLuca's protection doesn't extend to New York." Then changing his focus to David Tanner, he whimsically announced, "You better call an ambulance; I think your buddy fell down the stairs."

CHAPTER 68

Two days later Bart woke up in Mount Sinai Hospital in Long Island City. As he began to emerge from unconsciousness, his first reaction was this had to be the worst hangover he ever experienced. Fighting to regain his wits from the medications and concussion, he suddenly became aware of the pain. To say it was intense would be like describing Bo Derrick, running along the beach in the movie *10*, as attractive. Every time he took a breath, he felt like someone was stabbing him in the chest with a knife. That was from his three broken ribs and punctured lung. His face felt as if he was wearing a hockey goalie's mask with nails on the inside. This was from his broken nose, dislocated jaw, and fractured cheekbone, exacerbated by five teeth that had been knocked out. He tried to move his arms, but his left one was secured tightly across his chest in order to keep his reset shoulder in place.

The first thing he recognized, even before he could focus his eyes, was David, John, and Don having an animated conversation about him. When his eyes began to focus, he saw Patty Jo sitting in a chair staring at him with a very concerned look on her face. Struggling to speak, he realized that he couldn't open his mouth. All he could manage was a guttural groan. Patty Jo was the only one who recognized his feeble attempt to get their attention, "Was that him . . . I think he's coming around!"

John leaned over the bed, scrutinizing Bart for signs of consciousness. "Yeah, he's awake! Don't try to talk. Boy, were we worried about you."

Still unable to focus clearly, Bart forced out a painfully muffled "Where am I?"

John smiled tentatively. "I told you not to try to talk. Your jaw is wired shut."

David moved closer to the bed. "You're at Mount Sinai Hospital and you've been unconscious for two days. If you understand what I'm saying, just nod. Do you remember what happened?"

Bart grimaced as he moved his head left, then right.

"Do you remember Gina's funeral?"

This time he nodded in the affirmative and let out a soft moan.

Thrilled with Bart's comprehension, David continued, "OK, well after the cemetery, there was a small reception at Neidermeyer's. You and Al had some words so I decided to get you out of there before it got physical. As we were leaving, you decided to hit the men's room. The next thing I knew, Al came over to the car and told me you fell down the stairs. Are you beginning to remember now?"

In spite of the pain and wired jaw Bart forced out a guttural "Yeah!"

"So was it Al who did this to you?" John asked.

Bart nodded yes and with his free arm held up three fingers.

"There were three of them who beat you up?" John tried to confirm.

Bart nodded positive again.

"Damn that coward," John spit out angrily.

"The police will probably be back later to talk to you; you can file charges then," David declared. Then he continued, "You've had some pretty serious injuries; you'll probably be in here for a few days. Lots of people are very concerned about you. John and I have been requesting they not come by to see you yet. When you think you can handle visitors, let me know and I'll put the word out. The only other people that have been here besides us have been your sister and her husband. I just got a hold of Betty last night. She's on her way here as we speak. Meantime, don't worry about anything except your recovery. Gary and Doug are all set to take care of the business indefinitely. They'll both be up here this weekend to see you and resolve any business issues."

"I am really glad you regained consciousness today," John said. "I have to get back to Phoenix tomorrow. I have a lot of patients who need tending to back there."

Having finally regained his wits, he wasn't about to let a broken jaw and swollen face prevent him from communicating with the last people on earth he cared about. From deep down in his throat and without moving his jaw Bart told his friends, "Don't worry about me. How bad could I be hurt falling down a few steps?"

They all looked at each other with quizzical expressions. David was the first to respond. "What are you saying, Bart?"

"I'm saying that, as far as anyone outside this room is concerned, I tripped and fell down the stairs."

John was incredulous. "But what about my brother, you're not going to let him get away with this? Are you?"

Now starting to get the hang of talking with his jaw wired shut, Bart answered back in a very determined tone, "Oh no, that bastard isn't getting away with anything; I just haven't figured out how I am going to get even with him yet. But I guarantee this time, no smooth-talking lawyer or disappearing witness is going to get him off."

The day after John and Patty Jo left, David had to fly to a meeting in the Caribbean and Don drove back to Springfield. Except for Betty and his sister Fran, the only other visitors Bart had were Gary and Doug. Of course, there was the brief visit by

NYPD, but after Bart told them he fell down the stairs, they never came back. Bart got the impression they were not surprised he claimed it was an accident.

■ ■ ■

A week in the hospital gives a person plenty of time to think. By the time David Tanner came back with his private jet to take him home with him to Palm Springs for more recuperation time, Bart had developed the framework of his scheme to get even with Little Nicky. He hadn't worked out all the details yet; but he knew whatever he did, he would have to do it alone. It would be dangerous and afterwards, if he survived, he would have to permanently disappear.

On the three-hour flight from New York to Palm Beach, Bart revealed to David Tanner that he planned on getting his revenge on Al Nicosia, not only for the assault, but also for the role he played in both Peter and Gina's deaths. Initially, David was vehemently opposed to Bart's plan. Not only did he doubt his friend's chances of success against a Mafia boss, he couldn't see the logic of putting one's self at risk of criminal charges. In spite of David's objections, Bart remained steadfast in his intentions. Realizing he was probably not going to talk Bart out of it, David Tanner reluctantly began giving Bart whatever help he could. It was on this flight to Palm Springs David Tanner outlined the four key elements of a successful disappearance. He told Bart the first thing he needed was plenty of money. Bart already had plenty. The next thing he needed was to find a way to move his money without anyone, including the government, being able to trace it. That led to the third criteria: establish a new identity. The last element was the actual plan of attack and his escape.

David also pointed out that, as a result of his injuries, Bart had the opportunity to have some facial modifications done to go along with his new identity. David suggested that as soon as the swelling went down he would take him to a plastic surgeon for a consultation. Bart liked the idea, since he would probably have to have his nose and cheek worked on anyway.

The most critical thing David provided was a plan for moving all Bart's investments in Tanner's US real estate operations to his Caribbean holding company in Costa Rica and then converting those investments into untraceable bearer bonds. Through his connections in the Caribbean, David was also able to hook Bart up with the right legal advice for establishing his own shell corporations once he worked out his new identity. Perhaps the most important advice his friend gave him was to stay away from the Cayman Islands. Although you always read how the characters in various novels were able to hide all their ill-gotten treasures in the banks of the Caymans, by the mid-1980s that had all changed. Under pressure from the US over laundered drug money, the island nation agreed to make their banking transactions available to law enforcement agencies. It was inevitable someday there would be no safe banking haven from the scrutiny of US and European law enforcement, but in the late 1990s there were still a few places that believed it was in their best interest to maintain banking secrecy from foreign countries. The Caribbean island nation of Dominica was one of them.

CHAPTER 69

Bart's recovery was slow. The swelling on his face was gone within two weeks, but he wasn't able to chew meat for almost a month. His broken nose left him with a deviated septum, which made it necessary for him to breathe through his mouth most of the time. His cheek was now misshapen and still hurt when he touched it or tried to sleep on that side of his head. Because his ribs did not fully heal for almost three months, he was unable to play golf. Although his dentist recommended he get implants for his missing teeth, Bart figured removable dentures might be an advantage when he needed disguises.

Over the next several months, the plan for his revenge against his former brother-in-law really started to take shape. Initially,

Bart sought Don Serafina's advice, but when Don told him about Al's threat of not being under Bruno DeLuca's protection, he decided he didn't want to put Don at risk. That was the last time Bart talked to his friend leading up to the attack on his brother-in-law. He then confided in Doug Carbone, the former Mountie. Doug, unlike David Tanner, thought Bart could pull it off and actually disappear. On the other hand, Doug insisted he would help Bart only if it didn't result in a murder. Doug reasoned that, short of murder, law enforcement probably wouldn't get too worked up over the Mafia kingpin's troubles. At first, Bart didn't like Doug's stipulation, but the more he thought about it, the more he began to like the idea. After all, death is so final, whilst living years with the constant memory of a humiliating defeat would be maddening, especially for someone with an ego like Al Nicosia's. So Bart eventually agreed to Doug's terms, and in return, Doug provided him with his first new identity. Doug was the sole survivor in his family and had in his possession the birth certificate of an older brother who had died as an infant. Doug assisted Bart in submitting an application for a passport in his brother's name, Charles Carbone. The passport pictures included with the application were not flattering. Bart's nose had healed with a noticeable bump and his left cheek was misshapen from the fracture. In order to keep the procedure simple, they used the address of the family farm in Canada which Doug was leasing. After mailing in the application, Doug called his tenants and told them to keep a look out for an important government envelope addressed to Charles Carbone. When it arrived, Doug instructed them to FedEx it to him in the States. Two months later Bart LaRocca had his first new identity.

With the Charles Carbone passport in hand, Bart was ready for the next phase of his disappearance. First he got a green card in Charles's name through Doug's sponsorship. Then he rented a studio apartment just over the border from Charlotte, in Fort Mill, South Carolina. Using his new South Carolina address he proceeded to take, and pass, the South Carolina driver's license exam. His green card, South Carolina address, and driver's license gave him the credentials to obtain a Social Security card. Next he opened up a non-interest bearing checking account at South Carolina Bank and Trust and got a credit card.

Having established an ironclad alternate identity, Bart could work on moving the rest of his US finances. Bart had started selling off his stock holdings right after his and David's conversation. His timing couldn't have been more serendipitous, beating the dot com crash by a few months and netting almost $1.5 million after taxes. He started withdrawing between $5,000 and $9,000 a week and depositing it in the South Carolina checking account. David had cautioned him to keep his deposits under $10,000 in order to avoid government scrutiny, but at that rate it would take him almost five years to move all his money. He needed to find a faster method. In the meantime, whenever he traveled to one of David's Caribbean real estate company's board meetings, he brought a suitcase full of cash on David's corporate jet. After the meeting he would charter a boat and make his way to Dominica where he had set up bank accounts in the name of Charles Carbone. By the end of the summer of 2000, he had moved $350,000 to the Dominican accounts. Frustrated by how slow it was going, he was constantly searching for a more efficient, untraceable method for moving his money. One Thursday as he was delivering cash to his Chinese client, a new scheme popped into his head. Every week, for the last couple of years, he had been withdrawing almost $40,000 for the Chinese. A couple of days later they wired that plus the interest back into his account. So it dawned on him, if he could convince the Chinese to wire the money to an account in the Caribbean instead of in the States then he could replace the monies in his business account with his own money. It was a brilliant scheme; if he could pull it off, by the end of the year he would have his remaining $1.2 million in an offshore account.

The next week when he made his cash delivery to Raleigh, he handed his client a letter requesting they begin wire-transferring the payment to his shell corporation's account in Costa Rica. On Monday, to his amazement, the funds did not show up in his Charlotte business account. A quick telephone call to his bank in San Jose confirmed the funds were deposited in the corporate account of one of his companies. He was home free; he could now begin converting the cash into bearer bonds.

Bart began cleaning up the loose ends of his businesses by selling the entire ATM business to Doug and Gary for the depreciated value of the equipment plus the cash in the machines. That left him with only the Chinese business, which he still needed to move the remainder of his US cash.

About the same time, he received a call from the administrator of the Sunshine Nursing Home in Matthews, North Carolina. Apparently, one of his AARP tax clients, by the name of Carl Diaz, had died, and Bart's name was listed on his vital information record as his executor. The man, two years older than Bart, had contracted mesothelioma while working in the Norfolk shipyards during the 1960s and 1970s. He had never married and had no known relatives. He required constant oxygen and had been in the nursing home for the last ten years. One of his few trips out of the nursing home each month was to the senior center where Bart prepared income tax returns. After the first year of Bart doing his taxes Carl wouldn't let any of the other volunteers prepare them.

As his executor, Bart discovered in Carl's personal effects a couple of valuable documents. He found a will that bequeathed all Carl's assets to St. Mark's Catholic Church and the birth certificate of one Carlos Diaz y Vargos, born March 12, 1942, in Madrid, Spain, to Jorge Diaz and Isabella Vargos. He also found Carlos's and his parents' US naturalization documents. What a windfall for Bart! He could now attempt to obtain a Spanish passport in Carlos's name for himself. Rather than try to get the passport at that time, he decided to wait until after his plastic surgery so the picture on the passport would be closer to his new appearance.

CHAPTER 70

The plan for his revenge on Little Nicky was a lot harder for Bart to pin down than his vanishing act. From the first moment he awoke in the hospital and began to remember what had happened, he started fantasizing ways to get even with his former brother-in-law. At first it was a shotgun blast to the face, but he discarded that idea when he recognized the unlikelihood of getting close to Al with a shotgun. He then began envisioning more complex clandestine schemes. One of his initial favorites was the one where he'd introduce a toxic gas into the HVAC system of the Elmhurst Italian-American Social Club, forcing all the wiseguys to flee to the street. Concealed on the roof of the building across the street, he would then toss Molotov cocktails at the gasping mafiosi. At one point Bart even began researching the use of blow guns and poison darts. It didn't take him long to realize, however, it would be easier and he'd have a better chance of success if he just used a hunting rifle from a nearby rooftop. However, after his agreement with Doug not to fatally harm anyone, he revised his fantasy to tossing battery acid instead of Molotov cocktails. It wasn't until he actually staked out the social club that his final plan started taking shape.

■ ■ ■

Betty Rice was one of the founding members of the Association of College Administrative Professionals. Living and working in Radford, Virginia, Betty had the opportunity to become actively involved in the ACAP, whose headquarters were located just up Interstate 81 in Staunton, Virginia. Due to her proximity to the association's headquarters, Dean Rice was often a speaker at its conferences and workshops. During the second week in April 2001, she was attending one of those conferences in New York City, hosted by NYU, when she found herself having dinner at the same restaurant in Manhattan as Al Nicosia. He didn't recognize her, but she immediately recognized him. Al was at a table with three bimbos and two of his other middle-aged horny associates. Even after thirty years, seeing her rapist made her nauseated. She excused herself from her dinner companions and stumbled into the ladies' room, where she immediately surrendered her dinner. It took her a few minutes to clean up and regain her composure before returning to her colleagues. For the next half hour, feigning interest in the conversations of her associates, she was mesmerized, watching the dirty bastard. To her surprise, she secretly returned to the restaurant's bar after saying good night to her friends. Sitting there sipping a ginger ale, Betty Rice continued to watch, as if in a trance, until Al and his party were leaving. On their way out, a chill ran up her spine when Al declared, "Let's go someplace where we can get to know each other better." Those were the exact words he used on her at Bart's wedding.

Returning to her hotel, feeling almost as humiliated and angry as she did thirty years earlier, she called Bart, the one person with whom she could talk. During their emotional telephone conversation, Betty reiterated he was still the only person she ever told about the rape. After decades of unsuccessfully trying to forget what happened, she finally needed to see Al Nicosia pay for what he did to her. Bart then told her he was working on a plan to extract retribution from his brother-in-law. Betty excitedly declared, "Whatever you decide to do, count me in." Before they got off the phone, Betty had convinced Bart to meet her in New York to begin planning their joint revenge.

Bart arrived at Betty's room in the Gramercy Park Hotel shortly after she had finished her morning seminars. She had already changed out of her business attire into jeans, a sweatshirt, and boots. Not knowing what to expect when he arrived in New York, Bart flew up dressed in gray woolen dress slacks, blue button-down cotton shirt, Harris Tweed sports jacket, and a pair of Cole Haan two-tone penny loafers. In his overnight bag, he had the foresight to also pack a sweatshirt, jeans, and sneakers.

While he changed, Bart started filling Betty in on his unfinished plan to attack Al and disappear. Although he was initially reluctant to risk Betty's safety and reputation on his personal vendetta, she convinced him she needed to do this for her own reasons. After he grudgingly agreed to her help, she made her first contribution; she suggested the first step in the battle plan was to become familiar with the terrain. Since most of his plans included an assault at the Elmhurst Italian-American Social Club, Betty insisted they make their first reconnaissance that afternoon. While walking over to the Sixth Avenue subway station at Twenty-Third Street, Bart enumerated the many evolutions of his plan, expressing frustration he still hadn't hit on the right scheme. Sympathetic, Betty Rice suggested perhaps her strategic and tactical military planning courses at the Air War College could help him solidify a doable plan.

After they jumped on the M train, he quietly continued to brief her on the planning for his disappearance. She was overwhelmingly impressed with the ingenuity of his money-laundering plans and the cleanliness of his new identities. By the time they exited at the Woodhaven and Queens Boulevard station, they had agreed Betty would have no active involvement on the day of the attack. The couple almost looked like locals as they walked the several blocks toward the social club. On the way they stopped at Sal's, a small, four-table pizzeria that sold pizza by the slice. As they virtually inhaled their huge slices, a man about their age came into the joint and ordered a slice with sausage and onion. Bart thought the man looked vaguely familiar. When the man began talking excitedly about the Mets chances that year, it became clear to Bart he did know him. It was Gina's mentally challenged cousin Paulie. Bart recalled John had mentioned Paulie still lived alone above what used to be his father's bar and was now his cousin's headquarters, the social club.

Bart whispered to Betty, "Look at the guy at the counter. You saw him at my wedding. He's Paulie Nicosia, Gina's cousin. His father owned the bar that's now the social club. He's always had some kind of mental handicap. Based upon what John told me, after the kid's old man died, Al took him under his protection by turning the bar into the club and paying Paulie rent and charging dues to each of the members of his crew. Paulie gets half and the rest goes for booze and cigars. I also think Al paid to have the upstairs four-room apartment split in two; Paulie lives on one side and Al uses the other one for private meetings and who knows what else."

"You know, I do remember Paulie. He was hanging around Al for most of the reception. It disgusts me to say it now, but while Al and I were trying to get it on, Paulie wouldn't let Al alone long enough for him to even cop a feel. Between the kid and our Air Force buddies acting like mother hens, we were both getting pretty horny. Finally, Al suggested we go someplace where we could get to know each other better; that's when Al asked you for the house keys. Before we could sneak off together, the other Air Force guys virtually dragged me back to the base. I sometimes wonder if standing him up that way is what pissed him off. Perhaps if I had gone with him right then, things would have been different."

"It probably didn't make any difference. Al is Al. He leaves a path of destruction wherever he goes. Don't beat yourself up anymore; you may have wanted to get laid, but what he did to you wasn't about satisfying a carnal urge. It was about dominance and humiliation."

"You're right; let's focus on the task at hand, planning our humiliation of Little Nicky Nicosia."

The couple leisurely finished their beers and slices as the owner of the pizza parlor feigned interest in Paulie's analysis of the Mets' chances of meeting the Yankees again in the World Series. Just then the phone rang; the owner answered and started taking down an order. After he hung up he called to the back, "Four of the usual pies for the boys, six hoagies, two capicola, two salami with provolone, and two combos." Realizing his audience was no longer paying attention, Paulie left and walked the last few blocks to his apartment. Bart and Betty waited thirty seconds then casually followed him out the door. Trailing, hand in hand, the couple nonchalantly followed a half block behind Paulie. After they had turned onto Sixty-Ninth Street, Bart pointed out the unassuming and unmarked social club. There were two cars parked near the building and a half dozen more in the vacant lot next to it. But the parking spot right in front of the club was empty, apparently left open in case the boss showed up.

The couple continued strolling down the street like two lovers on their way home. Betty's military training took in everything, making a detailed mental note of every building, alley, fire hydrant, light post and vacant lot. Later, back at their hotel in Manhattan, she put it all down on paper. As they reached the next intersection, Betty stopped, turned, and said, "This is good; the first floor of all these buildings is occupied by small businesses. They'll all close down by 8:00 p.m. at the latest and the apartments on the second floor look empty. I wonder if either the NYPD or FBI ever uses them to stake out the place. Besides the rental unit above the small appliance repair shop on the corner of Queens Boulevard, there are a couple of other good second-floor windows that could be used for surveillance of the club. If the cops have the club staked out, that would be a showstopper."

"Shit," replied Bart, "I never thought of that. How are we ever going to find out if there is a stakeout?"

"I know a guy back in DC who used to be an assistant director with the bureau. He's retired now, but he still likes to keep up with what's going on. He always enjoyed telling stories about how the bureau screwed over organized crime. Maybe I can goad him into finding out if there are any ongoing stakeouts. I'll tell him I saw Little Nicky at a restaurant while I was in New York and I was surprised the FBI hadn't put him away yet. In the meantime, that shouldn't stop us from renting the apartment on the corner and starting our own observation of the place. If we find out the street is under regular surveillance, we'll just have to come up with an alternate plan. Let's take a walk up the two streets on either side of this one. I want to see what's on the back side."

They walked around the block and back down Queens Boulevard. Betty stopped at the corner of Sixty-Ninth and wrote down the telephone number on the Apartment for Rent sign. They continued across Sixty-Ninth to the next street and walked down it as Betty continued her mental observations. When they were finished, Betty suggested they walk past the club again. Just as they turned onto Sixty-Ninth, a black Lincoln Town Car turned off Queens Boulevard and pulled up in the vacant parking spot right in front of the club. The driver, a huge man, got out and quickly made it around to the passenger side. After a quick survey of the street, he spotted Bart and Betty. He hesitated for an instant, but must have figured these two middle-aged lovers posed no threat, so he opened the back door and Al Nicosia got out.

"How about that," Betty whispered, "I don't see the bastard for thirty years then whammo, twice in a couple of days. That must be some kind of an omen." Before they finished their second survey of the club, a beat-up Toyota Corolla with a Sal's Pizzeria dome light screeched around the corner and double-parked in front of the social club. The owner of Sal's jumped out, grabbed four pizza boxes and two large brown paper bags from the passenger seat, and rushed to the front door of the club. Bart and Betty watched as the door of the club opened and the huge hulk, who had just driven Al to the club, took the bags and boxes. As far as they could tell, no money changed hands. The pizza owner immediately hurried off as fast as he came.

"I wonder if he always personally makes the deliveries, or if there is a chance he might sometimes use hired help," Bart questioned out loud.

Betty immediately caught on to Bart's train of thought. "Are you thinking you could get inside by delivering pizza?"

Bart smirked. "Maybe."

When they got back to Queens Boulevard, Betty found a pay phone and called the number from the Apartment for Rent sign. After about five rings, a man with a Russian accent answered.

She asked, "Is the second floor apartment on the corner of Sixty-Ninth Street and Queens Boulevard still available?" After a slight pause she replied, "Great, I'm interested in renting it for a couple of months; how much is it?" Another pause as the landlord gave some thought to a short-term lease and what he would charge. A slight smile came over Betty's face as she responded to an apparent attempt by the landlord to make it sound as if he had another tenant waiting in the wings so he could jack up the rent. Betty didn't let him get too far down that line of thinking, abruptly telling him, "Look, tomorrow I will bring you three grand cash for three months' rent. You think you can hold it for me until then?" A pleased grin spread across her face as she listened to the landlord struggle to find the right things to say so three grand in cash didn't slip through his fingers. "OK then," Betty responded, "I'll meet you at noon tomorrow at the apartment."

Hanging up, she turned to Bart. "OK, this reconnaissance mission has already been a success. We have a great perch from which we can scout out whether this location will work as a battlefield. Tomorrow morning I'll have to convince an old friend, who is a SVP at Chase, to cash a check while you're getting some business cards printed up for a Marion Webster, Vice President of Sales for Acme Import/Export Company out of Atlanta, Georgia. You'll have to come up with an appropriate address and phone number."

CHAPTER 71

Bart spent the next two weeks cleaning things up in Charlotte so he could devote full time to surveillance and planning. First, he permanently transitioned the Chinese over to Doug and Gary, telling them he was going to be traveling too much to adequately support the business. He paid cash for a 1999 Maxima, identical to the one he was already driving. He registered it in

South Carolina under the name of Charles Carbone. Using the Bridgeport, Connecticut, Craigslist, he found a garage near the ferry terminal which he rented under Charles' name. His plan was to park the Maxima with South Carolina plates there and take the ferry over to Port Jefferson

While he was sanitizing his apartment for anything that might lead authorities to his plans, new identities or money, he found the note from the apartment manager with Ben Miller's phone number. Out of curiosity he dialed the number and Ben answered.

Ben was ecstatic to hear from Bart. He began apologizing for not calling Bart and thanking him for his role in connecting him with his American grandparents. Rita Ryan had contacted Ben and arranged to meet him at a doctor's office in Dallas where blood samples were taken and DNA analysis eventually proved he was Robbie's son. It took several months, but the general had eventually agreed to meet his grandson. Ben's relationship with his grandmother was wonderful, and grandpa seemed to be warming up to his only grandson.

■ ■ ■

At Betty's urging, he then took a side trip to Toronto. She wanted him to test his nerves at a border crossing using his new Canadian passport. Before he applied for his false passports and started moving his money into secret offshore accounts, Bart had never done anything even close to illegal. Betty was concerned his guilty conscience would be a telltale sign to the trained border agents. In those days before 9/11, it only required a valid driver's license to cross the border. Bart used his new Canadian passport, however. At the Niagara Falls crossing on the way over, he was really nervous. The morning he waited in line for the Canadian officials to get to his vehicle, it was a chilly 52 degrees. Yet, even with his windows open, he could feel the moisture under his arms. He felt nauseated and his head felt as if someone had blown up a balloon inside his skull. To his relief, after a brief scan of his passport and a quick look inside his vehicle; the guard passed him through. He was even more scared on the way back. He thought the US guards would be more observant, but they let him through without even a second glance. He continued to test the creditability of his new passport; first with US immigration authorities on his way back from a cruise on which he also rented a safe house in Rousseau, Dominica; then again passing through customs at the international airports in Costa Rica and Miami when he finalized his Costa Rican finances. By the time he presented his documents to the passport control agent on his return trip from Costa Rica, he no longer experienced any apprehension; he was by all accounts Charles Carbone, Canadian citizen.

▪ ▪ ▪

On a sunny day when the temperature is above 50 degrees, the one-hour, forty-five-minute ferry ride between Bridgeport, Connecticut, and Port Jefferson, New York, is quite pleasant. Port Jefferson is a quaint little seaside village with decent places to eat and cute little shops. Bridgeport, on the other hand, has no redeeming aesthetic features. The only thing that makes the ferry to Bridgeport worthwhile besides avoiding the drive through New York City is its proximity to the Amtrak station, I-95, and the Wilbur Cross Parkway.

Port Jefferson is also blessed with rail transportation; there's a LIRR station less than a mile from the harbor. Bart found the combination of ferry and train to be a great way to remain totally anonymous during his trips to and from New York. He liked to use a circuitous route driving to and from Bridgeport. He had two objectives on his drive: avoid the congestion on Interstate 95, and avoid the toll booth cameras around New York City. He accomplished this by taking a combination of Interstates I-77 out of Charlotte and I-81 in Virginia. He would then take I-81 to the Harrisburg area and either continue on I-81 all the way to I-84 in Scranton, or cut over to New Jersey on I-78. Depending on which route he took, he eventually crossed the Hudson River at either Bear Mountain Bridge or the Newburgh

Beacon Bridge. This route may have taken longer to drive, but any photographic record of him at a toll booth was too far north to prove he was ever in the City. Once across the Long Island Sound in Port Jefferson, he could catch a train almost anywhere on Long Island or the City.

His first solo reconnaissance trip to the Elmhurst Italian-American Social Club didn't happen until the second week in May. On the drive up, he stopped off in Radford to get Betty's latest thoughts on the surveillance. She had one bit of good news; her friend, the former FBI assistant director, had been more than anxious to talk about the New York Mafia. He told her Al Nicosia had gotten so good at uncovering bugs and doing most of his business through underlings, the FBI and NYPD had discontinued their constant wiretapping surveillance and bugs at the club. He also said at one point the FBI was able to plant undercover agents in his organization, but when the first two turned up floating in the Hudson with their throats cut, they realized somewhere high up in law enforcement there was a mole. He went on to say over the last several years authorities had focused on the lower levels in Al's organization hoping to get one of his subordinates to roll on the boss or give them a clue about who the mob's mole was.

Upon hearing this last tidbit Betty couldn't contain her cynicism by asking, "So how's that working since your last informant ended up in a dumpster?"

The AD was visibly embarrassed. "So what do you suggest we do?"

Sarcastically Betty replied, "How about setting him up on a date with a honey that has some kind of contagious fatal disease?"

Laughing, her friend replied, "Hell, we don't have to do that; Little Nicky does that himself every Tuesday night."

Surprised, Betty asked, "What do you mean?"

"Oh, I exaggerated some. They might not have fatal diseases but those S&M professional girls who show up every week at his social club apartment will, if they haven't already done so, eventually give him something."

Betty thought if this was really a weekly routine, there was a good chance Bart could somehow use it to get to Little Nicky without worrying about the rest of his gang.

■ ■ ■

The accommodations at the apartment Betty had rented were quite simple. The apartment consisted of a bedroom in the back, a combination living room and kitchen, and a small bathroom. There was no air conditioning and the heat was still supplied by cast iron radiators. Surprisingly, everything was relatively clean. The bedroom had a window providing an excellent view only fifty yards from the social club. Bart could only see half the parking lot used by the crew, but after a few days he realized there was rarely anything going on in the other half.

Bart installed a small window air conditioner and cheap shades. He pulled the shades all the way down. His furniture and goods consisted of an air mattress with pillow and blanket, a fold-up director's chair, a radio, an old-fashioned coffee pot, and a Styrofoam cooler which he resupplied every couple of days with dry ice. Whenever he came or left the apartment during daylight, he always had on a hooded sweatshirt with sunglasses. During the first month, he rarely left the apartment while there was activity at the club. Then he hit upon the idea of befriending Paulie. He wanted to get a look at the upstairs of the social club. If this was the right place for an attack on Little Nicky, he needed to know as much as possible about the inside of the building.

He planned on staying two weeks in the apartment then one week back in Charlotte. On his drive back to Charlotte at the end of May, he stopped at Betty's to discuss his idea of getting chummy with Paulie. At first she wasn't excited about the idea, and told him it would be too dangerous; but the more she thought about it, the more she liked it. If the attack was going to happen in or around the social club, she agreed it was important to understand the lay of the land. A relationship with Paulie could provide that opportunity; the only problem was would Paulie or anyone else recognize Bart? He sure as hell couldn't let his ex-brother-in-law get too close a look at him without a real good disguise. Betty suggested they drive over to Charlottesville and meet with another one of her retired acquaintances — one who "knew something about disguises."

Dr. James Hamel was a professor in the University of Virginia's history department. He was another one of Betty's acquaintances from her days at the Pentagon. Neither Betty nor Dr. Hamel ever said from which government agency he had retired, but he didn't come across as ex-military. It was apparent Jim and Betty were more than casual acquaintances. They seemed to have known each other for a very long time and, based upon the side chatter, Bart concluded they had worked together on some undercover operations. All Betty would say was over the years Jim had gathered some very valuable information for her, enabling the government to put some very corrupt people away for a long time. Bart suspected it had something to do with government procurement contracts, but beyond that, he couldn't venture a guess. At any rate, Betty said she trusted her old friend with her life and got Bart's permission to fill him in on their preliminary plans.

At her friend's suggestion, Betty had brought along a picture of Bart and her from before Al and his cronies messed up his face. The two-year-old injuries had healed, leaving two very noticeable facial differences which Bart planned on having fixed after he disappeared. The first was the bump on the bridge of his nose and the second was a three-inch scar and a misshapen right cheek from the fractured bone. Dr. Hamel commended Bart for his forethought not to have these obvious anomalies surgically repaired. He also liked Bart's new hair length and week-old beard. When Bart took out both his dental fixtures, the disguise expert was very pleased. He suggested Bart leave out the smaller of the bridges. He then opened one of his file cabinets and handed Bart a pair of black-framed glasses. The lenses were uncorrected. He also suggested Bart could really divert attention from his facial details by putting white adhesive tape around the bridge of the glasses. This trick also creates the impression the wearer is either too poor, or cheap, to buy new frames.

He then went on to explain to Bart the importance of complimenting his facial appearance with the right wardrobe and other subtle alterations such as skin tone, hair color, and the appropriate smell and walking gait. Dr. Hamel felt fairly certain that incorporating these few simple tricks into his already altered features would make Bart virtually unidentifiable to anyone who hadn't seen him since he received his facial injuries. Finally, he recommended Bart not to carry any of his Charles Carbone identification with him while he was on his stakeout. He instructed Bart to call him in a few days when he would supply him with a Social Security number and a couple of other complimentary IDs that would be usable for a few months. Buoyed by the expert's approval, Bart drove to Bridgeport confident about venturing right into the lair of his nemesis.

CHAPTER 72

Bart originally figured the best place to meet Paulie was at Sal's Pizzeria, and the easiest way to make his acquaintance was by wearing a Mets baseball cap and being seen reading the sports pages in the *New York Daily News* or *Post*. During his previous surveillance, Bart had noticed Paulie's schedule. Monday through Wednesday Paulie left the apartment at about 7:30 in the morning and came home between 2:00 and 3:00 p.m. On Thursday and Friday he didn't leave his place until almost 11:30 and didn't get home until almost 6:00 p.m.

On the morning of June 5th Bart watched out his window as Paulie left his apartment and headed up Queens Boulevard. Just as Paulie turned onto the boulevard, Bart stealthily emerged from his doorway and followed a few yards behind. Bart was surprised when Paulie stopped and waited at the bus stop with a half-dozen other morning commuters. Bart never figured Gina's simple-minded cousin would take public transportation on his own. Momentarily undecided as to how to proceed, Bart decided to get a cup of coffee at the convenience store on the corner. As he waited in line to pay for his coffee, he saw the bus pull up. Abandoning his place in line, he hurried back out the door and made it onto the bus just before the door closed. Not expecting to encounter Paulie face-to-face that morning, Bart was not in full disguise. He did have on his hooded sweatshirt, but he had all his teeth in and the rest of his clothes were normal.

Paulie got off the bus at Steinway Street. Bart followed suit. Paulie waited for another bus that would take him north on Steinway Street. Bart, as inconspicuously as possible, waited a few yards from the bus stop and again hopped on just before the doors slammed shut. When his subject got off at Broadway, Bart stayed on the bus, watching out the back window to see where Paulie was headed. Bart pulled the cord, alerting the driver to stop at the next intersection. Just as he stepped out onto the street, he saw Paulie disappear into a building on Steinway Street. When Bart finally arrived at the building, he discovered it was a Goodwill Industries donation and retail center. *Interesting*, he thought. *Paulie must work here since the retail shop doesn't open for another half hour.* Wandering aimlessly back down Steinway Street toward Queens Boulevard, he remembered Dr. Hamel had promised him a Social Security number. He began conjuring up a plan to get a job at Goodwill in order meet Paulie at work.

Besides a Social Security number, Bart needed an address; he certainly couldn't use the apartment on the corner of Sixty-Ninth and Queens Boulevard. He needed a place where his residency left as little traceable information as possible and from which he could disappear at a moment's notice. When he called the professor on a pay phone to get the Social Security number, he asked him if he had any suggestions for a temporary residence. Dr. Hamel had two suggestions, a cheap motel where he could pay cash or a homeless shelter.

The Social Security ID was for a Walter Jones, born March

16, 1945, in Rome, New York. Mr. Jones had died the previous weekend at the VA hospital in Elsmere, Delaware. Dr. Hamel assured Bart the ID should be clean for up to six months. "Just don't apply for benefits with it," he joked.

He also said he would get Bart Walter Jones' driver's license. He added, "Don't worry about the picture on the card. All that matters is Walter was an ugly, old white guy about the same height and weight as you."

The following weekend, Bart and Betty met at the Shawnee Inn in the Poconos to review his new scheme. She really liked his idea right from the outset. They spent much of the weekend perfecting his disguise. In this depressed area of northeastern Pennsylvania, the couple had no trouble finding a secondhand clothing store with the perfect ratty-looking clothes for his new wardrobe. The garments even possessed the right odor. Bart had not had a haircut since early April and he hadn't shaved in over a week. His hair was appropriately unruly and his beard was scruffy but not so long as to mask his misshapen right cheek. He added a cheap pair of sneakers from Walmart, with a thumbtack under the insole, and a Mets baseball cap to complete his disguise. He wore his new outfit all day Sunday so by Monday morning as he rode the LIRR into Jamaica he was mentally ready to be Walter Jones, homeless transient, looking for work and a place to sleep.

On Monday night he paid cash for a cheap motel room on Queens Boulevard in Elmhurst. Tuesday afternoon he found St. Benedict's Homeless Shelter in Woodside. It was run by Timothy Boyne, who was rumored to have been, or still was, a Paulist priest. He founded this well-endowed facility ten years earlier on the site of a former nursing home. It had space for thirty male residents sleeping two to a room. After making a number of inquiries, Bart learned the facility currently had a couple of openings.

Tim, as he preferred to be called, personally conducted an exhaustive, hour-long interview of potential residents. He only accepted about one out of every four that he interviewed. Besides surviving one of Tim's interviews, residents had to adhere to very strict rules: no alcohol, no smoking, no drugs, and no women in the rooms. All residents had to bathe regularly — that is, pass the smell test — and each was given a regular chore that contributed to the livability of the facility. If you had a job, you had to contribute 15 percent of your weekly earnings to the house. If you were not working, Tim would find you a job.

Bart was both surprised and concerned when Tim had him fill out an application before he would even interview him. Besides the standard name, Social Security number, date of birth, nearest living relatives and last address, the application also asked for the last two jobs the applicant held and for what kind of household chores he would volunteer. For "nearest living relative" Bart indicated "none;" for "last two jobs held," he wrote down "inventory counter" and "census taker." The question that concerned him the most was his last address. After debating with himself for a few minutes, Bart decided to put down the VA hospital in Delaware, figuring it would elicit some sympathy from the former priest.

To Bart's utter shock, the first thing Tim mentioned in the interview was he had already talked to a Dr. Singh at the VA hospital. "She spoke very highly of you, Walter. She asked how you were doing and requested you drop them a note when you get on your feet."

Bart was astounded, not just that Father Tim had called the VA hospital but that Professor Hamel had somehow arranged a contingency plan just in case someone contacted the hospital.

"I had a hard time understanding her accent," the priest continued, "and she wouldn't tell me why you were staying at the hospital, but I surmise it has something to do with that limp in your left leg. Did you get that in Vietnam?"

Recovering quickly from the padre's revelation, Bart answered with the story he and Betty made up when he put the tack in his sneaker. "Yeah, I dropped a case of ammunition on it, breaking virtually every little bone in the foot. Every once in a while one of those little buggers floats around to where it gives me incredible pain and I can hardly walk. When that happens, I go back to the VA and they fix it." Now, seeing an opportunity for his out, he continued, "But that wasn't the only reason I was there. Ever since I broke it, I've been addicted to pain killers and booze. After the last time the doctors fixed it, they convinced me to stay in for six more weeks of rehab to kick my dependency."

"Oh, you are aware of our policy on drugs and alcohol, right?" responded Tim.

"Sure, I'm OK now. I've been sober for 114 days."

Following the rest of what turned out to be one of the most grueling interviews he had ever been through, the priest's final comment to Walter Jones was "I suspect you have not been completely honest with me; that aside, I believe you will be a pleasant addition to our little community. Now let's see if we can get you that job you want at the Goodwill in Astoria."

That day, after the interview, Bart got his first indication Father Tim Boyne knew everyone who was anyone in Queens, if not all of New York City. He immediately picked up the phone and called the manager of the Goodwill in Astoria. After the usual greeting and bantering of what sounded like two old buddies, Father Tim said, "Look, I have a good guy here who needs a job and who I think could be a valuable addition to your retail operation. How about me sending him over and you talk to him?"

The manager apparently agreed, since after a short pause, Tim said, "Walter Jones will be there within the hour."

The store manager's interview was a cakewalk compared to Father Tim's. By late afternoon June 14, 2001, Bart, aka Walter Jones, had both a job and a place to live. He now could begin to foster a friendship with Paulie Nicosia.

Bart found Paulie easy to get to know again. All he had to do was mention something about the Mets and Paulie was glued to him like a poster on a construction site fence. It took about two weeks for the two of them to go for a couple of slices at Sal's Pizzeria. To Bart's surprise, Paulie liked to have a beer with his pizza. Telling Paulie he was a recovering drunkard, Bart always ordered a coke. During those days at work and the few times they went out to eat together, Bart realized Paulie might have an IQ of about 70, but he had made substantial social progress since his father passed away. Although he still loved to talk about the Mets, he did seem to sense when his listener became bored. For short intervals, Bart actually began to enjoy Paulie's company.

They had been working and hanging out together for almost a month, and Paulie had not picked up on any of Bart's attempts to get an invitation into his apartment. Bart finally hit on the idea of inviting Paulie to a Mets game. He bought two bleacher tickets to the Mets versus Cubs on the Fourth of July. The morning of the game, when Bart showed up at Paulie's, to Bart's shock Little Nicky and his driver, Tony "The Animal" DeMateo, were waiting for him in front of the social club.

Shit, thought Bart, *I guess I'll find out how good my disguise is. Hell, if I'd known he'd be waiting for me today, I could have been prepared to take him out right now. Yeah, right in broad daylight, me against two made men.* Not knowing what else to do, Bart LaRocca continued hobbling up the street toward his nemesis, hoping his elaborate masquerade would hold up under close daylight scrutiny. The closer he got to the two men the more pressure seemed to build in his head until, by the time they were just a few feet apart, it was like standing next to a roaring jet engine.

"So, you're the guy who wants to take my cousin to the ballgame!" Al announced in a tone and manner designed to scare the shit out of you.

Bart was virtually frozen with apprehension; he hardly heard his ex-brother-in-law's words.

"Hey, numbnuts, I'm talking to you," Al said with annoyance. "The priest said you were smart, but he didn't tell me you were deaf and dumb."

Finally, Al's words registered with Bart. "Uh, sorry; I was just thinking about something else." Starting to calm down, Bart continued, "Yeah, I invited Paulie to the game . . . look, if that's a problem, I can always scalp his ticket at the stadium."

"No, that's not the issue," Al replied. "I just wanted to meet you and make sure you weren't some kind of asshole looking to take advantage of Paulie. Do you understand where I'm coming from, Walter?"

"Ye . . . ye . . . yes, sir," Bart managed to stammer.

Al grinned. "Do you know who I am?"

Now feeling quite comfortable he wasn't recognized in his disguise, Bart confidently replied, "Sure, you're Paulie's cousin, Al. He told me you used to take him to the games. I heard you're not someone I want to cross."

With a far-off look in his eyes, Al ignored Walter's final comment. Seconds later he smiled and replied, "Yeah, we used to go to games together. I miss that. We need to start doing that again." Obviously reflecting on fond memories, Al Nicosia hesitated for a brief moment then continued, "OK, I gotta meet a couple of guys here, but Tony's gonna drive you guys over to Shea. Here's fifty bucks, buy yourselves some hot dogs and peanuts."

It was a nice day at Shea Stadium, and the Mets won 2–1. After the game, they took the subway back from Willets Point to the Sixty-Ninth and Roosevelt Avenue stop. As they got off the subway, Bart suggested they pick up a couple of hero sandwiches at Sal's and eat them at Paulie's place. Paulie liked the idea, so that Fourth of July evening Bart finally got to see the inside of Paulie's building. The front of the building contained a small six-foot-square alcove. The alcove was one step up from the sidewalk and its floor was covered with well-worn white ceramic one-inch-square tiles. Two doors led off the alcove; an aluminum and glass door on the right led to the social club while an old heavy wooden door was straight ahead. Inside the wooden door was a staircase that led to the two upstairs apartments. The wooden door had an electronic security lock on it. Paulie sheepishly told Bart he kept losing his key so Al had the electronic key pad installed; he then proudly announced he could never forget or lose that code. He then told Bart to turn around and not look while he entered it. Bart turned, but facing the glass door leading to the social club, not the street. Its glass was painted black on the inside, preventing anyone from looking into the club. This had the effect of virtually turning the door into a mirror. Bart was able to watch Paulie enter 3, 2, and 1 into the key pad. *OK*, he thought, *that might come in handy.*

As soon as they entered the building, Paulie bent over and picked up several pieces of junk mail the mailman had slid through one of those old brass mail slots at the bottom of the door. Bart found himself at the foot of a sixteen-step staircase. There was a narrow hall to the left side of the stairway apparently leading back to a storage closet underneath the steps. At the top of the stairs were two doors. The hallway then doubled back around to another set of steps. Bart figured they probably led to the roof.

The door to the right was Paulie's and the other to the left Paulie called "Al's love nest." When he said those words, he sort of blushed and giggled. As he opened his door, which had no lock, he half-turned to Bart and declared, "You wanna hear what my cousin lets the girls do to him?"

"Later," replied Bart. "Let's have our subs and beer."

Even after all the weeks of being around Paulie, Bart didn't think of Gina's simple-minded cousin as an adult, doing adult things, so he was still surprised when Paulie had two beers with his salami, ham, and provolone hero.

When he was finished, Paulie said to Bart, "Al makes me go to the movies on Tuesday nights, but every once in a while I sneak back and listen at the wall in my bedroom. Al's bedroom is right on the other side. I saw in a movie once that if you put a glass up to the wall you can hear almost everything that goes on. There is a lot of yelling and cursing, and I think he lets the girls beat him with stuff."

"What makes you think that?"

"I can hear stuff that sounds just like when my daddy used to beat me . . . you know, like naked skin being hit. Besides when I hear those noises, Al makes sounds like he's hurt."

"You better be careful, Paulie. If Al catches you, he might get mad."

Paulie's eyes widened and sheepishly he whispered, "He won't catch me, he's too busy. Besides I haven't done it in a long time. Wanna see Al's place?"

"Are you telling me you have a key?"

"No, but I got a little hole in my closet where you can look in his room."

"So you didn't just hear what was going on. You watched, didn't you?"

Paulie didn't answer but a devious smile crossed his face. Bart was again surprised at Paulie; perhaps he was not the simpleton everyone thought. Deciding not to pursue it any further, Bart said, "No, I don't need to see it, Paulie, but I'd like to go up on the roof and look around the neighborhood if we can."

"Sure, Walter, I love to go on the roof. I see everything from up there."

The roof door was only secured by a dead bolt. That was good to know if Bart wanted to use the roof in his plan. On the roof was the HVAC system and a couple of air vents. There was also a dilapidated pigeon coop. Paulie said his father used to have lots of pigeons. When Bart asked what he did with the pigeons, Paulie answered, "I don't know. My daddy once told me the phones were bugged so he and Uncle Pete used to use the pigeons to deliver messages to their friends." He hesitated for a moment and got an excited look on his face before he announced, "Hey, it's the Fourth of July; we can stay up here and watch the fireworks like I do every year. You want to stay and watch with me, Walter?"

Sensing Paulie's loneliness, Bart couldn't help but agree to stay another couple of hours to watch the fireworks.

After he left Paulie's, about 10:00 p.m., Bart sneaked around the corner and entered the apartment on the corner of Sixty-Ninth. He immediately wrote down everything he could remember about the inside of the building and the roof. He added this to the detailed notes he had been accumulating for the last ten weeks. Soon he would take another trip to meet with Betty so they could put together the final plan or decide this wasn't the right battlefield.

CHAPTER 73

Over the next ten days Bart made several more visits to Paulie's. He also began a detailed surveillance of Al's Tuesday night events. One Tuesday, after the girls left, Bart, out of curiosity, followed them until they headed down to the subway platform on the inbound side. By July 15th he felt he had enough details to get back together with Betty to plan the attack. When he called her she insisted that before they plan the attack she wanted to spend a week doing her own surveillance from the apartment.

Betty took a week of vacation and arrived in Queens on July 18th. Betty insisted they both stay in the apartment. By Friday evening Betty was also convinced the best time to get Little Nicky was on Tuesday night. Her only reservation was that she hadn't had an opportunity to see the inside of the building.

After some thought, Bart offered, "Suppose we try to get you in there the same way I got in for the first time?"

"You mean you and I take Paulie to another ballgame, assuming he'll invite us up to his place?"

"Yeah. Why not? You could be my new girlfriend. Heck, we could pick you up a Daisy Mae outfit at Goodwill. You could color your hair purple or orange and get it spiked. Jeez, we could even get you a tattoo! It could be fun."

"Sure you can spruce me up to look like one of those thirty-year-old hussies that hang around Al?"

"Well, not exactly, but we could fix you up to look like someone who might be interested in a middle-aged loser like me."

"The only problem is, suppose Al shows up when we go to pick up Paulie; just like he did when you took him to the game?"

"Ah, he's used to me being with his cousin. He won't give it a second though. Even if he does, he'll never recognize you after all these years in your floozie costume."

"No, but if he gets close to me, I might panic."

"I know you better than that. You'll be just fine."

"I hope so . . . OK, let's try it. It's probably my only chance

342

of getting inside unless I want to try to get on Al's menu next Tuesday night. So what's my name going to be?"

"How about Daisy . . . Daisy Duke? I bet you can still conjure up a mean southern Appalachia twang."

"Real original, Walter," Betty sarcastically replied.

Bart bought three tickets to the Mets' Sunday afternoon interleague game against the Toronto Blue Jays. When Paulie heard the two of them were going with Walter's new girlfriend, he couldn't wait to meet her. On Saturday Betty got her hair cut and spiked; she first had her color restored to its natural dirty blonde and a sort of pale orange added to enhance the spikes. She purchased couple of pairs of tight, very pre-worn jeans at a consignment shop. When she got back to the apartment, she cut one down. At almost sixty years old, she still had very firm and shapely legs. She accentuated the look by putting on a halter top with no bra. Looking in the mirror, Betty declared, "Finally all the years of working out at the gym and running fifteen miles a week are paying off, even if it is only to look like an over-the-hill stripper." Actually Bart thought the effect made her look ten years younger and pretty sexy. He especially liked the two henna tattoos she had added earlier that day, one of a dove on her right shoulder and a rose on her left ankle.

Paulie succeeded in making some surprising personal improvements himself. He had gone to Sears and bought a new pair of tan chinos and an Izod checkered, short-sleeve, button-down shirt. He even bought a new pair of Reebok sneakers and got a haircut. Up close he oozed the aroma of Aqua Velva instead of his normal reheated garlic bread. Bart hated the term "dude," but that day he was tempted to call Paulie "DUDE."

The three of them actually did have a wonderful time at the game. Paulie developed an instant crush on "Daisy," and she found Paulie's innocence to be refreshing. Just as they hoped, Paulie invited them upstairs and Betty got a really good look at the inside of the building.

■ ■ ■

On the short walk back to their place at the corner of Sixty-Ninth, Betty jokingly said in her best southern accent, "You know, I kind of like this look; maybe I'll keep it for a while. You know I was hit on a couple of times on the way to the ladies' room!"

Bart played along. "I find it desirable, too. I sure want to jump your bones right now."

"Well, what's to stop you, big boy?" Betty purred seductively.

The now-anxious couple checked to make sure no one was nearby before they took a fast hard right into the building and virtually sprinted up the stairs to their air mattress.

The next morning they began sanitizing the apartment, wiping down every surface with ammonia and water. They dumped everything in the dumpster behind the building. Queens being what it was, Bart figured by the next day scavengers would have carted off every last piece, including the half-full box of Cheerios.

While they were cleaning out the apartment, they agreed an in-depth planning session was necessary. Betty suggested they pick up the Maxima in Bridgeport and get a room off I-84 near Port Jervis. When Bart agreed it was a good idea, Betty told him Professor Jim Hamel had expressed an interest in participating in any planning session. Bart was apprehensive about adding another collaborator and witness to his planned attack. But Betty was adamant that her long-time friend was more of an asset than a liability. She added he was the best detail planner she ever met. Reluctantly Bart agreed; Betty called the professor, and he committed to meet them in Port Jervis by midnight. He said he would arrange the rooms at the Best Western off US Routes 6 and 209.

They caught the 6:30 p.m. ferry out of Port Jefferson and didn't arrive at the motel until almost 2:00 a.m. At the desk they discovered Jim was already there, and he had reserved just one room for the two weary travelers. Before he had gone to bed, he left a voicemail on their room phone informing them he would meet them for breakfast in conference room 112 around nine in the morning.

The next morning when a refreshed Betty and Bart arrived in

room 112, James Hamel was already waiting for them. He had put a hand-printed sign on the door which read "WB TV Pilot Script Development." Bart chuckled, recognizing Jim Hamel really did think of everything. The room was set up with an easel stand and two pads of 18-inch by 24-inch paper; it looked like a real business meeting was about to take place. Boxes of markers and tacks lay on a single rectangular table in the middle of the room surrounded by four chairs. They had hardly greeted each other when a waiter arrived with three breakfasts. "I took the liberty of ordering us breakfast. I know Betty only eats yogurt and cereal, but I make you out to be an eggs, sausages, home fries, and white toast kind of guy. I hope that's OK?"

"That sounds good to me. I'm so hungry, I'd eat anything," Bart asserted.

After breakfast and several cups of coffee, Jim stood up and said, "In order to get this started, I thought Bart could walk us through how he perceives this going down."

Bart laid out the plan from the notes he had been formulating for the last couple of months. Jim acted as the recorder, outlining Bart's plan in bullet format on the easel pads. As he filled a page, he tore it off and tacked it up on the wall. Bart felt as if he were back at IPC at one of their strategic planning sessions. An hour later Bart had laid out all of his thoughts and the professor had repapered one wall with his bullet notes. They took a short break and then Betty and Jim critiqued the plan. They talked and Bart transcribed their thoughts on the easel.

By lunch Bart was feeling pretty depressed about all the details he had overlooked. Betty suggested they get out of the war room for lunch. Hamel offered to buy. Over lunch both Betty and Jim attempted to reassure Bart the foundation of the plan was still good. Both Betty and the professor were adamant about the attack taking place outside the building, and all that was left for them to do was dot the i's and cross the t's to assure a "successful operation and clean withdrawal."

Over the next day and a half, they worked out every little detail. Jim's details were so exhaustive he even suggested the kinds of foods Bart should avoid the day of the attack. He suggested when Bart should sleep, and that he needed to take a piss before arriving in the alley. Before they split up, Bart and Betty agreed they would meet in Philadelphia after he had executed the first three phases of their now very meticulous plan. Bart drove back alone to Bridgeport. On his way back, he stopped and bought a can of bear spray at a rod and gun shop. The heavy-duty pepper spray was guaranteed to stop a full-grown black bear from twenty feet away. The three of them had agreed to add pepper spray to Bart's arsenal after he relayed the story of Al's second wife. On the drive back, Bart felt pretty confident about his chance for success.

CHAPTER 74

After missing three days of work without giving them so much as a telephone call, it was pretty easy for Bart to begin to plant the seeds for his dismissal from Goodwill. It only took a couple of ounces of whiskey on his clothes along with an argumentative attitude with customers for the store manager to give him his walking papers and call Father Tim. Father Tim was angry with him, but not yet ready to write him off. They had a long heart-to-heart talk. Bart tearfully explained he had been seeing a woman but she dumped him for a younger, more successful man. Father Boyne was sympathetic but told Walter, in no uncertain terms, that drunkenness would not be tolerated at St. Benedict's. Feigning remorse, Walter promised the priest he would straighten himself out and get another job. Two days later he boisterously showed up in the shelter's dayroom reeking of whiskey. Within the hour Father Tim Boyne, true to his word, ejected Walter Jones from the homeless shelter. Bart had successfully pulled off phase one of the plan.

Phase two was to make sure Al Nicosia and his crew knew Walter was fired, run out of the shelter and on the streets as a useless drunken bum. The plan called for Bart to show up at Paulie's, begging for a place to sleep. When Bart showed up, Paulie was elated his one friend wanted to stay at his place. That elation and Paulie's hospitality lasted until Tuesday when Al found out he had been sleeping on Paulie's sofa. Al called Father Timothy and got the sad story of Walter Jones's tumble off the wagon and his resulting firing and eviction. Early Wednesday morning, shortly after Paulie left for work, Al burst into the apartment; he physically dragged Walter down the steps and tossed him onto the sidewalk, roaring, "Stay away from my cousin, you drunken deadbeat." Thus began phase three.

Over the next several weeks, Walter Jones was seen scrounging through garbage cans and dumpsters, collecting bottles and cans for their deposit value. The locals in the neighborhood saw him sleeping under cardboard boxes in the alleys and on park benches; he was rousted by the cops on more than one occasion. At first, when he scouted through the garbage and dumpsters at the social club, the wiseguys left him alone; when Al saw him he directed his guys to "run the bum off and keep him away from Paulie."

The first night he tried to sleep outside, under the awning of a truck dock, he didn't sleep a wink. Every time he heard a noise, whether it was a car on the street or a cat in the parking lot, he sat straight up, anxiously waiting for some unseen danger to present itself. The next night he tried to bed down behind a stack of large cardboard boxes in the back of a furniture store. This time he caught a few catnaps, but he was still too wired against threats to get any real restorative sleep. The third night he found one of those by-the-hour motels on Northern Boulevard. He paid cash from his stash that he kept in the sweat band of his Mets cap for a good night's sleep. Neither the seedy nature of the motel nor the filth and grime of his room could prevent him from achieving a wonderful eight hours' sleep. Over the weekend he escaped on the ferry to Bridgeport, where he picked up his car, drove to one of the Indian casinos in Connecticut, and lived in the lap of luxury until Monday morning. While he was playing at a $25 blackjack table, Don Serafina inadvertently showed up and sat down at the same table, two chairs away. Bart had been intentionally avoiding all contact with Don, fearing that after Al realized who had attacked him Don would be one of the first persons he would go after to locate Bart. They played at the same table for over an hour, but Don never recognized Bart. When Don got up to leave, Bart was tempted to follow him and make himself known; sadly he let the opportunity escape. By the middle of his second week on the streets, he managed to get a reasonable amount of shut-eye.

On his third Monday night sleeping as a homeless vagrant, at about one o'clock in the morning he was in one of those semiconscious states and he heard loud sounds. It was young boisterous voices. As they got closer he tried to quietly slither deeper under the cardboard that protected him and find the three-foot length of pipe he kept nearby. Unfortunately, his movements triggered a noisy avalanche of trash. Alerted, the voices stopped. After a brief pause, Bart heard one of the youths declare, "What have we here must be a big rat." Bart could hear the footsteps headed toward his hideout. As they got closer, they began picking up rocks, bottles, cans or whatever was available and tossing them at the cartons. Reaching his position, one of the youths, perhaps fourteen or fifteen years old, began pulling off Bart's flimsy fortification.

"Looky what we got here!" the smaller of the two said to the other.

Bart recognized them. He had seen the two teenagers hanging around the convenience store on Woodside Avenue. They had harassed him several times; the last time he ran across them, they followed him until he turned down Sixty-Ninth Street near the social club. One of the things Bart noticed during his surveillance of the social club was the local toughs seemed to avoid walking past the Mafia hangout. The few who did venture down the street did so with a sense of urgency and always walked on the opposite side of the street. So he had not been surprised when these two didn't follow him down Sixty-Ninth Street.

Bart didn't think they had followed him this night but that

didn't make any difference now. They were there and obviously bent on harassing him.

The bigger one gave Bart a long look. "You're blitzed, aren't you, old man?"

Bart made a monumental effort to mask his fear. "No, just trying to get some shut-eye. What are you *kids* up to?"

Ignoring or perhaps reacting to the old man's "kids" barb, the big one pulled out and flicked open a switchblade. "Got any of your bottle deposit money left, grandpa?"

Besides the four $20 bills he kept hidden in his Mets cap, he had a $100 bill under the insole of each of his sneakers. Figuring that giving them some money might satisfy their craving, he took off his cap, pulled out a twenty and tried to hand it to the big one. As the youth reached out to take the bill, the other one stepped forward and snatched Bart's hat and shoved him down to the ground, exclaiming, "How much you got stashed away in there?"

Realizing they probably wouldn't stop until they beat him and did a thorough search of the rest of his clothes, Bart's mind raced for a way out. Then it hit him, he had the can of pepper spray in his windbreaker. Reacting with a speed that caught his younger attackers off guard, he pulled it out and gave them each a long hard dose of the stinging liquid.

The first reaction was from the smaller of the two. "What the fuck!" he screamed. Then the burning kicked in on both of them. Desperately trying to rid their faces and eyes of the fiery substance, they totally forgot about their victim.

Bart, experiencing a surge of adrenalin, tossed aside the cardboard and searched for the pipe. Finding it, he turned and, with his best home run swing, smashed his weapon across the left knee of the larger assailant. Hearing the loud cracking of bone and cartilage, he didn't even watch as his helpless victim crashed to the ground. Turning his attention to the smaller one, who was now staggering aimlessly twenty feet away, Bart rushed toward him ready to deal him a vicious blow. As the second youth frantically tried to rub away the blistering fluid from his eyes, Bart landed a devastating blow across his forearms. Again he heard bones crack.

Not waiting to see how badly he had hurt his antagonists, he picked up his cap and backpack and started to walk toward the nearest lighted street, still carrying the pipe in his right hand. Then he remembered Betty's rule, disable and disarm.

Turning back he cautiously approached the now-disabled assailants, scouring the ground for the knife. He didn't see it, but what he did see sent a chill up his spine. The one he had clobbered across the arms was kneeling on the ground with his face buried in his limp hands; protruding from his waistband was the dark handle of a revolver. Carefully he reached down and pulled the weapon out from the boy's pants, scanned the ground one more time for the knife, and not finding it, turned to beat a hasty retreat. He was pretty sure these two would not be bothering any more homeless drunks for quite some time. Hurrying along the chain-link fence that protected the LIRR tracks, he wiped his prints from both the pistol and the pipe. First he tossed the gun over the fence and then a hundred yards later the pipe.

When he finally made it back to Queens Boulevard, he found the first sleazy motel and tried the door. It was already close to two o'clock in the morning. The doors were locked but he pressed the buzzer; after a long minute the night clerk, still half asleep, staggered out of the back. Seeing, what looked like a vagrant, he shook his head and began to retreat to the backroom.

Bart, not willing to take no for an answer, leaned on the buzzer with one hand and took off his sneaker with the other. When the angry clerk turned to threaten the persistent vagabond, what he saw was Bart holding up a $100 bill. Staring in disbelief, he watched as the penniless bum mouthed, "This is yours if you give me a room." Greedily, the clerk unlocked the door and let his meal ticket in.

A half hour later, after taking a shower, Bart lay in bed reflecting on his harrowing encounter. Replaying the entire confrontation in his mind, he realized that although he had been scared, he had remained in control both physically and emotionally. Smiling, he recalled Major Slaughter's words decades before in Vietnam, "I'm a pretty good judge of character and I'd bet my life you would do whatever you had to in order to keep yourself and your troops from getting killed." *Well, I guess Slaughter was right*, he acknowledged to himself.

That was the last night Bart attempted to sleep on the streets. Although he never stayed at the same motel two nights in a row, he was always able to find a night clerk willing to accept cash without having him register or show identification.

■ ■ ■

When Bart felt certain his new homeless identity was firmly imprinted in the collective mind of the neighborhood, he called Betty from a pay phone to initiate phase four.

They met at a hotel near Philadelphia International Airport. Bart drove the Maxima with the South Carolina plates. Betty flew in and took the shuttle to their hotel. After spending what they believed would be their last night together, Betty drove Bart to the Amtrak station and then returned home. Bart had signed the South Carolina registration over to her. The plan was for Betty to sell it for cash to one of those auto auction dealers and keep the South Carolina license plates. The day after Bart's attack on his brother-in-law, she was to put the old South Carolina plates on the North Carolina–registered vehicle, drive to a mall parking lot just off Interstate 81 in Harrisonburg, Virginia, put the North Carolina plates back on, and wait for Dr. Hamel to pick her up.

Bart took Amtrak back to New York with the suitcase Betty brought containing several changes of clothes and personal items, all of which he had purchased while on his first Niagara Falls border crossing. All the labels were from stores in Ontario. Also in a carry-on size suitcase was $50,000 in cash and the Charles Carbone Canadian passport and South Carolina driver's license. He would deposit the baggage in a locker at Penn Station. His final takeaways from Betty, which she had placed in a leather briefcase, were an untraceable stun gun baton, a new can of bear pepper spray, and a typed, three-page bullet listing of his time and events schedule for the seventy-two hours surrounding the attack. As Betty told him when she gave him the listing, "Making it to the last bullet probably means you are free and clear." As they embraced before parting company, Betty repeated for the umpteenth time, "Remember the first two rules in an assault: immobilize and disarm the subject, not necessarily in that order."

Before Bart left Penn Station on the F train, he got a haircut on the concourse. He then took the MTA train to Grand Avenue and took a taxi the rest of the way to his new motel on Sixty-First Street, just south of Roosevelt Avenue.

CHAPTER 75

The original attack on Little Nicky was scheduled for Tuesday evening, August 28, 2001. The day before Bart began the first task on his to-do list. At the local hardware store he used cash to purchase the rest of his arsenal: liquid drain cleaner, bottles of ammonia and bleach, a spray bottle of Armor All, and rubber gloves in a color that would not be too noticeable in dim light.

After returning to his motel room, he put on the wig that mimicked his hair before he got it cut. He changed into the rest of his Walter Jones disguise and sneaked out the back door of the motel. He began his afternoon routine of scouring the neighborhood between Queens Boulevard and Roosevelt Avenue for bottles and cans he could redeem for cash. In the weeks he had gone through this shameless routine, he made sure the locals and merchants in the area became accustomed to the limping homeless vet rummaging through their trash cans and dumpsters. A couple of hours later he could be seen cashing in his bottles at one of those automatic redemption machines at a supermarket on Roosevelt Avenue near the BQE. After collecting his cash, witnesses would report he purchased a pint of Four Roses at the liquor store back on Queens Boulevard near Sixty-Ninth Street.

He then aimlessly wandered the neighborhood, apparently polishing off his pint to the disdain of the citizenry.

On this Monday afternoon, as planned, he deviated from his previous routine; this time he staggered down Sixty-Ninth Street, apparently collapsing alongside the social club on the parking lot side. There were still a couple of cars in the lot, but he knew from his previous surveillance they would all soon be leaving. In all the times he kept watch on the social club, not once was there anyone at the club between 7:00 and 10:00 p.m. except for Tuesday nights when Al had his rendezvous. Sure enough, he was only sitting there for a few minutes when the last two wiseguys came out of the club and headed to the parking lot. One of them noticed the drunk slumped upside the wall; motioning with his head and eyes, he nudged his companion. "Isn't that the lush who used to hang out with Paulie?"

The second hoodlum, whom Bart recognized as Tony the Animal, replied, "Yeah, and if Al catches him hanging around here, he'll beat the living crap out of him."

Tony slowly ambled over to the drunken figure slouched against the wall, hovering over him. Tony, a 6-foot 260-pound Neanderthal who probably whacked his first victim before he reached puberty, growled, "Hey, numbnuts, didn't you hear Al warn you not to hang around here anymore?" Without waiting for an answer from the drunk, he continued, "Look, I'm gonna give you a pass this time only because you got screwed up in 'Nam, but if I catch you hanging around here again, I'm gonna have to beat the crap out of you. *Capisci?*"

Bart didn't have to fake the fear resonating in his voice. "OK Tony, I'm out of here."

Convincingly playing the drunken Walter Jones, Bart staggered to his feet. Struggling to stay upright, he stumbled and weaved his way back toward Queens Boulevard while the two goons watched with contempt. He made his way to his motel down the side streets between Queens Boulevard and Roosevelt Avenue. Unnoticed, he used his key card to gain entry to the motel through the back door. An hour later he exited through the main lobby in his running shorts, a NYU T-shirt, and a new pair of sneakers, sans the thumb tack, and a new Titleist cap. This was his first test to see what kind of a reaction a jogger would get running through the streets of Queens after dark. An hour later he returned through the motel's lobby entrance. He was now fairly certain the following night he could expect to be ignored by police and residents alike.

As hard as he tried, he could not get to sleep before 1:00 a.m. and the next morning he woke with the first glimmers of light. Just in case it turned out to be a long night, he would have to catch a quick nap sometime during the day. The only two things on the "time and events schedule," until late morning, were to eat a good high-protein breakfast and tear up page one of the schedule, flushing the pieces down the toilet. After disposing of the list, he showered, shaved his entire beard off, then dressed in his "getaway" clothes and headed for a leisurely breakfast at the same Fifty-Third Street diner where he had met Agents Sardo and Eastland after Peter's death.

Two hours later he returned to the motel to begin preparing for that evening's event. From the previous days collection of recyclables he had saved four empty capped plastic bottles: a 7-Up, a Mountain Dew, a Sprite, and a Poland Springs. Wearing rubber gloves, he filled the 7-Up bottle with drain cleaner, the Mountain Dew with ammonia, the Sprite with bleach, and the Poland Springs with tap water. After making sure the caps were secure, he rinsed the 7-Up, Mountain Dew, and Sprite bottles with tap water then wiped the outsides of all four clean of prints. He put the newly filled ammonia and bleach containers in opposite side pockets of his daypack. The drain cleaner, water bottle, and spray bottle of Armor All went in the front pocket. He washed the remainder of the chemicals down the sink, wiped the original containers clean of prints, and threw them in the motel's dumpster. Back in the room he packed his now-familiar army fatigue shirt, a football quarterback's flak jacket, the wig and his faded Mets cap. He then preset the four cable ties into loops by inserting one end into the clasp. Doug had warned him that under stress and with his adrenalin flowing, it would be difficult to quickly thread one end through the small clasp in order to make them into cuffs. He placed the cuffs in the center compartment. Next, he checked to make sure the baton stun gun was still fully charged and placed it into the day pack with his disguise. He located the bear pepper spray and placed it next to the Armor All.

Feeling his anxiety building, Bart decided to go for a jog. This time he thought he had better run a different route than the night before. Instead of south toward Queens Boulevard, he headed north on Fifty-Eighth to Northern Boulevard, then west to Honeywell, where he crossed back over the train tracks before picking up Skillman and heading back to the motel. Arriving back at the motel, he was feeling the effects of his lack of sleep the night before.

At the motel in Port Jervis the three planners had debated long and hard as to whether Bart should follow his normal routine the last afternoon and scout for bottles. Finally, they concluded it was better for Bart to conserve energy rather than reinforce his persona. The plan called for him to arrive in the alley across the street from the social club shortly before dusk and not garbed in his Walter Jones disguise. With nothing to do before he went to dinner at five o'clock, he decided to close the blackout curtains in the room and lie down on the bed. Not expecting to be able to sleep, he was surprised when the next thing he knew he awoke at 4:00 p.m.

The last task on the schedule before heading toward the social club was to get a substantial dinner, nothing too heavy, spicy or salty. Bart noticed the diner where he had breakfast offered half a roasted chicken for their Tuesday night special. That sounded substantial and harmless. It was a nice afternoon. Granted, 87 degrees in New York can feel stifling, but to someone who just spent the last couple of summers in North Carolina, the walk seemed quite pleasant. He was not disappointed with his dinner choice.

He timed dinner perfectly, finishing with twenty minutes to

spare before his scheduled arrival in the alley. Following his task list, he went to the men's room before leaving the diner. Catching the bus, he was at Sixty-Ninth Street in fifteen minutes. The planned entry and egress to the alley was from the next street over, Sixty-Ninth Place. He was settled into the alley by 7:15. Once he was in place alongside the dumpster, the anxiety he had experienced earlier returned. Unlike the sensation he felt when Al met him at the social club a few weeks earlier, this was more like the stomach butterflies that accompanied the national anthem before one of his football games decades earlier.

As soon as the Lincoln Town Car turned the corner from Queens Boulevard, the butterflies subsided. That was, until both front doors opened and Tony the Animal got out and was joined by another of Little Nicky's henchmen. *Damn*, he thought, *what now? I can't take on both of them. Do I wait and see if he sticks with Tony all night or should I just call it off right now?*

Everything followed the expected script except now there were two goons instead of just one checking upstairs and returning to the car. After squatting in the alley another couple of minutes, Bart finally made the decision to walk up to Pepe's and look inside to see if both wiseguys were having dinner. Sure enough, as he walked past the front window, he spotted the two men at one of the tables. He didn't have to ponder over his decision any longer; this was not the night he would get revenge on his ex-brother-in-law.

Stopping at one of the few pay phones left on Queens Boulevard, he called Betty to tell her what had just happened. When she saw the 718 area code on her caller ID, she feared the worst. It was way too early for Bart to be in the clear. When she heard his voice, she was relieved. After he explained the situation, she said, "Tonight, next Tuesday, the following, it doesn't make any difference as long as you get away clean. So what are you going to do now; stay there and continue your vagrant charade or get away for a few days?"

"You know, I really haven't had time to think about it. But now that you bring it up, since I already shaved off my beard, it would be hard for me to continue the Walter Jones thing. I should really get out of the City, but I no longer have the car over in Connecticut. Any suggestions?"

"How about spending a few days with your sister?"

"I don't know. So far I've avoided telling her I've been in New York. I always figured if the police or Al's boys came around, she could convincingly deny seeing me for the last couple of months."

"Yup, that still makes sense," Betty agreed. "Like you said, you still should get out of the City. Do you want me to pick you up somewhere?"

"That would be nice, but it's such a long drive for you and this is Labor Day weekend. Do you think you're up for it?"

"No, but I'll do it anyway, if that's what you need."

"No, forget about it; I'll figure something out. I'll call you Tuesday morning at the latest."

Heading back to the motel, he made up his mind he was getting out of the City and spending the weekend at the beach. The next morning he used the computer at the library to book motel reservations. Even though it was a holiday weekend, he was able to find a motel room on the North Folk near the Long Island Sound in the town of Southold only a few blocks from the train station.

CHAPTER 76

Tuesday, September 4th, Bart arrived back at Jamaica Station in the early afternoon. He was revitalized by his six-day seaside getaway. He called Betty from the station pay phone to confirm he was back and ready for action. He checked into the same motel where he had been staying the previous week and, except for the nap, he duplicated the previous Tuesday's routine.

It was such a stifling hot and humid late summer day that he cut his afternoon run short. He took the bus to the diner instead of walking and ordered the same chicken dinner. He remembered to take a leak before he left the diner and caught the same bus, arriving in the alley at 7:16 to wait for Al's and Tony's arrival and to begin his final preparations by putting on his vagrant costume.

This time Tony was the only one accompanying Al, and everything went according to script right up to 8:45, when the door opened and the two working girls strolled out of the building laughing. There is something unique about the saunter of a pro; it's like a moving billboard saying, "I got it, you want it, come get it."

OK, gotta move fast, I've got less than ten minutes before Tony shows up again. Grabbing his daypack he calmly but swiftly crossed from the alley to the alcove of the social club. When he reached the small portico, he put down the pack and began taking out his weapons. First, he put on the rubber gloves, then he took out the bottles of ammonia and bleach along with the letter-size piece of cardboard he'd torn off an old pizza box he found in the alley's dumpster. He rolled the cardboard into a make-shift funnel, inserted it into the letter slot, and poured in the ammonia. He followed that with the bleach. He then took out the four cable ties and stored them in his back pocket with the ends hanging out for quick retrieval. Next he armed himself with the stun gun baton and pepper spray. Looking at his watch, he saw he had less than six minutes left. As he put the two empty soda bottles back in his pack, it started raining, sending little clouds of steam off the asphalt street. At first it was just a trickle, but before he had himself positioned, half sitting and half lying on the white ceramic tiles, it was a downpour. He situated himself against the one wall without a door. His left side was facing out with his left hand containing the pepper spray hidden behind the backpack. His right arm and hand were concealed behind his body. The rain continued to fall, causing streams of water to cascade out of the rain spouts, across the sidewalk and into the gutter. *Maybe the rain will help,* Bart almost said out loud. *It's one more diversion.*

At 8:56 p.m. the Lincoln pulled up in front of the club with its windshield wipers going full blast and the raindrops dancing in front of its headlights. Bart pulled the bill of the Mets hat down but still allowed himself enough space to see Tony jump out of the car with a newspaper held over his head. Quickly, Tony moved around the back of his vehicle and headed for the door. Two steps onto the sidewalk he spotted the drunken Walter Jones, apparently passed out on the entrance. Tony stopped dead in his tracks, stood there for a few seconds, then erupted into the animal from which his nickname is derived. "I warned you, asshole, that if I caught you around here again, you were gonna get a beating." He dropped the newspaper and moved incredibly fast for a big man. In two strides he was in the alcove and out of the rain. Without hesitating, he lashed out with his right foot into the slumping vagrant, catching him with his pointed shoe right in the left rib cage. His victim was lifted a full six inches off the ground. Quarterbacks will tell you that flak jackets are a gift from God, but they don't work miracles against a direct hit by a 260-pound linebacker. It still hurts like hell for days, but in most cases it will prevent broken ribs. Though momentarily stunned by Tony's size 12 into the flak jacket, Bart was still ready when Tony attempted to deliver a second blow. Before Tony could start his leg forward, Bart hit him with a shot of the pepper spray. Tony didn't utter a word; he just stumbled backwards, clawing at his face. He bounced off the Lincoln's back quarter panel. Bart was after him like a lion on a wounded water buffalo. Tony had hardly hit the ground when Bart jabbed him in the chest with 800,000 volts from the stun gun. A five-second burst was supposed to take down any man; Bart gave him a full eight seconds. As Bart pulled the baton away, the big man was sprawled on the sidewalk, his muscles totally disabled. Quickly Bart reached under Tony's jacket and found his gun in an underarm carry holster. He removed it and stuck it in his belt. He then pulled out two of the pre-looped cable cuffs from his back pocket and swiftly slipped one over Tony's ankles. He then rolled the hulk over, pulled his arms behind his back, and secured them together at the wrists with the second cable cuff. He grabbed Tony's feet and pulled his rigid body to the back of the Lincoln and rolled him into the gutter now rushing with water.

Having immobilized and disarmed his first target, Bart moved swiftly back to the alcove. He reached into the backpack one more time and pulled out the Armor All and bottle of water. Meticulously, he sprayed every square inch of the tiles lining the floor of the portico with the Armor All. When he finished, he poured the water on top of it. If you have ever tried to pull out of a car wash lot too fast, you know wet Armor All is one of the slickest surfaces on the planet.

He checked his watch one more time and saw it was a few seconds to nine. Al could be coming down at any moment. Pinning himself against the wall outside the alcove, he waited. Fifteen seconds later he heard Al exclaim, "What the fuck is this?" As Bart had anticipated, Al had apparently exited the apartment and ran smack into the toxic fumes from the combination of ammonia and bleach. Bart heard the loud thumping as his brother-in-law ran down the steps trying to escape the fumes burning his eyes and lungs. He hit the door, flinging it open and desperately attempting to reach the clear air of the street. When his front foot hit the slick tiles, it went straight out and up. His back leg followed but still bent behind him. Up and out went the lower part of his body, out and straight down went his upper body. His shoulders slammed into the edge of the step. His head slammed on to the tile floor. He bounced and settled on his back with his right foot and calf tucked under his right thigh. Blood flowed from the back of his head and mixed with rainwater to make a cherry Kool-Aid color. Bart only saw him from the time he was airborne until he crashed to the sidewalk, but he later described the scene as "reminiscent of the ski jumper who missed the end of the jump on the Wide World of Sports film clip."

Bart waited a second after Little Nicky landed before he rushed out, pointing Tony's gun at Al's chest. Al didn't move; he was unconscious from his head bouncing off the step. Knowing he'd better move swiftly, Bart pulled out the remaining cable ties and secured Al the same as Tony. Just as he was finishing with Al's ankles, the mobster started to stir. Before his brother-in-law became fully alert, Bart did a quick pat-down looking for a weapon. Surprisingly, Al was unarmed. Besides pain, the expression on Al's face was one of puzzlement. His head and body hurt like hell, and there was this guy who looked like Paulie's friend, Walter Jones, standing over him holding a gun. His first words were "What the fuck is going on here? Who are you? What the hell happened?"

"There's no time for explanations, Little Nicky, you'll figure it out. All you need to know is that this is payback for Peter, Gina, Dede, Betty Rice and all those innocent Vietnamese women and children."

"If you're going to shoot me, asshole, pull the damn trigger and get it over with."

"Shoot you? Hell, I'm not going to shoot you. I want you to live the rest of your pathetic life with what I'm now going to do to you."

"LaRocca, is that you?"

Without answering, Bart reached in his backpack and pulled out the 7-Up bottle. Bart's intention was to pour the drain cleaner over Al's face, figuring nothing would hurt his narcissistic brother-in-law more than to spend the rest of his life as the same scarred, detestable monster on the outside as he was on the inside. Standing over his pitiful victim, poised to deliver the blinding and disfiguring potion, Bart had an epiphany; instead of pouring the acid on his face, as he had planned, he emptied the bottle on something Al prized even more than his gorgeous Italian features, *his genitals*. Having saved a small portion of the liquid, Bart poured it on one of his rubber-gloved hands. He then reached down and smeared it on Al's agonized face. It took a few seconds before the acid started doing its damage. When Al felt the searing pain, he let out a scream reminiscent of 1920s damsels in distress. Fortunately, all the shops in the buildings across the street were already closed and the proprietors were

safely home with their families. Between the rain and the street
traffic noise from Queens Boulevard, Little Nicky Nicosia's pitiful
screams went unnoticed.

Al's howls of agony jolted Bart out of his "attack" mentality
back to "survival" mode. He stuffed the empty 7-Up bottle into
the backpack and searched the alcove for his glasses that went
flying when Tony kicked him. Finding them in the corner, he
picked them up and wiped them clean of any potential prints.
When he was satisfied they were clean, he dropped them on the
sidewalk and stepped on them, breaking the frames and one
of the lenses. He then did a quick scan of the area, finding the
only thing left was the Mets cap, which had also been lost sometime during the melee with Tony. Briefly he hesitated, deciding
whether or not he should leave it as one more clue the attacker
was the homeless Walter Jones. Since it wasn't in the original
plan to leave anything behind except the glasses, he picked up
the now-soaked hat and put it on his head as he walked back
across the street to the alley, not too urgently but with a sense
of purpose. Once in the alley, he stripped off the hat, wig and
shirt, stuffing all the wet articles in the backpack. Two streets
over he ditched the empty bottles and wig down a storm drain.
He hadn't heard any sirens, so he figured Al was still lying on the
sidewalk writhing in pain. Actually the rain was a blessing for Al
Nicosia; it diluted the acid and helped wash it away. But in spite
of the rain, Bart was confident there would still be destructive
burns to Al's genitals and some scarring to his face.

The plan had been for Bart to strip off his pants and jog back
to the motel along the same route he had used for his previous
runs. Since it was raining, he thought he might look stupid jog-
ging and he'd attract more attention than he wanted. Making a
decision to disregard their well-thought-out plans, he continued to walk on the backstreets between Queens Boulevard and
Roosevelt Avenue. During his twenty-minute walk, he disposed
of the pepper spray and stun gun down storm drains. Slipping
in the back door, he entered his room without anyone seeing
him in the halls. He immediately stripped off his clothes and

showered. When he was done, he threw his still-soaked pants, T-shirt, and backpack in the motel dumpster. Then he tried to sleep. That's when all the emotions he had been suppressing hit him: fear, guilt, and a sense of loss for his life as Bart LaRocca. He didn't lose consciousness until after 3:00 a.m. and by then his left side was throbbing from Tony's kick.

He awoke in a sweat from a horrible dream at 6:15. He dreamt Al and two of his henchmen were chasing him down a dark subway tunnel. He kept falling down, and each time he fell, they would gain on him. He forced himself to wake up just as Al was about to catch him. He was almost as wet with sweat as he was the night before from the rain. He got out of bed, grimacing. He didn't know if his ribs were broken, but he couldn't raise his left arm above his head. He immediately popped four ibuprofens, then showered, dressed, and went out for breakfast and a paper.

The front page of the *New York Post* had a picture of Little Nicky being loaded into an ambulance on a gurney. The headline read "Mafia Don Attacked." The article on page three went on to explain Little Nicky was found by his nephew when he returned from the movies around 9:45 p.m. Paulie Nicosia had found Little Nicky and his driver Anthony DeMateo (aka Tony "the Animal") tied up in front of the Elmhurst Italian-American Club; a picture of the club was included. The article went on to explain that Little Nicky had incurred a head injury, and both he and Tony looked like they had burns on their faces. Police and hospital spokesmen declined to offer any further details on either the attack or the victim's injuries.

■ ■ ■

By the time Bart returned to his motel room, he was antsy to leave Queens. He disposed of all his belongings except for the clothes on his back, his cash, and the key to the locker at Penn Station. He checked out at the front desk, paying cash for his last night, and headed out with the rest of the morning rush hour commuters toward Queens Boulevard to catch the subway to Penn Station.

By 9:45 a.m. he was part of the throng of travelers at Penn Station. He now had in his possession his Charles Carbone Canadian passport and South Carolina driver's license, the $50,000, a suitcase with two days of new clothes, and the last page of the time and events schedule. He paid cash for a ticket on the Empire Service to Niagara Falls. At 10:00 a.m. he boarded the middle car and waited for the train to leave the station. Nine and a half hours later he checked into a motel on the American side of the Falls under his new identity. The next day, along with hundreds of other international commuters, Charles Carbone crossed back over to his native country. His first stop was at a travel agency where he booked a first-class round-trip ticket on the Friday morning flight out of Toronto to the island of St. Lucia in the Caribbean. The agent was more than happy to accept payment in cash after Mr. Carbone slipped her an extra twenty bucks. He then took a bus to Toronto International Airport, where he used the hotel reservations phone in baggage claim to book a room at a motel with an airport shuttle.

When the captain turned off the seat belt sign, passenger Charles Carbone got up and went to the lavatory. Once inside, he tore up the last page of his time and events schedule, flushed it down the commode, and returned to his seat, confident he had made a clean getaway.

■ ■ ■

It was amazing how different the heat and humidity of the Caribbean felt compared to New York; or was it just that now Bart was free from a stifling burden? St. Lucia was a wonderfully exotic island with remnants of both British and French cultures. Bart found a room in the capital, Castries, but he couldn't stay there long. He had to make sure his trail was completely cold. After just two mesmerizing days lying out on the beaches, he took the L'Express des Îles ferry to the neighboring island of Guadalupe where he had a leisurely breakfast in the hotel restaurant. This leisurely breakfast occurred on Tuesday morning, September 11, while the Twin Towers were being attacked.

Back in New York, the NYPD got little cooperation from Al Nicosia in identifying and finding the assailant. Both hoodlums claimed they did not get a good look at their *attacker*. At the same time, rumors were circulating on the street Al's boys were trying to find a homeless drunk by the name of Walter Jones. Bruno DeLuca made a personal visit to Don Serafina. Following up on these rumors, investigators soon discovered Walter Jones had been a resident at St. Benedict's Shelter and just weeks before the attack had been kicked out of the shelter for drunkenness. Father Tim supplied police with Walter's application and informed them he had spoken to a doctor at the VA hospital in Delaware. When investigators tried to talk to Dr. Singh, they were told by the hospital administrator there was no Dr. Singh on staff, but a Walter Jones had been a patient at the hospital before his death several months earlier.

On Friday, an FBI informant reported there was a $500,000 bounty on Bart LaRocca. At this point, the FBI became involved in the investigation and sent agents to visit his sister Fran and Bart's apartment in Charlotte. Fran could claim without any reservations that she hadn't heard from Bart in months. The FBI's search of his Charlotte apartment and questioning of his friends at the country club turned up nothing except that Bart had told all his friends in early June he was going on an extended fishing trip to western Ontario but would be home for a golf tournament on September 8th and 9th. On September 10th an all-points bulletin was put out on the East Coast for Bart and his blue Maxima with North Carolina plates. September 11th brought a screeching halt to the investigation. It was never to be reopened, and all indications were the $500,000 was never paid.

Bart LaRocca, using the pseudonym Charles Carbone, made his way to the island of Dominica, where he lived for the next two years. In the spring of 2003 he booked passage on the *Sea Dream 1* from Barbados to Malaga, Spain. In his carry-on luggage were almost $2 million in bearer bonds.

After disembarking in Malaga, Spain, Charles Carbone fell off the grid. One month later retired American citizen Carlos Diaz, with his Spanish birth certificate, a new nose, cheek structure, and with his scars virtually invisible to the naked eye rented a condo on one of the Costa del Sol's most prestigious golf courses. Six months later he had a chin implant; shortly after, Carlos Diaz applied for and received his first Spanish passport.

CHAPTER 77

June 18, 2012

It was shaping up to be another hectic week for me. I was driving into the alumni office at Bishop Ott High School in Mineola to see if any last-minute RSVPs arrived for the Class of 1962's fiftieth reunion; I was scheduled for three book signings that week and an appearance on *The Late Show with David Letterman*. If I had known how much the book and the trial were going to change my life, I would have never taken on the chairmanship of our class reunion. I thought to myself, *Well, at least they scheduled these book signings for times when I don't have to fight rush-hour traffic, unlike the freaking trial.*

The thought of Al Nicosia's trial for the forty-year-old murder of a New York state trooper triggered a whole myriad of memories from the last two and a half years; the mysterious call from Monaco, my first meeting with the surreptitious Bart LaRocca, and the weeks of anxiously waiting for Bart's next revelation about his life with Gina. But that was only the beginning of the end of my quiet retirement. The real upheaval began after Bart finished telling his epic tale and disappeared as mysteriously as he had appeared. Things really started getting hectic when I unretired and resumed the role of Attorney Charles Stanfield.

First thing on my agenda was calling the US attorney general's office for the Southern District of New York. I left a message informing Assistant US Attorney General Sam Sardo that I was calling on behalf of my client Bart LaRocca. When Sam anxiously returned my call, things started steamrolling. Following our first meeting at the US attorney general's offices in Manhattan, Sam was euphoric over the prospect of getting his hands on indisputable evidence of Al Nicosia's involvement in a capital crime.

Problems arose, however, when Sam reported the exciting news to his superiors. The newly appointed US attorney general for the Southern District of New York, Roger Newman, had been promoted out of the attorney general's office in Washington, DC. Unfortunately, he was an ass-kissing, publicity-seeking egotist with designs on running for public office. What better way to get his name and face on the evening news than to personally prosecute one of the five most powerful men in the New York Mafia? In spite of the government's intense desire to nail the Mafia kingpin on murder charges, Sam Sardo's new boss started out the negotiations by insisting Bart turn himself over to him personally and be put under the protection of the FBI.

This was when I mentally got back in the lawyer game and began earning my client's money. Turning toward Sam Sardo, I said, "Is this guy kidding? Isn't he aware there is a major high-level leak somewhere in the law enforcement community?" A subtle grin crossed Sam's face as I continued, "Not to mention that Bart LaRocca has done fine these last ten years under his own protection." Turning back to Roger Newman, I added, "Now if you want to grandstand and not play this exactly the way I laid it out for Sam, perhaps my client will forget where the evidence is hidden. After all, it has been almost forty years already, and his memories are beginning to fade."

The attorney general's face turned beet red. He started to say something then thought better of it. After a brief pause, he composed himself and responded, "OK, let's talk about all this immunity bullshit. I can't authorize blanket immunity from crimes I don't even know about or for people who aren't even identified."

OK, I thought, *this guy intends to play hardball. Two can play that game.* Gathering up my notepad and pen, I stood up, made a project of putting my stuff in my briefcase and said, "If that's the way you want to play this, Mr. US Attorney General for the Southern District of New York, so be it. Call me if you change your mind."

Twenty minutes later, back in the temporary office my former partners were loaning me, I made two calls. The first was to David Tanner. I explained the situation to him. David, over the last thirty years, had been a major donor to the political campaigns of numerous elected officials, both Republican and Democrat. When David put a call in to one of his friends, if they couldn't take the call immediately, they usually called him back the same day. The second was to United States Senator William Kehoe, an alumnus of Bishop Ott High School, Class of 1964.

It only took three days before Sam Sardo called me at home requesting we meet over lunch at the Garden City Hotel. Over lunch Sam explained his boss had another pressing, high-profile case requiring his attention; therefore he had turned over all the Bart LaRocca negotiations to him. However, at a later date he might be able to participate in the prosecution of Al Nicosia. With that resolved, it took less than a week for me to have the written immunity documents, signed by the attorney general himself, in my possession. The next day Sam and I drove up to Attorney Bob Byrnes' office in Danbury to pick up the evidence and Attorney Byrnes' affidavit that he had been in sole possession of the evidence since John Nicosia gave it to him for safekeeping in 1971.

■ ■ ■

Al (aka Little Nicky) Nicosia was arrested on the ninth anniversary of Bart's attack on his brother-in-law. The arrest and trial became the most sensational media event in New York since September 11, 2001. In all his previous arrests the television footage and newspaper photos showed a smiling, confident media darling laughing and joking with the press. In stark contrast to those earlier scenes was a dejected Al Nicosia being led in handcuffs to a back door of the federal courthouse for his arraignment while attempting to hide his scarred face from the cameras. Instead of his usual braggadocio responses to reporters, all Little Nicky could utter was "No comment." If it hadn't been for the attempted jury tampering, the trial would have been a cakewalk. As it turned out, this time Al picked the wrong juror to try to buy off. The retired New York City schoolteacher, whose deceased husband had been a preacher, reported the incident to the trial judge. In a move that shocked attorneys for both the defense and the prosecution, the judge, rather than declare a mistrial, sequestered the jury and continued the trial.

The evidence Dr. John Nicosia had saved from his brother's gunshot wound was impeccable. Forensics proved the bullet had come from the slain officer's gun; the blood traces on the bullet were an exact DNA match to Alfonse Nicosia; and the X-rays of the bullet lodged in Al's left femur were in exactly the same location as new X-rays showed there was now calcified bone. The jury deliberated for less than a day and recommended the death penalty. Unfortunately, the way appeals go these days, Little Nicky will probably die in prison before he gets the lethal injection he so richly deserves.

After the government's evidence was released to the defense in the discovery phase, word came back the open contract on Bart's life had been raised to $1 million, and there was another $250,000 on the life of Al's sister-in-law, Patty Jo. To me, neither the increase of the contract on Bart's life nor the new one on Patty Jo's seemed to present an eminent threat. After all, Bart had successfully eluded detection for almost ten years, and Patty Jo had not been seen since her husband's funeral. That all came crashing down when, a few days after Al's conviction, I received a call from the Portuguese authorities. They found my business card in the abandoned vehicle of Carlos Diaz, a Spanish citizen vacationing in Portimão. The authorities wanted to obtain information on the whereabouts of any relatives of Mr. Diaz. I lied, and said Marie and I were only passing acquaintances of

Mr. Diaz's from our last vacation in the Algarve, and we didn't have any personal information on Mr. Diaz. I asked what this was all about, but all they said was he had gone missing.

I immediately called Sam Sardo and told him about the call and that Carlos Diaz was the alias Bart used when I was with him in Spain and Portugal. Sam called back two days later to say the authorities in Portugal believed Mr. Diaz had either fallen, jumped, or was pushed while fishing off the cliffs at Cabo São Vicente. Although they never found his body, his tackle box and car were found nearby. The authorities said two lovers had seen a man fishing off the cliffs at dusk; they then witnessed another man approach him. They really weren't paying much attention to what was going on, being preoccupied with each other; but when they looked up, both men were gone and the fisherman's tackle box and bait bucket were still at the edge of the cliff. By the time the couple reported the incident, it was too dark for a search. That night an Atlantic storm blew in and prevented search boats from venturing near the cliffs. By the second day, the waters were calm enough for a search, but no evidence of a body was found. They did find one sneaker, about Carlos' size, washed up on the rocks. Sam Sardo requested Portuguese authorities send him fingerprints from either the car or fishing gear so he could run them against Bart's Air Force top secret security clearance prints. Examination proved the prints were Bart LaRocca's.

I called his sister Fran, David Tanner, and Betty Rice to inform them of the sad news. Fran was very upset, ranting again about that bastard, Little Nicky, and how she hoped he would burn in hell. David and Betty had almost identical reactions, as they both unemotionally said something like, "Well, I guess Al finally caught up with him."

I didn't think much of it at the time, but now, after what happened today, I wonder if they knew all along. You see, today when I was opening the last few RSVPs for the class reunion there was an envelope postmarked from Port Elizabeth, South Africa. Inside the unsigned, typed note, on letterhead from the Zuuberg Mountain Inn, read:

September 21, 2012

Dear Chuck,

I am writing you from South Africa to send my
regrets that Patty and I will not be able to attend our
50th class reunion over the weekend of October 13.

During our last meeting in March, I believe I told
you of our plans for an around-the-world excursion.
Our original plans were to be back in New York in time
for the reunion; however, last week, while touring the
Elephant Park near Port Elizabeth, Patty was bitten by
a poisonous snake. She is recovering in the hospital
here in Port Elizabeth, but doctors have advised us
she shouldn't travel for at least another two weeks.

We are so disappointed; we had been looking
forward to seeing everybody again, especially you
and Marie. We have such fond memories from our
visit with the two of you in Southampton last winter.

Again, we do regret not making the reunion;
please give my regards to all our classmates.

Sincerely yours,

Jim Gerhardt

I looked at the postmark again; then I read the letter again
slowly. It wasn't a cruel joke. It was a coded message. Jim had
actually been the backup halfback to Bart on our high school
football team. He died of a heart attack twenty years ago at age
forty-eight; his wife's name was Carol, not Patty. This letter had
to be from Bart LaRocca! He was alive, and he was telling me
he and Patty Jo were touring the world!

ACKNOWLEDGMENTS

Writing a first novel is like diving off the starting platform in a swim meet without knowing how to swim. Fortunately I had a few lifeguards ready to keep me afloat and teach me to swim.

First and foremost is my wife and best friend for fifty years, Angela. Without her hand-holding and encouragement I would have drowned in my own convoluted ramblings shortly after I hit the water.

Then there is my golfing buddy, John Mueller, the first outsider to read the initial draft, who provided invaluable advice that kept me afloat. Without my sister Connie's tenacious preliminary editing, my copy editor Robin Calkins would have spent a lifetime fixing my spelling and grammar. My brother Gerry's experience provided me with the authenticity for many scenes and his enthusiasm propelled me forward. Thanks, Gerry, for fitting this into your hectic schedule.

The novel reads more smoothly since Jan Smith provided me with her valuable insight. Finally, Carla King and all the people at her Self-Publishing Boot Camp gave me the confidence and technical advice to strike out on my own and make it to the finish line. I may not win, but I didn't drown.

ABOUT THE AUTHOR

Born Francis X. Biasi Jr. during the waning days of WWII in Queens, New York, Frank grew up on Long Island and attended Catholic grammar and high schools, where he excelled in football, baseball, and track. He married a "city girl," Angela, in 1966. The couple have four children and six grandchildren. Frank graduated from the University of Maryland and later attended Harvard Business School. From 1966 to 1971 Frank served in the United States Air Force.

Following military service, Frank's business career included positions as a financial and operations executive in the packaging, pharmaceuticals, and electronic industries. Frank retired in 1999 but has remained active as an independent consultant.

During their more-than-four-decades marriage, the Biasis have lived in Amarillo, Texas; Washington, DC; Baltimore, Maryland; Scranton, Pennsylvania; Milwaukee, Wisconsin; Lexington, Kentucky; Danbury Connecticut; Springfied, Massachusetts; and Charlotte, North Carolina.

Frank and Angela moved in 2008 to the Sacramento area, where he was inspired to write his first novel, *The Brother-in-Law*.